Power Rising

Guardian from Trandor Series #2

By Phoenix Halloway

Thank you, God. Without you, none of this is possible.

Table of Contents

Chapter 1

As the spaceship Acadia traveled through space, Kiara worked hard to keep her eyes open. This trip was straightforward and routine, and she was having a hard time staying focused. Frankie, the pilot, was at his station behind her, whistling softly. Dark-haired and light-skinned, Frankie was a mixed-race human from Earth, and his charming, happy demeanor hid the calm and courage a pilot needed. Frankie favored bright shirts with his dark pants, and today was no exception, with the neon pink shirt he was currently wearing. Kiara blinked her purple eyes and shifted her position in her seat in a futile attempt to wake up her brain. Leaning forward, her dark blue hair shifting around her face, she checked the ship's position and heard a soft snoring sound down by her feet. Kiara giggled as she looked down at Elvis, curled up at her feet. Elvis was a drayek, a small dragon-like creature that she had rescued during a junk-hauling trip. He was curled in a tight ball, his little wings snug up against his back, his long tail wrapped around his nose. She had rescued him, but he had saved her life more than once. They were telekinetically bonded, evidenced by his skin taking on her own bluish skin color. To Kiara, he was more than a pet, but not quite like a child. He was currently at her feet, snoring, and the snoring was increasing in volume. Kiara glanced over her shoulder at Frankie to see if the noise was bothering him.

They were on the ship's bridge, and, like most cargo ships, the bridge and any other spaces not used for cargo were small. A few consoles and seats, a large view screen in front with several side screens, and seats that folded out of the walls. Any noise by Elvis was going to be heard by everyone on the bridge. Similar to other cargo ships, the design was minimalistic, with upgrades few and far between. The ship's interior matched the exterior in a dark, metallic-gray color.

Frankie was looking in her direction, but he, too, was smiling. Kiara looked back at Elvis and sighed. Evidently, watching the little drayek snoring was going to be the most exciting event of the day. Ever since they had exposed the Senior Logistics Officer at the Galactic Transgate Alliance for her corruption and attempted murder of Kiara, their lives had been normal. Normal cargo runs, normal trips through the transgates, normal days. She had to admit, when she and the crew were fighting for their lives, battling CyRAINs, and fighting corrupt Rangers, she had wanted life to go back to normal. Now that things were normal again, it was almost—she didn't want to say it—boring. Reaching up to braid her long hair, she tried not to sigh loudly again. Watching Elvis snore and braiding her hair were the highlights of the trip so far.

Even her dad had gone back to being retired on Earth. After helping expose the SLO, he went on to complete a few missions with the Rangers. When the attacks on the transgates and space stations began to taper off, he found he was no longer needed. He wasn't an official Ranger, and he had only been helping because the Rangers were short-handed. The Rangers were the law-enforcement division of the Galactic Transgate Alliance (GTA). They were needed the year before, when attacks on the transgates began. Because the transgates connected different sectors by creating artificial wormholes, the need to keep ships safe for travel and supply runs necessitated activating more Rangers.

Kiara nudged Elvis with her foot to get him to stop snoring. He woke with a start, blinking and snorting before climbing her leg into her lap. He reached up to her face with his little front paws and made a chirping noise at her. Kiara smiled at him, sending thoughts of love to him while she scratched the tufts of hair on top of his head. She could feel the beginnings of horns growing under the tufts of hair, reminding her again of how much time had passed since she had found him. Elvis had come into her life around the same time as the first transgate attack. Shortly after finding Elvis, she discovered her power. She was from Trandor and learned that some women from her planet were called Guardians with varying degrees of telekinetic power. Not all women from Trandor were Guardians or had power, and she was thankful she discovered hers.

Kiara sighed again as she thought back to that time of discovery and danger. She had power, and with help from the little drayek, had developed it into something that eventually saved her friends, family, and herself. Now that things were back to normal, the only time she used her power was when she was in the flex-space, working out with a holographic program.

Still scratching the little drayek's head, she thought about Trandor. The planet was now dead, destroyed long ago in the battle with Galdor, Trandor's sister planet. Her people, blue-skinned like herself, were now scattered. Trandor's sister planet, Galdor, was also a dead planet. Fortunately, or unfortunately, that made all Trandorians and Galdorians 'protected'. Kiara frowned slightly. Sometimes, being a Protected Race brought extra trouble.

Her adoptive dad had found her in a damaged ship, floating in space, when she was around five Earth years old. He'd taken care of her since he'd found her, and their bond couldn't be stronger.

Captain Blackburne entered the bridge, interrupting her thoughts. Taller than Kiara's own six-foot height, the captain was fair-haired, broad-shouldered, with a scowl that matched his name.

Dressed in his usual dark pants, shirt, and dark leather jacket, Kiara thought the scowl looked a little more severe today. Blackburne nodded at Frankie, and when he glanced over at Kiara, she raised an eyebrow in question. He headed over to her station, and a feeling of dread hit Kiara.

"Is my dad okay?" Kiara asked. She couldn't think of any other reason that Blackburne would look that serious.

Blackburne immediately relaxed his face, realizing he had caused her to panic. "Your dad is fine," he hurriedly assured her. At her doubtful look, he quickly continued, "Really, your dad is fine."

"Then what is it?" Kiara asked. She could tell he had bad news. Her anxiety was transmitting to Elvis, and the little drayek tried to burrow into her mid-section to help comfort her.

Blackburne took a deep breath. "I received a message that the SLO is dead."

"Dead?" Kiara's head swiveled from Frankie to Blackburne. "What do you mean, dead? What happened?" Kiara's voice raised slightly in alarm.

Frankie adjusted some settings at his console and joined Kiara and Blackburne, waiting to hear the answer.

Kiara couldn't imagine what could have happened to the SLO. The Senior Logistics Officer at the GTA had been behind the attacks on Kiara and the transgates. The SLO also had a corrupt Ranger working for her who had tried to end Kiara's life. The SLO, after being confronted by Kiara, had suffered a psychotic break and was supposedly under sedation and heavy guard at a mental facility. Kiara, her dad, and Blackburne had always suspected that the SLO wasn't the only one at the GTA that was corrupt, but they couldn't prove it. They had been hoping that the GTA would eventually get more information, once the SLO had recovered.

Blackburne's frown turned severe again. "They found her dead in her room. Surveillance showed an orderly from the mental facility entered her room and gave her an overdose."

Kiara's mouth opened, but no words came out. She didn't know why, but the news was filling her with dread. She supposed she should be relieved that she didn't have to worry about the SLO anymore. Still, the situation sounded very suspicious to her, as if someone were tying up loose ends. She looked from Frankie to Blackburne, trying to find the words to express what she was feeling. Elvis climbed onto her shoulder, placed his paws on her face, and quietly chirped at her.

Blackburne could see her distress and knew, without Kiara saying anything, what was going through her mind. He was sure he was thinking the same thing. "There's more," Blackburne said as he looked up at the front view screen.

"More?" Frankie asked.

Blackburne nodded. "They went to arrest the orderly and found him dead in his home. They ruled the orderly's death a suicide." Blackburne looked back at Kiara. "He apparently left a suicide note."

"That's convenient," Kiara said sarcastically.

"I agree," Blackburne said, "but we don't have a say in it."

"Did they give a reason why the orderly killed her?" Frankie asked.

"Supposedly, his suicide note said he was angry over her betrayals," Blackburne said as he shook his head. "The worst part is that I just found out about this, but her death happened several months ago."

"How could that happen?" Kiara asked. "I thought you had someone monitoring the situation?" Kiara tried hard to keep her tone from sounding accusatory. She trusted Blackburne with her life and knew that there had to be a good reason why he hadn't known about the SLO's death right away.

"I did," Blackburne said, taking no offense at her question. "The GTA kept her death and the death of the orderly under wraps. My contact got suspicious a few weeks ago. He was finally able to uncover what happened and sent me the message a little bit ago."

"What about John?" Kiara asked. "Is he still in a coma?" John was the corrupt Ranger who was working for the SLO. Kiara's power had thrown John out of the building at the SLO's office after the confrontation. She hadn't killed him, but his injuries had been severe enough that the hospital had induced a coma.

"As far as I know," Blackburne told her. "The hospital is still saying that he has irreparable brain damage. That may be why he's been left alone."

The bridge was quiet as everyone digested the information. Finally, Blackburne broke the silence. "Kiara, you might want to let your dad know."

Kiara nodded and turned back to her navunit. She looked down at Elvis, who had moved back down to her lap, now that she had calmed down. She scratched his chin, checked their position. She had some time before she would be needed again. She let Frankie know she was leaving and headed to her cabin to get in touch with her dad.

She headed down the corridor to her cabin. At six feet tall, thin, with an athletic build, the corridor could be cramped with more than one person. It was just her and Elvis, currently riding on her shoulder, one paw clutching her long dark braid of hair, his long tail draped down her back. She was wearing her usual black skinsuit, with a light-blue, asymmetrical tunic over it. Her black boots with soft soles carried her silently through the ship.

As she entered her cabin, she checked to see if her roommate, Curly, was in the room. Curly was a Bendanite, a large, bear-like creature from the planet of Bendan. Curly, along with two other Bendanites—Larry and Moe—were part of the crew that helped load and unload the cargo. Bendanites were usually around seven feet tall, with legendary strength, and they had helped to save her life. Kiara considered the Bendanites in this crew to be family.

Curly wasn't in the room, so Kiara assumed she was in the cargo area with Larry and Moe. Their cabin was small because this was a cargo ship, and having the large Bendanite in there with her made the room almost claustrophobic. Kiara hooked up her com unit to the ship's booster and attempted to contact her dad. Since he had returned to retirement on Earth, he was usually easy to find. He finally answered, and his face swam into focus in front of her.

"Hey, Dad!"

"Kiara! How's my girl?" Kyle McAllister's face came into focus. Fair-haired like Blackburne, but with an Irish father's smiling face. They weren't related by blood, but he knew he couldn't love her any more than if she were his biological child. He studied her face—something was going on, he could tell. "What's wrong?"

Kiara smiled at his question. He always knew when something was bothering her. "Blackburne got some bad news today." Kiara paused, knowing that his response was going to be like hers.

"What's happened?" Kyle impatiently asked when she didn't continue right away.

"Blackburne had someone monitoring the SLO, and he just found out that she was killed a few months ago," Kiara said.

"Someone killed the SLO? Do they know who? And why did it take so long to find out?" Kyle peppered his daughter with questions.

"I know, I know, I had the same questions for Blackburne. I couldn't understand how he didn't know since he had someone keeping an eye on her," Kiara told her dad. "Apparently, an orderly killed her and then killed himself. Blackburne thinks the GTA covered it up, but we are all suspicious about the situation." Kiara could see a thoughtful, concerned look on her dad's face. "What are you thinking, Dad?"

"Probably the same thing you are," Kyle replied. "I don't think this is a good development. We were all hoping to get more information about others involved in the attacks on the transgates and space stations. We'll probably never know what she knew and who she was involved with, but, to me, this points toward more corruption in the GTA."

"I think so, too," Kiara said worriedly. She studied her dad's face, noting that he needed a haircut.

"What about John? Did Blackburne get an update on his condition?"

"Yes, he did. John is still in the same condition, which is probably why no one has bothered him." Kiara told her dad. "What do you think we should do?"

"We probably shouldn't do anything right now. Let me make some discreet inquiries about any rumors or other issues with the GTA and the transgates." Kyle looked hard at his daughter. "Stay safe and watch out for trouble. Now that they have gotten rid of the SLO, they may start to make a move again."

"Okay, but I guess I don't understand. They tried to blame everything on the SLO. If they start back up again, they run the risk of exposure."

"I agree," Kyle said. "However, the people behind all of this aren't just going to abandon their plans. The scope of the attacks before suggests extensive planning and resources. I can't believe they would stop because of the risk of exposure."

"I hope you're wrong, but what you're saying does make sense," Kiara sighed. "I'll tell Blackburne what you said, and we'll be extra careful."

They said their goodbyes, and Kiara closed the connection. She briefly considered reaching out to Jax, but wasn't sure what she would say to him. Jax had been brought in to help her understand her heritage and train her. He understood her powers in a way no one else could. He had also helped to save her life a few times. Jax was from Soltus, and his rugged, wolf-like looks, and their time together ended with her developing feelings for him. He was off helping others now, and she probably shouldn't bother him, but she did miss him. They'd seen each other a few times since they had parted ways months ago, but for her, the feelings she had for him hadn't dimmed in the least. She wasn't sure how he felt anymore, since they hadn't discussed it. He was usually so busy that it was hard for them to have meaningful conversations.

After briefing Blackburne on her dad's thoughts, Kiara headed to the flex-space to burn off some energy. She was silently scolding herself for the adrenaline spike she'd gotten from the conversation about possible danger. She'd wanted less risk, not more. She thought of the Earth saying she'd heard her dad mutter a few times. Be careful what you wish for. Well, she'd wished for normal, and that is what she'd received. So why was she so bored?

She entered the flex-space and found it empty. The flex-space was a workout room, storage space, conference room, or whatever else they needed. Setting the holographic program for one of her more strenuous workouts, she removed her tunic and boots in favor of her skinsuit. She set Elvis on the bench by the door and smiled at him while she warmed up. She would have him rejoin her with just a thought when she was ready. Her tall, athletic frame worked easily through the warm-up part of the program, and with a thought, she asked Elvis to join her. He jumped from the bench, and with a couple of flaps of his little wings, landed on her back and grabbed the braid of her hair. Kiara immediately set a protection field around them with her mind. She began a series of spinning flips and jumps that Jax had taught her. She worked in some martial arts and boxing moves she learned from her dad. After about 30 minutes, she began her cool-down exercises and let Elvis return to the bench. She wished she could practice throwing some energy, but the flex-space was just too small. She was limited to defensive training while on the ship.

When she worked out in the flex-space and practiced using her powers, she was reminded of the battle on Earth Delta Nine. She'd had to use both defensive and offensive powers to get to the SLO's office to expose her corruption. She'd nearly lost her dad in that battle. Shaking her head, she headed over to the bench and scooped up Elvis, heading back to her cabin to clean up. Using her powers also reminded her of her ancestor, Mirona. When Kiara first became aware of her powers, she had started dreaming of one of her ancestors, Mirona. Her ancestor had guided her and, at one point, had helped save Kiara's life. Kiara grinned as she thought of all the people who had helped to save her life. She was lucky to be surrounded and supported by so many people willing to help her. Kiara's grin faded as she realized that she hadn't dreamt of Mirona in months. She supposed it was a by-product of the normalcy that had returned to her life, but she missed talking with her. Jax had tried to teach her how to contact Mirona through meditation. Still, Kiara had never successfully contacted her that way. She thought she'd been close a couple of times, but wasn't successful.

Kiara entered the bridge to find Frankie sitting up in his pilot's seat, looking more alert than the last time she was here. Her eyes moved around the bridge until she found Blackburne, deeply engrossed at his monitor. His posture, too, suggested a more alert status.

"What's happening?" Kiara asked.

Blackburne looked up from his monitor and met Kiara's eyes. "Nothing. I was looking for anything suspicious that may have happened since the SLO's death."

"Did you find anything?" Kiara asked and had to hold back a laugh. Apparently, everyone was a little bored with the normal routine.

Blackburne raised an eyebrow when he realized that Kiara was trying not to laugh at him. "What's so funny?"

"Us," Kiara said, finally letting the laugh out. "It seems like I wasn't the only one who was getting tired of the normal routine."

Blackburne had been looking severe, but at Kiara's comment, he chuckled and looked at Frankie. "Guilty," he said. "I was perfectly happy with our routine until we got involved in your adventures."

Kiara liked how he phrased the battles, poisonings, and near-death experiences as 'adventures'.

"I miss being able to use the modified engines on the Acadia for something more than just boring cargo runs," Frankie interjected.

"We are a sorry group," Kiara said. "The whole time we were battling and trying to keep me safe, I wanted things to go back to the way they were, and to keep all of you out of danger. Now, here we are, back to the normal routine before I found my power, and we're all wishing for something different."

All three nodded before Blackburne returned to Kiara's question. "I might have found something, but, then again, I might be trying to make something out of nothing."

"Well?" Frankie asked when Blackburne didn't continue. "Don't leave us hanging. What did you find?"

"Remember those attacks on the transgates with the CyRAINs? CyRAINs - Cybernetic Robotic Artificial Intelligence soldiers - use a specific set of components for their artificial intelligence chips. It appears that a huge amount of those chips are being shipped to a couple of different planets."

Kiara frowned. "How would you even know to look for something like that?"

"I bid on a few of those shipments for transporting, not knowing at the time exactly what the shipment was. When we were repeatedly rejected for the cargo run, I became suspicious," Blackburne said as he looked from Frankie to Kiara. "At the time I bid for the transport, we were the closest cargo ship, and I know our bid was competitive. The only reason not to use us was our involvement in the exposure of the SLO's corruption."

"So how did you figure it out?" Frankie asked.

"I didn't figure it out right away and actually forgot about it until I got the information today about the SLO's death." Blackburne pointed to his monitor as he continued. "I looked up the cargo ship that did get the contract, and come to find out, it was a ship owned by a buddy of mine. I contacted him, and he just sent me the manifests." With a couple of swipes on his console, Blackburne had the manifests displayed up on the big front screen.

Kiara studied the information for a moment, thinking, at first, that Blackburne was making something out of nothing. However, the analytical side of her brain kicked in, and she started noticing the pattern.

"They hid the part numbers in larger part numbers!" she exclaimed.

"Exactly!" Blackburne confirmed.

Frankie just kept frowning at the screen.

"Here, let me show you," Kiara said quickly, and with a few swipes at her console, highlighted the same part number, hidden within a larger number, but repeated throughout the document. "My guess is that these larger part numbers don't actually mean anything, right?"

"That's correct," Blackburne nodded as he entered a few commands into his console. "The shipments were all from the chip manufacturer, and the part numbers you see on the screen don't correspond to anything, but if you take off the extra numbers and letters, the same chip part number is there."

"How many do you think were shipped?" Kiara asked.

"Half a million in these two shipments alone."

Kiara gasped at Blackburne's statement.

"I'm sure there were more, but we just know about these," Blackburne told her.

"Do you think they are making more CyRAINs for more attacks?" Kiara asked him. "Is it going to start up again?"

"That's the question, isn't it?" Blackburne asked her back. "I think we have a bunch of separate information that looks bad, but nothing conclusive."

Kiara nodded, her thoughts jumping around, when an alarm signaled on her console and her com unit. She looked down and realized they were approaching the transgate. She needed to coordinate with the transgate controllers for their journey through the artificial wormhole. Blackburne nodded at her, so Kiara headed to her navunit, trying to refocus her attention on the task ahead.

The journey through the transgates was uneventful, and Kiara left it to Blackburne to continue his investigation. She made sure to update her dad on the latest information Blackburne had found. Still restless, she had a hard time pinpointing the source. Sure, they had discovered some unsettling information, but she just wasn't sure that was the source.

Kiara scooped up Elvis and moved him up to her shoulder, and headed to the kitchen to grab a snack. Elvis, sensing her restlessness, touched her hair and chirped at her. Kiara stopped outside the kitchen, closed her eyes, took a deep breath, and connected to Elvis. Through the connection, she felt calmer and more centered. Thankful that she had Elvis for times like these, she opened her eyes and continued into the kitchen.

She grabbed a couple of snacks and then played a favorite game with Elvis. She threw a couple of snacks into the air, then caught them in separate energy bubbles. Concentrating, she moved the snacks around the kitchen individually. She silently asked Elvis to get them. The little drayek was waiting, rather impatiently, for her to ask him to grab the snacks. He was on her shoulder, his hind legs moving him up and down, his gaze fixed on the snacks. When he received the request from Kiara to grab the snacks, he shot from her shoulder to the first one, his tail whipping out behind him. He grabbed the snack in his front paw, his momentum carrying him to the cabinet on the far wall. He pivoted his body and springboarded off the cabinet, his little wings flapping a couple of times. He grabbed the second snack as his body fell gracefully to the floor. With a snack in each hand, he jumped and flapped his way to Kiara's shoulder, his long tail wrapping around her upper arm to steady himself.

Kiara smiled at him and rubbed her forehead against his. She loved to watch the little guy in action. His wings didn't let him really fly, but they helped push him forward and keep his momentum going. She opened one of the snacks for him and took the other snack for herself. Exercises and games like this helped keep her power in focus and stay bonded to the little drayek.

As she headed out of the kitchen, Kiara's com unit signaled that they had arrived at their destination. She hustled up to the bridge to help coordinate their arrival at the space station. This space station was large enough for them to land in the docking area. Once Frankie completed the docking maneuvers, Blackburne gave them a few hours before they had to load the cargo.

Kiara watched the three Bendanites lumber off the ship. Curly had told her that they had some Bendanite friends who worked on this space station, and she assumed that they were headed to visit with them. Kiara didn't need any personal supplies, so she took Elvis to one of their favorite places, the gardens up on the observation deck.

They reached the gardens and found quite a few patrons enjoying the area. With an artificial sky and several decks of plants and walkways, this garden area was one of the largest that Kiara and Elvis had ever been to. Checking their surroundings and the scarcity of people nearby, Kiara thought it would be safe to let Elvis run. He loved the gardens, and Kiara really enjoyed watching him run through the plants and rub on his back in the grassy areas. She had to keep a good eye on him, though, as he sometimes found the plants irresistible and tried to eat them. She silently told him to go play and watched a few people in the gardens take notice. They were smiling, so she didn't worry about them and turned her attention back to Elvis. Jogging to keep up with the little drayek, they went through several sections of the gardens before Elvis finally slowed down. With the little drayek rolling in the grass, Kiara sat on a nearby bench, smiling at some of the people walking by. She watched a couple of Earth women walk by, then a small group of Volterrans. Volterrans were reptilian-like creatures, intelligent and multi-tasking. She had worked with a few of them and even had a couple of them help to identify who was after her when Ranger John had drugged and kidnapped her. A couple of other humanoid races walked by her, and Kiara told herself to relax.

She was in a relaxing area, had just spent a few minutes chasing Elvis, and yet, she still felt anxious. Jax had coached her to use her senses, and she wondered if her abilities or powers were trying to tell her something. When the Galdorian had been hunting her, there had been a few times that she had sensed him, and when Stryker had been looking for her, she had sensed him as well. Stryker, also from Soltus like Jax, had found her and was the first to talk with her about her power. Stryker and Jax worked together to help those in need.

This anxiety felt different, and she still didn't think it was because of the information that Blackburne had discovered. It was steadily building, and no matter what she did, it wasn't getting any better. Elvis, sensing her rising anxiety, came back to her and poked his nose into her calf. Reaching down, Kiara brought him up into her lap and looked into his trusting eyes.

"Can you sense anything, little man?" Kiara quietly asked him. Elvis clenched his feet slightly, and Kiara felt a rush of power through her. The gardens around her seemed to fall away, and Kiara felt like her consciousness was expanding beyond the gardens and the space station. The feeling was so foreign to her that she pulled back and broke the connection with Elvis.

"What was that? Was that you, Elvis?" she whispered to him. He reached his front paws up and touched her face, chirping quietly at her. "I'm sorry, little man," she whispered to him. "That scared me a little." She ruffled the little tufts of hair on his head. "Should we try again?"

Elvis gave her an answering chirp, and after a quick look around, she took a deep breath and closed her eyes, hoping that it would keep the shock factor to a minimum. Elvis clenched his feet again, and the feeling started again. Her consciousness quickly went beyond the gardens and the space station, heading out into space. Kiara tried to focus her breathing as the rush of seeing not just what was in front of her, but all around her hit her. Suddenly, everything focused on one point, and in Kiara's mind, she saw several squadrons of Mercenary ships, piloted by CyRAINs. Their intentions were coming through loud and clear to Kiara. They were heading to the space station she was at!

With a loud gasp, she snapped her eyes open, her head whipping back in shock. That feeling of anxiety was now full-blown terror, as she realized that she had been seeing or sensing an attack on the space station. Elvis had moved to her shoulder, his feet clenched, and a strange growling noise coming from him. Kiara stood and grabbed her com unit, intent on sounding the alarm. She looked around the gardens at all the patrons, smiles on their faces, oblivious to the coming danger. She didn't want to cause panic, but she needed to warn them.

She knew that the space station security staff wouldn't believe her, so she contacted Blackburne instead. She enabled audio only when she reached him and tried to find a section of the gardens where she wouldn't be overheard.

"Kiara, what's wrong?" Blackburne's voice came through the audio. He knew something was wrong when she hadn't enabled the video part of the connection.

"Blackburne, the space station is going to be attacked! There are several squadrons of Mercenary ships on their way here!" Kiara tried hard to control her breathing, but panic was bubbling up. She didn't think there was any way the space station could withstand an attack of the magnitude that was coming.

"What are you talking about?" Blackburne calmly asked her. "The space station hasn't sounded an alarm or sent out a warning."

"I've been feeling anxious, and apparently, with Elvis' help, I had some sort of vision. I could see them coming!" Kiara was whisper-shouting, trying to convey the urgency of the situation to Blackburne while still keeping the patrons in the garden from hearing her.

"When?" Blackburne shouted the one question that came foremost to his mind.

"I don't know," Kiara said, nearly in tears. "I could see them coming, but I couldn't tell where they were, or how far away they were."

"Get yourself back here, now! I'll start running some long-range scans and see if I can get the space station to run some as well," Blackburne quickly said. "Hurry!"

Without saying anything else, Kiara disconnected and, silently telling Elvis to hold on, took off at a full run back to the Acadia. She knew she was getting a few strange looks aimed at her, but she didn't care.

It didn't take her long to get to the Acadia, and as she shot onto the bridge, she could see both Blackburne and Frankie on their com units. Blackburne's conversation sounded heated. Frankie, catching sight of Kiara, disconnected and came over to her.

"Take a deep breath, Kiara. Blackburne hasn't been able to see anything on the scans. Whatever is coming is still pretty far away."

Kiara took a couple of deep breaths, bending over at the waist to recover from her sprint to the ship. Elvis adjusted his position to her back, still holding her braid.

"Who's Blackburne yelling at?" Kiara asked from her bent-over position.

"Space station security," Frankie said to the back of her head. Bending over to get his face even with hers, he continued. "They don't want to listen to him, and he doesn't necessarily want to tell them that he is basing his information on your vision."

Straightening up, Kiara nodded. "That's probably a good idea."

Frankie straightened up and went over to his console to see if anything was coming up on the scans. Blackburne finally finished yelling at the security person and, after disconnecting, walked over to stand next to Frankie and Kiara, a disgusted look on his face.

"That went well," he said sarcastically.

"We could tell," Frankie told him.

Blackburne looked at Kiara. "Anything else you can tell me? How many ships, that sort of thing?"

"At least ten squadrons of three Mercenary ships in each squadron," Kiara said, trying to pull the memory out. "Somehow I knew they were coming here, but I don't know how I know that." Kiara, calmer now, looked from Blackburne to Frankie. "Maybe we should leave? I can protect us better if we aren't in the space dock."

At her suggestion, Blackburne's frown turned black.

"What?" Kiara asked in alarm.

"They won't let us leave," Blackburne growled. "I raised too many suspicions when I tried to get them to scan for the threat."

"We can't leave?" Kiara squeaked it out, her panic bubbling up again. Could she keep them safe in the space dock? Elvis clenched his feet on her shoulder, her panic transmitting to him.

"We'll be fine," Blackburne said, trying to sound confident. He was worried, though. He was sure that the space station defenses wouldn't hold against thirty Mercenary ships.

"We should contact my dad," Kiara finally said. "He should be able to talk the Rangers into coming here, don't you think?"

"Good idea, Kiara," Blackburne said, turning back to his console. "I'll keep working on the space station security, and Frankie can keep working on scanning the area."

Frankie nodded, his eyes still on his console. Kiara could see that he hadn't detected anything yet, so she told herself that her dad could probably get the Rangers here in plenty of time. Kiara connected her com unit to the ship's booster at her navunit console and made the connection to her dad. She knew the call would be tough—she was going to tell her dad that they were in imminent danger, and there wasn't going to be anything he could do about it, except to call the Rangers. She was right. There was a lot of yelling on his end, and she knew that he was also going to see if he had any pull with the space station security to get them permission to leave.

Kiara disconnected with her dad and turned back to Frankie to see if he had found anything. She was considering trying to see if she connected with Elvis if she could figure out more about the attack, when she saw Frankie stiffen. She knew then that it was too late; it was apparent that Frankie had detected the ships.

"Blackburne, I see them," Frankie said calmly.

"How much time do we have?" Blackburne asked as he crossed over to Frankie's seat. Before Frankie could answer, Blackburne turned to Kiara. "Tell the Bendanites to brace for battle."

Kiara nodded as she heard Frankie tell Blackburne that they only had a matter of minutes before they would be under attack. She sent the warning to Larry, Curly, and Moe, and then headed to her seat. They were confined in the space dock, so they couldn't even use the ship's weapons to help. As she sat, the space station alarms went off, and she heard warnings broadcast throughout the space dock.

Now that the Mercenary ships were here, she felt strangely calm. She'd been so panicked before, she couldn't understand why she wasn't screaming or crying. Perhaps she was in shock? Elvis moved from her shoulder to her lap, his eyes locked onto hers. She felt the first shudders from the weapon's fire and could hear small explosions in the distance. The space station had excellent shielding, but it would only last a short time with all the heavy fire they were taking. With her eyes still locked onto Elvis, she knew she had to do whatever she could to keep them safe. She also knew that she wouldn't be able to ignore the thousands of people on the space station. She could hear Blackburne and Frankie relay the status of the space station to each other and to a Ranger that had contacted Blackburne. She knew the Rangers were trying to get here, but she also knew it wouldn't be in time. Keeping her shipmates and those on the space station alive was going to be up to her.

She considered her options. She could try to put up a protection field, but she knew there was no way to encompass the whole space station. She could try to monitor the shielding and protect the areas that failed, but she guessed she'd still end up trying to protect the whole station, and she'd be right back to the first problem: the station was too big. Okay, that left trying to take out the Mercenary ships themselves with offensive energy. Looking at Elvis, she felt his agreement. With the decision made, she jumped up from her seat and headed off the bridge, intent on reaching a better vantage point inside the space station.

As she shot out of the Acadia, she could hear Blackburne and Frankie yelling behind her, but she didn't want to take the time to explain. They would follow her or not; her mind was focused on getting to the upper observation deck. It had the best vantage point and would allow her the best opportunity to use her powers.

The space station was shuddering violently when Kiara reached her destination. She spun a quick circle and moved Elvis to her shoulder. Breathing hard from her run, she closed her eyes and focused her power. Like one of the early battles she had been involved in while on the Acadia, she could see the battle and the enemy ships in her mind. The Mercenary ships were running in their trademark pack of three, and Kiara smiled fiercely as she realized their predictability would work in her favor.

Focusing on a squadron coming in fast, she sent twin pulses of energy out. The energy immediately impacted the two outer ships, pushing them as they exploded into the middle ship. All three ships were destroyed. Without pausing, she turned her attention to the next squadron, sending out pulses of energy. She could feel how much energy she was expending and hoped she had enough to keep the space station safe. The space station was firing at the Mercenary ships, and she could see a few of the enemy ships explode. She spent a few precious seconds rebuilding her energy and sent pulses out to a squadron approaching quickly. She could tell from the impact that her energy pulses weren't as intense, and she was starting to feel drained. Breathing hard, she nearly lost her balance as an explosion rocked the space station. Elvis, clenching her shoulder tight, growled in her ear.

"I see them, little man," she whispered.

Two squadrons were coming in from opposite sides, their constant weapons fire causing explosions and destruction. Kiara could see debris from the destruction floating out into space, and an alarm within the space station went off, warning of imminent loss of gravity and life support. Shooting both arms out to the side, she sent energy pulses at both squadrons simultaneously. She only managed to destroy two of the ships, since the amount of energy she was able to send decreased each time she tried. Kiara bent over, breathing hard. She felt as if she had run a marathon, and there were still several squadrons left. If humans or some other life form had piloted the ships, she was sure they would have broken off the attack by now. But because the ships were being piloted by artificial intelligence, they wouldn't stop until the mission was complete, or the CyRAINs themselves were destroyed. She worried that she wouldn't have enough power to get them all, but she knew she had to try. The alternative was to die.

Straightening again, she took a deep breath and targeted another squadron. She sent the pulse of energy, but she was weak, and the ships merely wobbled before continuing their destruction. Kiara fell to her knees, her breath leaving her in a whoosh. Elvis jumped to the floor, chirping and jumping in front of her. On a sob, she opened her eyes and looked at Elvis.

"I can't do it, I can't," she sobbed.

Hearing a noise behind her, she turned her head to see Blackburne and Frankie. The space station shuddered hard, and Kiara could see their despair mirror her own. She thought of the

Bendanites on the Acadia, she thought of Jax. She turned back to Elvis and closed her eyes. The little drayek reached up and touched her face, his touch sending a pulse of energy through her. Kiara didn't think she had enough energy to stand up, so, still on her knees, she took a couple of deep breaths. Gritting her teeth, she focused on one of the squadrons circling the space station. With one more deep breath, she screamed as she sent the pulse of energy at it, Elvis letting out a screech as well.

It worked! She saw the squadron explode as the ships collided. Blackness was starting to creep in around her vision, and she fought to stay conscious. There were still several squadrons circling the station. She struggled to stay upright as her vision went completely black. Elvis was chirping at her, and she could feel Blackburne and Frankie trying to hold her up.

"I'm sorry," she mumbled, her despair at having failed coming through in her voice.

"It's okay," Blackburne said into her ear. "The Rangers are here. You bought us enough time."

Blackburne's statement finally penetrated Kiara's brain, and with a sigh, she gave up trying to stay conscious.

Kiara woke in the med-bay aboard the Acadia. She felt disoriented and exhausted. She slowly sat up, searching her mind for the circumstances that would have put her into the med-bay. Elvis was curled into her side, snoring softly. He appeared to be okay. She scrubbed at her face, and suddenly, everything came flooding back. The CyRAINs, the battle, the destruction. Swinging her legs to the side of the bed, she slowly slid her feet to the floor and stood up, making sure that her legs would support her. Elvis, with a chirp, stood on the bed next to her and reached out to touch her arm. As she slowly started across the room, she could feel the rumbling of the engines and assumed they had left the space station. Stopping near the door, Kiara looked around for her com unit. She spotted it over by the bed and, grinning, walked back. Next to her com unit was a glass of water, some of the protein gel that Jax liked to give her when she used her powers, and her supplements. She'd been so disoriented when she'd woken that she hadn't seen any of it. She was glad that her supplements were there. She needed them to replace the minerals that were once inherent on her home planet of Trandor.

She took her supplements and quickly swallowed the gel. Kiara knew from experience that the gel would work quickly to restore her energy level, but would also wear off just as fast. Grabbing her com unit, she moved Elvis to her shoulder and headed to the kitchen while she checked their position. She couldn't tell where they were headed, but she was sure that Blackburne would tell her when she reached the bridge.

She entered the bridge, still eating some of the food she had grabbed. Frankie saw her first and immediately jumped up from his seat and crossed to her.

"Hey, are you doing okay? Do you need anything?" Frankie asked as he put his hand under her elbow and led her to her station, as if she were a frail older woman.

"I'm okay, Frankie, really," Kiara told him, trying to pull her arm away from him.

Blackburne walked over and seemed to be studying her, trying to determine whether she really was okay.

"Seriously, I'm fine," Kiara said to both. When they just continued to stare at her, she finally said, "Who's piloting this thing anyway?"

Blackburne and Frankie both grinned before Frankie walked back to his seat.

"Is everyone okay? How long was I out?" Kiara asked Blackburne.

"Our crew is fine, and the Acadia came through without a scratch," Blackburne said. "The space station took some serious damage, and there were quite a few casualties. You've been sleeping for about twelve hours."

Kiara looked down and nodded. Tears came to her eyes. She should have done more.

Blackburne reached down and slowly pulled her chin up. "You did everything you could. We all did," he told her. "Space station security wouldn't listen to me, and the Rangers did everything they could to get there as fast as they did." It would have been a lot worse if you hadn't tried to destroy as many of those ships as you did."

Kiara clamped her lips together in an effort to control her emotions. She nodded at Blackburne, not trusting herself to be able to say anything without crying.

Blackburne, uncomfortable, awkwardly patted her shoulder. "Make sure you talk to your dad. We contacted him to let him know you were okay, but I know he wants to hear from you."

"I will," Kiara said, finally feeling like she could talk. "Where are we headed? Were we able to get the cargo loaded before the attack?"

Blackburne nodded and, crossing back over to his console, sent Kiara the information she needed to coordinate and plan their trip. Falling back into her job's routine, Kiara sent navigation information to Frankie before heading to her cabin to talk to her dad.

Chapter 2

At the GTA headquarters on Earth Delta Nine, news of the latest space station attack prompted varied reactions. Most focused their efforts on determining who was behind the attack and coordinating recovery efforts. But for one office on the executive floor, the news was poorly received. Slamming his fist on his desk, the executive who occupied that office stood and walked to the window, his anger evident in every step he took.

The report he had received was vague on details. Still, he knew, without a doubt, that the female Trandorian responsible for the trouble before was also behind this latest setback. He muttered a few expletives as he paced in front of the window. He thought, once things had settled down, and they had gotten rid of the SLO, the Trandorian wouldn't be a bother to their plans. Maybe it was bad luck that she was there, but perhaps she had somehow found out about the attack and gone there to prevent it. Because of her interference, most of the ships were destroyed, and he had to self-destruct the remaining ones so that the Rangers wouldn't get access to the CyRAINs on board.

Taking a deep breath, he headed back to his desk to formulate a plan to get rid of her, once and for all.

On the Acadia, Kiara headed back up to the bridge after spending the last ten minutes trying to convince her dad that she was okay. She knew he hated being away from her, especially when she was in danger. She'd talked him out of trying to meet up with her, but she knew he might try anyway. She thought briefly about contacting Jax, but didn't know what she would say to him. Elvis was trailing behind her, alternately huffing and chirping. She knew it was because of her mood. She stopped in the hallway before she reached the bridge, taking a second to compose herself. Quite a bit had happened in the last day, and she felt like she couldn't catch up. It reminded her too much of all that had happened when she had first discovered her powers.

Kiara entered the bridge and thought for a second that she was hallucinating. She had just been thinking about Jax, and there he was, on the front monitor of the bridge, talking to Blackburne and Frankie. Kiara walked slowly in until she was far enough in to be included in the picture that was being transmitted to Jax. She felt like all eyes were on her, and it made her feel awkward. She forced her feet to move and reminded herself to breathe. In. Out. In. Out.

Jax's face transformed from a serious look to a relieved smile when he saw her. Obviously, Blackburne had told him what had happened.

"Kiara, are you well?" Jax asked, his eyes never left hers. "Did you take your supplements and the gel that I left for you?"

"Of course," Kiara said, a little embarrassed that he seemed to be treating her like a child.

Jax, always in tune with her feelings, immediately tried to fix it. "I'm sorry, I don't mean to sound like you don't know how to take care of yourself. We heard about the attack, and when Blackburne told us that you were involved, I was worried about you." Jax looked from Blackburne to Kiara. "We understand it was pretty bad."

Kiara felt like they were keeping something from her, but before she could ask, Blackburne jumped in.

"Jax and Stryker have actually contacted us to ask for help," Blackburne said. He nodded at Jax to continue.

"Yes. After you deliver your cargo, we could use your help to rescue some people out on Havernon 3."

Kiara quickly brought up the sector they were traveling through on her com unit, seeing that Havernon 3 wasn't that far away.

"I thought you had a network to help with these kinds of missions," Kiara said. "Why do you need us? And what race of people are you talking about?"

Jax smiled. He knew she would ask those questions. "Your ship happens to be the closest, and we need to move quickly. We have reports of human trafficking," Jax said as his look turned serious. "They're trafficking women and children from Earth. Besides, Kiara, we might need your skills."

Kiara looked from Jax back to Blackburne. "We have to help, if we can," she implored Blackburne.

Blackburne nodded at her. "We didn't have anything lined up after this cargo drop, so we are available to help." He knew she would want to help. She had a big heart. He had watched her nearly destroy herself trying to protect the space station and all the people on it. He had meant it when he had told her that there wasn't anything else she could have done. He turned back to Jax.

"Frankie has already agreed, but we need to make sure that the Bendanites are okay with the mission. We'll contact you back in a few minutes," Blackburne said before disconnecting with Jax.

Blackburne headed to the cargo area to talk to the Bendanites, and that gave Kiara a moment to corner Frankie on what everyone was keeping from her.

"Frankie, what is it that no one wants to tell me? Is it about this mission?"

Frankie looked uncomfortable. He couldn't seem to figure out where to look, as his eyes darted around so he wouldn't have to meet Kiara's stare. "What do you mean?" he finally stammered out.

Kiara nearly laughed. He was going to be easy to crack. "Come on, Frankie. You can tell me."

Frankie looked down, his indecision coming across loud and clear.

"I won't tell them that you told me," Kiara said. She bent over and put her face in his line of sight. "Please."

"Look, Kiara, they didn't want to tell you because they didn't want to upset you." Frankie moved over to his seat and sat down heavily. "You gave everything you had on the space station, trying to save everyone. Blackburne was worried about how you would take it."

"How would I take what?" Kiara asked. She was dreading what Frankie would say next.

"He was worried about how you would take it when you found out how many people died on the space station."

Kiara walked unsteadily over to her station and sat down. Elvis immediately jumped into her lap, detecting her distress. Reaching down, she scratched the top of the little drayek's head. The tears started as she thought about all the people she hadn't been able to save.

"Maybe if I had started sooner, or if I had tried harder..." Kiara whispered.

"Kiara, don't," Frankie said as he came over to her station and squatted down next to her. "You did everything you could. We all did."

With tears streaming down her face, she asked Frankie to tell her how many had died. The number he told her caused her to sob.

"It would have been worse, much worse, if you hadn't helped when you did," Frankie said, trying his best to reassure her. He felt completely out of his element here.

Blackburne walked back into the bridge to see Kiara crying, and Frankie and Elvis trying to comfort her. He sighed. He knew exactly what had happened. "Frankie, you shouldn't have told her."

Frankie, looking chagrined, stood up and walked over to Blackburne. In a quiet voice, he said, "She knew something was going on. I didn't think it was right to keep it from her."

Blackburne walked over to Kiara, unsure how to proceed. He opened his mouth to say something, but Kiara interrupted him.

"I know, you're going to say that I did everything I could. My head knows that, but my heart aches for those who died."

Blackburne nodded and awkwardly patted her shoulder. Kiara seemed to be steadier now, much to his relief. "Larry, Curly, and Moe are good with the mission, so if you're okay, let's contact Jax and find out what he needs us to do."

Kiara nodded and hastily wiped at her face. She hated crying and knew it made everyone else uncomfortable, too. She took a couple of deep breaths. She didn't want Jax to see her crying either, even though he'd seen her cry a few times when he was with them before.

Blackburne quickly contacted Jax and worked out the logistics for a meeting point after the Acadia dropped their cargo. Logistics finalized, Blackburne asked Frankie to increase their speed. They needed to get to the rendezvous point as soon as possible.

The cargo drop went smoothly, and the Acadia reached the rendezvous point quickly, orbiting Havernon 3. A small spaceship was waiting for them, and Kiara quickly made contact. Jax's serious face floated into view on the large screen; his relief at seeing them was apparent.

"Thank you," Jax said to Blackburne. "Our source on Havernon 3 informed us that the traffickers are getting nervous and are trying to move their captives. We need to travel quickly."

"I looked at the information you sent us," Blackburne responded promptly. "We've studied the details about this planet. We shouldn't have any issues bringing the Acadia down to the surface."

The tricky part about this mission had been figuring out how to get the captives back aboard the Acadia. The atmosphere was thin and shallow, allowing the Acadia to reach the planet's surface easily. The hardest part would be landing where the traffickers wouldn't detect them and then getting the captives back to the Acadia. Jax hadn't been sure how many captives there were, and Kiara hoped that they had enough room for them.

"Kiara, are you ready?" Jax asked. "Our source has told us that the traffickers are heavily armed."

Before Kiara could answer, she saw Stryker join Jax on the screen. Seeing Stryker here drove home the severity of the situation. Stryker was from Soltus like Jax, and the two of them, tall, muscular, with wolf-like features, were intimidating to those who didn't know them. Stryker was the first person to contact her when her powers had started to manifest. She'd found out later that Stryker had also contacted her dad after her dad had first found her. Stryker, Jax, and their friends helped Protected Races, like Kiara's. They also jumped into situations like today, with human trafficking. Kiara knew that some of these situations fell between the Rangers' and the local governments' jurisdictions. Havernon 3 was a planet with little in the way of local government. Because the planet was inhospitable to most races, the population was sparse, making it an excellent place for smugglers and traffickers.

"Stryker!" Kiara exclaimed. She was genuinely glad to see him. He was responsible for bringing Jax into her life. "Are you coming with us on this mission?" Elvis, on her shoulder, chirped a greeting at Jax and Stryker.

"Yes, I will be with you," Stryker answered. "The situation is very serious."

"Remember, we'll need suits and breathers," Jax said. "Our source is tracking the group on the ground. We'll most likely have to improvise once we land, because the information we have been receiving is spotty, at best."

"Understood," Blackburne said. "The Bendanites have the cargo areas ready, and they will stay on the Acadia to protect it and monitor us."

Jax looked at Kiara and Elvis. "Kiara, it is my understanding that Elvis will not need a breather or suit on this planet. His body should be able to adapt to the atmosphere with no problem."

"Thank you, Jax. I was trying to figure out what to do with him. I didn't want to leave him behind." Kiara looked at Elvis and smiled. He chirped back his agreement.

"Are we ready?" Jax asked. After receiving a 'yes', he continued, "Okay, let's go. Follow us to the surface."

The Acadia followed the smaller ship, with everyone strapped in their seats. Kiara knew it would be a very bumpy ride. The atmosphere was thin and shallow, but it still presented issues trying to get through it. With their shielding at maximum, the Acadia bumped and rocked through the atmosphere. Frankie was keeping a safe distance from the smaller ship, and Kiara could see that the smaller ship was being buffeted and rocked even more than the Acadia. They entered the lower atmosphere of red and orange gases, and Kiara checked their distance to the ground since the gases blocked their view. They were coming up fast to the surface. Still, Frankie was already leveling them off, since the bigger Acadia would need more time to make maneuvers than the smaller ship. The gases suddenly disappeared, and the ground seemed to shoot up towards them. This area of the planet was relatively flat, but Kiara could see jagged-looking mountain formations in the distance. She hoped that the traffickers weren't close, because both ships were clearly visible.

Jax's voice came over the ship's com unit. "We're heading towards that distant rock formation. Stay low."

Both ships reached the rocks, and Kiara was surprised to see how big the formation really was. The jagged rocks were a mix of orange, red, and brown, and extended toward the sky for several miles. Frankie landed the Acadia with a soft thud, and everyone immediately unstrapped to get ready for the mission. Larry, the Bendanite, joined them on the bridge, and with his massive height and bulk, the bridge seemed really crowded. Blackburne gave Larry a few last-minute instructions before heading out.

Blackburne joined Kiara and Frankie near the back of the ship. The Acadia had a special pod that could lower them to the surface without letting any of the ship's atmosphere escape. One by one, they lowered to the surface. The suits they wore weren't bulky, but they did limit their movements. Each member of the group carried a pack with water, food, and medical supplies. Kiara adjusted the visor on her suit helmet to see more clearly in the reddish haze on the surface of the planet. She mentally checked Elvis and found him relaxed and breathing well. Jax and Stryker soon joined them, and Kiara stared at them. She wasn't used to seeing them without their usual hooded cloaks. She did notice, however, that both men still carried the batons they used for both defense and offense. The group took a moment to check their suits and sync up their com units before Jax led them toward the jagged mountains.

Kiara looked around as they walked, noting the area was devoid of vegetation. Kiara suspected the lack of direct sunlight was responsible. They were walking through hard-packed rocks and dirt, the same color as the jagged mountains they were heading to. She couldn't believe that anyone could or would live on this planet.

The small pockets of population on the planet had indoor gardens to sustain them, as well as trade with other planets for food.

Jax had them moving at a good pace, and as they approached the jagged rocks at the base of the mountains, Kiara could see a path that had been cleared through the rocks. Jax's voice came through the com unit in her helmet, telling the group that their contact here on the planet was meeting them on the other side of the pass. He was supposed to be bringing transport to take them to the traffickers.

Kiara heard Blackburne check in with Larry on the Acadia. All was good on the ship, and Larry wasn't picking up anything on his scans of the area. As they continued their trek, Kiara was glad she spent so much time in the flex-space working out. She didn't want to be the one who slowed the group down. She adjusted Elvis to her other shoulder, reluctant to let him run on the ground.

After a few hours, they finally reached the other side. They exited the rocky path into an area that looked almost identical to where they'd just come from. Off to their right, Kiara could see someone under a large overhang of rocks.

"Jax, is that your contact?" Blackburne asked.

"Yes, that is Ridon. He is from this area," Jax answered as he raised a hand in greeting.

Kiara looked around but didn't see any buildings or vehicles. Where exactly did Ridon live, and where was their transport? She could see that he was wearing a dark scarf and protective clothing with a hood, but he apparently didn't need the breathers like her group did.

As they approached the overhang, Kiara could sense something else in their vicinity. Going on full alert, Elvis let out a screech that had everyone halting. Jax turned to Kiara.

"What is it, what do you see?" Jax asked her, his gaze going from Elvis to Kiara.

"Something, or someone, is under that overhang with your contact," Kiara whispered.

Stryker turned, and together with Jax, they popped their batons out and slowly approached Ridon. Kiara had already extended a protection field around them, just in case.

Ridon, sensing that something had frightened his guests, immediately left the overhang to approach Jax and Stryker.

"What is wrong? Are you picking up something on scans?" Ridon hurriedly asked.

"Ridon, who's in the cave with you?" Stryker demanded.

Ridon's steps faltered, and he looked genuinely confused before realization dawned on him.

"No, no, you misunderstand," he hurriedly rushed to reassure them. Ridon, about a foot and a half shorter than Stryker, looked almost childlike as he approached them. Stryker's reputation, even on this planet, was legendary. He didn't want to be killed before he had a chance to explain. "It is our transportation." He gestured to the overhang and let out an ear-piercing whistle.

Elvis let out another screech before going strangely quiet. Kiara watched in amazement as creatures emerged from the overhang, six in all, about the size of an Earth elephant. Kiara smiled as Elvis began to huff at them. She could feel his unease.

The creatures were the same mix of colors as the landscape, most likely to help camouflage them from any predators. Most of their bodies seemed to be taken up by what appeared to be lungs, and Kiara thought their bodies must have adapted over the centuries to the thin atmosphere. They walked on four legs, and their heads were dominated by long noses. The noses didn't appear to be flexible and weren't long like an elephant's, but Kiara supposed it helped them breathe. Each animal was outfitted with a harness and saddle. Looking at their feet, she could see large, flat, flexible, calloused feet, perfect for walking on sand or rocks.

She thought they might look like a cross between an Earth horse and elephant, but she couldn't see any hair on them, certainly none of them had a tail. Their ears were tucked close to their heads, and as she looked closer at their heads, she could see that each animal had four eyes.

They were absolutely incredible, and Kiara quickly used her com unit to take a quick picture of them. She knew her dad would enjoy seeing them.

"Ridon, this is perfect!" Styker said with a laugh.

Blackburne and Frankie both looked doubtful.

"Are we supposed to ride on them?" Blackburne questioned.

"But of course. They are perfectly safe." Ridon brought one toward Stryker. "They are from my own herd."

He had a herd of them? Kiara was delighted. She had always wanted to ride a horse, but the opportunity never seemed to present itself. Riding on one of these magnificent animals was going to be as close as she could get. She sent feelings of protection to Elvis and slowly approached Ridon and his animals.

"This is going to be great!" Kiara told the group.

Blackburne gave her a serious frown, but Jax was delighted with her enthusiasm.

Ridon turned to Kiara, curiosity in his gaze. He bowed low to her. "Hello. I am Ridon. I am at your service."

Kiara was unsure how to respond. She hadn't studied the planet's culture, not anticipating that they would encounter any local inhabitants. She looked at Jax, and he gestured for her to bow back and say thank you.

Bowing, Kiara thanked him for his hospitality and introduced herself. It appeared to be the proper response, since Ridon's face was beaming at her when he straightened up. He smiled at Elvis and, grabbing one of the creatures, brought it forward.

"This is Namiba, she will take good care of you," he told her.

Kiara approached the animal cautiously, surprised and delighted when she discovered she could sense the animal's feelings.

"She is very fond of you," Kiara told Ridon.

"You have the gift!" Ridon exclaimed.

"The gift?" Kiara looked confused.

"Yes, yes, the gift!" Ridon looked excited. "You can speak to them, right?"

"No, not really. I just sort of sensed that she was fond of you."

Ridon looked disappointed for a second before he brightened again. "Ask her to come down for you, so that you can gain her back."

Kiara looked doubtful, but after connecting with Elvis, she supposed anything was possible. She reached her hand out and touched the neck and face of the creature. She sensed that the animal liked it, so following that thought, she pictured Namiba folding her legs and Kiara climbing into the saddle.

Kiara watched in amazement as it did just that. The giant creature folded her legs and came down onto her belly. Ridon unfolded an extra strap from the saddle, and Kiara was able to climb up. Elvis made a couple of rumbling noises from unease, but once Kiara was seated and Namiba remained steady, Elvis quieted down.

Kiara looked at a beaming Ridon. "What are these wonderful creatures called? I don't remember reading anything about them."

"They are called Amdrolans. They are from this planet, but not much about this planet is reported correctly." Ridon patted the massive animal with affection. "Because you can communicate this way with her, you can direct her with your mind. The others will have to use the harness."

Ridon helped the others gain their mounts, each outfitted with a harness for control. Blackburne studied the harness assembly with some doubt. A small cloth-like harness was fitted over the animal's head. The controls were mounted to the saddle and were connected wirelessly.

"Are you sure this will work?" Frankie asked what Blackburne was probably thinking. To Frankie, as a pilot, what he was looking at didn't make sense, but he was willing to give it a try.

Ridon, smiling, gave everyone a quick demonstration of the controls and, after a few maneuvers, deemed the group ready to travel.

Before they headed out, Ridon approached Kiara and Elvis, reached into his suit, pulled out a small piece of fabric, and gave it to Kiara. "This will help him," he said.

"Thank you," Kiara said, and quickly wrapped Elvis in it. She moved the little drayek to her lap, hoping to shield him further from the harshness around them.

"What about the traffickers? How far are they?" Stryker asked as they set off.

"We should catch up to them in about two hours," Ridon said. "They are moving slowly—I believe some of the captives may be sick or very weak, and it is slowing them down."

Stryker nodded grimly and exchanged a look with Jax. "It will help us to catch them, but it will complicate the situation when we try to get the captives out."

Ridon, behind his scarf and hood, looked solemn. "We are glad you are here for them. We have some from my village that will help in whatever way they can, once the captives are free."

"Thank you, my friend," Stryker replied.

The Amdrolans moved gracefully, despite their bulk, and Kiara was enjoying the ride. Her mount followed the others, so there wasn't much she had to do to control it. She could feel Elvis start to relax, and Kiara used the moment to try to sense others nearby. The landscape was just as barren on this side of the rocks as it was on the other, so there wasn't much to look at. Looking at the barren landscape, Kiara wondered what the Amdrolans, or Ridon for that matter, ate. Her curiosity getting the better of her, she reached down to touch her mount and pictured them next to Ridon on his mount. Kiara's mount immediately increased her pace until they caught up to Ridon, who was leading the group.

"Kiara, you are doing well with her," Ridon said when she caught up to him.

"Thank you, Ridon. She is a joy to ride," Kiara said with a smile behind her breather mask. "Ridon, what do they eat? I don't see anything but dirt and rocks. And what about water?"

Ridon nodded at her. "Aahh, it is not like other planets you have visited?" Ridon chuckled. "The Amdrolans eat roots that are just under the surface. The roots supply the water they need as well."

"How do they get to the roots?" Kiara asked. She pictured the feet of the Amdrolans, and they didn't seem capable of digging through the rocky soil.

"They have a bony protrusion on their tongue. It is used to dig through the dirt, along with their nose."

Kiara tried to picture it, but she just couldn't.

Ridon saw her confusion. "When we stop for a break, I will show you."

"Thank you, Ridon." Kiara thought about her other questions. "What do you and the other villagers eat?"

Ridon, eager to share information about his planet and village, told Kiara about their underground gardens and the aquifers that supplied their water. Apparently, the gardens didn't require sunlight as they did on Earth. Kiara knew she would look up some of the information to understand it better. This planet, which had looked so barren and inhospitable, definitely had a lot more to it.

Kiara moved her mount back towards Jax, just wanting to be near him. Jax returned her smile through his breather mask. Kiara searched for something to say, but it was Jax who finally broke the silence.

"You are okay?"

"Yes, I'm okay. How about you?" Kiara rolled her eyes. Really, could she sound anymore childish?

"It is okay, Kiara," Jax said softly, his empathetic nature sensing her unease. "We haven't seen each other for quite some time, so it is bound to be a little awkward."

Kiara let out a sigh, and Elvis, wrapped up in his blanket, poked his head out to chirp at her. Kiara quickly patted him and covered him back up. There was already a fine dusting of the reddish dirt on the fabric.

"How is your father doing?" Jax asked into the silence.

"I think he's bored," Kiara said with a grin. "He's trying to be retired again, and I think it's killing him."

Jax nodded, picturing her dad trying to do nothing, and shaking his head. "I cannot imagine him being retired. He is too active, too involved in all that is going on."

"I agree, so we'll see how long it lasts."

"What about you, Kiara? Are you bored as well?"

Damn him and his empathetic nature! He could tell she was bored. Before she could answer, he tried to reassure her.

"It would be natural for you to feel this way, after everything you have been through."

Kiara nodded. "I think we are all feeling a little bored. There was so much going on for a while—excitement, trying to stay alive, discovering my powers. It's been hard to go back to the normal routine."

"It is understandable."

Suddenly, Kiara could sense someone else's presence. She sat up straighter in the saddle, and Elvis immediately poked his head out of the fabric and stuck his nose in the air.

"What is it, Kiara?" Jax signaled Stryker, and the group slowed down.

"I sense someone or something," Kiara said, trying hard to determine what it was. "I think they are too far away for me to really understand what they are."

Ridon brought his mount back to Jax and Kiara. Stryker, Blackburne, and Frankie went on full alert, looking for anything that might be a threat.

"Ridon, are we close?" Jax asked him.

"Yes, I believe we may be close. It was hard to estimate where we might see the traffickers, as their pace has been erratic."

Kiara tried hard to see through the haze, but it just looked like endless sand and rocks to her.

"Where do you think they are? How far away are they?" Jax fired rapid questions at their guide.

Ridon rushed to reassure them. "There is a ridge of rocks just ahead. They have been traveling on the other side of the ridge." Ridon looked from Jax to Kiara. "We are not in danger. They cannot know that we are here."

Jax nodded, feeling slightly relieved. He looked at Kiara and noticed that she had her eyes closed, and even through her breather mask, he could see that her skin had flushed a darker blue.

"Kiara, anything?" Jax asked her.

Kiara slowly opened her eyes and turned her head to look at Jax. "I can't tell where they are, but I'm not sensing any alarm from them."

"Can you sense the captives?" Blackburne asked her.

Kiara turned sad eyes towards Blackburne. "Yes, I sense their despair. It is almost overwhelming."

"The ridge of rocks is not that large; we will be able to scale it and see where they are," Ridon quickly told the group.

"We can't see anything through this haze," Jax said, looking around. "Ridon, did you bring anything that would help us see through this haze?"

With a nod, Ridon opened his pack and handed Jax a small lens. Jax raised the lens to his mask and quickly scanned the area before giving it to Stryker.

"That will work, Ridon, thank you. I can see the ridge up ahead and didn't see anyone else in the area."

The group set off again, heading to the ridge. They reached the rocks, and Jax and Ridon dismounted and headed to a spot where they could see the other side. It only took a few minutes, and the pair came stumbling back down the rocks.

"We see them, up ahead of us, moving slowly," Jax quickly told the group. "We need to get closer so we can get a better idea of how many traffickers there are, what kind of weapons they have, and how many captives there are."

Jax and Ridon mounted quickly, and the group set off at a quick pace. At the point where Ridon estimated they had caught up with the traffickers on the other side, they halted. Once again, Jax and Ridon dismounted and climbed the ridge. This time, they were gone considerably longer, but Kiara could sense that Jax was fine, so she didn't worry. She supposed that they were gathering information. When they finally came back down, Kiara knew it was bad, both from the look on their faces and the feelings pumping off of Jax.

"What is it, what's wrong?" Kiara asked before she could stop herself.

Jax looked at her but addressed the group. "They have at least two hundred women and girls, some of them appear to be near death." Jax looked at Stryker. "We counted ten heavily armed traffickers. They are making the women and children walk, and most of them look ready to collapse. The traffickers are riding single-occupant quads. The videos are on your com units."

Jax, Stryker, Ridon, and Blackburne discussed strategies for a few moments before deciding they would attack them from three sides. Jax, Ridon, and Frankie would approach from behind, while Stryker and Blackburne approached from the front. Kiara would stay near the middle and protect or fire energy pulses as needed. Jax and Stryker readied their batons, and Ridon pulled a few weapons out of his pack, giving one to Frankie and one to Blackburne. Blackburne recognized the weapon as a laser-firing weapon and hoped it was accurate. Ridon approached Kiara and offered her a weapon as well, but she politely refused. Ridon looked confused.

"How will you protect yourself?" Before she could answer, he turned to Jax. "One of us should go with her to make sure she is protected. She is in danger without a weapon."

Jax chuckled. "She is the weapon."

Ridon looked more confused than ever at that statement, but followed Jax and Frankie up the rocks. Kiara headed for her position, watching Stryker and Blackburne hustle to get in front of the traffickers. They wouldn't be that far from her, so she quickly protected everyone with a protection field, including herself and Elvis.

"Ready, little man?" Kiara asked him as she reached up and touched his toes. Elvis was sitting on her shoulder, his tail wrapped around her upper arm, his smaller front legs touching her breather mask. He chirped at her in answer, and she took that to mean that he was ready.

Crouching low, she approached the top of the ridge. She had to work hard to block out the despair that was coming from the captives. She reached the top and looked down, seeing the women and children, stumbling along, barely moving. Some of the women were trying to carry the smaller girls, and Kiara wondered how they managed to do it. All the women looked too fatigued to carry their own weight, much less the weight of a child. The traffickers were wearing breathers and protective suits. They rode their quads around the captives, yelling at them to keep moving and shouting insults. Kiara was surprised that they were mistreating the captives. If a bunch of the captives died, or they arrived too sick to be able to sell, didn't that cut into their profits? The more she watched, the angrier she got.

She heard over her com unit that everyone was in position and waiting for Stryker to give the go-ahead. Kiara had a better idea. She told everyone to hold their position and just watch for any traffickers that might run. Blackburne yelled back into the com for her to stand down, but Kiara calmly told him that this would be safer for everyone, including the captives.

Closing her eyes, she reached up and touched Elvis, gathering her power, using her anger to intensify it. When she was ready, she opened her eyes, which were now dark violet, and her skin was a dark blue. Using her hands to control and aim her power, she shot an energy pulse at the nearest quad rider. As the energy pulse hit him, he flew backwards off the quad about fifty feet, landing in an unconscious heap. A few women close to him screamed and jumped back, and the chaos started. A couple of the riders who were near the first rider quickly rode their quads over to him, scanning the area for the threat, their weapons ready. Kiara knew she couldn't waste any time. She shot more pulses out, taking out one after another. She watched as one of the traffickers ran and picked up one of the children to use as a shield. He spun in a circle, trying to keep the child between him and whatever was taking them out. Kiara smiled. That would not protect him. Shooting a smaller pulse at his head, he dropped to the ground when the energy hit him. The child was scared, but unharmed.

Through her com unit, she could hear Ridon shout in surprise, and then Jax telling her where the other traffickers were. It only took a few minutes, and all the traffickers were lying on the ground. The others in her group left the ridge and approached the caravan. Jax and Stryker secured the traffickers, while Blackburne, Frankie, and Ridon tried to reassure the women and children. They were having a tough time; to the captives, the rescuers looked just as violent and scary as their previous captors. Kiara knew it didn't help the situation that her group was in suits and masks.

Kiara hurried down to see if she could help. Seeing a woman may help calm the captives down. She approached the chaotic scene in front of her; some of the women were weeping hysterically, others huddled in small groups, trying their best to shield the young girls. Taking a deep breath, she removed her breather mask and made eye contact with one of the women in front of her. She saw shock, then relief crossed the woman's face.

"We're here to help," Kiara said quietly.

The woman hobbled over to her and threw herself on Kiara, weeping with relief. Elvis made quiet chirping noises and tried to stay out of the way of the woman's wildly swinging arms as she grabbed Kiara. Slowly, the other women and some of the girls saw Kiara and Elvis and made their way over. Kiara gently disengaged the woman's arms and, with a hand under the woman's chin, raised her chin so she could make eye contact again.

"We're here to help. Please let the others know so they won't be scared." Kiara could feel the pressure on her lungs to keep breathing, so she needed to make this quick. She had no idea how any of these women or children were still breathing. "I need to put my mask on now. Please let the others know that they can trust us."

The woman nodded at her, and Kiara quickly donned her breathing mask, taking a few deep breaths to relieve the pressure in her chest. The woman turned and spoke to those closest to her, and in turn, they told others. The crying stopped, and most of the women and children tried to huddle around Kiara. She could hear Blackburne congratulate her over the com unit, and Jax and Stryker grunting as they moved the unconscious traffickers to one area.

Suddenly, she could hear yelling, and some of the women started screaming again. Turning, she saw that one of the traffickers had woken up before Jax and Stryker had gotten to him, and he was headed straight for her. She didn't have her protection field up, and he was closing fast. Out of the corner of her eye, she saw Blackburne trying to get his weapon out, and Jax and Stryker running for her. Thinking first of protection, she raised a protective field around herself and the other women. The field was large, and Kiara could feel it stretching her limits. The trafficker, seeing all the women between him and Kiara, and knowing that he was running out of time, pulled a large dagger out and threw it at Kiara. Kiara knew, an instant before it hit her, that it was going to penetrate her protection field.

The dagger hit high in her shoulder, penetrating deep. She started to fall, but the women surrounding her caught her and gently lowered her to the ground. She heard Elvis howl and tried to tell him to stay with her, but it was too late. He jumped from her shoulder as she started to fall and shot straight at her attacker. She couldn't see him because of all the women surrounding her, but she heard her attacker's screams of pain and agony. His screams only lasted a few seconds before he was silenced. Kiara could hear Blackburne and Jax yelling for her, but the pain was so bad she couldn't respond.

The wall of women surrounding her with concerned looks suddenly parted, and Jax was running up to her, his eyes on the dagger still protruding from her shoulder. Kneeling next to her, Jax removed his pack to get to the medical supplies. He performed a quick scan with the portable med scanner and then looked at her with concern.

"I can't remove it yet," he grimly told her.

Kiara nodded, still in too much pain to answer. She was surprised at how much pain she was in.

"I'm going to give you something for the pain," Jax said, reaching into his pack again.

Kiara used her uninjured arm to stop him. Gritting her teeth, she shook her head 'no' at him when he looked at her.

"Kiara, you need something!" Jax implored her. He could see how much pain she was in. It suddenly dawned on him that she was worried about protecting everyone. "How about a half dose?"

Kiara reluctantly nodded, and Jax quickly administered the meds. The relief was immediate, and Kiara felt like she could breathe again.

"Thanks," she whispered.

Jax nodded and produced some compacted bandages from the pack. After letting them open and expand, he started wrapping her shoulder, working to stabilize the dagger so it wouldn't cause more harm. The women helped to hold her steady and assisted Jax in completing the task.

"I've got to stabilize this until we can get back on the Acadia," Jax whispered.

Kiara nodded her understanding. Now that the pain was subsiding, she was becoming more aware of her surroundings and what was happening. On her com unit, she could hear Blackburne talking to Larry, asking him to bring the Acadia to their location. She looked at Jax in alarm.

"Can Larry pilot the Acadia?" Kiara whispered the question. The painkiller was working, but it was making her a little woozy at the same time. She felt like she couldn't talk above a whisper.

"Let Blackburne and Frankie worry about that," Jax told her.

"You're so handsome," Kiara whispered.

At the look from Jax, Kiara slapped her good hand over her eyes in horror. Had she said that out loud?

Jax let out a small chuckle. He slowly reached out and gently moved her hand from her face. Their eyes met, and she saw his emotions for her. He always kept them hidden, but his concern for her was overriding his usual control.

Kiara felt those feelings deep inside and sighed. She desperately wanted to close her eyes and let the pain meds work. Still, she needed to stay alert for everyone's safety here. And where was Elvis? She tried to look past Jax, but he was busy trying to stabilize her and wouldn't let her move. There were still so many women standing around her, looking concerned. Jax finally finished with her shoulder, saw the anxiety on her face, and quickly realized what she was thinking.

"Elvis is fine," he quietly told her. "He's keeping watch just outside the circle of women. I think he wants to make sure he sees the next threat coming."

Kiara, finally able to calm down, closed her eyes and connected to Elvis. She sensed his anger, but also his watchfulness, and his concern for her. She sent him feelings of love, and he relaxed slightly.

The women around her parted again, and Blackburne joined them. Squatting down, he looked at the portable med scanner and then at the dagger in her shoulder. His frown firmly in place, he finally looked at Kiara.

"We've got the Acadia on its way. You're going to be fine," he said gruffly.

Kiara smiled weakly. "I didn't know that Larry could fly the Acadia."

"Frankie's been practicing with him. He's in constant contact with him right now. He'll get it here."

Kiara nodded. She hoped the ship would get here quickly. The pain was quickly overriding the painkiller, but since she was already woozy, she didn't want Jax to give her anymore. She became aware of a couple of young girls who had pushed their way into the circle of women and were trying to get close to her. One of the women brought them forward and told them to be careful as they knelt next to Kiara. One of the girls, Kiara thought her to be no more than ten Earth years old, scooted as close to Kiara as she could. The little girl's face was gaunt, her blue eyes taking up most of her face. She could see discoloration in the whites of her eyes and wondered briefly at the cause.

"Thank you," the little girl whispered, and reached out to hold Kiara's hand.

Kiara smiled as tears streamed down her face. The pain was worth it. To save these little girls and the other women was worth every moment of pain.

Chapter 3

Kiara could hear the thunder of the Acadia's engines as it approached them. She struggled to keep her eyes open. The pain and medication were making it hard for her to stay in the moment. She looked down at her hand, seeing the little girl's hand still holding hers. She smiled; at least she thought she was smiling as she looked at their joined hands.

Dirt and haze flew into the air around them, and several of the women used their own meager clothing to help shield Kiara. She was grateful but didn't have the energy to thank them. She heard the engines cut out and knew that the Acadia had landed. Kiara acknowledged in the back of her brain that Larry had successfully piloted the ship to their present location. She could hear Elvis chirping in the background, and she suddenly received a very happy feeling from him. The women around her parted, some looking fearful, some with a look of wonder on their faces. Kiara realized why when Curly's light brown, bear-like form approached her. Curly towered above all the women and children surrounding Kiara.

"Kiara!" Curly exclaimed.

"I'm okay," Kiara whispered.

The little girl holding her hand squeezed hard. Kiara looked at the little girl's face.

"Don't let it hurt us," the little girl whispered.

"It's okay," Kiara whispered back. "She's my friend." The little girl still didn't look convinced. Kiara tried again to put the little girl at ease. "What's your name?" Kiara whispered.

The little girl stopped looking at Curly and turned her attention back to Kiara. Leaning close to Kiara, she whispered, "Zara."

Kiara nodded. "Zara, this is Curly. She is my very good friend, and she will keep us safe."

When Zara heard the words 'keep us safe', she relaxed slightly. It seemed to be what she had been waiting for. She smiled shyly at Curly.

Curly stood next to Kiara, waiting for an opportunity to help Kiara. Kiara looked up at Curly and nodded to her large Bendanite friend. Curly bent over and effortlessly picked up Kiara. The little girl wouldn't let go of Kiara's hand, so the three of them made their way to the Acadia. About halfway there, Elvis joined them, positioning himself on Curly's shoulder and chirping at Kiara in between his scans of the area.

Curly took Kiara straight to the med-bay. After getting Kiara comfortable on the bed, she looked at the little girl still holding Kiara's hand. "You come with me?" Curly asked in her softest voice. "Kiara rest."

The little girl looked at Kiara in alarm.

"It's okay, you can go with her," Kiara reassured Zara. "She will take you to be with the others. You're safe now."

Zara reluctantly let go of Kiara's hand and looked up at Curly. Curly slowly held out her large hand, and the little girl tentatively reached her small hand out and touched Curly's hand. She looked at Kiara in wonder.

"It's soft," she whispered.

Kiara smiled at the little girl as Curly led her out of the med-bay. Elvis was curled up against her side, alternately chirping and huffing. Kiara snuggled him closer, grateful to have him with her.

They were soon joined by Blackburne, with his usual frown still in place.

"Kiara, you look like hell," Blackburne said as he pulled out scanning equipment and bandages.

Kiara smiled weakly. "Thanks." She closed her eyes for a brief second before continuing, "Is everyone else okay? Are you getting them on board?"

"Stop worrying about everyone else besides yourself," he quietly admonished her. "Everyone is fine, and we should be loaded shortly."

"They're going to need medical attention," Kiara said. When Blackburne frowned harder at her, she shrugged her good shoulder. "I noticed the little girl's eyes. I assumed it was a lack of oxygen and poor nutrition, so just getting them on the ship isn't going to be enough."

"I agree, but Ridon's village isn't equipped to handle it, so we'll have to make do until we can meet up with a medical ship."

Kiara nodded while Blackburne finished the scan. He looked over at her, concern interrupting his usual frown.

"The dagger is up against the bone and is pressing against a major artery." Blackburne showed her the scan. "That's why we couldn't take it out before."

Kiara nodded her understanding. The painkiller was starting to wear off, making it challenging to talk again. At least now she knew why it was so painful. The dagger was pressed against bone. Taking shallow breaths, she asked Blackburne what the next steps were.

"Jax is going to come up and assist me as soon as they get everyone loaded." Blackburne began to connect her to monitors and readied an anesthetic. Noticing that the pain was starting to get out of control, he quickly gave her another shot of painkiller. "Frankie is going to wait to clear the atmosphere until we're done.

We don't want the bumpy ride out of here to jostle something loose."

Kiara could feel the engines rumble to life and supposed that Frankie would at least take them back to their landing point so they could pick up Stryker's smaller ship.

"What about the traffickers?" Kiara asked, feeling the pain start to subside again.

"Ridon and his village are going to hold them until the Rangers can get here."

"You were able to talk the Rangers into coming?" Kiara was surprised. She didn't think the Rangers could be bothered.

"We sent video, and it got their attention."

The Acadia shifted slightly as Frankie got the ship in the air, heading to their original landing point. Inside, the ride was smooth, and Kiara knew Frankie was doing everything he could to keep it steady.

Jax joined them in the med-bay, and Kiara knew it was time to get the dagger out. She was trying to be brave, but she was scared. She'd seen the scans and knew, even with all the medical advances and technology on this ship, it was going to be a tricky surgery. Elvis gently climbed onto her stomach and touched her face. Her worry blended with his worry.

Jax approached the bed and gently cupped the side of her face with his hand, his eyes full of concern.

"Don't worry, we'll take care of you," Jax said quietly.

"Your eyes tell me that you're worried," Kiara said. To her embarrassment, tears started to stream down her cheeks.

Jax gently wiped her tears, knowing she hated to cry. "Yes, I'm worried, but I also know how tough you are."

Kiara smiled, and when she saw Blackburne approach the bed, she moved Elvis away from her shoulder, silently asking him to stay out of the way. He chirped his worry at her, but Kiara firmly told him to stay there. He quieted down and snuggled into her again, his eyes watching every move that Jax and Blackburne made.

Blackburne administered the anesthetic, and Kiara slowly floated away.

Kiara?

Mirona? Kiara slowly became aware of her ancestor speaking to her. She struggled to remember where she was and what was happening. Her brain seemed to be fogged.

I can sense that you are not well.

*Yes....*Kiara struggled for another moment before the events of the day came flooding back. She must still be under anesthesia.

What has happened, Kiara?

We were helping to rescue some women and children who were being trafficked across different worlds. One of the traffickers threw a dagger at me.

You weren't able to protect yourself?

I had thrown up protection around myself and the women around me. I think the field was too large. I could feel how stretched it was.

Did you protect the women around you?

Yes, we were able to rescue them.

So, you have become a Guardian?

Kiara thought of all the people she hadn't been able to save on the space station. Her sadness was transmitted to Mirona.

What is it, Kiara? Why are you so sad? You saved the women and children.

Mirona, I wasn't able to save many people on a space station. I tried, but I wasn't able to do it.

Kiara, you can't save everyone. Did you give all you had to save them?

Yes, I gave it everything I had.

Then, as a Guardian, that is all you can do.

Did you ever lose anyone? You always seemed so powerful.
Yes, Kiara, there are those that I wasn't able to save.
How do I get stronger, Mirona?
You must practice. That is the only way.
Yes, I understand.
Have you been saving many others?

Kiara thought about the normal routine that she and her shipmates had fallen back into.

Not really. After all the danger and battles from before, I thought I wanted things to go back to normal. We went back to hauling cargo, and I only practiced small stuff after that. I didn't want to put myself or my shipmates in danger.

Kiara, you are a Guardian. It is your destiny.

Kiara slowly woke up in the med-bay, aware of the dull, throbbing pain in her shoulder and the weight of Elvis on her stomach. She lay for a moment, thinking of her dream with her ancestor, Mirona. Mirona, who looked so much like Kiara that they could have been sisters, had come to her while she'd been under anesthesia. Her destiny, that's what Mirona had said.

Blinking her eyes open, she wanted to laugh at the absurdity of what she was seeing. Elvis, trying to be careful of her wound, had sensed that she was awake and had positioned himself so that the first thing she would see would be his face. His eyes stared intently at her, and his worry blasted into her head. Kiara reached up with her good arm and stroked the top of his head. Her mouth felt like it had cotton in it, so she was pretty sure she wouldn't be able to talk.

"Kiara?" Jax spoke her name from across the room.

Turning her head slightly, she saw that he had pulled in a box from somewhere to use as a makeshift chair. She tried to smile but wasn't too sure she had pulled it off.

Jax got up from the box and checked her monitors before standing next to her. He patted the happily chattering Elvis as he looked at Kiara.

"Any pain?"

Kiara shook her head. The dull, throbbing pain in her shoulder didn't really seem to qualify.

"Your mouth is dry?" When she nodded again, he grabbed something from the table next to the bed and asked her to open her mouth. He quickly sprayed something in her mouth.

The relief was instantaneous. "Thank you," Kiara croaked out.

Cupping her cheek, he nodded.

"Did everything go okay?" Kiara asked him. "I assume it did, since I'm here and the dagger is gone."

"Yes, it went well. I was grateful that we had the computer-assisted program onboard. I don't think we would have been successful without it." His voice dropped to a whisper. "You would have bled out if we did not have the assistance." He bent over and kissed her brow.

"Thank you," Kiara whispered back. She knew it was bad, but didn't really comprehend how close to death she may have been. "Did anyone contact my dad?"

Straightening, Jax rechecked her monitors before answering. "Yes, Blackburne contacted him after we finished repairing your shoulder."

Kiara grimaced. "How bad was it?"

Jax smiled at her. "Let's just say I was glad it was not me." He grabbed her com unit from the nearby table and put it next to her. "Better contact him before he tries to fly out here."

Kiara looked at her com unit before meeting Jax's gaze. "How long have I been out?"

"About six hours."

"Are the women and children still on board?" Kiara remembered the little girl who had been holding her hand.

"Yes. We'll meet up with a medical ship big enough to handle all of them in about an hour."

"Are they doing okay?"

Jax smiled at her. She had a big heart, he knew. "They are doing the best they can. We have plenty of water, and we were able to give them small amounts of food. Just being in a good oxygen environment has been a tremendous help."

Kiara nodded. "I'm glad. Where will they go, do you know?"

"We sent the video to the GTA, and they have agreed to help them. For those who have a home, they will get them home; for the others, they will try to find a place for them on Earth Delta Nine." Jax chuckled while he looked at her monitors again. "All of them have asked to come in and thank you and see if you are alright."

"Really?"

"Yes, the little girl who was holding your hand has been very persistent. She greets us at the door every time we go in and asks about you."

"I'm glad we were able to help them."

"Me too. Now, stop stalling and call your dad," Jax said as he headed to the door.

When Jax shut the door behind him, Kiara looked at Elvis. "I guess I'd better call him," she said on a sigh.

Her dad answered immediately, so Kiara knew that he had been waiting for her to contact him.

"Hi, Dad," Kiara said quietly. She made sure to enable the video portion of the call because she knew he would want to see how she was doing, not just hear it.

"Kiara, how are you?" Kyle McCallister let his worry come through his voice. He never imagined, when he had decided to adopt her, that he would have moments like these.

"I'm doing okay," Kiara replied, and tried to look at ease. She noticed her dad's hair looked like he'd been constantly running his fingers through it, a sure sign of his worry.

Her dad squinted his eyes at her through the connection. "How much pain are you in?" He knew that she was trying to keep him from worrying.

"Not too much, right now." Kiara smiled at him, trying to reassure him. "Jax and Blackburne are taking very good care of me."

Kyle looked down, but not before Kiara saw the anger in his face.

"Why are you mad?"

"Why didn't they protect you?" Kyle finally let his anger out in a shout.

"Protect me?" Kiara was genuinely baffled. "I'm supposed to protect them."

Kyle growled low in his throat and let out an expletive.

"Dad, it was my job! I was protecting those women and children!" Before he could say something, she continued, "I'm a Guardian, that's what I'm supposed to do. I just wasn't good enough."

Her dad muttered another expletive.

"Dad!"

"You shouldn't have to worry about being good enough!"

"Dad, you can't be mad at Blackburne or Jax. They did their job. I went off script, so it was probably my fault anyway."

"What do you mean?"

"I saw those women and children, and their despair was hitting me, and I got so angry." Kiara took a deep, calming breath. "I thought I could take out all the traffickers, without endangering any of my shipmates or the captives. I was wrong."

Kyle seemed to calm down a little bit at her explanation. "I didn't realize. Did Blackburne give you hell?"

"Not yet, but I'm sure it's coming," Kiara said, looking chagrined.

"Blackburne told me about your injury and the tricky surgery." Her dad was back to looking worried. "Are you sure you're okay?"

"I'm a little sore, but the pain isn't bad. I haven't tried to move my arm yet." Kiara was afraid to move it. She knew that with advanced medical techniques, her arm would be nearly healed within a day, but the scan of her injury scared her.

They both fell silent, Kyle trying to control his anger and Kiara unsure of what to say.

"Is Elvis okay?" Kyle finally asked.

"Yes," Kiara answered quickly and moved Elvis over so her dad could see the drayek. Elvis chirped at her dad, but Kiara wasn't sure the little drayek knew precisely what was happening. "He protected us, again."

Kyle made a face, picturing the last time that Elvis had protected Kiara. The little drayek had ripped out the throat of a man who was trying to kill Kiara.

Kiara, seeing her dad's face, knew what he was thinking. "Yeah, it was like that," she said with a nod.

"I'm glad he's on our side," Kyle said with a grimace.

"Are you going to try to come out here?" Kiara asked him.

With a sigh, Kyle shook his head no. "It would take me days to reach you, and from what I understand from Blackburne, you guys are on the move, anyway."

"Oh, okay. I haven't spoken to him yet, so other than dropping off the captives, I don't know what our plans are."

They spoke for a few more minutes before disconnecting. Kiara was relieved that her dad wasn't going to try to fly out to be with her. She loved him and missed him, but didn't want to try to explain her decision to him just yet. Her dream with Mirona and the satisfaction she had found in helping the captives had shifted something in her. She looked down at Elvis, remembering her boredom and dissatisfaction before Jax had asked for their help. She knew now that she couldn't go back to the normal cargo-hauling routine that had been her life before. Mirona was right—she was a Guardian, and she needed to embrace that. Reaching down, she ruffled the tufts of hair on Elvis's head.

Closing her eyes, she asked Elvis, in the only way she knew how, if he was okay doing more 'Guardian' things. She pictured cargo hauling, sitting at her navunit, then helping the captives and protecting the space station. Granted, neither of the Guardian scenarios had worked out to the best, but she knew she could get better. Kiara kept replaying the scenes in her head, trying to sense which one Elvis wanted, or at the very least, which of the scenes he absolutely hated. At first, she couldn't seem to get anything from him. She opened her eyes and looked at him. It seemed to be what he was waiting for. Standing on his hind legs, Elvis reached out and touched her face with his smaller front feet, bringing his face close to hers. An image popped into Kiara's head. It was she and Elvis, together, with nothing else around them.

Kiara smiled at Elvis. He was telling her that he just wanted to be with her; it didn't matter what the circumstances were. "I agree, little man."

Now, if she could only figure out what to do next. Kiara loved working with Blackburne, Frankie, and the Bendanites, but she was pretty sure this decision would take her in a different direction than theirs. She also wasn't sure if Jax and Stryker would want her help on a more permanent basis, but if they didn't, perhaps they could help her find someone or something that did need her.

With her decision made, she supposed that she had put off trying to move her arm long enough. Setting Elvis aside, she slowly raised her arm, and when she felt only dull pain and stiffness, she tried some other movements. Pleasantly surprised that the movements didn't hurt, she slowly got off the bed, her intention to get cleaned up and change her clothes. Elvis already looked cleaned, so she supposed that Curly had probably come in and cleaned him up while she was sedated.

She headed to the bridge later, feeling refreshed and clear-headed. Wearing a clean black skinsuit and a light blue tunic, her hair clean and braided, she was ready to talk to the others. She had decided to speak to Blackburne first. No matter what direction she moved, she wouldn't leave him short-handed.

Checking the time on her com unit, she knew they were close to meeting up with the medical ship. She wanted to help get everyone settled and make sure she had a chance to say goodbye to Zara.

As she entered the bridge, she caught Frankie's eye first—he gave a relieved smile—then Blackburne. Blackburne was sitting at her navunit, and Kiara was surprised to see that he looked more relieved than Frankie. She wasn't sure if it was because she could take over the navigation duties or because she was up and about. She approached her navunit, and Blackburne jumped to his feet. As she sat down, he quickly briefed her on their position. Kiara's fingers flew over her console as she listened to Blackburne. She was up to speed instantly and looked up at Blackburne when he finished speaking.

"Got it," Kiara told him.

"Are you up for this?" Blackburne asked her.

"I'm good." Kiara nodded emphatically.

Blackburne studied her face for a moment before he turned and headed for his seat.

A short time later, they rendezvoused with the medical ship, and Frankie expertly guided them next to it so they could dock. Kiara was relieved to see that it was a large medical ship and bore the markings of the GTA. Kiara quickly rechecked her sensors. Everything looked normal, and she didn't detect any ships approaching their position, so she headed to the cargo area.

Kiara entered the cargo area and saw that one of the Bendanites had already set up the docking tunnel to the medical ship. Several crew members from the medical ship were setting up on the other side with hover chairs and stretchers. Before she could take more than a couple of steps into the cargo room, a small shape flew at her from the right side of the room. Kiara recognized Zara a moment before the little girl's body slammed into her side. Elvis wobbled slightly on her good shoulder, huffing at the little girl.

"You're here!" Zara exclaimed, hugging Kiara as tightly as she could.

Kiara reached a hand down and stroked the little girl's hair, smiling at the exuberance from her. She could tell that the oxygen and a small amount of food had already worked wonders for Zara.

"You're better, I can tell," Kiara told her. As she looked up from the little girl, she saw that many of the women and children were crowding around her, smiling and murmuring their thanks. She could sense their feelings of gratitude and knew that her decision to help others in need was the right one.

Squatting down next to Zara, she looked into the little girl's eyes. She had spent a little time looking up information about the little girl and had been relieved to discover that Zara did have family to go to.

"Are you feeling better?" Zara asked Kiara. Zara liked having Kiara down at her level. She reached a small hand out and stroked Kiara's long, dark braid.

"Yes, I'm much better, thank you," Kiara responded. She waited, sensing that the little girl had more to say.

Zara looked down, shuffled her feet, and clasped her hands together in front of her. Kiara waited, knowing that if she spoke, the little girl wouldn't say anything else. Finally, Zara looked up, looked at Kiara, and then swung her eyes to Elvis.

"Can I pet him?" she quietly asked.

Kiara smiled. That was not what she was expecting. She could sense fear, curiosity, and affection coming from Zara. At the same time, Elvis realized what was happening, and she could feel apprehension and suspicion emanating from the drayek. Elvis danced around on Kiara's good shoulder and made huffing noises before she finally quieted him with a quick thought of reassurance. She silently asked the little drayek to come down to the floor between herself and Zara, then spoke aloud to the little girl. "Of course, you can pet him." With Elvis now on the floor, Kiara took the little girl's hand and gently placed it on Elvis's back. "Be gentle."

The little girl's eyes popped open wide at the contact with Elvis, and as she slowly moved her hand gently down his back, she quietly giggled. "He doesn't have any hair," she whispered to Kiara. "It's not like Curly."

Kiara nodded, noting that both the little girl and Elvis were relaxing and starting to enjoy the moment. The little girl removed her hand, and Elvis chirped at her. Zara turned questioning eyes to Kiara.

"He wants you to keep petting him," Kiara said, surprised at how quickly Elvis had warmed up to the little girl.

Zara immediately obliged, and, still petting him, she sat down and crossed her legs. All suspicion of the little girl from Elvis was now gone. Kiara watched in amazement as Elvis climbed into the little girl's lap, curled up, and rumbled for her. As she watched, tears flowed down Zara's cheeks, even though she was still smiling.

"What's wrong?" Kiara quietly asked her.

"He reminds me of my kitty," Zara sniffed back. "I hope he's still there."

"Me too," Kiara whispered back.

One of the women approached Zara and touched her on the top of her head. "Time to go, Zara."

Elvis jumped onto Kiara's good shoulder as everyone stood up. Zara hugged Kiara one more time before joining the others on the medical ship. Most of the captives had already left, and a few that were making their way to the docking tunnel turned and waved at Kiara before boarding the medical ship.

With the last of the women and children loaded onto the medical ship, Kiara headed to the bridge as the Bendanites closed the cargo bay. She was deep in thought, trying to decide the best time to talk to Blackburne, and rehearsing what to say. A chirp in her ear from Elvis brought her back to the moment at hand, and she realized that Blackburne was approaching her, a serious look on his face. He'd just left the bridge, and Kiara looked down at her com unit to see if she had missed a message from him.

Blackburne saw her look at her com unit, rushing to reassure her. "You aren't late for anything."

Kiara nodded, but since he was still looking straight at her, she thought he must have been looking for her. "Did you need me to do something, or should I go help Frankie?"

"Actually, I wanted to talk to you," he told her, that serious look still firmly in place. "Frankie is okay for now."

"Sure, do you want to go to the kitchen?" Kiara asked as she turned and headed back down the hallway. As she entered the small room, she knew that this was the time to tell him about the decision she had made, as soon as he finished whatever he needed to say. She was so focused on what she was going to say to Blackburne that it took a moment for the situation to sink in. Blackburne was looking serious, and he wanted to talk to her? Her mind jumped to the worst conclusion.

"Is my dad okay?"

"Everyone is fine," Blackburne reassured her, his frown increasing over his agitation. He was never any good at touchy-feely conversations; it's why he was a captain. He just ordered people to get things done, and that was that. "Go ahead and sit," he told her, and gestured to one of the chairs. When Kiara continued to stare at him, he heaved a huge sigh. "Everyone is fine, I just wanted to talk to you about your future."

"Oh," Kiara said, plunking into the seat closest to her. Elvis flapped his little wings to get his balance and huffed at her. Why did he want to talk about her future? This could be bad. "I wanted to talk to you about that as well."

"Really?" Blackburne's frown turned into confusion.

"You go first," Kiara told him. While she waited for him to get started, she moved a small bowl of fruit closer to her and silently let Elvis know that he could have some. The little drayek happily jumped down to the table and grabbed a piece of fruit.

Blackburne's frown returned. "I think there have been some feelings of discontent lately with the crew and myself."

When Kiara opened her mouth to interject something, he silenced her with a look.

"It's nothing you've done," he said, looking toward the doorway, "well, at least not negatively."

Kiara could see he was struggling to find the right words. It suddenly dawned on her that he was probably referring to the same feelings of boredom that she had been experiencing. She smiled, and her smile stopped whatever Blackburne was going to say next.

"Why are you smiling?" he asked her instead.

"I think you guys are bored, like me."

Blackburne chuckled. "You too, huh?" When she nodded, he continued. "Is that what you were going to talk to me about?"

"Yeah," Kiara said a little sheepishly.

"Well then, you go ahead and tell me what you were thinking."

"I came to the decision that I needed to use my powers to help others, and not hide on a cargo ship," Kiara blurted out. She winced. That wasn't exactly how she'd been rehearsing it in her head, and she hoped Blackburne didn't take offense at the 'hide on a cargo ship' comment. She watched her captain's face for a sign of anger or something, but his usual frown was still there. Suddenly, he nodded.

"That's it, exactly," he said. He started pacing around the little kitchen. "We should be helping those in need, like we just did with all those hostages we just rescued." He nodded again. "Hiding is exactly what we're doing. We have someone like you, and we should be taking advantage of it."

Blackburne stopped pacing and turned to look at Kiara to gauge her reaction. His eyebrows went up. She was staring at him, her mouth open.

"You'll catch flies," he teased her, using an old earth phrase.

Kiara snapped her mouth shut. Smiling a little, she said, "That's exactly what I was thinking! I was so worried about how to tell you about my decision, but I want to help people." Unable to sit herself, Kiara stood to pace, and Blackburne threw himself into the nearest chair, not wanting to get in her way.

"I love what I do here," Kiara continued, gesturing with her hands. Elvis, alarmed at her pacing and gesturing, jumped and flapped his way from the table to her shoulder. Kiara distractedly patted his feet and continued. "But after all that excitement on Earth Delta Nine, and the conspiracies, and all that," Kiara threw her arms out wide, her gesture meant to encompass all of the adventures of the past year. She looked at Blackburne to make sure he agreed. He nodded at her.

"At first, I wanted to go back to being normal, to have my old, boring life back." She started pacing again. "But it didn't feel right, and I was bored. Then Jax asked us to help." Winding down, she sat across from Blackburne. "It felt so good to help those people!"

"I agree," Blackburne said. "Frankie thinks so, too. We were both talking about it while you were recovering, but we weren't sure how you were going to feel about it since you were hurt so badly."

"There's risk in everything we do." Kiara thought back to her dream with Mirona, her ancestor. "Mirona told me that I should be a Guardian and to use my powers to help. It made sense to me." She looked at Blackburne hard. "Helping those people was worth getting hurt."

"We thought there was a chance you would think that way."

"Did you talk to the Bendanites?"

Blackburne shook his head. "Not yet, I wanted to talk to you first."

"If they agree, are we going to try to work with Jax and Stryker? I planned to talk to them after I talked to you." Kiara reached up, grabbed the disgruntled Elvis from her shoulder, and hugged him. He chirped at her. "Elvis is okay with the plan, but I haven't talked to my dad yet."

Blackburne winced, and Kiara let out a little laugh. "Yeah, I'm not looking forward to it either. He was pretty mad that I got hurt this last time." Kiara's eyebrows went up at the look that came across Blackburne's face. "He yelled at you, too?" At Blackburne's nod, Kiara rushed to apologize, but he stopped her.

"Your dad and I have an understanding."

Kiara jumped up from her chair, jostling Elvis again. "What the hell does that mean?"

"Look." Blackburne tried a soothing tone. "It's nothing, really. I promised to look out for you, and he was pissed that I let you get hurt."

"You didn't 'let' me get hurt!" Kiara was trying hard not to shout.

"I know that, and you know that, but it was hard to convince your dad." Blackburne seemed unfazed by her angry outburst.

Kiara mumbled an apology.

"It's okay. He loves you very much. If I had children, I would probably be the same way." Blackburne looked at his com unit. "And to answer your other question—yes, I was going to talk to Jax and Stryker and see if we could join their 'team'. I know they use different resources, depending on the situation, so maybe we could be one of their resources."

Kiara saw him glance at his com unit again. "Does Frankie need us?"

"Soon." Blackburne stood up. "I'll go back and talk to Larry, see what the Bendanites are thinking, then we can decide whether or not to continue with the new plan or if we should stay with cargo hauling."

Kiara watched the captain head out and moved Elvis to her shoulder. She stroked his toes, feeling a sense of relief, but also a sense of excitement for what was to come.

"Well, little man, for better or worse, our decision has been made."

On Earth Delta Nine, just outside the crowded city of New London, a man hurried down the sparsely-lit street, heading for the small tavern at the end. He was wearing black, from head to toe, his cap pulled low to hide his face. He kept looking side to side, darting glances behind him to make sure he wasn't being followed. He knew this meeting was a little cliché—low-population area, dark street, wearing black. He also knew that he needed to take every precaution to keep his identity and this meeting a secret. As a Director at the GTA, his involvement in this plan was very dangerous. He could be fired, put in prison, or even worse. But he believed in his boss, and his boss's cause, so here he was.

Darting another glance down the street, he entered the poorly lit tavern and immediately took a seat in the back, where he could watch the door. He was early, just as he planned. His arrival at the tavern wasn't a concern for anyone, and the other patrons ignored him, nursing their own drinks and involved in their own conversations. Using the display at the table, he ordered a quick drink and took a large sip to steady his nerves when the drink arrived. He took a couple of deep breaths and settled in to wait.

He didn't have to wait long. The man he was meeting entered the tavern and immediately headed to the back table. The two men nodded at each other before the newcomer sat down across from the Director.

"Do you have my payment?" the newcomer asked in a low, gravelly voice.

The Director slid a small bag across the table. The man across from him opened it, a gleam in his eyes when he saw the rare jewels inside. Money and some gemstones could be traced, but these jewels were illegal to begin with and could not be traced. It had been his stipulation.

"My boss wants an update as soon as you know she has it," the Director said, sliding a larger bag across the table.

The cap on the man across from the Director slid slightly to the side, revealing human-like features. The Director knew he was a Galdorian, and since Galdorians could pass for many different races, he was perfect for the job. The Galdorian's hatred of everyone from Trandor was simply a bonus.

"You are sure this will work?" the Director questioned. "Finding this stone wasn't easy."

The Galdorian across from him gave him a smug look. "Of course."

Stuffing both bags into his coat, the Galdorian stood, took a quick look around, and left.

The Director stood as well. He sent a quick message to his boss that the plan was now in motion. He hoped this latest plan worked, or there would be hell to pay.

Chapter 4

Kiara sat in the gardens on Darlarnia Station, a space station several quadrants away from Earth Delta Nine. The Acadia was docked here while they waited for Stryker. Jax was still on the Acadia waiting for Stryker to arrive, so it was just her and Elvis in the gardens. Kiara suspected Jax knew what this meeting was about, but he was respecting her decision to wait until everyone was together before they discussed it. She'd been awkwardly avoiding Jax anyway, afraid of the decision, what he might say, and hoping her face wouldn't give away her feelings for him. If the Acadia crew worked with Jax and Stryker, would Jax push her away to keep her safe, or would he pretend he was just her friend?

Keeping a mental connection to Elvis, Kiara wandered the gardens, her mood bittersweet. She was excited to meet with Jax and Stryker to discuss their roles, but she was sad that the crew of the Acadia wasn't all together. Sitting on a bench, she sent a silent 'no' to Elvis to keep him from eating one of the plants in the garden. She shook her head and smiled. No matter how many times she told him no, he still tried to eat the plants when they visited a garden.

She glanced at her com unit but knew that Stryker hadn't arrived yet. Blackburne would notify her as soon as he did. She sighed as Elvis joined her on the bench. He touched her face, sensing her sadness.

"I miss them already, Elvis."

Blackburne had met with the three Bendanites to propose the new mission for the Acadia crew. Bendanites were a peaceful race, only dangerous when riled. Kiara knew that they didn't look for trouble and preferred a peaceful, hard-working way of life. Larry and Moe had wanted to continue working cargo runs; the familiarity of moving cargo had been their reason for joining the crew of the Acadia. They had helped Kiara with her initial journey of self-discovery and power, knowing they would be returning to cargo hauling. When presented with a choice, they preferred the familiar. For Kiara, their decision hadn't been a surprise, but she had still hoped they would stay. What had been a surprise was Curly's response. The female Bendanite had chosen to stay. When Kiara asked Curly why she stayed, Curly simply told her that Kiara was her friend and that she needed to protect her. Kiara suspected that Curly was also a little attached to Elvis, since the Bendanite had once had a drayek on her home world. In either case, she was grateful that Curly had stayed, but she missed Larry and Moe. Blackburne had already arranged for them to join another reputable ship, and they'd seen them off early this morning.

Kiara's com unit signaled a message from Blackburne. Stryker had arrived. Moving Elvis to her shoulder, Kiara headed back to the Acadia. Her thoughts were whirling in her head. She was anxious about the upcoming discussion with Jax and Stryker and what her future would hold.

She boarded the Acadia and followed the sound of voices to the flex-space, the room that doubled as their meeting area when needed. Earlier that day, she had completed a rigorous workout with Elvis, using the hologram feature in the room.

Her thoughts were still jumping around when a familiar voice penetrated her consciousness. Her dad?

She walked into the flex-space and let out a squeal of delight. Her dad was here!

72

"Dad!" Kiara yelled as she launched herself into his arms. Elvis, hanging onto her long braid, squeaked and chirped at her dad. "What are you doing here?" she finally asked him, pulling back slightly in his embrace, but reluctant to completely let go of him.

"I missed you," Kyle teased her.

Kiara gave him a disbelieving look before turning to greet Stryker. In his usual hooded cloak, his dark, wolf-like features barely visible, he approached her, a smile on his face.

"Kiara, you look well," Stryker said as he embraced her. Elvis chirped at him before jumping and flapping his way over to Curly. Stryker's hug was long, and Kiara suspected that he had been just as worried about her as everyone else had been.

"It's good to see you again," Kiara told him when he finally released her. "Were you able to get all the hostages settled?"

"Yes, they are being cared for, and for some, they are already home." He could see the next question she had, even before she asked. "Yes, Zara is home."

Kiara smiled. Stryker and Jax were both empathic, so it didn't surprise her that he knew what she was going to ask.

Stryker reached into his cloak and produced his com unit. "Zara requested that she be able to keep in touch with you," he said as he keyed in some information. "I have sent you her contact information."

Kiara smiled her thanks and immediately sent a quick message to Zara. Sensing her dad next to her, she looked up into his face.

"Who's Zara?" he quietly asked her. He could tell that Zara meant a lot to her, just by the look on his daughter's face when Stryker had said to her that Zara was home.

"She was one of the hostages that we rescued," Kiara told her dad. "She was only a little girl, and she and Elvis had a moment before they left us."

Kyle nodded his understanding, just as Blackburne cleared his throat.

"I appreciate everyone being here. Kiara and I wanted to discuss a decision that the rest of the Acadia crew and I came to a few days ago." Blackburne looked at each individual's face as he spoke.

Kiara silently asked Elvis to join her, and as the little drayek hopped over to her, she noticed that Frankie was standing next to Blackburne. The pilot's bright yellow shirt was in stark contrast to the serious look on his face. She hadn't had a chance to discuss the decision with him, and she hoped that he wasn't regretting his choice. She darted a glance at her dad, unable to detect what he was thinking. She'd discussed her decision with him shortly after her talk with Blackburne, and though he hadn't been happy about it, he had accepted it. She wondered now if that's why he was here. Was he going to try to talk her out of it?

"Even though Kiara suffered a grave injury on the last mission with Jax and Stryker, we both felt as if helping others, in that kind of capacity, was something we were meant to do." Blackburne looked directly at Stryker. "We were hoping to be a resource for you and Jax, for other missions, to help those in need."

Stryker stepped forward into the middle of the group, turning his head to look at Kiara. "Jax and I discussed that you would perhaps go one of two ways, after the last mission." Glancing briefly at Jax, he continued. "You would either refuse to do missions with us anymore, or you would wish to join us on a more permanent basis."

Kiara's eyebrows went up.

"We had hoped that you would choose to join us," Stryker said into the silence.

No one said anything for a moment. Kyle looked at the bewildered expression on his daughter's face.

"What's wrong?" he asked her.

"Nothing really, I just feel like everyone knew I was going to make this decision, but me." Kiara shrugged, "It's just a weird feeling."

"Changing your mind?" Kyle asked hopefully.

Kiara gave her dad a slight frown. "No, of course not." Her expression cleared. "I know in my heart, this is what I was meant to do."

Kyle nodded at her with a resigned sigh.

Stryker looked around the room. "Is everyone from your crew onboard with this decision? Some missions will be mundane, but some will be even more dangerous than the last."

Blackburne nodded. "Yes, everyone here is in agreement. Two of our Bendanite coworkers decided that they wanted a slightly less exciting life, so we helped them find a new cargo ship to work for. Curly wanted to stay."

Kyle noisily cleared his throat to get everyone's attention. "What can we do to keep Kiara safe?"

Stryker and Jax turned to look at Kiara's father. Kiara sighed.

"Perhaps if I trained more with Jax?" Kiara asked into the silence.

"Training is always a good idea," Jax said, "but we can investigate other ways to help keep you safe. If you are busy trying to protect others, and us, we must do our part to help keep you safe."

Kyle nodded. That would have to do for now.

Back in her cabin, Kiara connected her com unit to the main booster and opened a connection to Zara. The little girl had answered Kiara's initial message and had asked if she could see her. Kiara did the next best thing. Opening audio and video, Zara's little face swam into focus. Kiara could see her bouncing in her chair, her eyes and complexion showing a healthy, vibrant little girl.

"Hi, Zara!"

"Kiara! Kiara!" Zara shouted into the connection.

Kiara laughed, grateful to see the health and exuberance bursting through the connection. At Kiara's laughter, Elvis jumped onto her shoulder. Kiara wasn't sure how much of the holographic image in front of her he could see, but she could feel affection coming from the little drayek.

"Elvis!" Zara yelled at the sight of the little drayek. Her enthusiasm was barely controlled. Suddenly, she jumped from the chair she was bouncing on and raced from the room.

"Zara?" Kiara called out, but didn't receive a response. Kiara looked at Elvis, wondering if she should try to talk to the little girl later. She didn't know anything about kids. Was this normal behavior? She was just about to terminate the connection when Zara shot back into the room. Kiara gasped in happy surprise when she saw that Zara was carrying a small cat. She remembered the little girl saying that Elvis reminded her of her cat.

"Kiara! See! I have a kitty!"

Kiara winced as the little girl squeezed the kitten and shoved it toward the holographic image. She wondered briefly if the kitten was drugged, as it seemed indifferent to the rough handling. She changed her mind when she watched the little girl cuddle the kitten, and the kitten began to purr loudly. Kiara turned her head and watched Elvis. He was looking at the holographic image, his head tilting back and forth. Kiara giggled.

She talked to Zara for a few more minutes before disconnecting. The little girl was thriving, and Kiara knew, once again, that she was making the right decision. She thought about Jax and discovered that because of this, she understood him a little more and why he did what he did.

Kiara checked her com unit to see if she had an update from Blackburne or Jax. Before adjourning their meeting, Jax let everyone know they had a mission in the pipeline and were working out the details. Stryker was heading out again to work on something else, but for now, she supposed that Jax would be with them again. Since she didn't have an update, she grabbed Elvis and went in search of her dad to see if he wanted to go for a walk with her. They were still docked at Darlarnia Station, and she wanted to take advantage of it as much as possible.

She found her dad deep in discussions with Blackburne and Jax in the kitchen. Walking in, the conversation immediately stopped, making her suspicious. Raising an eyebrow, she looked from person to person.

"What's going on?" she quietly asked the three of them.

"We were discussing ideas to keep you safe," Kyle answered his daughter. He didn't look the least bit contrite, talking about her when she wasn't in the room.

"Don't you think I should be in on those discussions?" Kiara demanded. Elvis huffed his displeasure as well.

"Of course, hon, you should," Kyle immediately soothed her. "This was an impromptu meeting, and I didn't want to interrupt your conversation with the little girl."

"Oh, okay," Kiara answered, still a little suspicious. She glanced at Blackburne and Jax, but neither was showing any emotion on their faces. "Did you come up with anything other than what we discussed before?"

"Actually, Jax thinks he might have something," Kyle said, as he nodded in Jax's direction.

Jax looked directly at Kiara. "I don't know if we can make it work, but there's a guy on Earth Delta Nine that makes body armor."

Kiara quickly interrupted. "Body armor? That stuff is heavy, constrictive, and half the time it fails."

"I agree," Jax said, "but this guy has something new."

Kiara didn't look convinced.

"I am hesitant to use him, as he is trying to keep from being noticed by the GTA," Jax continued. "His inventions have attracted the attention of the GTA before, but not for good reasons."

"What's he been working on that attracted the attention of the GTA?" Kiara wanted to know.

"He's a genius with nanotechnology and has been caught a few times using it for personal gain."

Kiara frowned. "That doesn't sound so bad."

"He used it to rob a bank."

Kiara started laughing. Physical banks were few and far between, as most banking transactions were handled digitally. Kiara had a picture in her head of an old western movie her dad had let her watch when she was young. "An actual bank?" She managed to ask in between laughs. Her laughter had the rest of them laughing with her. Elvis, on her shoulder, joined in with a few loud chirps.

When the laughter died down, Jax, serious now, answered her. "He went to a remote outpost on Earth Delta Nine, where they still had a physical bank, and tried to use the nanotechnology to disguise and protect himself to get into the bank."

"Is he in jail?" Blackburne asked, a grin still on his face.

"Lucky for us, he is not," Jax replied. "He was not successful in his bid to rob the bank but managed to get away. We convinced him not to try again, and we have been funding some of his research to help keep him out of trouble."

Kiara looked hard at Jax. "How do you know him?"

"His genius attracted the attention of several groups that wanted to use his inventions for their own. He was kidnapped and was being held on one of the moons around Earth Delta Nine." Jax shook his head. "They were forcing him to develop weapons with his technology. His mother contacted us for help. We liberated him and destroyed the weapons he was working on."

"His mother? How old is this guy?" Kyle wanted to know.

"He is about twenty, which explains the poor decision-making when it came to robbing a bank," Jax replied. He stood up, grabbed some fruit from the counter, and coaxed Elvis down to the table with it. Feeding Elvis, he continued. "We got a glimpse of his research and encouraged him to make something useful. We moved him and his mother to a protected location, but without direction, he did not make good choices. We have since fixed that error."

"You have someone with them?" Blackburne asked.

"Yes, we moved a retired scientist and his wife in with him. He keeps an eye on him and helps him with his research as well," Jax continued, his focus on feeding the little drayek. "Unfortunately, his mother did not want to stay. She went back to Earth. I think the situation is now healthier for him; I don't think his mother had been the best influence." Jax shrugged slightly. "In any case, he sent a message to us some time ago that he thinks he has perfected the body armor. I contacted the retired scientist after our earlier meeting, and he confirmed that it is working rather well. They've done some testing, but I think we would need to test it more."

"This actually sounds promising," Kyle said quietly. He looked at Kiara. He needed to do something to help keep her safe. This genius on Earth Delta Nine may have the answer for them.

Jax looked at Kiara. "It's up to you. The armor is for you, so it is your decision on whether or not to pursue this."

Kiara was intrigued by the thought of using nanotechnology, and she thought it was worth investigating, even if it turned out to be something she didn't want. "I think we should at least check it out." Kiara looked at her dad and Blackburne. "What do you guys think?"

"I agree, we should go," Blackburne said with a nod.

Kyle agreed as well.

Blackburne stood. "I'll get the Acadia ready to go. Kiara, get the navigation information to Frankie." He turned to Jax. "I'm assuming you will stay with us, at least for now?"

"Yes, of course."

"Good, let's plan to head out first thing in the morning."

Kiara turned to her dad. "Do you want to go for a walk with Elvis and me? I wanted to explore the station a little more."

Kyle looked down at his com unit. "I'm sorry, Kiara, I need to clean up a few loose ends before we leave."

"Are you coming with us?"

"I wouldn't miss it."

Kiara smiled. She loved having her dad around and was glad he could look at the armor with her. She trusted his judgement.

Before heading out, Kiara went to the bridge to get the route planned and give the information to Frankie. She walked onto the bridge and found Frankie at his station, looking at his console.

"Hey, Frankie," Kiara called out.

Frankie turned to her, his usual broad smile on his face.

"I've got a new destination for us," Kiara quickly told him.

Frankie's smile widened. "Alright! Is it our first mission?"

"Sorry to disappoint you, but no." Kiara headed to her station and began entering information. "We're going to Earth Delta Nine to rendezvous with someone Jax knows."

"Then we're heading out to our first mission?"

Kiara wanted to laugh. So much for being worried that Frankie wasn't completely sold on the idea of doing missions with Stryker and Jax.

"I'm not sure when or where our first mission will be. Jax and Stryker are being quiet about it."

Frankie looked disappointed for a moment before he thought to ask why they were going to Earth Delta Nine. "What's on Earth Delta Nine, besides somebody that Jax wants to see?"

Kiara finished entering her information and turned back to Frankie. "This person that Jax knows has developed some type of body armor that we're going to check out."

"Body armor? Really?" Frankie looked at her in disbelief. "You know that stuff is bulky, you can't move in it, and half the time it doesn't work."

Kiara opened her mouth to respond, but Frankie interrupted her, his ire growing with every word.

"Jax should know that!" Frankie shook his head. "With your athleticism and martial arts training, something like that would never work."

Kiara laughed. "Thanks, Frankie, that's exactly what I told them. However, this person on Earth Delta Nine has made some advancements with nanotechnology that might be worth looking at."

Now Frankie looked intrigued. "Really? That sounds interesting."

"That's the general consensus. We're heading out first thing in the morning. Nav information has been sent to you," Kiara said as she headed out.

With Elvis firmly planted on her shoulder, Kiara headed into the space station. Bypassing the administrative areas and dining areas, she headed to the shopping area. Never one to spend a considerable amount of time shopping (she frankly thought it was a waste of time), the shopping area on Darlarnia Station was supposed to have some unique shops to look through.

Her first stop was at a small shop that had her supplements. She had to keep a good supply of the supplements on hand, since she never knew when she would find them. The supplements helped replace the minerals found on Trandor. Grabbing her supplements, she paused at a display that boasted chocolate from all corners of the Galaxy. Kiara let out a small snort. Yeah, right. She found some Earth chocolate at the bottom of the display and added it to her items. She quickly paid and headed out of the shop to see what other shops were in this area.

Foot traffic was light, making it easy to navigate some of the narrow hallways of the space station. Kiara paused in front of a display showing a piece of fabric that seemed to change color. The shopkeeper noticed her and hurried out to try to make a sale.

"Please, please, come in," he gestured at her. He even made a point of smiling at Elvis.

Kiara went in. The shop was so full of different glowing textiles, she didn't know where to look first. However, the shopkeeper knew what he was doing. He gestured her to the side of the shop and pulled a tunic, similar to the dark purple one she was wearing, off the rack of clothes.

"See, it is perfect for you!" The shopkeeper exclaimed enthusiastically. "Here, here," he said as he gestured her to a privacy area where she could try it on.

Feeling a little rushed, Kiara hesitated.

The shopkeeper, sensing that he might be pushing too hard, tried a different tactic. "Here," he gestured to a small pocket sewn into the hem of the tunic. "Power cell is connected to fiber optic threads sewn into the garment." He demonstrated how to turn it on.

Kiara smiled. It couldn't hurt to try it on, could it?

A few minutes later, Kiara left the shop, wearing the new tunic, and trying not to think about how much she had just paid for it. Elvis, on her shoulder, was chirping at her, and he kept touching the fabric on her shoulder. Kiara thought he liked it too. She continued, browsing the various shops that held everything from food to clothes to knick-knacks. She smiled as she approached a shop that touted gifts from the 'known universe'. Gift shops appeared to stand the test of time and were always present in any shopping environment.

Kiara stood looking at the gift shop for a moment, a strange feeling coming over her. She looked around, but no one was paying any attention to her. She didn't think this feeling was the same as when Stryker had been watching her, but she definitely felt something. Elvis, sensing her thoughts, quieted down and began looking around. Looking back at the dimly lit shop, Kiara was undecided whether to enter, but felt drawn in. Maybe someone in the shop needed her help? She quickly chided herself. Don't look for trouble where there isn't any.

Deciding to go in, she sent a quick message to her dad so he would know where she was in case of trouble. Reaching one hand up to touch the little drayek's toes, she put up a small protection field around them and entered the shop. It took a moment for her eyes to adjust to the light, and she almost giggled when she realized that her shirt was glowing slightly. There was a small, thin woman of unknown race behind a counter in the back of the shop. Tables and shelves seemed to take up every square inch of the place, and Kiara had a quick thought that Curly would never fit in here. Objects, large and small, filled every table and shelf. Kiara recognized some Earth memorabilia, but for most items, she couldn't tell where they were from. Everything was covered with a layer of dust, and Kiara began to question why she had even entered. The woman never even looked up at Kiara's entrance, which was a stark contrast from the last shop she was in.

Elvis huffed in her ear, and Kiara could feel him fidgeting on her shoulder. He wasn't comfortable in here either. Kiara wandered a little further in, looking at the table that had Earth memorabilia on it. She let out a little sound of surprise when she saw a little figurine of her drayek's namesake. A small human figurine, decked out in a white pantsuit with glittering sequins, dark hair, and sideburns, sat on the table. The figurine was positioned in the singer's classic pose and was about four inches tall. Pulling her protection field back slightly, she reached out and picked up the figurine. It had a small on-off switch on the back, and when Kiara switched it on, it began to dance around in her hand, the scratchy sounds of one of his famous songs filling the air around them.

The toy's sound and movement startled Elvis, and he let out a screech, jumping from Kiara's shoulder, with his claws out. Kiara nearly dropped the figurine, but steadied it and quickly calmed Elvis. She took a quick peek at the clerk, but the tiny woman still hadn't looked up from the tablet she was reading. Kiara frowned. Maybe the woman wasn't reading, perhaps she was sleeping? Kiara looked from Elvis to the clerk. Surely, Elvis' screech would have woken her up. Kiara's heart was still pounding from being startled. Well, they would find out soon enough, since Kiara wanted to purchase the little figurine.

Still holding the figurine, Kiara started to turn toward the clerk when a flash of blue from a shelf behind the Earth memorabilia caught her eye. Intrigued, she maneuvered around a few tables to the shelf, searching the dust-covered items for what she had seen. This shelf had a collection of rocks and sparkling stones, and at first, Kiara thought maybe it had just been one of the sparkling stones that had caught her eye, but none of them appeared to be the right color. Still searching, she reached her hand forward to move a large, ugly, brown rock and felt a vibration in her hand. She quickly pulled her hand back, and Elvis, already jumpy from the figurine in her hand, twitched his feet and tightened his claws into her shoulder.

"Ouch!" Kiara whispered.

Elvis immediately loosened his grip and quietly chirped into her ear. Kiara knew the chirp was his way of apologizing. Kiara soothed him and returned her attention to the rock display in front of her. What caused the vibration in her hand? She looked for some sort of protection field, but there didn't appear to be anything electronic in this corner of the shop. She glanced at the clerk but didn't see any help coming from there. Mentally preparing Elvis, she slowly reached her hand toward the big, ugly brown rock, but nothing happened. She slowly touched the rock, but still nothing happened. Okay, she thought, maybe she had imagined it? She set the figurine down in front of her and, with both hands, moved the big, ugly brown rock slightly to the side. She gasped. Behind it was the most beautiful, blue, jewel-like stone she had ever seen. About the size of her fist, it didn't have a speck of dust on it, with the shape of an intricately cut, multi-faceted diamond.

Kiara slowly reached toward it, and as her hand got closer, she could feel a vibration start in her fingertips and work its way through her hand and up her arm. The vibration wasn't painful, but Kiara was reluctant to touch it. She pulled her hand back and stared at the stone, unsure of what to do.

"It calls to you," a woman's voice said from behind Kiara.

This time, both Kiara and Elvis screeched, and it took all of Kiara's control not to throw a protection field around them that would have destroyed half of the shop.

"My apologies," the tiny woman from the shop spoke again. "I did not mean to startle you."

Kiara thought the woman's voice matched her stature—tiny and thin. She wore a plain brown skinsuit that hung loosely on her small frame.

"That's okay," Kiara finally managed to get out. Elvis was once again gripping her shoulder painfully, and Kiara mentally begged him to loosen his grip. He immediately complied, but his attention was on the little woman who had sneaked up on them. Kiara could feel his need to leave the shop; it was almost overwhelming. She soothed him, telling him that she had them both protected. Feeling a little more in control, Kiara tried to smile at the tiny woman.

"You have visited Bedi," the woman said, gesturing to Kiara's shirt.

Kiara looked down at her slightly glowing shirt. "Yes," she hesitantly responded.

The little woman nodded her approval before gesturing behind Kiara to the blue stone.

Kiara turned to look at the stone and remembered what the woman had said. "Why did you say it called to me?"

The little woman shrugged. "It won't hurt you."

Torn between trying to touch the stone and Elvis' overwhelming need to leave, Kiara shuffled from foot to foot. "Where did it come from?" she finally asked the clerk.

"A trader brought it here a few years ago," the clerk said, studying the stone with a critical eye. "It did not look like this. It is responding to you." The clerk gestured to Kiara to grab it.

Kiara, mentally preparing herself again, slowly reached toward the stone. Why did the clerk say it was responding to her? The vibrations started again, intensifying as her fingers got closer.

"I can feel it vibrating," Kiara told the clerk, still reluctant to touch it.

The clerk nodded again. "It is for you."

It still wasn't painful, so Kiara pushed her hand forward the last inch and touched the stone. The vibrations immediately stopped. She closed her hand around it, stunned to feel that the stone was warm. She picked it up, surprised that it was also heavier than she thought it would be.

Turning back to the clerk, Kiara asked for a price. The clerk quoted a ridiculously low price, telling Kiara it included the stone and the figurine. Kiara quickly agreed before the clerk could change her mind and stood impatiently while the clerk slowly and methodically wrapped everything up for Kiara.

Kiara stepped out into the hallway, and both she and Elvis took a huge breath. Checking her com unit, she was astounded to see that they had only been in there for a few minutes. She felt like it had been much longer. Taking a glance at the other shops, she instead headed for the Acadia. Her appetite for browsing and exploration had evaporated. She kept thinking about the stone. Where did it come from? Why did it vibrate when she got close to it? Maybe Jax or her dad would know something about it?

Kiara entered the Acadia and could hear Blackburne and Frankie talking on the bridge. Closing her eyes for a moment, she concentrated on sensing Jax, discovering him in the flex-space. The door was open, and as she entered, she could see he was using the space as a temporary office area. He had enabled the holographic display on his com unit and was scrolling through pictures and documents.

"Am I interrupting?"

Jax looked up from his perusal of the documents, a ready smile on his face. "Not at all." His smile broadened when he saw her slightly glowing tunic. "I see you've been shopping."

Kiara glanced down at herself, a little embarrassed. "Yeah, I couldn't resist."

"It looks good." Jax's smile turned a little serious. "Why does it bother you?"

Kiara shrugged. She didn't do things that drew attention to herself, like clothes and facial enhancers, so when someone noticed her clothes, it made her uncomfortable.

Jax was about to press the point, but as she got closer, he felt alarmed. He quickly looked Kiara over, and not seeing anything, looked at Elvis. Still not understanding where the feeling was coming from, he stood up quickly from the chair he was sitting in, startling Kiara and Elvis.

Kiara stopped, sensing his alarm. "Jax, what's wrong?"

"I'm not sure," Jax responded, still looking her over. "Are you feeling okay?"

"Yes, I feel fine," Kiara said hesitantly.

"Did anything happen while you were shopping? Has anyone approached you who threatened you?"

"Jax, what's wrong?" Kiara was beginning to feel seriously alarmed. "Nothing happened while I was shopping."

Jax, still trying to figure out what was wrong, zeroed in on her shopping bag. "What's in the bag?"

"It's just a figurine and a rock," Kiara said as she reached into the bag. She remembered the tingling in her hand, but before she could say anything, Jax was reaching for whatever she was bringing out of the bag.

Elvis let out a loud hiss, just as Jax grabbed the little singing figurine. The hiss startled Jax, and he bobbled the figurine. "What's this?" he asked harshly, trying to cover up his embarrassment at being startled by Elvis.

"It's just a little singing figurine of Elvis' namesake," Kiara said, trying not to laugh.

Jax frowned at it while he studied the figurine. Kiara reached over, hit the button to start it singing, causing Elvis to screech and Jax to nearly drop it.

This time, Kiara did laugh, while the little figurine belted out lyrics that talked about hound dogs. Jax, still frowning, handed the figurine back to her. Kiara turned it off and reached into the bag to grab the stone. It didn't vibrate this time, and as her hand closed around it, Kiara was surprised to find it cool to the touch. She let out a sound of dismay at the sight of it. It was a dull brown color, and even the multi-faceted diamond shape was gone. It now looked like a chunk of concrete. She handed it to Jax.

"I think I've been duped."

Jax was slowly turning the rock over in his hand, his look thoughtful. "Why?"

"The clerk must have done something to it while I was in there because when I first saw it, it didn't look like that." Kiara frowned at the rock in Jax's hand. "I don't know how she did it, but it was the most beautiful blue color, and the shape of a multi-faceted diamond." Kiara slowly shook her head. "No wonder she didn't charge that much for it."

Jax looked up at Kiara, sensing that there was more to the story. "What else happened?"

"Well, it made my hand tingle when I first got close to it."

At her statement, Jax hastily put the stone back into the bag.

"What?" Kiara looked from Jax to the bag and back to Jax. "What is it?" She could feel Jax's alarm and fear. She gingerly put the bag on the floor and backed away from it. Elvis hissed at the bag, clenching his feet into Kiara's shoulder and flapping his little wings.

Jax took a deep breath. "I'm not completely sure, but it could be part of a weapon that was on Galdor, your sister planet."

Alarm arrowed through Kiara, and she shot her hand out, enveloping the bag in a protection field. "Is it a bomb?"

"No, it is not a bomb, and by itself, I don't think it is dangerous."

"How do we know for sure?" Kiara whispered.

Jax walked back over to his com unit and quickly began a search. "There isn't much information, as you know, about either planet, but there are some stories, or legends, about the stones from Galdor." Jax was busily swiping at the holographic display, trying to find the correct document.

"Ah, here we go." Jax enlarged the display so that Kiara could see it. "It says here that there are reports of at least four stones, but some speculate there to be as many as eight. The Galdorians made them to help in the war against your planet." Jax swiped the display; two pictures now dominated the display. The first was a computer drawing of a rock; ugly and brown, with rough edges—the second, a computer drawing of a smooth, multi-faceted stone.

"That's close, but the stone is the wrong color. When I saw it in the shop, it was blue. That drawing shows it to be green," Kiara said as she looked through the writing in the document. "Oh, wait, it says here that the stones can appear to be different colors, depending on who is looking at them or holding them."

Jax enhanced another portion of the document. "Look, it says they are called the Stones of Kreelon, named after the Galdorian who created them." Jax read a little further. "It seems that these stones were supposed to be the ultimate weapon to end the war between your two planets." He looked thoughtful for a moment. "I think it is similar to Earth's history, when nuclear weapons were first introduced. The ultimate weapon to trump all weapons and end whatever conflict was happening."

"Do you think this is what ultimately destroyed our planets?" Kiara asked. The document was heavy on speculation and light on facts.

Jax looked thoughtful. "It is hard to know. According to what we read here, that was their purpose, but whether or not the Galdorians were desperate enough to use them, it doesn't say." He kept searching through archives until he found another document. "Okay, here is some additional information. If all the stones are together, they have enough power to destroy a planet, but separate, they are thought to be harmless."

"It says they were designed that way to make it easier to transport and smuggle." Kiara read further into the document.

"That makes sense," Jax said, still suspicious of the stone in the bag.

"Why do you think I was drawn to it?" Kiara walked over to her bag and peered into it. "Why did it make my hand tingle?"

Jax shook his head. "I don't know, but I will try to find out more information."

"Maybe I should try to take it back to the shop?"

"Take what back to the shop?" Kyle asked as he entered the room. He'd just caught the tail end of the conversation between Kiara and Jax.

Kiara looked at Jax, then back at her dad, not sure what to do. If the stone was dangerous, Blackburne wouldn't want it on the Acadia, she was sure of that.

"Well?" Kyle asked when no one answered him. He had a feeling that there was something more going on than just buyer's remorse for a trinket.

Kiara hesitantly walked back over to the bag in the middle of the room. "I found this stone at a shop on the station, and there is something strange about it." Kiara felt an overwhelming urge to reach into the bag and pull out the stone. The feeling alarmed her, so she backed up a few feet.

Kyle watched his daughter's actions, and then, with a sense of alarm, watched Jax back up a few steps. "What's strange about it?" To be on the safe side, he backed toward the door.

"Maybe we should scan it and see what it's made out of?" Kiara whispered to Jax.

"Maybe we should get it off the ship?" Kyle was thinking like a captain. He was pretty sure Blackburne wouldn't want something on the ship that was making both Kiara and Jax nervous.

Kiara rolled her eyes. "Oh, for Pete's sake!" Marching over to the bag, she ignored the hiss from Elvis and reached into the bag and grabbed the rock. It was now the deep, dark blue she remembered from the shop, heavy and warm.

Kyle let out a whistle. "How much did that cost you?"

"Not as much as you might think," Kiara said quietly. She looked at Jax. "I'm going to take it back to the shop. Even if she won't give me my money back, I'll give it to her, and then we won't have to worry about it."

Jax nodded. "I will accompany you."

"I'll go too, and maybe somebody can explain what this is all about?" Kyle said, looking a little irritated.

As they headed off the ship, the rock now heavy in the bag, they ran into Blackburne and Frankie. Kiara took the opportunity to explain the stone, how she had acquired it, and what she and Jax had uncovered about it. Kiara felt like crawling into a hole with the frown she received from her father and Blackburne.

"Stop frowning at me, I'm taking it back," she told them, somewhat defensively.

"We'll all go and make sure the shop takes it back," Blackburne said, his disappointment still heavy in his voice. "We may want to let the GTA know about it as well."

Now it was Jax's turn to frown. "I thought of that, but with the corruption we have seen, I'm a little worried about it falling into the wrong hands."

They all digested that bit of information while they headed to the shopping area. Kiara led the way, finding the shop where she bought the tunic, and heading a few doors down to find the gift shop. She stopped after a few steps, looking around, feeling confused. She was certain that this was where the gift shop was. The gift shop wasn't here. Instead, there were several shops with clothes, and the doorway that should have been the gift shop was now a well-lit bakery.

"What's wrong?" Kyle approached his daughter, her alarm evident on her face.

"The shop isn't here." Kiara spun in a circle. There was the shop she bought her tunic from, so the gift shop should be right here. She pointed to the tunic shop. "That's where I bought this," she said, pointing to her shirt. "The gift shop was right where the bakery is now."

Jax entered the bakery and asked the clerk about a gift shop. The clerk just looked confused.

"I'm not imagining this—the gift shop was right there!" Kiara fairly shouted it.

Jax immediately soothed her; Blackburne's frown intensified.

"Something is very wrong here," Kyle said from behind her.

"I agree," Jax said.

Blackburne nodded. The group stood, a little indecisively. No one wanted to take it back to the ship.

"I know it's not the best solution, but we should take it to the GTA office here on the station," Kyle finally said.

Jax looked resigned, and Blackburne nodded his agreement. "We can't keep something potentially dangerous on the Acadia."

"I'm so sorry," Kiara said, feeling terrible about the situation. Elvis chirped his apology.

Blackburne walked over to her, awkwardly putting a hand on her shoulder, before simply reaching up and scratching the top of Elvis's head. "No one blames you. These things happen. We'll fix it."

They spent a few more minutes asking other shop owners about the gift shop, but got the same reply. No one had seen or heard of the shop. Kiara herself even went into the tunic shop but got the same response. It added to the mystery of the stone.

Luckily, the response they received at the GTA office was one of help and compassion. Security arrived immediately and placed the now-ugly, brown rock in a special case. Kiara breathed a massive sigh of relief as they left the GTA office, and her feelings were mirrored on the rest of the faces in the group. She was ready to move on from this and was looking forward to the next part of her journey.

Chapter 5

Kiara woke up the next morning, feeling restless and out of sorts. With a headache building behind her eyes, she dressed in a dark skinsuit and light-colored tunic. Looking in the mirror, she could see that her blue skin looked pale. She hadn't slept well; her vivid dreams had bombs and green or blue stones that turned into bombs.

Looking at her com unit, she had some time before she would be needed on the bridge, so she headed to the flex-space for a good, hard workout, Elvis trailing behind her. Kiara supposed that this was one of those times when being bonded to her was bad for Elvis. He looked as bad as she felt.

On Earth Delta Nine, word of the stone being found had made its way to the Director. Worried, the Director sent a message through secure channels to the Galdorian, setting up a meeting with him in a local park.

Arriving at the park early, as was his habit, the Director looked around to make sure he wasn't followed. He knew this was a very visible place to meet, but since he wasn't giving the Galdorian anything, he supposed it was a low risk. For anyone watching, it was just two people talking on a park bench. Again, it struck him how cliché all of this was, but he supposed that was why it worked.

Sitting on a bench, he pretended to read something on his com unit. The Galdorian joined him on the bench after a few minutes. Neither man looked at the other.

"The stone is on its way here," the Director said conversationally.

The Galdorian snorted.

The Director frowned. "A report came across my desk this morning. She turned the stone into one of our satellite offices, and they have it in a protective case, on its way here for further study."

On a sigh, the Galdorian finally reassured the Director. "She took it, just as planned." Before the Director could continue, the Galdorian waved an impatient hand. "Do not worry, the stone will still be with her and will do its job."

The Director looked doubtful, but there wasn't anything he could do about it until the case arrived.

"Just make sure you have it in a secure place when it arrives. The only way she can break its hold on her is by destroying the stone," the Galdorian said.

The Director sent a quick message to be notified as soon as the stone arrived and stood up from the bench. Looking relaxed, he headed back to his office.

Kiara, sitting at her navunit, nudged Elvis with her toe. He was curled up at her feet, snoring quietly. The workout in the flex-space had invigorated both for a short time, but she was tired again from lack of sleep. Elvis woke with a snort, gave her a huff, and curled back into a ball. Kiara rolled her eyes in response and stood up to stretch. They were due to arrive at Earth Delta Nine shortly. Frankie had the docking information for the station above the planet. The plan was to leave the Acadia at the station and take the shuttle down to the surface.

She was excited to meet Jax's contact and explore the possibility of functional body armor. Her thoughts returned to the stone they had turned over to the GTA. She gave herself a quick mental shake.

She was thinking about that stone way too much. It was gone, and she needed to push thoughts of it out of her head.

Frankie was guiding them in when Jax joined them on the bridge, followed by Blackburne.

"Frankie and Curly are going to stay on the Acadia," Blackburne told the group. "The rest of us will head down to the surface."

Kiara signaled her dad, wondering why he wasn't on the bridge. Her dad quickly sent a message back—he was wrapping up a conversation with one of his buddies in the Rangers. Kiara knew that he was still trying to figure out who or what was behind the attacks with the CyRAINs. The attacks were ongoing but still rare, with no apparent purpose they could see. Kiara had a feeling the attacks were more like practice runs, with the major ones still to come. She didn't have anything to base that on, just a gut feeling.

Later, as they pushed their way onto the public shuttle, Kiara tried to keep a positive attitude. The shuttles to the surface were always packed with people and cargo, and today was no exception. With Elvis on her shoulder, she squeezed in tight against Jax. Jax, smiling down at her, moved his arm protectively around her shoulders, pulling her tight against his side. Kiara enjoyed being pulled in close and took a deep breath of his musky scent. Elvis quietly chirped his approval as well. Jax was dressed in his usual hooded cloak, and with his height and menacing look, Kiara noticed that many of the patrons on the shuttle were trying to squeeze over to give him more room. Maybe she should try a cloak and a mean look, and see how people respond?

Of course, now that she was really looking at the people around them, she couldn't tell if they were moving away from her or Jax. Her blue skin gave her away as a Trandorian, a GTA-protected race. Sometimes that designation helped, sometimes it didn't.

As the shuttle bumped its way through the atmosphere, one of the passengers swayed and bumped into Kiara, earning a loud huff from Elvis and a fierce look from Jax. Kiara found she didn't have it in her to look mean, so she smiled instead. Jax rolled his eyes, as if sensing the whole conversation she'd just had with herself. She didn't need to be mean; Jax and Elvis were there to take care of that.

They finally reached the surface, and Kiara took a deep breath as soon as she exited the shuttle, grateful to have the breathing room. She was never comfortable in large crowds.

Jax had arranged for them to use local transportation, so they all followed him around the corner of the shuttle drop-off building to a lot full of land vehicles and air shuttles. Most of the travel on Earth Delta Nine was through the air in mass transit shuttles or private shuttles. As a result, most of the available land-based roads were in disrepair and difficult to navigate.

Luckily, Jax led them to a shuttle big enough for the group, but small enough to maneuver easily through the local air traffic. Jax took off with ease, and Kiara could see that he had experience piloting shuttlecrafts like this. Blackburne occupied the seat next to Jax, ready to help navigate or pilot if needed. Multiple engines provided quick vertical lift, and once airborne, Jax set the autopilot to guide them along the designated flight paths out of the city's central area. When they were clear, Jax disengaged the autopilot and turned off the shuttle's location services. Checking to make sure they weren't being followed, he veered to his left and shot out over some dense trees, keeping the shuttle as close to the tree canopy as possible to help cloak them.

Kiara walked back into the cramped cabin to talk to her dad. Elvis immediately jumped from her shoulder and flapped and wobbled his way over to her dad. Landing gracefully on the arm of the seat, Elvis chirped at Kyle to get his attention.

Kyle looked up from his com unit, his brow furrowed.

"Trouble, Dad?" Kiara asked him. "You've been glued to that screen for a while."

"I'm not sure," Kyle answered with a sigh. "My contacts suspect that the attacks are going to ramp up soon. They think whoever is orchestrating this is waiting for something before launching more wide-scale attacks."

"How do they know?" Kiara looked at her dad, doubt on her face.

"I have a couple of buddies observing orders for ships and CyRAINs ramping up over the last few months, but whoever is behind this hasn't begun any big attacks. It's just been these one-off kinds of attacks, like the one you got caught up in a while back." Kyle shook his head. "We're just speculating on the waiting thing, because it's the only idea that makes sense right now."

"What do you think they're waiting for?"

"That is the question, isn't it?" Kyle looked down at his com unit again. "I don't know if they are waiting for more assets or if they are waiting for everyone to become complacent. It's the one piece of this that I can't get a handle on."

Kiara looked at her dad. There was still more he wasn't telling her. When he remained silent, she moved to sit across from him and nudged his foot with hers.

"What aren't you telling me?"

With a sigh, he finally told her. "There have been some intercepted communications that mention the Trandorian that keeps causing problems."

"You think they are talking about me," Kiara said it as a statement, her dad's face confirming it. "Are there any threats?"

"No, they've been cautious, covering their tracks. My sources haven't even been able to tell who the communications are coming from and who they are going to."

Kiara frowned. That didn't make any sense. She'd been able to decode the overhead in the message her dad had retrieved from the space station.

"I know, I know," her dad said, forestalling her next question. "I had my source set up a universal search for anything mentioning Trandor or you by name."

Kiara's eyebrows shot up. "Why would you do that?"

"I was trying to find a way to keep you safe," Kyle quickly told her, trying to keep her from getting too upset. "I was hoping to catch any threat to you early and help you defend yourself." At her look of disbelief, he hurriedly continued, "I was also thinking it might lead us to whoever is behind this."

Kiara nodded. All of them had been wondering who else was behind the attacks. Since the SLO's death, that possibility seemed even more threatening. "So why can't they get more info?"

"I think they figured out how we tracked the SLO last time, and they are coding false information in the messages. Every time we decode one, it leads to a dead end." Kyle handed his com unit to Kiara, pointing at the displayed message. "See?"

Kiara fiddled with it for a moment before she reached the same conclusion as her dad.

"I guess we just keep monitoring the messages and see if we can get more information?"

Kyle nodded, his face grim. He was worried, though.

Kiara looked down at Elvis as he crawled into her lap, and her thoughts turned to the stone that they had turned into the GTA. Visions of the stone swirling in her head, she dozed off. She began to dream almost immediately, her dreams centering around the stone. In her dream, she was holding the stone, sleeping with it, and carrying it everywhere she went.

She woke with a start when the shuttlecraft dipped slightly. She looked at her dad, "Why didn't you wake me?"

"You looked tired," Kyle told her. "Were you having bad dreams?"

"Not really, why?" Kiara didn't know why, but she didn't want to tell him about the stone.

"You seemed restless, even when you were sleeping."

Kiara shrugged and looked away, her thoughts going to the stone again. Maybe they should have kept it? If it had power, perhaps she could have used that power? Realizing that she was starting to obsess over the stone again, she pushed thoughts of it away and looked out the shuttle window. The landscape was hilly and densely wooded.

The trees in this area of Earth Delta Nine resembled Earth pine trees, but the needles of the trees were different colors of red and slightly broader. It was hard to judge the height of the trees from their position, but she thought she remembered they were several hundred feet tall, with smaller trees growing beneath them. It made it nearly impossible to see the ground from the air, and doing more than walking through these forests was almost impossible. No wonder Jax and Stryker had wanted their safe house out this way.

Jax yelled from the front that they were almost at their destination, just as the shuttle started to slow. Kiara frowned. Jax and Stryker had really worked to hide this place away. She couldn't see any buildings, just trees and more trees. The shuttle came to a hovering stop above the trees, and as Kiara watched, the tree canopy began to draw back, revealing a camouflage dome. She smiled, appreciating how much effort had gone into hiding this place.

They landed with a soft thump, and Kiara could hear the hum of the dome as it closed over them. Still looking out the window, she could see that the land here had been cleared of trees and now consisted of several large buildings, a few smaller outbuildings, and beautiful landscaping with rocks, small trees, bushes, and ornamental plants. As Kiara got up from her seat, she noticed three people exiting one of the large buildings that she assumed was a residence.

The young man leading the way must be the inventor that Jax spoke of. His excitement at seeing the shuttle was evident in his body language. An older couple trailed behind him, smiles of welcome on their faces. Kiara moved Elvis to her shoulder and followed the others off the shuttle. Jax was already greeting the young man, who was alternately shaking Jax's hand and embracing him. To be honest, it was not the reaction she had expected. From Jax's description, she'd been expecting a spoiled, belligerent young man.

After greeting everyone, Jax turned and gestured for Kiara to come forward. "Cory, this is Kiara, the one I told you about."

Cory, the young scientist, took one look at Kiara and fell hopelessly in love. He was dressed in dark trousers and a wrinkled T-shirt, and he hastily brushed at his shirt before trying, unsuccessfully, to smooth down his dark, unruly hair that framed his pale face. His intense feelings made him awkward, and he rushed toward Kiara. First, he stuck his arms out like he wanted to hug her, changed his mind, pulled his arms back, and then threw out his hand like a handshake. Changing his mind again, he pulled his hand back and stuck it in his pocket and hunched his shoulders. Tripping over his words, he tried to greet her.

Kiara frowned at the weird squeaky noises coming out of his mouth. She had thought he was human—was he really some species she'd never heard of? Elvis flapped his wings and huffed loudly, drawing Cory's attention to Kiara's shoulder. Cory's mouth froze, halfway open, a squeak trailing off to nothing as his dark eyes widened at the sight of the drayek. Kiara wondered how he hadn't noticed the drayek when Jax introduced her because Elvis had been on her shoulder the whole time.

Jax started laughing and punched Cory in the shoulder, hard enough to move him over slightly. "Wake up, Cory," he said, still laughing.

Cory's mouth snapped shut, his eyes darting from Jax to Kiara to Elvis. "S-s-sorry," he managed to stammer out. Finally pulling his wits together, he stuttered out 'hello' before looking down and shuffling his feet.

Kiara, not sure of how to proceed or what was wrong with Cory, mumbled a 'nice to meet you' before sending a questioning look at Jax.

Jax, still laughing, introduced Cory to Kyle and Blackburne. The elderly couple moved forward, and Jax introduced them to the group. Randall and his wife, Shiandra, looked to be about Kyle's age. Kiara thought Randall looked exactly like a scientist or professor might: slightly rumpled brown trousers and a darker brown coat. His brown hair, with grey at the temples, and brown eyes also fit her idea of what she thought he would look like. His wife, Shiandra, was dressed in flowing lengths of fabric in greens and blues, her long blonde hair flowing down her back. The wrinkles on her face added to the character of her face, but Kiara could tell they were lines from laughing and smiling. Piercing blue eyes smiled kindly at her. Randall and Shiandra were about the same height, both shorter than Kiara.

"Is that a drayek?" Shiandra asked, moving forward slightly, her gaze now on Elvis.

Elvis clenched and unclenched his feet on her shoulder, but Kiara didn't sense any fear coming from him. Apparently, Elvis was withholding his judgment of the older couple at this point, but she could feel some animosity from the little guy toward Cory.

Probably because Elvis didn't understand the young man's actions any more than Kiara did.

Kiara nodded at Shiandra, "Yes, his name is Elvis."

"Is he bonded to you?" Shiandra asked, extending her hand up to Elvis. Elvis pretended to sniff her hand.

"Yes," Kiara answered, somewhat surprised that Shiandra knew about drayeks.

Cory moved closer to Kiara, earning a huff from Elvis. Trying to keep Kiara between himself and the drayek, he angled closer to her, hoping to get her attention. He was nearly a foot shorter than Kiara, but that didn't stop his hopefulness.

"Um, Kiara?" Cory's earnest face was looking at her.

Kiara turned to him, and as her gaze landed on him, his cheeks reddened slightly, and he struggled to get the words out.

"Are you thirsty? Can I get you something to drink?" Before Kiara could answer, he rushed on. "Maybe you're hungry? We have some snacks ready for you."

"Cory, give the poor woman some space," Shiandra admonished quietly. Cory moved back quietly, but kept his earnest smile directed at Kiara.

Shiandra invited them into the house and pulled Cory forward with her. Kyle moved up to Kiara's side, a smile on his face.

"A little bit of puppy love, I see," he chuckled at her.

"Puppy love?" Kiara looked around for a dog. She loved dogs.

"No, I don't mean an actual dog," Kyle said, and Kiara's face fell. "I mean Cory. He's fallen for you already, and the old earth phrase 'puppy love' means a young fella is in love, or thinks he is."

"Oh." Kiara frowned. "What do I do about that?" She looked ahead at Cory, who kept turning around and smiling at her.

"You're going to have to let him down gently," Kyle said, still chuckling.

"I don't know what that means either," Kiara said in a slightly panicked voice.

"It's okay," Kyle said with sympathy, and hugged her with one arm. "Just be nice, but not too nice, and you'll eventually have to tell him that you aren't interested in him, or something along those lines."

"Ah, you are speaking of Cory?" Jax asked as he came up on Kiara's other side. "He is very infatuated with you."

"So I understand," Kiara said wryly. "This is awkward."

Both men just chuckled as they entered the house behind Shiandra and Cory. Randall and Blackburne were behind them, and Kiara could hear them discussing space formations.

Now it was Kiara's turn to gape. From the outside, the house seemed to be a simple two-story home with architecture reminiscent of traditional old Earth homes. Even the size, from the air, had seemed smaller. Inside, the layout was grand yet still homey, with dark wood and stone features throughout, an enormous two-story foyer upon entering, and windows everywhere she looked. Tasteful art hung on the walls, and comfortable-looking furniture filled the common area as they walked further into the home. Kiara searched her brain for the name of the common room and finally settled on family room.

Shiandra gestured everyone into the large family room and disappeared to grab the refreshments. Kiara waited until Cory sat down before deliberately choosing a seat across from him. She sighed as she sank into her seat, attempting to remember the name of the piece of furniture she was sitting on. She spent so much time in space and was so used to sitting at consoles and piloting stations. Homey things, like the furniture she was sitting on, were foreign to her. Her dad, seeing her confused look, leaned over and whispered to her.

"Couch."

Kiara giggled quietly—such a funny name for a piece of furniture.

Cory leaned forward, ready to try to engage Kiara in another conversation, but Jax forestalled him.

"So, Cory, how's the body armor testing going?" Jax asked, drawing Cory and Randall's attention to him.

Cory turned to Jax, his excitement at this new topic evident in his body language. Even Randall seemed to perk up quite a bit.

"It's going really well, Jax," Cory said. He turned to look at Kiara. "Jax gave me some basic information about you, so I could get something started. I have something ready for you to try out, whenever you're ready."

"How does it work?" Kiara asked.

"Please, please," Shiandra injected into the conversation. "Let them settle and catch their breath before we start on all this technical talk." She set a tray of drinks and snacks on the low table in the middle of the room. "Please, help yourself to some refreshments."

"My wife is right, of course," Randall said. His gravelly voice washed over the room. "We have plenty of time for that. Please relax and refresh."

Shiandra smiled gratefully at her husband. "I assume that you will be staying for a few days, so I have some rooms ready for you. I can show them to you after you eat." Reaching down to the tray, she picked up a small bowl of fruit. "I brought this for your little drayek—do you think he will like it?"

Elvis, seeing Shiandra hold up the bowl of fruit, chirped at her and reached out his front paws for it.

"Is it okay if he eats it here, next to me?" Kiara asked, not sure of the protocol with their hosts.

"He is welcome anywhere," Shiandra reassured her.

Setting a napkin under the bowl, Kiara moved Elvis to her side so he could eat. Content for now, Elvis happily dug into the fruit, making chirping noises as he ate.

"Thank you," Kiara told Shiandra. "How do you know about drayeks?"

With that question, the conversation turned to more mundane topics, as they discussed the house here, and Blackburne and Jax talked about working in space. Kiara could see that Cory was starting to relax, and he even began to join the conversation, injecting his take on some of the happenings around Earth Delta Nine.

Kiara could tell from the way that Cory talked about Randall and Shiandra that he thought of them like grandparents, and that the feeling was mutual. She could sense genuine affection.

Shiandra turned to Kiara. "Jax tells us that you have some telekinetic abilities."

"Yes, some of my people are born with these abilities. Jax helped me to develop them."

Shiandra nodded. "Jax and Stryker have helped many."

Cory, interest piqued again, asked Kiara if she could demonstrate something. Kiara shrugged and floated a small piece of fruit in front of him. Cory was thrilled.

"Wait till you see what she can really do," Jax said.

"What do you mean?" Cory asked. "That was really cool! It's like magic."

"Yes, there is quite a bit more," Jax said with a laugh. "Were you able to set up the holographic room as I asked?"

"Just as you asked," Randall replied.

Shiandra frowned at Jax and Randall, but Kiara was anxious to get started.

"I'm sorry if it seems like we are pushing too fast," Kiara said, looking at Shiandra. "We are used to moving fast to get things done, and I know that all of us are anxious to see what Cory has." Kiara glanced at Cory and sent him a small smile. "I'm sure he's anxious to get started as well."

Shiandra sighed. "I know. Cory has been talking about this nonstop and working with Randall every waking moment."

Randall got up and walked over to Shiandra, giving her a quick kiss. "You are a wonderful hostess, my dear."

Shiandra's cheeks turned a delightful shade of pink. "Okay, you guys go play with your toys, and I'll start working on dinner. Let me show everyone where their rooms are before you head out."

Kiara's room was on the second floor, overlooking the back of the house and gardens. A huge bed dominated one wall, and after Kiara closed the door to the room, she took a running leap and landed, face down, on the bed. Elvis, with a slight squawking noise, jumped from her shoulder just before she landed. Kiara had never slept in something so huge before. She rolled around on it, giggling, and was soon joined by Elvis, her lighthearted mood transferring to him. Chirping, jumping, and rolling, Elvis played in the covers with Kiara, enjoying the new game.

Getting up from the bed, Kiara walked around the room, looking at all the furnishings in the large room. Small wooden tables flanked the bed, with an old-fashioned clock on one of the tables. Kiara picked it up, wondering how it worked. Putting it down, she walked to the wide bank of windows and looked out over the garden area. She hoped that they would be able to stay here for a few days; this area was the most beautiful she had visited in quite some time.

Turning back to the room, she saw something blue out of the corner of her eye, on the table next to the bed. Turning more fully to the bed, she stared at what appeared to be the Galdorian stone. She blinked a couple of times, thinking she was imagining it. She looked around the room before her eyes moved back to the stone.

They had turned that stone over to the GTA; there was no way that it could be here. She moved forward, almost in slow motion, her hand reaching out for the stone. She felt an overwhelming need to touch it again, hold it again. It didn't matter that Jax thought it was dangerous; she needed it.

Alarmed, Elvis jumped from the bed with a screech and flapped his way to Kiara's shoulder. The screech made her jump, turning her attention away from the stone. Blinking a few times as if awakening from a dream, Kiara turned her head back to the little table, but the stone wasn't there. She frowned. Did she imagine it? Was she having some sort of weird, waking dream? And why would it center around that stupid stone?

She shook her head and took a couple of deep breaths, willing herself back to normal. She looked up at Elvis, grateful that he had pulled her from whatever was going on. She should probably tell Jax about it, but for some unknown reason, she wanted to keep it a secret. Elvis huffed at her, but she ignored him. She told herself she imagined the whole thing and pushed it from her mind. Besides, she wanted to explore her room a little more before she had to leave with the others.

Moving to the other side of the room, she opened a door to find a smaller room that looked like it was meant to hold clothes. It had a few racks and built-in drawers that intrigued her. Leaving that small room, she opened another door to find a beautifully furnished bathroom with gleaming tile and copper fixtures. Lotions, soaps, and other assorted bottles were artfully arranged around the room, and several small plants were placed near a window. The window had privacy screening, which was a relief. She looked at the large container on the floor and struggled to remember the name for it. Yes—a bathtub! It was for bathing, she thought, although why anyone would do that in the large container, she didn't know. Maybe she would try it out one night to see if she liked it. Perhaps it would be a little like swimming? Her father had taught her to swim at one of the space stations they had stayed at when she was little, and she had enjoyed it very much. Her father had told her that she took to the water like a fish.

Elvis, it seemed, was fascinated by the bathtub as well. Perched on the side of it, he kept turning his head from side to side. Kiara thought maybe the way the tub was made was somehow messing with his depth perception. Watching him, Kiara wondered if drayeks could swim. She'd have to look up that information at another time.

Hearing a knock on the bedroom door, Kiara walked over to open it. Her dad stood outside the room.

"How's the room?"

"This is great!" Kiara said with a smile. She gestured over to the bed. "Does your room have a huge bed, too?"

Kyle smiled at her enthusiasm. "Yep, mine has a huge bed, too." He reminded himself that she had chosen her current lifestyle and that she wasn't a deprived little girl. He didn't have to feel guilty that she didn't get to sleep in a large bed every night. "You ready to head over to the lab?"

With a nod, Kiara silently called Elvis to her. It appeared that he was still investigating the bathroom.

With Elvis trailing behind her, they followed Cory and Randall to one of the other buildings in the compound. The building had a small lab at one end and a holographic room on the other. Cory seemed to have regained some of his equilibrium, now that he was in the familiar environment of the lab. He immediately engaged Jax in the lab, showing him some of his notes on a computer screen.

Jax turned to Kiara. "Let's show Cory a little of what you can do, so he can see if his preliminary design will be able to keep up."

Kiara followed Jax over to the holographic part of the building. "I gave Cory one of the holographic programs that I put together for you. It's the one with the two-headed Gorlican."

Kiara nodded, did a little stretching, and coaxed Elvis up to her shoulder. "Ready, little man?" Elvis, his front paws holding her braid, clenched his feet on her shoulder, signaling that he was ready. Crouching slightly and moving up to the balls of her feet, Kiara nodded at Jax.

The room changed to show another planet of barren soil and large rocks. With a roar, a two-headed Gorlican charged out from behind a large boulder to her right, his four front legs up off the ground, swinging wildly at her. The Gorlican stood about eight feet tall, with both heads sporting wickedly long teeth; spit dripping from its mouth. Kiara immediately threw up a protection field, blocking the blows of the Gorlican. Two more Gorlicans appeared, and she was now surrounded. One of the Gorlicans began to throw rocks at Kiara, bouncing them off her protection field. From behind her, the cries of a small child could be heard. Two of the Gorlicans heard it too and began to move in that direction. Kiara took a couple of running steps and, using the nearest boulder, launched herself with a front somersault over the head of the nearest Gorlican. Elvis clenched his feet on her shoulder and tightened his grip on her braid to stay with her. Using an energy pulse, she drove the Gorlican back a few steps and used an energy field to trap the other. The third began to charge her, so Kiara, using an energy field, picked up a rock about the size of her head and threw it at the charging Gorlican. The rock connected with the Gorlican's head, but it only slowed him down slightly. Kiara smiled. Apparently, Jax had made some adjustments to the program.

The Gorlican in the energy field was slowly pushing his way toward her; the other that she had hit with the energy pulses had run around her in the direction of the child's cries. Taking a deep breath, Kiara wrapped an energy field around the one who was getting closest to the child, and, with a scream, threw him nearly fifty feet in the other direction. The one wrapped in her energy field was still pushing forward, so Kiara began shrinking the energy field, with the Gorlican in it. Panicking, he tried to rip his way out, but Kiara held on while she threw energy pulses at the other. She could feel her own protection field begin to fail, and knew she had to end this quickly, or she would run out of energy, and they would get to her.

Reminding herself that this was only a hologram, she used her energy field to crush the one wrapped in it, leaving her with the last, seriously pissed off Gorlican. He charged her, throwing rocks in rapid succession. Kiara dodged, jumped up on a boulder, and led the Gorlican between two towering rocks. When he followed her, she used her energy to move the stones and crush him. Breathing hard, she propelled herself over the rocks, looking to see if Jax had other Gorlicans for her to battle, or if the one she had thrown had come back. She didn't see anything, and out of the corner of her eye, saw Jax at the computer console. The barren landscape disappeared, and the holographic room reappeared.

Still breathing hard, hands on her hips, Kiara walked back to where the others were waiting. Her dad, Blackburne, and Jax were smiling; they'd seen her in action before. Randall had a look of astonishment on his face, but Cory's face was the most amusing. His expression was a cross between excitement and terror, his mouth open, his eyes wide.

"Cory, you okay there?" Jax asked him as he followed Kiara's amused gaze.

Cory finally closed his mouth and, with a smile, said, "That was really awesome!"

It reminded Kiara a little of how Frankie reacted when he'd found out about her abilities.

"If you can do all of that, why do you need body armor?" Once the initial excitement had worn off, the scientific part of Cory's brain kicked in.

"Good question, Cory." Jax walked over to stand next to Kiara. "One, she doesn't have unlimited power. Two, very small, pointed objects—knives, lasers, bolts, bullets, that sort of thing, can sometimes penetrate her protection field, especially if she isn't focused or she's tired. Three, if she's trying to protect too many with a protection field, she's vulnerable." Jax looked at Kiara. "We found that out the hard way."

Cory nodded, his brain already working to solve the problems. "I have a small prototype ready to try now, but getting all of her protected will take some more programming." All business now, Cory walked over to a small case on the table and, opening it, pulled out something that looked like a chunky metal bracelet. He handed it to Kiara and asked her to put it on one of her wrists.

Kiara hesitated, just for a second. Was it safe? She didn't want to hurt Cory's feelings, but she didn't want to get hurt either.

Cory looked up and saw her hesitation. A small look of impatience crossed his face. He grabbed the bracelet and put it on his own wrist. Turning, he swiped at the holo-display of the computer, and Kiara watched in amazement as the bracelet expanded up his arm and down over his hand in a flow of light silver. He held out his hand, and Kiara could see that it moved with his hand and wrist.

"See, perfectly safe," Cory told her. He did a few more swipes, and the armor retreated into the bracelet form. "Ready to try?"

Kiara nodded, and this time, when he handed the bracelet to her, she immediately put it on her right wrist. She silently asked Elvis to go to her dad, and when he did, she tilted her head to Cory to let him know she was ready. He did the swipes at the computer, and Kiara felt the bracelet expand up to her elbow and over the back of her hand. It was a curious sensation, almost like water flowing up her arm.

"It will move with you, and I don't imagine it will block any of your power, but we can test it to make sure." Cory looked at the computer display, then over at Kiara. "How does it feel?"

Kiara experimented with moving her fingers, then her wrist. The armor didn't inhibit her movements, and in fact, she could barely tell it was there at all. The water-like sensation faded as soon as the armor was fully deployed.

"How well will it protect her?" Kyle asked, watching his daughter move her hand around.

Cory disengaged the bracelet and moved it to a fake arm that he had set up inside a safe box. Closing the box, he engaged the armor and fired at it with a laser and a conventional bullet. Opening the box, he took a knife from the table and sliced and speared at the armor. Standing back, he gestured for the others to look. They crowded in, looking for any signs of damage.

"I can't see any marks on it at all," Jax murmured.

"I can't either," Kyle said. He turned to Cory. "Can we take it off and see if there is any damage underneath?"

Cory disengaged the armor and walked over to the box. "It will protect her from any penetration, but less from the blows themselves. So, she won't have any open wounds but will have plenty of bruising."

Kyle frowned. "So, she could still suffer broken bones, do you think?"

"What about trauma to the chest, which could cause her heart to stop?" Jax asked.

Cory looked thoughtful for a moment. "I think I can make some adjustments to the armor over the chest—make it thicker, more shock absorbent, as it won't need to be as flexible, as say the wrist area. But right now, I don't think I can do anything about her limbs, without compromising the flexibility of the armor." Still looking thoughtful, Cory continued, "It will give some protection, more than nothing at all, but less than, say, a sheet of metal."

Randall walked over to stand next to Cory, putting his hand on the young man's shoulder. "You've done a good job here."

"I agree," Jax said. "This is amazing work, Cory."

Cory smiled but looked a little embarrassed, now that they weren't discussing specifications.

To help him get his equilibrium back, Jax steered the conversation back to the armor. "How long will it take to make the adjustments and have more to test?"

Cory brightened up immediately. "The adjustments will take a few hours, but I have other pieces ready to test." He reached down and brought up a larger case, then opened it. "Due to the nature of how this technology works, it will have to be several pieces, placed strategically on the body." Cory lifted out two other cuff pieces. These would be for your legs. You would need one for a belt, one on each arm, and one to be worn around your neck."

Kiara studied the cuffs, trying to picture them on her legs.

Cory, entirely in his element now, walked over to Kiara to show her the cuffs. Her presence no longer had him tongue-tied or nervous, now that he was talking about his invention.

"We have a lot of flexibility here. We can incorporate them into clothes, make them look like jewelry, whatever works for you."

Kiara nodded, still fascinated by the whole thing. "I think we can figure something out." At that moment, her stomach rumbled loudly. Laughing, she put a hand on her stomach. "Using my power makes me very hungry. Maybe we can throw around some ideas over dinner?" She turned to Randall. "If we're early, I can eat some of the snacks I brought. I don't want to be a burden."

Randall checked the time. "It looks like it's time for dinner, so let's head back to the main house." Steering Kiara toward the door, he threw out another idea. "Shiandra is great with designing—clothes, houses, you name it. I bet she would have some ideas on how to incorporate the armor into something usable for Kiara."

"That sounds great," Kiara said as her stomach rumbled again. She was looking forward to eating something other than ship food. The small demonstration of her powers had sapped her strength, and she needed to refuel. Elvis jumped to her shoulder, voicing his hunger in her ear and in her head.

As they left the lab, Cory hustled up to walk next to Kiara. He looked suspiciously at Elvis before focusing on Kiara.

"What did you think, Kiara?"

Kiara looked at his face. His expression didn't show the 'puppy love' from before, and his question seemed genuine. "I was very impressed."

Cory nodded, his gaze turning thoughtful. "But you're wondering how it will protect all of you, and how it will work?"

"Yes, exactly. I know you've only had a little time to work on it for us, but I can't picture how it will protect, let's say, my face."

"I can make adjustments there, just like I can for your chest." Cory's eyes went to her chest as he said it, but he immediately looked away, a look of embarrassment on his face. He mumbled an apology.

"It's fine, Cory. We have to talk about it, or how else will we figure it out?" Kiara thought about his life here, isolated, with only an elderly couple for company. "Do you go into the city very much?"

Cory looked back at her, careful to keep his eyes on her face. "We don't much, it's too risky. Ever since I got into that trouble, we've had to keep a low profile."

Kiara frowned. "I don't think it's good to keep you isolated out here. You need to have friends, do things with other people your age." Kiara wanted to giggle. She sounded like one of those moms from an old movie she'd watched, but she thought that the situation was similar. It couldn't possibly be good for him to be isolated. Isn't that how serial killers got started? Before she could expand on that thought, Cory interrupted her.

"I have friends that I video chat with all the time," he told her. "We also make sure we take at least one trip off planet, visit someplace new, at least once a month."

"Oh," Kiara felt silly for worrying about it.

"Thanks, though. You're the first person, besides Jax, who seemed to be worried about it."

"You're welcome."

"I think, if we could come up with some designs, we could place the launch point for each of the body armor modules at your wrists, your neck, your waist, and just below your knees. I did a similar design when I tried to relieve the bank of its money." Cory let out a small laugh. "Jax was not happy with me that day."

"I bet he wasn't," Kiara laughed with him. "Why did you do it?"

Cory shrugged. "I was bored and read too many graphic novels."

Kiara searched her memories for what a graphic novel was.

Cory saw her confused look. "You know, like *Superman*, or *Batman*?"

Kiara's confusion cleared immediately. "Yes, I've seen those." She frowned again. "But you were acting like the villain, not the hero." She tilted her head toward Cory. "Is that how you see yourself?"

Cory looked back at Jax. "For a while, I was pretty confused about who I was and what my purpose was. I met Jax, and he helped me figure it out." They were getting close to the main house, so Cory slowed his steps. He thought it was essential to tell Kiara who he was now and that he wasn't a villain. "I went with Jax and Stryker on a rescue mission once. It completely changed my view. What they do, the people they help, opened my eyes." He stopped, his gaze earnest. "I was pretty selfish, pretty immature before. Sure, I had this genius for inventing things," he grinned as he said it. "But I was totally in it for me. Seeing the people out there that needed help—it changed me. I knew I could do something to help—to help Jax help those others."

Kiara nodded. "I have helped them as well, and you're right. When you see the ones that need assistance, and you realize that you have a way to help, it changes your thinking." She smiled at Cory. "Have you tried to go back out with them?"

Cory looked appalled. "No way! What they do is really awesome, but really scary. I nearly wet myself that one time I did go with them."

Kiara laughed, hard.

Cory looked at Elvis again. "Will you help me make friends with the drayek?"

Kiara was surprised that he asked. "Sure, I can do that." She looked from Elvis to Cory and back to Elvis. "Is there something about him that bothers you?"

Cory looked down and shuffled his feet. He mumbled something, but Kiara couldn't make it out.

"I'm sorry, Cory, what did you say?"

He was mortified. Taking a quick look around to make sure that his hero, Jax, couldn't hear him, he spoke a little louder.

"He scares me."

Kiara knew it would hurt his feelings if she laughed, so she worked to keep a straight face.

"He won't hurt you, unless you try to hurt him, or me." Kiara saw that Shiandra was out on the back terrace of the house, waving them in. "Let's make friends after dinner, okay?"

Cory nodded. "Don't tell Jax, okay?

"No problem."

Power Rising

Chapter 6

Shiandra had prepared an enormous meal of roasted meat, root vegetables, and the Kalana fruit that was native to the planet. Kiara vaguely remembered something similar on Earth once, when her father's friends had prepared a meal for them. Kiara savored every bite of the food Shiandra made, praising her often. Kiara knew she was hungry, and that accounted for some of it, but the meal was excellent. Obviously, she wasn't the only one who thought so, as everyone had cleaned their plates.

Kiara helped Shiandra clean things up once they were done eating, giving Shiandra time to ask questions. Kiara had sensed that Shiandra was quite curious.

"Jax said you are from Trandor—that's a protected race, right?"

"Yes, it's a protected race."

Shiandra studied Kiara's face. "Isn't that a good thing?"

Kiara laughed a little. "You'd think so, but it makes some people avoid you altogether, and it makes getting a job pretty tough."

"Oh, I hadn't thought of that." Shiandra paused in the act of loading the dishes into the cleaner. "Your dad isn't from Trandor."

"No, I'm adopted." Kiara handed her a couple more dirty dishes. "He found me after my ship had been attacked and rescued me." The love for her dad was on her face. "He's been my dad ever since."

Shiandra nodded; she could see the bond between those two. "How old were you?"

"We're not exactly sure, maybe five Earth years?" Kiara took the small, empty fruit bowl from Elvis and handed it to Shiandra. "Thanks again for the fruit for Elvis."

"My pleasure. How long have you had him?"

"Elvis?" at Shiandra's nod, Kiara continued. "About a year. I found him on a cargo run. He bonded with me right away."

"I think Cory is scared of him," Shiandra whispered.

"Yes, he told me. He wants me to help him make friends."

"He actually told you he was afraid?"

Kiara nodded. "Do you know why he would be afraid?"

Shiandra closed the dish cleaner and programmed it before turning to answer Kiara's question. "Before we knew him, when he was very young, one of the dogs in his neighborhood bit him. He's been afraid of anything like that ever since."

"That's so sad."

"I know," Shiandra said, her face full of sympathy. "Randall and I talked about getting a dog, but we didn't think Cory could handle it."

"Maybe Elvis and I can help." Kiara moved Elvis up to her shoulder. "Since Cory wants to make friends with him, I think it will be successful."

Changing the subject again, Kiara questioned Shiandra about the body armor they were working on. "What do you think about Cory's body armor project?" Kiara couldn't tell what Shiandra's role was in the technological part of Cory's life. She seemed slightly removed from it, concentrating instead on housekeeping and home life.

"I'm very excited for him," Shiandra said as they walked back into the large common area of the house.

Kiara waited, sensing that she wanted to say more.

"It's refocused him again," Shiandra continued as she gestured Kiara ahead of her into the room. The rest of the group was huddled together, gesturing and swiping at a computer screen. Kiara smiled at the chaos that swirled in the air. She turned back to Shiandra, wondering what she meant by 'refocusing'.

Shiandra saw her questioning look. "I think he was starting to get bored." Shiandra shrugged. "There's only so much he can do here, and to tell you the truth, we aren't exactly the best company for him." She hurriedly went on, not wanting Kiara to get the wrong impression. "Don't get me wrong, we all love each other like family, but a once-a-month excursion off planet is surely not enough to keep someone young, like Cory, from going crazy."

Kiara nodded; it was exactly what she had been thinking.

Cory looked up as they entered and hurriedly waved them over.

"We've been experimenting with some designs," he pointed at the screen, "tell us what you think."

Kiara and Shiandra looked over Randall's shoulder, and for a moment, neither one spoke. Kiara straightened up and looked at Shiandra, trying to figure out what to say that wouldn't hurt anyone's feelings.

Shiandra started laughing. "That's what we get when we leave the designing to a bunch of men!"

Randall looked affronted for a moment before he, too, started laughing.

"I think we designed something very functional," Jax began, before Shiandra cut him off.

"Functional, maybe, but that is the ugliest thing I have seen in a long time," Shiandra said, still laughing. "Kiara is too polite to say so, but I have no such qualms. Besides, she doesn't have a body like a troll."

"Troll?" Jax looked confused.

"Mythical Earth creature," Kyle mumbled, still looking at the screen and trying to figure out where they had gone wrong. Now that Shiandra had pointed it out, he did admit that the drawing on the screen did look like a troll in body armor. Ugly body armor.

"Besides, who has boobs that big, anyway?" Kiara wanted to know.

A couple of the men looked at the floor at Kiara's comment, and Cory turned an interesting shade of pink. Blackburne cleared his throat and coughed slightly.

"Shiandra, my love, will you help us?" Randall asked his wife. He deliberately used 'my love' to smooth over any hurt feelings.

Cory looked apologetically at Kiara. "We were just trying to keep the momentum going."

"I know, and I appreciate it." Kiara looked at the screen and shuddered a little. "Why don't we let Shiandra give it a try?" She couldn't think of anything else to say.

Shiandra, all business now, reached into a nearby cabinet and pulled out a large tablet of paper and some pencils.

Kiara was fascinated. Nobody used pencils and paper anymore, at least nobody she knew.

Shiandra, catching Kiara's look, patted the seat next to her at the table. "Come, sit by me, and brainstorm with me." Settling in with the paper, she began drawing some curves. "I have always preferred to use paper for my sketching. It connects me to the drawing."

Kiara watched as first her face, and then her body, in a ghostly form, took shape on the paper.

"We want the armor to complement her skin and hair coloring," Shiandra murmured as her pencil flew on the paper. "I think we also want some sort of symbol or crest on the base pieces." She turned and looked at Kiara. "You might want to think of something to use for that."

Kiara nodded, "I have some ideas."

"Cory, how many foundation pieces will she need?" Shiandra continued the sketch, with Kiara's blue skin now showing up.

Cory cleared his throat. "One at the waist, one on each arm, one on each leg, and something in the neck or throat area." Looking thoughtful, he continued, "and one on the chest to protect the heart."

"We should incorporate the foundation pieces into her clothing, if we can," Shiandra said, and looked at Cory for confirmation.

Cory, finding his footing again, moved forward in his seat. "Yes, yes, we could incorporate the leg ones into boots," he said excitedly. "Bracelets or jewelry type ones for the arms, and a belt for the one at the waist." Cory looked at Kiara, not wanting to offend her again. "What do you think?" he quietly asked her.

Kiara could see it, with the help of Shiandra's drawing, and liked what was taking shape. "Yes, and a matching choker at the neck that would match the bracelets." Too excited to sit, she jumped up from the chair, earning a huff from Elvis. She looked back down at the picture. "All of that could be put on when needed. I'm not sure about the chest piece."

"I have an idea for that," Cory said quickly. "I have something that I can put the nanotechnology onto, and it attaches to pretty much anything. We can make the chest piece out of that, and you could attach it to whatever skinsuit you are wearing that day."

Kiara looked thoughtful. "Would it be bulky?"

"Not if you didn't want it to be." Cory looked thoughtful. "It could be as thin as a piece of paper, and as small as a button, if that's what you wanted."

"I always wear tunics, like today. I'm not picturing how that would work."

Cory nodded. "This is just the chest piece. It's in addition to the other armor, to help protect your heart. It would expand underneath your tunic, so it shouldn't be a problem."

Jax walked over and put his hand on Cory's shoulder. "When do you think we can have some pieces to test?"

"We can test the prototypes tomorrow, if you want. It will probably take a few more days to put together something that looks like Shiandra's drawings."

"Kiara, did you have any ideas about an emblem or crest?" Shiandra asked her without looking up from the drawing.

"Actually, yes. My ancestor, Mirona, had a tattoo or something similar on her arm that I saw once." Kiara walked over to Shiandra and looked at the picture taking shape. She didn't think she could describe it accurately, but maybe she could try to draw it? "May I?" Kiara asked, gesturing to the pencil and paper.

"Of course!"

Kiara sat down next to Shiandra and, flipping the page over, began to draw what looked like a flower with eight overlapping petals. The petals were almost teardrop-shaped and joined together at the base. She encased the flower in a Celtic knot circle, and then a simple circle around the entire design. It was a rough design, but Shiandra immediately expressed how much she liked it.

"That's pretty close, although I'm no artist." Kiara turned her head slightly, looking at her handiwork.

"Here, let me work on it a little," Shiandra said, taking over the drawing. Now that she had the basic idea from Kiara, she could work it a little more, smooth out the rough edges. With Kiara directing her, she redrew the design in dark blue and placed it on a light blue background. The image fairly popped off the page.

"That looks great!" Kiara said, hugging Shiandra with one arm.

Cory peeked over Shiandra's shoulder, still making sure that he kept his distance from Elvis. "I like it." His eyes looked thoughtful for a moment. "You know, we could make something that looks like a pendant, with that design. You could wear it on a long chain, or attach it to your clothes, and either way, it would protect you."

Kiara nodded. It would be like having her ancestors protect her.

Shiandra put the finishing touches on the drawings before standing and stretching her back. "I think I'm done for the night. Randall, are you coming?"

"Yes," Randall responded on a huge yawn.

Cory looked around Shiandra at Kiara, hoping to catch her eye. He didn't want to turn in for the night; maybe he could talk Kiara into staying. He could use the excuse of getting to know Elvis.

Kiara was still energized from the drawing session and trying to figure out how to burn off a little excess energy before bed. She wondered if the compound was big enough to take a run in. Running through actual nature rather than a holo-program might be an exhilarating experience. She turned to ask Shiandra about it, only to catch Cory trying to get her attention. Smiling, she realized she could use the time to introduce Cory to Elvis.

"Hey, Cory, you want to spend some time with Elvis?"

Cory looked excited and terrified at the same time, and Kiara struggled to keep a straight face. She didn't want to hurt Cory's feelings.

They headed outside, and Elvis immediately began to chirp at Kiara.

"Can you tell what he's saying?" Cory asked her, intrigued by the noises that Elvis was making. He was still keeping his distance, though.

"No, I don't know what he's saying, but I can sort of tell what he's feeling." Kiara reached up and touched Elvis' toes. "He's excited to be outside. I think he likes the trees."

Cory led them to an area with trees, a few benches, and a bubbling water feature. Sitting on a bench, Cory looked nervously at Elvis.

"I'm going to tell you that you don't have to be afraid of him, but I don't think that will help you to get over your fear." Kiara sat down on a bench across from Cory and moved Elvis to sit next to her. "He's very in tune with your feelings, so if you think positive, friendly thoughts, he will feel those."

Cory nodded, trying valiantly to control his fear. He extended a shaky hand out toward Elvis, and when Elvis turned his head to look at Cory's hand, Cory quickly snatched his hand back.

"Sorry," he mumbled, looking at the ground, his cheeks turning pink.

Before Kiara could reassure him, Elvis turned around and slowly climbed down the bench and crossed over to Cory. Cory, still staring at the ground, his hands hanging down, held his breath as Elvis approached him. Elvis, so in tune with the situation, merely turned around to look at Kiara, and then slowly moved over until his little body touched Cory's leg. Sitting down, he chattered happily at the two of them.

Cory released a shaky laugh. "It's like he knew what was happening."

"Yes, I think he did." Kiara sent feelings of gratitude to Elvis. He was amazing. "Why don't you slowly reach down and touch the top of his head?"

"He won't mind?"

"Not at all."

Cory slowly moved his hand to the top of the little drayek's head and released his pent-up breath when he was able to touch the little guy without incident. When Elvis continued to sit next to his leg, still chirping and chattering, Cory started to feel more confident. Moving his fingers, he played with the tufts of hair on top of Elvis's head, which earned an almost purring noise from Elvis.

"This is awesome," Cory whispered.

"I think he likes you," Kiara whispered back.

"Can you ask him to sit next to me on the bench?" Cory whispered to Kiara.

Kiara knew she didn't have to ask the little drayek. At Cory's question, Elvis slowly turned and climbed the bench, still chirping. Kiara thought the noises the little drayek was making were helping to relax Cory. Cory's eyes widened, and his posture stiffened, but when nothing happened, he began to relax again. Elvis curled on the bench next to Cory, still chirping, and Cory slowly moved his hand to stroke down the little drayek's back.

"He doesn't feel like I thought he would," Cory whispered.

Kiara smiled. She didn't think he would get to this point with Elvis, but, since Cory was willing, anything was possible.

Cory's posture slowly started to relax, so Kiara asked him questions about living on this planet and more about what he wanted to do with his life. Cory's answers made Kiara wonder whether there was something Cory could be doing for their little band of rescuers. She made a mental note to talk to Jax about it. Cory seemed happy here, but he also seemed to be on the verge of wanting something more. She could hear it in his comments. Not that he was cut out to do any field work, but didn't every band of rescuers need a behind-the-scenes computer pro? She thought Cory and Frankie would probably hit it off right away.

By the end of their conversation, Elvis was curled up in Cory's lap, seemingly without Cory realizing that he had gotten there. Cory looked down and smiled.

"I'll probably still be terrified of a stray dog, but I don't feel fear toward this little guy anymore. Thanks Kiara."

"It was our pleasure, Cory," Kiara said as she stood. Elvis stood as well, and with a last look at Cory, jumped and wobbled his way back to Kiara's shoulder. Kiara yawned, finally feeling ready to get some sleep. They walked up to the house in easy companionship, Kiara feeling the start of a friendship she hoped Cory felt as well.

Kiara entered her bedroom and marveled again at the size of the bed and the room overall. Now that she was alone in the quiet room, her thoughts once again turned to the Galdorian stone. It just seemed to make sense to her that she should be using the stone, for good, of course. If it had power, shouldn't she be using it? She pictured the stone in her mind, in all its beautiful glory.

Unknowingly, her thoughts of the stone were slowly putting her into a trance. So deep into the trance, she didn't notice that Elvis was screeching at her. The little drayek knew something was wrong; whatever was happening to her was breaking their bond.

Kiara, fully immersed in the trance, walked to the window and held out her hand, willing the stone to be with her. Surely, she could call it to her. What was the harm in that? She'd be careful with it. Elvis screeched louder, physically feeling their bond begin to break.

Kyle, in the next room, woke with a start, his heart hammering in his chest. Sitting up in his bed, he strained to hear what had shocked him awake. At first, he didn't hear anything, but his heart was still hammering, his adrenaline running high. He'd had this feeling before, when something had happened to Kiara. They may not be related by blood, but they were family, and as close as any blood family could be, maybe closer, due to her powers and their love for each other.

In his sleep-fogged, over-energized state, he couldn't imagine that anything could be wrong with her while they were here. Still struggling to make sense of his feelings, he heard Elvis screech from the next room. It sounded like the little drayek was in pain. He shot out of bed and out the door and nearly collided with a sleepy Jax. They were both heading toward Kiara's room.

They reached her door at the same time, just as Elvis screeched again. Kyle pounded on the door, and Jax yelled her name. Neither cared if they woke everyone else; they could hear the panic in

Elvis's screech. Kyle tried the door, and even though the knob turned, the door wouldn't budge. Both men shoved their weight against it, but it wouldn't open. Blackburne joined them; the noise they were making had also brought him out of his room.

Randall and Shiandra came running down the hall, fear and concern on their faces.

"What is it, what's wrong?" Shiandra yelled her question to raise her voice above Jax yelling Kiara's name.

"We can't get in, and something's wrong," Kyle huffed out, in between his attempts to push the door open.

Randall looked confused. He could clearly see the knob turning, but the door wasn't budging.

Inside the room, Kiara held her hand out for the stone; her other hand was palm up, facing the door, keeping the others out. Elvis, in a full panic now, jumped at her, claws out. Kiara shifted the hand holding the door to push at Elvis, and Kyle was finally able to get the door open.

Jax, Blackburne, and Kyle pushed into the room, each trying to understand what was happening. Kiara was holding a hissing Elvis in an energy bubble, a few inches from her outstretched hand. She was looking out the window, her other hand reaching out to whatever she was looking at. She didn't seem to notice the group that had just pushed into the room.

Kyle rushed forward, grabbing her shoulder to turn her toward him. At first, he couldn't move her, and her eyes, deep blue, were glazed and unseeing.

"Kiara!" Kyle shouted her name, but got no response. He looked helplessly at Jax.

Jax moved forward, seeing the glazed look and the lack of response to everyone in the room. "She's in some sort of a trance. We need to break it." Receiving a nod from Kyle, Jax produced his baton and touched it to her upper arm.   The effect was instantaneous.

Kiara screamed in pain and crumpled to the floor, Elvis falling to the floor next to her. The little drayek crawled to her, making small whimpering noises.

Jax dropped to his knees next to Kiara, feeling for a pulse. He hadn't hit her with that much power, but he wasn't sure what kind of trance she had been in. He'd never seen anything like it.

"Is she breathing?" Kyle asked from behind him.

"Yes, she is breathing, and her pulse is strong. Help me get her and Elvis to the bed."

By the time they had her in bed, her eyelids were beginning to flutter. Shiandra appeared with a glass of water, and Cory had now joined them in the room, fear and concern on his face. His look mirrored the feelings of everyone in the room.

"Jax?" Kiara looked around the room at the concerned faces and back to Jax. "What's going on?" She winced as a full-blown headache hit her.

"Do you remember anything?" Jax quietly asked her.

Kiara opened her mouth to answer when she heard a slight whimpering sound coming from her side. She looked down to see Elvis. Alarm shot through her. Why couldn't she feel him?

"Elvis!" She reached down and pulled him up to her. He looked like he was in pain. "What's happened to him? Did someone hurt him? Why can't I feel him?" She pulled him close, tears streaming down her face. The little drayek was a grayish shade of blue and lethargic.

Jax looked from Blackburne to Kyle. He had no idea how to deal with this. Had the trance somehow broken the bond between Kiara and Elvis? If he remembered his drayek teachings, wasn't a broken bond a death sentence for the little guy? He quickly turned to Blackburne, intending to ask him to get Curly on his com unit. Maybe she would know what to do.

"There you are," Kiara murmured.

Jax turned back to look at Kiara and was relieved to see that Elvis was once again Kiara's blue color, and the whimpering had stopped.

"Can you feel him again?" Jax asked as he stroked the spot on her arm where he had shocked her.

Kiara nodded. "It's not very strong, but it's there, and getting better." She looked at everyone in the room. "What happened? Were we attacked?"

"What's the last thing you remember?" Kyle asked her.

Kiara furrowed her brow. "Cory and I were outside, letting him get to know Elvis. We came back in, and" Kiara's voice trailed off.

"And?" Jax prompted.

Kiara looked away from his gaze.

"Kiara?" Jax looked at the others in the room. When she stayed silent, he looked at Shiandra, Randall, and Cory and quietly asked them for some privacy.

"You will let us know how she is?" Shiandra asked as they left the room. "We won't be able to sleep until we know everyone is okay."

Jax nodded. "Why don't you wait downstairs for me, and I'll be down in a bit to give you an update."

He walked back into the room. Kyle was sitting on the bed, hugging his daughter, who was now sobbing on his shoulder. Blackburne was pacing at the end of the bed.

"Kiara, please," Jax implored her. "Tell us what happened."

Kiara pulled back from her dad and took a couple of deep breaths. "I should have told you sooner."

"Told me what?"

"It's the stone."

"Stone?" Confusion cleared as he immediately thought of the stone they had turned in. "The Galdorian stone?" At her nod, his look turned to confusion again. "What about the stone?"

"I can't stop thinking about it, and earlier today, I think I was falling into some sort of trance thinking about it."

"Earlier today?"

She nodded. "Elvis snapped me out of it. I kept thinking that I should have it, that I could use its power."

"But Elvis was able to snap you out of it?" Kyle asked her.

"Yes, and I was going to tell you, but for some reason, I thought I should keep it a secret." She looked down, shame flooding through her. "When I came back to my room this evening, the same feelings came over me, but stronger. I couldn't fight it. Even when Elvis tried to help, I couldn't stop it. It was almost like I was watching myself, and not really myself." She looked at Jax. "I'm not making sense."

"No, you're making sense. I don't understand the power behind it, but the stone, or something with the stone, is trying to influence you."

"It almost broke my bond with Elvis," Kiara said on a sob. "I wouldn't have willingly done that." She touched her forehead to Elvis, sending him feelings of love and comfort. His feelings, still shaky and faint, came back.

"We need to figure this out, but in the meantime, you should talk to Curly," Blackburne told her.

"Talk to Curly?"

"Yes, she may have some advice on how to strengthen your bond with Elvis."

Kiara nodded. She hoped it wasn't too late, and that she hadn't done irreparable damage to their bond.

"Until we figure this out, you aren't to be alone," Jax told her.

Kiara nodded, hugging Elvis, stroking his head, murmuring to him.

Jax turned to look at Kyle and Blackburne. "I'll take first shift, after I go down and let our hosts know that everything is okay."

Kyle nodded. "I'll see what I can dig up about the stone and see if any of my contacts know anything."

"I will check as well," Jax said as he left the room.

Blackburne walked toward the door, his look thoughtful. "I'll see if anyone I know has information about it."

Kyle looked at his daughter, at a loss for what to say to comfort her. She still looked distraught at the pain she had caused the little drayek.

"We'll figure this out," he whispered to her, his arms going around her again.

Kiara woke up the next morning, and the headache from the night before was still going strong. Jax was across the room, in a chair, and Kiara could see that he had finally fallen asleep. Guilt hit her again, seeing how uncomfortable he looked, slumped in the chair. Elvis, still plastered against her side, gave her a quick chirp when their gazes connected. Kiara, relieved that she could feel his thoughts again, quickly hugged him before swinging her legs off the bed. The movement instantly woke Jax, and Kiara winced in guilt.

Jax immediately joined her by the bed, studying her. "How do you feel?" He reached out and gently touched her face.

"I've still got that headache, but I don't know if it's from the stone or your baton, or both." Kiara could feel his concern, but his touch on her face was comforting.

Jax was still studying her, and Kiara squirmed uncomfortably.

"Did I grow a third eye or something?" Kiara finally asked him.

Jax smiled. "No, you're fine. I was trying to gauge if something was going on in your head, with my limited abilities." Jax turned back to the chair he had been sleeping in and grabbed a small bag next to it. "I thought you might still have a headache, so I got you something for it." He returned to the bed and handed her a tube containing a greenish gel.

"What's in it?" Kiara asked, eyeing the tube suspiciously.

"Vitamins, electrolytes, and some natural pain reliever."

Kiara knew he would stand there until she took it, so she quickly squirted the gel into her mouth and was pleasantly surprised by its mild minty flavor.

"How's the bond with Elvis?" Jax quietly asked her.

"Stronger this morning," Kiara said, looking down at the little drayek. "Curly said it would either get better, or it wouldn't; there really wasn't anything I could do but wait."

Jax nodded. The little drayek looked nearly normal this morning, so he hoped Curly was right.

Kiara scrubbed at her face before heading to the bathroom. Elvis immediately jumped onto her shoulder to accompany her. She eyeballed the huge bathtub that dominated the bathroom and vowed to try it out before she had to leave. As she cleaned up, she could hear her dad come into the bedroom and begin talking to Jax. She could hear the word 'stone', so she hurried through her morning ritual so she could be part of the conversation.

She exited the bathroom to see Jax and her dad, deep in conversation. She crossed over to them, and her dad stopped talking and gave her a big hug.

"You look better this morning," he said into her hair.

Kiara started to pull back, but noticed that Elvis was holding onto her dad's head. She giggled, and it felt good and normal.

"I'm starting to feel quite a bit better, thanks to Jax." She slanted her eyes towards Jax and mouthed a 'thank-you' at him. He nodded, smiling at the picture they made.

Elvis finally let go of Kyle, and Kiara pulled back. "What did you find out?"

"Why don't we head down and grab some breakfast, and I'll fill you in," Kyle said as he headed for the door.

Shiandra had left some simple items out for them to eat, but she was nowhere to be seen. Kiara assumed everyone else had already eaten. Kiara was grateful that Shiandra was such a good host. Fruit, rolls, and juices were left out for them. After filling their plates, the three of them sat down to go over what they had learned. Kyle started first.

"I told Kiara on the way here that it seems as if 'they' are waiting on something. We don't know who 'they' are and what they want, but they are amassing a large army. However, they haven't used that army or any of the resources yet." Kyle looked at each of them before smiling down at Elvis, who was busy shoving fruit into his mouth. "I've heard some rumblings that they are trying to take out Kiara before they launch any attacks, since she seems to be pretty good at disrupting some of their plans."

"Do you think the stone is supposed to be taking me out?" Kiara asked in alarm.

"Well, that would make sense," Jax said thoughtfully. "The shop you bought the stone in was gone when we went back, and you seem to be very susceptible to whatever power it holds."

"Speaking of that power," Kyle said quietly, "I didn't get very far with my research on the stone."

Jax agreed. "There just isn't that much out there, beyond what Kiara and I found the first time."

"So, we're stuck?" Kiara asked with a disheartened sigh.

"I didn't say that," Jax said with a small laugh.

"What are you thinking?" Kyle asked him.

"I talked to Stryker late last night. He's going to find a Galdorian and see if they know something about the stone. He may have to question a few of them, but I think it's the best shot we have."

"That's a good idea, but why would they tell Stryker anything?" Kiara questioned.

Jax's smile was evil. "Stryker has a way."

"When do you think we'll know something?" Kiara asked, her voice reflecting her worry.

"Stryker understood the urgency, so I hope it is soon," Jax responded, trying to calm her fears. "I just don't know how long it will take to find a Galdorian."

They had just finished cleaning up their breakfast mess when Shiandra joined them. She immediately crossed to Kiara and hugged her tight. Kiara's eyes filled with tears. She thought this must be what it was like to have a mom. It wasn't something she thought about since her dad was always there for her, but at times like this, she wished she had a mom.

"It's okay," Shiandra whispered, rocking her slightly.

Kiara took a deep breath and pulled back slightly. "Thank you," she whispered back. "I really needed that."

"Thank you for cleaning up," Shiandra said as she turned to the others. She kept one arm around Kiara's waist, sensing that Kiara still needed the contact. "Randall and Cory are out in the lab—they wanted to keep busy and help you out in any way they could."

"That's much appreciated," Kyle told her. He turned to Kiara. "Do you feel up to working in the lab?"

"Absolutely," Kiara said, nodding her head for emphasis. "I can't just sit around and wait for another episode."

With one last hug for Shiandra, they headed to the lab. Kiara was excited to see how far Cory had gotten and knew that working on the body armor would help to keep her centered.

When they entered the lab, music blared through the room, and Cory was hunched over a computer terminal, typing on the screen and swiping at a holographic image of what appeared to be body armor. His head bopping to the beat, he didn't hear them come in. When Kiara touched his shoulder, he jumped and let out a yelp of surprise. Elvis let out a shriek and clenched Kiara's shoulder. Cory's surprise quickly turned to irritation, and then to concern. With a flick toward his terminal screen, he shut the music off. Silence filled the room.

"Are you okay?" Cory quietly asked Kiara.

Before she could answer, a bellow came from the back of the room.

"It's about damn time!" Randall's irritated voice filled the room. "I couldn't even hear myself think!"

Cory rolled his eyes but smiled. "Seriously, are you okay?"

"Yes, thanks, Cory."

Randall appeared from the back of the room, carrying a tablet and muttering. "Are we ready to give this another try?" he asked without looking up. When no one answered right away, he looked up from the tablet and caught sight of Kiara with Kyle, Blackburne, and Jax standing behind her. Surprise had him nearly dropping the tablet before he recovered. He quickly crossed to Kiara, concern on his face.

"How are you, my dear?" Randall reached out hesitantly to touch her arm. He looked up at the little drayek perched on her shoulder. He supposed the little guy would be even more hesitant to leave her now.

Kiara took a deep breath. All this concern for her was a little unnerving and a little embarrassing. "I'm doing much better, thank you, Randall."

Randall studied her face, much like her dad would sometimes do when he was judging for himself if she was okay. Randall must have decided that she was, indeed, better. He nodded and walked back over to Cory.

"Good timing, I think we have another piece for you to try out," Randall said, and, receiving a nod from Cory, moved to the table where they had placed some of the equipment. He looked over the items on the table and selected a silver piece that appeared to be a bracelet. At the moment, it looked like a simple metal bracelet.

Walking back to Kiara, Randall gestured at her right arm. "May I?"

Kiara nodded and held out her arm. Randall slipped the bracelet around her upper arm, just below her shoulder. The piece immediately snugged up, fitting her arm perfectly. Kiara moved her arm around and was pleasantly surprised. Once it was fitted to her arm, she could hardly feel it.

"How does it do that?" Kiara asked, looking from Randall to Cory. Kyle, Blackburne, and Jax had moved in closer to inspect the piece.

Before Cory or Randall could answer, Jax spoke up. "You made this out of that experimental alloy you were working with."

Cory nodded, looking pleased that Jax remembered something he had been working on. "Yeah, you remember that we found that mineral on one of the moons. Once we added it to the metal alloy, it made the metal flexible while retaining its strength. We've been experimenting to find the right ratio of mineral to alloy and came up with the perfect blend a few months ago." Cory shrugged. "We really hadn't thought of too many places to use it yet."

"This is perfect," Jax muttered, his attention on the metal bracelet on her arm. The bracelet contracted and expanded, depending on how Kiara moved her arm and the way her muscles moved. "Do you have the nanotechnology in this piece?"

"Yes, and we ran some tests early this morning," Randall responded. "It's working really well."

Cory looked at Kiara. "Are you ready for me to expand it?"

Kiara nodded and braced herself for the watery sensation to run up her arm.

Cory made a few swipes at his terminal, and the bracelet expanded smoothly up and down her arm. It covered her shoulder and ended in a slight 'v' shape on her hand, wrapping around her middle finger. Elvis, seeing the armor expanding up towards his perch on her shoulder, let out a hiss and jumped to her other shoulder. He kept a suspicious eye on the armor. Cory checked the bracelet's feedback on his terminal and asked Kiara to perform specific arm movements. Up, down, bend at the elbow, all the while, studying the readout. Randall joined him, and with their heads nearly touching, they muttered, swiped at the screen, and kept asking Kiara to move her arm.

"Well?" Kyle impatiently asked. He wasn't sure if he was asking Cory or Kiara, but he wanted someone to say something.

Cory finally looked up from the terminal, a smile on his face. "It's working better than I thought it would. We designed it for her, and when Randall and I tried to use it, it just wasn't quite right. But, on her arm, it's perfect."

Jax nodded and turned to Kiara. "Let's test your abilities with that arm, now that it's covered." He took a glance at Cory and, receiving a nod from him, looked back and nodded at Kiara. "Anytime you're ready. Let's do something small and controlled, and then something bigger."

Kiara moved away from the tables and, concentrating, formed a small energy bubble. She moved it slowly around the room, judging if it felt any different, or if her power seemed to be impeded at all. So far, everything felt normal. She dissipated the energy bubble and walked back over to Cory.

"It didn't feel any different for me," she told him.

"All of these readings look normal as well." Cory could barely contain his excitement. "Try something bigger." He zeroed in on his screen again, waiting for readings from the bracelet.

Kiara smiled. Cory's excitement was contagious. She looked around and focused on a water bottle halfway across the room. Outstretching the arm with the body armor, she sent a small pulse of energy at the bottle, and watched in disappointment as the bottle wavered slightly, but stayed upright. She turned back to Cory, her look questioning.

Cory was swiping at the screen and muttering; his brow furrowed in concentration. Obviously frustrated with the progress he was making, he swiped at the screen and shot it up into the air, creating a 3D hologram in front of him. He spun it a few times before stopping the image and reaching into it to rearrange a couple of components and move a few connections.

Kiara could see that the holographic image floating in front of Cory was made up of connections and components, but that was all she could tell. Kiara was good with computers and technology, but Cory was a genius with it. The armor on her arm contracted and expanded as Cory made his adjustments. With a final nod, Cory collapsed the image and sent it back to the screen. The armor expanded one final time on Kiara's arm.

Cory turned to Kiara. "Give it another try."

Kiara nodded at Cory and looked at Jax before looking again at the water bottle. She wanted to laugh. Cory looked excited and hopeful, and Jax looked a little doubtful. To make sure it was a good test, she didn't try harder; she attempted to focus as she had the first time and sent a small pulse at the water bottle. And watched with satisfaction as the bottle went flying.

"Yes!" Cory shouted.

Kiara heard sighs of relief behind her as well. She looked at the table with the other components. "Should I try something bigger before we move on to the other components?"

Jax nodded at her. "Put up a protection bubble."

Kiara did as he asked, and Jax, whipping out his baton, did a side spin with a leap, swinging his baton at her. Her protection field held up, and the impact from Jax's baton vibrated up his arm, causing him to hiss in pain.

Kiara dropped her protection and rushed to his side. Jax brushed aside her concern, a wry smile on his face.

"Well, I guess that worked," he said with a chuckle.

Cory was looking at them, his mouth open, eyes wide.

Randall punched him in the arm to snap him out of it. Cory blinked, his mouth snapping shut. He tried to look casual, but he muttered 'wow' under his breath as he turned back to his console.

"When can we try the rest?" Kiara looked again at the table of other components.

Cory didn't hear her; he was already programming again, rearranging various components and muttering.

Jax came up behind her. "How are we going to test how well it protects you?" At her questioning look, he continued. "Cory demonstrated how well it holds up in that box, but, to be sure, we'll have to test it for real."

Kiara nodded. That seemed a little scary. To really test it, she'd have to be wearing it, and she wouldn't be able to use a protection field, like she just did with Jax.

Randall joined them. "He's going to be buried in that for a while. I suggest you head back to the house," he looked pointedly at Kiara, "and get some rest."

Chapter 7

Back at the main house, Kiara paced in the lower great room, her irritation clearly visible. Jax glanced up from his seat near the doorway. He knew she was feeling trapped in the house. No one would let her out of their sight; they had made that abundantly clear. When she first started pacing, Jax had tried to reassure her, and she'd nearly taken his head off for his trouble. He looked back down at his com unit. He wasn't going to try that again.

Jax knew they were doing well with the body armor. Cory would have the armor ready for them to test shortly, and Jax was confident that it would work well. His worry about her mental state was another matter. He wished Stryker would get back to him on the stone. He felt powerless to help her fight against whatever pull it had on her. He was more comfortable fighting an enemy that he could actually see.

Kiara finally stopped pacing and sat down across the room, and Jax could practically hear everyone let out a sigh of relief. He watched her out of the corner of his eye, trying to judge her mood. She wasn't relaxed, and even Elvis, perched on her shoulder, seemed to be on edge. The little drayek kept reaching out and touching her hair, as if to reassure himself that she was there. Jax waited, thinking it was odd that she wasn't trying to comfort Elvis. He willed her to look at him, and when she finally did, her face was set in a serious frown.

Worried, now more than ever, he got up and crossed to her. "Kiara?" He pitched his voice low.

"I'm okay," Kiara responded, working to smooth out the frown on her face. Jax didn't look convinced, so she assumed she hadn't been successful.

Jax squatted down next to her. "Tell me."

Kiara sighed in relief. He didn't ask her what was wrong; he just knew.

"I'm worried that I will do something stupid again." She reached up as she spoke and gently grabbed one of Elvis' little paws.

"Are you feeling it pull you again?" Jax worked to keep his face neutral. He wasn't sure how to handle it if she went into another trance. The last time, when he hit her with his baton to break the trance, it had almost hurt him as much as it hurt her.

"No!" Kiara rushed to reassure him. "But worrying about it seems to be just as bad." She moved Elvis to her lap to cradle him closer. "I could feel him trying to touch my hair, but I felt guilty about what happened earlier, so I was afraid to touch him." She nuzzled her face into his. "Stupid, I know."

"Not stupid, not at all." Jax reached out and touched her knee. "It wasn't your fault."

"You say that, but I feel like it is. I shouldn't have gone into that shop. I should have known something was wrong. I should have been stronger at resisting it."

Jax shook his head as she was talking. "You expect too much."

"You haven't heard from Stryker yet." She said it as a statement.

"No, not yet."

Kiara heard the worry in his voice. He didn't look worried, but she knew Jax, and she knew he worried.

"Let's go get some training in, that should help relieve some of this tension," Jax suggested. Sitting around waiting for something to happen was also driving him insane.

Kiara sighed in relief and nodded. "There's a good, flat spot out in back. I think it should work."

They headed out, and to Kiara's irritation, her whole entourage followed her.

Jax, sensing her irritation, whispered to her, "They worry."

They reached the small, grass-covered clearing in the back of the property, and after a quick warm-up, Kiara sparred with Jax. It felt good to work out the tension, and as she started to feel better, she grew more aggressive in her moves. Jax, sensing the change, upped his game as well. They threw punches, roundhouse kicks, and the occasional leg sweep. Jax charged at her, and she leaped into the air, executing a front flip and pushing him from behind as she came down. She was relieved to feel Elvis move with her effortlessly, helping strengthen their fragile bond.

Jax, with the additional momentum from Kiara's push, went into a seamless roll, gained his feet, and turned to face her. He had a sinister grin on his face, acknowledging that she had bested him with that move. Kiara watched him bring out the baton and knew he was turning up the intensity yet again. She smirked back at him, prepared to show him something he hadn't seen before. Narrowing her eyes, she connected with Elvis and charged at Jax. With her connection to Elvis, she slowed everything down, and as she approached Jax, she feinted to the left, swept to the right, and anticipated his baton swing. Easily dodging the baton, she spun back around and delivered a roundhouse kick to his back. Jax went flying again, a look of surprise on his face as he rolled and got to his feet.

Breathing hard, he lowered the baton and slowly approached her. "How did you do that? You anticipated everything I did and moved faster than I've ever seen you move before."

Kiara let out a short laugh, and Elvis chirped happily on her shoulder. "Something I've been practicing with Elvis. With his help,

I can slow down everything around me, allowing me to 'seemingly' anticipate your moves."

"Nice." Jax nodded his approval and stretched his back out where Kiara had connected.

Kiara moved behind him and rubbed his back. When she hit the spot where she had kicked him, Jax winced.

"Sorry!" Kiara said quickly. She was sorry that she hurt him, but was secretly proud that she had shown Jax something beyond what he had taught her before.

"It is okay," Jax whispered. "I am glad that you are practicing and expanding on what you learned."

"That was amazing!" Cory shouted.

Jax and Kiara turned to see that their practice session had drawn a larger audience. Kiara's entourage, as well as Cory, Randall, and Shiandra, were watching the sparring match. Kiara turned a darker blue with embarrassment.

Kyle walked up to his daughter and gave her a quick hug. "You looked amazing," he quietly told her. "All that training is paying off. Once we get you into body armor, you'll be unstoppable."

"I hope so," Kiara whispered back.

Cory stepped up and looked like a kid trying to hold in the biggest secret in the world.

"Cory?" Kiara grinned at him.

"It's ready," Cory nearly shouted. "Come on, let's go put it on, then we should come back out here, and you should do that again!"

"I don't know if I want to do that again," Jax mumbled as they headed to the lab.

Kiara heard him and laughed quietly. "Cory, do you have all the pieces complete?"

"Yep, and it has the design you wanted."

"That was fast!" Kiara marveled.

"It's the nanotechnology," Cory said. "It works fast. I had all the preliminary designs done, so refining them, especially after the test this morning, made it easy."

They reached the lab, and Kiara noticed that her dad kept checking his com unit. She frowned. He wasn't the one waiting for information from Stryker. Before she could ask him what was going on, Cory jumped in front of her and presented her with the body armor pieces. Kiara's focus shifted to the beautiful pieces before her. The arm bracelet pieces looked like fine silver jewelry, with a bluish tinge, her dark blue symbol a small piece in the middle. The belt looked like the finest leather, dyed dark blue, with the buckle in the middle containing her symbol. All the pieces matched, and it took her breath away.

"Cory, these look…" she stopped. She was at a loss for words.

"Amazing, awesome, works of art," Kyle filled in for her.

Kiara nodded. She slowly reached out, almost afraid to touch them.

"Go ahead," Cory urged her.

Kiara looked at him and noticed that he was holding a small tablet. He saw her look and rushed to explain. "For the first few times, I need to monitor the pieces and fine-tune changes as needed."

Kiara picked up one of the bracelets and put it on her upper right arm. It immediately snugged up against her tunic, but not too tight. Feeling more confident, she put on the second arm bracelet and reached for the belt. To her surprise, the belt looked like leather but had a metallic feel. She sent Cory a questioning look.

"It's the nanotechnology. I can make it look like anything you want."

Kiara nodded, added the ones on her boots, then slowly raised the necklace. She looked at it a little worriedly. The ones on her arms had snugged up pretty good. She didn't want to get choked, but she also didn't want to hurt Cory's feelings by questioning the safety of it again.

Cory walked over and whispered, "It's okay, I would be a little worried too. How about I try it first?"

Kiara took a deep breath and told herself to step up. With a slight shake of her head and a grimace on her face, she slipped the necklace on. It immediately snugged up, but like the bracelets, once it was fitted, she didn't even feel it. She moved her head around, surprised that she still couldn't feel it.

"How does it feel?" Kyle asked from behind her.

Kiara looked back at her dad. "I can't even feel it, it's great!" She turned back to grab the last piece for her chest and picked up a small, button-like piece, light blue, with her symbol on it. She sent Cory a questioning look, who motioned for her to put it on her chest, underneath her tunic. She didn't see anything to attach it with, but attached it to her tunic as Cory had shown her. When she took her hand away, the button stayed, and she felt a slight pull on the fabric of her tunic.

"So, Cory, do you have to activate it?" Kiara asked him.

"For now. Are you ready?"

"Yes," Kiara whispered, and took a deep breath, closing her eyes.

She heard Cory chuckle before he said, "Just relax."

Cory activated the armor, and Kiara felt that flowing sensation over most of her body. It was strange, but not unpleasant. She opened her eyes and saw the bluish armor, nearly translucent, with a silver reflective surface covering her arms, her legs, her chest. She could see, out of the corner of her eyes, a slight reflective surface near her eyes. The armor covered her head and face. She looked back at Cory, worried that the armor near her eyes would interfere with her vision.

"What is it? Is something not feeling right?" He was madly tapping and swiping at his tablet, looking for anything out of the ordinary.

"It's okay, I'm just concerned about the armor near my eyes—it might interfere with my peripheral vision."

Cory stopped swiping for a second, studying the armor around her face. He nodded, worked at the tablet for a bit, and then nodded again.

Kiara felt the armor adjust slightly and move out of her vision. Smiling, she turned to Cory. "That was awesome!"

She took a few hesitant steps and was pleasantly surprised to discover that she couldn't feel the armor. Once the sensation of the armor deployment was done, she couldn't feel it. She sent a smile back to Cory and walked in a small circle, moving her arms and shoulders, and even doing a few squats. Encouraged by the performance of the armor, she moved into a few jumps and executed some martial arts moves. With the more strenuous moves, she could feel a slight restriction. She turned to tell Cory, but he was furiously swiping and typing on his tablet. She heard him mumble 'yeah, yeah', then swiped and typed some more. When he finally looked up at her, Kiara couldn't read the look on his face.

"I need to work on a few adjustments," he finally said.

"Okaaaay," Kiara drew the word out, trying to gauge what was going on. She looked at Randall before swinging her gaze back to Cory.

Randall walked up behind her and whispered, "That's his 'I've failed, and I'm embarrassed' look."

"Oh," Kiara whispered back. Well, that wouldn't do. This armor was the best thing she had ever seen, and he definitely hadn't failed.

"Yes, I think a few more tweaks are needed, but other than that, I think this is just about ready." She looked at Cory as she made her matter-of-fact statement.

"I agree," Jax said emphatically, understanding, without being told, exactly what was happening.

Cory looked up from his tablet, confused. "You're not disappointed? I know that you could feel the restriction on those last moves. I could see it here."

"Disappointed? Are you kidding? We've never seen anything like this, and the fact that it works this well is beyond anything I could have imagined," Kiara said forcefully.

Cory's ears pinked up a bit, and he nodded hesitantly. "I always think it has to be perfect," he finally admitted.

"This is about as close to perfect as we can expect at this point," Randall said. "Let's disengage, and you can work on those adjustments."

As Kiara removed the now small pieces, she could see her dad, once again, frowning at something on his com unit. Concerned now, she removed all the pieces and walked over to her dad.

"What's wrong?" Kiara quietly asked him.

Kyle looked up at his daughter. "There's been more attacks," he responded without hesitation. "They're losing a lot of Rangers and other troops."

Kiara closed her eyes in sorrow. Then it hit her. "They're asking you to come back and help, aren't they?"

Kyle nodded grimly. Kiara schooled her features into what she hoped was a neutral expression. She would never get in the way of what her dad wanted to do.

"What are you going to do?"

"I'm not leaving you, not while you are battling this stone thing," he nearly shouted.

"But, you do want to go?" Before he could answer, she continued, "I can see it on your face. You feel a duty to help."

Kyle let out a resigned sigh. "I'm not leaving until I know you're out of danger."

"I love you, Dad," Kiara whispered as she moved in for a fierce hug. "But if you need to go, you need to go." She let go and moved back to arm's length, looking him square in the eye. "I have plenty of people here to keep an eye on me. Jax isn't going to let me out of his sight."

Kyle just shook his head, and Kiara knew he wouldn't change his mind.

Shiandra invited everyone back to the house for dinner, and they all trooped back, except Randall and Cory. She guessed that they would want to keep working on those adjustments. Shiandra confirmed her assumption when she said that she would make up some plates of food to take out to them.

After dinner, Kiara relaxed with the others in one of the house's gathering rooms. She liked this room; it had something that Shiandra called a 'fireplace' in it. When Randall had first lit the fire in the small space in the wall, Kiara had been alarmed. Lighting a fire inside the house? After Shiandra had explained it to her, and Kiara had felt the warmth coming from the fireplace, the room had become her favorite place.

Sitting in front of the fireplace, Elvis in her lap, Kiara relaxed. Jax walked by her on his way to a chair and brushed the side of her cheek. Kiara smiled and sent him thoughts of affection, which she knew he would feel. She stared at the fire, her eyes half closed. She smiled sleepily as Elvis began to softly snore and let her thoughts drift to the events of the day. Half asleep, thoughts of the stone crept in, so insidiously, so inconspicuously, that it didn't alarm her in the least. Thoughts of the stone swirled in her head, and she marveled at the beauty and power of it. She dreamed of holding it, feeling its power, using its power.

Jax looked up from his com unit, glanced at Kiara, and shot out of his chair. Her hair was floating, and she was once again holding her hand out in front of her as if reaching for something. With her other hand, she was doing something to Elvis, and as Jax reached her chair, he could see that she had encased him in a protective shield. Elvis looked panicked but seemed powerless to do anything about it. Knowing that she also had the power to stop him if she sensed him, he swiftly produced his baton to shock her out of the trance. He hit her in the shoulder, just as she was turning to him. Kiara screamed, Elvis screeched, and everyone else in the room shouted.

Jax caught Kiara just as she collapsed. He looked at Elvis and was relieved to see that the little drayek was still Kiara's blue color.

Kiara came to, quickly this time; most likely because the trance she was in had just started. She looked up into Jax's worried eyes and could see the others huddling around her as well. She began to panic about Elvis, but quickly tamped it down when she realized she could feel his bond, as strong as before.

Jax helped her sit up, and she shook her head to clear it. Jax was on one side, her dad on the other, both supporting her. She could hear Blackburne muttering in the background, something about Stryker getting his ass in gear. She hugged Elvis to her, while he chirped and stroked her hair.

"What happened this time?" Jax asked quietly.

"I think I was dozing off. I was really relaxed, which is probably why it happened."

"Did it feel like something had taken over?" Kyle was still puzzled by this whole thing and worried sick about his daughter. He knew he'd made the right decision, not to leave.

"No, not like that. My mind starts drifting, I think of the stone, and then I can't think of anything else but the stone, and getting it, using it, that sort of thing."

Jax looked thoughtful for a moment. "What about Elvis? It was different this time."

Kiara struggled to recall those moments, and suddenly, she sat up straight, her eyes wide. "I remember! I started thinking about the stone, and some part of me realized I was slipping under its power, and I knew I had to protect Elvis. I used my protection field to isolate him from the influence of the stone, but kept him bonded to that part of me that was still conscious of what was happening."

Jax and Kyle looked at each other before they focused on Kiara. Jax spoke before Kyle could say anything. "Maybe you can do that with yourself? Keep the influence of the stone from taking you over somehow?"

All three thought about it, with similar frowns on their faces. Blackburne was still pacing and muttering, glancing over occasionally at the three of them on the floor.

Shiandra shot into the room, a worried look on her face. "I heard yelling. Is Kiara okay?" She saw Kiara on the floor and immediately jumped over to her, pushing Jax out of the way. Jax just smiled. He could feel the maternal feelings pumping out of her.

"Sweetheart, are you okay?" Shiandra smoothed Kiara's hair and made clucking noises at Elvis.

"I'm okay, Shiandra. It was just a quick lapse this time. Jax was right on it."

"Elvis looks okay this time," Shiandra said, in between the clucking noises she was making at him.

"Yes, I protected him this time." Kiara slowly levered herself up off the floor, and with her dad supporting her elbow and Shiandra making room on one of the chairs, she sat back down, surprised that she still felt unsteady.

"Do you want something to drink, maybe a nice cup of tea?" Shiandra asked her, fluffing pillows around her like a mother hen.

"No, I'm okay. Thanks," Kiara told her and stilled Shiandra's hands. Holding Shiandra's hands, Kiara looked in her eyes. "Really, I'm okay."

Shiandra took a deep breath and nodded. "My heartbeat went through the roof when I heard you scream," she admitted.

"You and me, both," Blackburne said from behind her. He shot a look at Jax. "Heard from Stryker yet? I don't think we can take this anymore."

Jax shook his head. He was frustrated as well.

Kiara cleared her throat, "I have an idea."

Kyle and Jax both groaned, and Blackburne let out a sigh.

Shiandra looked at them. "What is wrong with Kiara having an idea?" she scolded.

Blackburne chuckled. "It's not that she has an idea, it's the way she said it." He shook his head. "When she says it like that, it means it's probably dangerous."

Shiandra looked at Kiara in surprise.

"It's not dangerous!" Kiara protested. "Probably not dangerous," she qualified when they all sent sarcastic looks her way.

"What are you thinking?" Jax finally asked her.

"Mirona, my ancestor, once told me that at some point, I should be able to reach her when I'm not dreaming."

"That doesn't sound so dangerous," Shiandra said into the silence.

Kiara shook her head. "I think the dangerous part will be when I'm trying to relax my mind and reach her. It will probably make me vulnerable to the power of the stone."

"What if I use my abilities to help focus you?" Jax asked her. "Your dad and Blackburne will be there—"

"And me!" Shiandra interjected.

"And Shiandra, to help snap you out of it, if anything goes wrong."

Kyle looked dubious, but Kiara looked determined. "We have to do something."

At that moment, Jax's com unit signaled. He looked down at it and sighed in relief. "It's Stryker." He left the room to hear what Stryker had to say.

With Shiandra still fussing over Kiara, Jax came back into the room. Instead of a look of relief on his face, he looked frustrated and angry.

"What's wrong?" Kiara jumped up and crossed to him, relieved that she felt strong again. "Didn't Stryker call with information on the stone?"

Jax grabbed her hands, looking into her eyes, his face serious. "Yes, he did find some information," Jax said, emphasizing the word 'some'.

When he didn't continue, Kiara squeezed his hands to continue. "Tell us. Whatever it is, we'll deal with it."

"He talked to several different Galdorians about the stone." Jax sat down heavily while he talked. His mind was desperately looking for another solution, even while he told the group what Stryker had found. "The first one didn't give him what he wanted, so he ended up talking to several different ones. They all said the same thing."

Everyone looked at him expectantly.

"Once the stone has a hold on you, there is nothing you can do to break it, except death, or destruction of the stone."

Silence filled the room.

Kiara's wobbly voice broke the silence. "Why me? What's the stone ultimately going to do to me?"

"Stryker thinks it will eventually give control of you to whoever put you in the path of the stone."

"They could use her to cause more destruction, to further whatever their agenda is," Blackburne commented.

"And keep her out of the way of all the CyRAINs out there," Kyle added.

"Control me?" Kiara squeaked out, her panic rising. The thought was utterly terrifying.

Jax immediately went to her. "We won't let it happen. I promise you." He put his arms around her and pulled her close.

Kiara buried her face in Jax's shoulder. She couldn't live this way, waiting for the next episode to happen. Elvis combed his paws through her hair, trying to find a way to comfort her. They wouldn't be able to help people, because they would always be waiting for the next episode. Her eyes filled with tears when she suddenly remembered her plan. She pushed back from Jax, determination in her stance.

"We have to try to contact Mirona, it's our only hope at this point."

With a grim look, Jax nodded. Kyle crossed over to her, resigned agreement on his face as well.

"No time like the present," Kiara quipped. Receiving nods from everyone, Kiara crossed to the fireplace and sat on the floor, folding her legs. Jax joined her, his legs nearly touching hers. Elvis sat on Kiara's lap; Jax and Kiara joined hands. Shiandra stood directly behind Kiara, ready to help if necessary. Blackburne and Kyle stood just to the side, Kyle holding Jax's baton. They opted to have Randall and Cory wait in the lab to keep things simple.

Jax and Kiara, eyes locked, began deep breathing in unison. Kiara expanded her mind, feeling for Jax. Her eyes turned darker, and her hair began to float around her head.

Power Rising

Shiandra felt goosebumps pop up on her arms. It was amazing and frightening, all at once.

Once Kiara was sure she and Jax were connected, she expanded her mind again, reaching out and searching for Mirona, using her previous dreams to guide her. Her thoughts racing through time and space, she could feel the stone, just outside her thoughts, pushing, taunting, reaching. Each time she could feel the stone breaking through, Jax would be there to shore up her defenses and bring her back to the task. It was tiring, and Kiara could feel frustration creeping in. Jax bolstered her up again, and with renewed determination, she forced the stone away and reached for Mirona.

Mirona!

I'm here, child.

Kiara was so relieved to hear Mirona's voice in her head that she nearly lost the connection.

I can't believe it worked. Is it really you, Mirona?

Yes, Kiara, I am here. You have done it; you have reached me when you are awake. I sense someone with you—not your drayek, someone else.

Jax is helping me. I'm desperate.

What is it, Kiara? What has happened?

Mirona's anxiety punched into Kiara's brain, and Kiara could feel Mirona strengthening their connection. Kiara quickly explained what she knew about the stone and its effect on her.

Kiara, I have heard of these stones. It is mostly legend, and my knowledge of them is limited.

Kiara's despair hit Mirona hard through the connection.

Do not despair, child. Even though I do not know much about the stones, I think I can help break the connection and the hold it has on you. Throughout our history, others have tried to control Guardians through any means possible.

You can help?

I believe so, but we will need others to help us, or we will not be successful in completely breaking the hold.

Can we connect with your family and our other ancestors, as we did before? Kiara hoped Mirona could connect them with her ancestors.

Yes, we will need them, but we will need others from Trandor, in your time. I know you told me there are not many left from Trandor. Can you find Trandorians to help? We will need them for the ceremony.

In Kiara's head, she could feel Jax agreeing, and she took that to mean that he could take them to the colony that he had spoken about before.

Yes, Mirona, we can do that.

Mirona left them with the ceremony instructions before they broke the connection.

Jax helped bring Kiara safely back to the present, and everyone in the room let out a sigh of relief when she let go of Jax's hands and looked around the room. She started to stand up but realized that her legs were a little wobbly. She looked at Jax, and he, too, looked exhausted.

"Well?" Kyle asked impatiently. He couldn't tell from their expressions if they were successful or not. They both looked exhausted.

Kiara nodded at her dad as she moved to a chair, Shiandra mothering her the whole way.

"We connected, and she said she could help us," Kiara finally said into the silence. She grabbed her com unit and quickly entered the instructions for the ceremony that Mirona had told her about. "There's a ceremony we can perform to rid me of the stone." Kiara took an exhausted look around the room. "Mirona wasn't sure it would work, but she thinks it is our best option."

"We'll have to get to the colony of Trandorians, though." Jax collapsed in the chair next to her. He looked at Kiara. "That was rough. It was almost beyond my abilities."

Kiara grabbed his hand. "I'm sorry," she said quietly. Before he could respond, she added, "But I am so glad you were there."

"We have to go to the colony you told us about? Where you secretly moved some of the Trandorians you have helped?" Kyle asked, looking for clarification.

"Yes," Jax replied, closing his eyes. "We should try to leave as soon as possible."

"What about the armor?" Kyle asked quietly.

No one answered for a moment. Kiara knew the whole reason they were here was to get her the armor, and to have to leave before it was ready was going to be a blow.

"It's not completely ready," Cory said from the doorway.

Everyone in the room turned to look at him.

"That's what we thought," Jax said quietly.

"Wait, that's not what I meant," Cory said quickly. "It's ready enough for her to use it, but I need to be with her in the beginning to monitor and make adjustments."

Kiara frowned. No one spoke. Kiara finally broke the silence.

"You need to come with us," Kiara said, waiting for objections.

"That's exactly what I was thinking!" Cory nearly shouted his response.

Shiandra crossed the room to him. "Are you sure, Cory?"

"It's only until she has it under her control and we have the kinks worked out."

Blackburne crossed to him and held out his hand. "Welcome aboard, Cory!"

"How soon can you be ready?" Jax questioned.

"Tomorrow."

With a nod, they finalized their plans to leave, and Cory shot out of the room to get a start on his packing.

Kiara glanced at Jax and saw him in a hushed conversation with her dad. She knew they were discussing her. She crossed over to them, determined to be part of the conversation.

Kyle recognized the look on his daughter's face and took a step toward her to head off the lecture and the temper he could see.

"We were working out a schedule to stay with you, and keep us rested at the same time," he quickly said.

Kiara stopped. Of course they were. She could still see the exhaustion on Jax's face and knew the whole situation was taking its toll on him. She nodded, her temper dissipating as quickly as it started. "Of course." She looked at Jax. "You're going to rest first, right?"

Jax chuckled. "I look that bad, huh?"

Kiara crossed to him quickly, remorse filling her. She wrapped him in a hug and whispered in his ear. "I'm so sorry this is happening, but I'm happy you are here. I couldn't have survived this long without you."

Jax returned her hug with a fierceness he knew she would understand. "There's no other place I would rather be," he whispered. He let go of her and answered her earlier question. "Yes, I'm resting first. Your dad will sit with you when you go to bed."

A part of her hated that she needed someone to sit with her, but the sensible part knew it was the right thing to do.

Later, as she got ready for bed, she reflected on her situation. She hoped that Mirona was right and that the ceremony she spoke to them about would help break the connection to the stone. She was worried, since Mirona didn't seem to know that much about the stones. She sighed and opened the door to the bathroom, only to find her dad right outside the door. She let out a squeak and jumped, glad that she also hadn't shot an energy pulse at him. At her jump, Elvis shot off her shoulder, letting out a hiss.

"Sorry, baby, I was just trying to stay close in case you needed me."

Kyle looked apologetic, but Kiara could see relief as well. Because she hadn't shot him with an energy pulse, or because she wasn't in a trance, she couldn't tell. She soothed Elvis after he landed back on her shoulder. They were all a bit jumpy, it seemed.

Once in bed, she tossed and turned, trying to get comfortable. Every time she rolled over, Elvis let out a grumpy sound as he repositioned himself to sleep. She was exhausted, but her mind was energized, worrying about the stone and what was to come. Her dad was pretending to read something on his com unit. Kiara rolled her eyes at their sorry predicament.

She finally fell asleep, and for a while, she didn't dream, just slept. When her dreams started, the stone was front and center, and even in her sleep, Kiara knew the danger. She tried to wake herself, but couldn't. In her dream, she was floating across a body of water, straight to where the stone waited. It was floating above the water, visibly pulsing with energy. She could feel the pull, and even as she resisted, it pulled her closer. She looked around for help, but all she could see was water.

Just as she felt that she was going to give in to the stone, she felt another presence in her dream. It wasn't Elvis, she could still feel him off to the side, not quite in her dream, but just outside of it, as if she was protecting him again. She concentrated on that other presence, her lifeline at the moment. Maybe her dad? Maybe her dad had gotten Jax? The image of the stone began to shimmer and fade, and Kiara found herself on the shore of the body of water rather than floating over it. In her dream, she turned away from the water and instantly recognized Trandor from her dreams with Mirona. She turned some more and saw Mirona standing in front of her. She sighed with relief.

Are you really here? It isn't the stone, trying to trick me?
Yes, Kiara, I am here. I was worried, so I have been waiting for you to fall asleep so that I may watch over you.
You can do that?
Yes, you will be safe now. Sleep. Rest well.

Kyle observed his daughter. He'd seen her tossing and turning, then settle. His relief was short-lived as he watched her tense up in her sleep, her breathing changed from restful to anxious panting. Elvis had sat up next to her, looking uneasy. Kyle had been ready to get Jax when she suddenly relaxed again. Her breathing had gone back to an even, deep pattern, with Elvis relaxing and lying down next to her. Whatever was going on in her dreams, for now, she seemed to be safe.

Chapter 8

The next morning, Kiara stood outside the shuttle, watching Cory in disbelief. Using a modified, small hoverlift, he brought out crate after crate from his lab. Elvis huffed at Cory every time he unloaded a new crate.

"Are we going to be able to get any lift with all that stuff?" Kiara asked, half joking, half serious.

Blackburne stepped up next to her, threw his small bag into the shuttle, and then frowned at Cory. "How much stuff are you bringing?"

"I know, I know," Cory huffed out, moving his crates into the back of the shuttle. "I have to make sure I have what I need for every contingency."

Kiara rolled her eyes and jumped into the shuttle, throwing her bag on top of the crates. She felt well rested, for the first time in a long time. She was very thankful that Mirona had watched over her. She waved out the doorway to Shiandra and Randall. Saying good-bye to them earlier had been difficult. She felt an attachment to Shiandra, as did Elvis. The only way that Shiandra had let go of her was for Kiara to promise to keep in touch and to return for a visit every chance she had. They were easy promises. Shiandra had sent Kiara with fruit for Elvis and snacks for the rest of the crew.

Kyle and Jax were already in the shuttle. Jax looked more rested as well, even though he had stayed up to watch her for half the night. When she had woken, she immediately reassured them that she was okay and explained about Mirona. To know Mirona was watching when Kiara slept had eased all their minds. Before Kiara had awakened, Mirona had promised to watch her every night until the ceremony could be performed.

Cory finally had all his gear on the shuttle and went to say his goodbyes to Shiandra and Randall. Even from the shuttle, Kiara could feel Shiandra's sadness and sympathized with her. Cory finally disengaged himself, jumping into the shuttle. Kiara could feel both his sorrow and his excitement. With everyone finally on board, the shuttle lifted off, the overhead dome opening to let them out. As Blackburne headed them back to the city, Kiara looked into the back of the shuttle at all the crates. How were they going to get those on the public shuttle and then up to the space station?

She turned to Jax and saw him realize it at the same time. He nodded at Kiara and moved up next to Blackburne. She saw Blackburne look back at the crates and roll his eyes before looking forward. He immediately had Jax get on his com unit. After a few minutes, Jax came back to join them. Cory looked apologetic, as he had finally figured out what was happening.

"I'm sorry, Jax. I really needed to bring all of it."

Jax patted Cory on the shoulder and smiled. "It's okay, Cory, we've got it handled." He looked at Kiara. "Unfortunately, we'll have to get a private shuttle to the space station, and it could bring unwanted attention. We're trying to get it done through some contacts that I have, but I wanted everyone to be aware, and stay on your toes."

Cory opened his mouth to apologize again, but Jax cut him off. "We need you, the armor you designed, and your expertise. We always have to think on our feet and make adjustments, so this isn't your fault."

Cory nodded, but frowned as he thought of something else. "Why can't we just take this one? Everything is already on it."

Jax smiled as he remembered that, as smart as Cory was, he hadn't spent that much time in space. "This shuttle is only rated for the lower atmosphere, so we'll have to get something else." He looked out the window as the forest gave way to the cityscape. "The government likes to limit how much traffic goes between the space station and the surface, since that trip is more hazardous than anything else. It will take a little more effort to get us something to the space station."

They landed in the shuttle lot, and Jax and Blackburne worked their com units to plan out the next leg of their journey. While they worked their magic, Kiara took the time to tell Cory about Frankie and Curly. She didn't know if Cory had ever seen a Bendanite before, and she didn't want him to panic. She contacted Frankie on the ship and brought up a holographic conference call to introduce them to Cory. Cory, seeing Curly, was suitably impressed.

"Finally," Blackburne muttered when Kiara disconnected the call.

Blackburne came to the back of the shuttle and nodded at Kyle. "Thanks for your connections, Kyle. One of your Ranger buddies was in the area, and he's on his way over to us. He's got room in his ship to take the cargo and one other. The rest of us will take the regular shuttle back to the space station."

"Glad you worked it out. I suppose we should send Cory?"

"Yes, Cory is the one who needs to accompany his gear. It's going to look suspicious if one of us came to the surface on the shuttle, but didn't go back up."

Cory looked thrilled. "I get to ride with a Ranger?"

Everyone smiled at his enthusiasm.

"How long before he gets here?" Kyle wanted to know.

"I caught him right before he was heading out, so he changed direction, and he's heading here. Should be landing any minute now," Blackburne said as he headed up to the front to button down the shuttle.

Kiara agreed that Cory needed to go with the Ranger, but she really hated riding the public shuttle to the space station.

The ride on the shuttle to the space station wasn't as bad as Kiara feared. Thankfully, the shuttle wasn't as full this time around. Once they were aboard the station, they headed to the Acadia, and Curly and Frankie met them at the bottom of the ramp. Elvis, when he saw Curly, jumped from Kiara's shoulder and flapped his way awkwardly to her. When Kiara caught up to him, she hugged Curly, while Elvis chirped and clicked, jumping from Kiara to Curly.

"You are okay?" Curly quietly asked her.

"Yes, I'm okay," Kiara told her, hugging her again. She had enjoyed her time on the surface, but she was relieved to be back in familiar surroundings.

Kiara heard a shout from behind her and turned to see Cory approaching, hauling his cargo with a borrowed hoverlift. His face was beaming, so she assumed he'd had a great time with the Ranger. His mouth dropped open when he looked at the Acadia.

"This is the Acadia?" Cory asked, his eyes wide as he tried to take it all in.

Blackburne came up behind him and slapped him on the back. "Let's get your stuff loaded. Jax says we've got a long haul to the Trandorian colony, so we need to get going." He turned to Frankie. "Did you get us all fueled up and the supplies loaded?"

Frankie, dressed in a bright orange and yellow shirt, nodded as he helped Cory load his cargo. Kiara could hear Frankie teasing and joking with Cory. They'd hit it off, just as she thought they would.

Kiara took her bag to her bunk before heading to the cargo area. She stopped short as she entered the cargo bay. Off to the side, Frankie had sectioned a small area of the cargo room to serve as

Cory's room and his lab. Kiara had been wondering where they would put him. She'd thought they would put him in the flex-space, but as she looked around the cargo area, she knew this was much better. Cory joined her, carrying one of his crates.

"Can I help you get set up?" Kiara asked him.

Cory looked doubtful.

"I know my way around computers and technology," Kiara assured him.

Still looking doubtful, Cory nodded, dropped his crate, and went back out for more.

With Kiara's help, it didn't take long to get his gear unpacked and mainly organized. Even Elvis helped, with Kiara silently directing him to hand her things or move a cable. Cory was pleasantly surprised and told her so.

Kiara smiled and headed up to the bridge. Her com unit had signaled that Frankie was ready for her to get their route to him. As she approached the bridge, she felt the rumble of the engines and the slight dip as Frankie took them out of the space station. She entered the bridge, with Blackburne seated in his chair, and her dad occupying one of the chairs that popped out of the wall. She sat at her navunit, entering the data that Jax had sent her for the colony. The planet was one she had never been to, and it was in an isolated sector. It was the only planet in that system that supported humanoid life. She double-checked her calculations and noted they would need to travel through two transgates to get there. She calculated the trip would take them two days.

She sighed as she sent the navigation information to Frankie's console. Two more days and nights of worrying that the stone would take hold of her. She knew her dad was watching her, and Jax would take a turn, and Mirona would watch her while she slept. It was still a worry. She hoped Mirona's plan would break the stone's bond.

As Frankie headed them toward the first transgate, he motioned Blackburne over. Kiara could hear them talking in low voices, and from her station, she could feel their distress. Elvis chirped quietly at her.

"I know, little man. Something has them worried."

Kiara got up and walked over to join them and saw her dad get up as well.

"What's going on?" Kiara asked. They had stopped talking as she approached.

Blackburne waited until Kyle joined them before he spoke up. "Frankie had to file a flight plan in order to use the first transgate. Space station control wouldn't let us leave without doing it. He didn't file the whole route, so the colony's location is still safe, but—"

"You think that puts us in danger?" Kiara saw the looks exchanged by her dad and Blackburne. "You think whoever is planning the attacks and trying to keep tabs on me might take the information on where we are going and use it to attack us?"

"It's a possibility," Kyle answered. He looked at Kiara. "We'll need to be on alert, even more than we usually are. I'll update Jax."

Kiara watched her dad leave the bridge and felt Blackburne watching her. She attempted to lighten the mood. "Your turn to watch me?" she asked with a smile.

Blackburne looked uncomfortable, but Kiara assured him she was okay with it.

They reached the first transgate without incident, but, as they had learned on previous travels, the greater threat was when they exited it. They would be essentially blind and vulnerable, and if an ambush were waiting, it could be fatal. Kiara contacted Transgate Control and received normal responses, which was a relief. She performed her own scan on the transgate and, finding nothing out of the ordinary, waited for Transgate Control to let them know when they could proceed.

While they waited, Cory joined them on the bridge, and Blackburne directed him to a pop-out chair. Kiara wondered why his eyes didn't just fall out of his head. His eyes were still so wide and full of wonder as he tried to take everything in. She knew he'd been off planet before, but he usually traveled in a big personnel transport, and it was nothing like traveling in a cargo hauler or smaller spacecraft.

Finally, Transgate Control gave them the go-ahead to enter. Kiara was surprised they didn't have to wait longer, exchanging looks with Frankie and Blackburne as they headed into the transgate. Kiara sent the navigation information to him and braced for the entrance into the transgate. She knew from previous experience that this transgate had a rough entrance and exit, but the middle was reasonably smooth. She also knew that Blackburne would get motion sickness from it, especially since the entrance would be rough. She glanced over at Cory, hoping that he would handle it okay. He was strapped into a chair and didn't look concerned.

They entered the transgate, the Acadia straining and groaning with the stresses put on the ship. The travel time would be short, so the anticipation for the exit wouldn't wear on them too long. Kiara glanced at Blackburne, who was now his usual shade of gray from the motion sickness, but she knew he wouldn't leave the bridge. The ride had smoothed out, and Kiara checked her scans, looking for anything that would spell trouble. So far, everything was normal, but Kiara's anxiety was building as they drew closer to the exit.

Elvis had been at her feet, but as her anxiety grew, he climbed her leg and sat in her lap, ready to help her in any way that he could. She looked down at him and thought, perhaps they could try to sense what was on the other side? She felt that Elvis agreed, and, checking her scans one more time, touched the drayek on his back and attempted to sense what was coming.

At first, she couldn't sense anything, and then she sensed too much, as she realized she was getting something from all the areas they were passing through with the transgate. She strained to focus on the transgate exit, and finally, she thought she had it. She could see the exit; she could see the space station just beyond it. That's when she saw them. The Mercenary ships, in their typical three-ship formation, were waiting just outside the exit. She struggled to figure out exactly where they were in relation to the transgate. She pulled back and turned to Frankie. Apparently, her attempt hadn't gone unnoticed. Frankie was staring at her expectantly.

"Are they waiting for us?" Frankie asked.

"Yes, Mercenary ships, three of them, right outside the exit. They are dead center."

Frankie nodded, adjusting his position in his seat as he readied himself for maneuvering as soon as they exited. Blackburne announced the warning to the ship so that Curly, Kyle, and Jax would be braced. Before he was done with his warning, both Jax and Kyle joined them on the bridge, and Kiara knew it was because they could help with firing weapons. They both strapped in, with Jax positioning himself at the second weapons station next to her.

For a moment, Kiara's thoughts went to the stone, but Jax quickly touched her arm.

"Stay focused on this battle," he forcefully told her.

Kiara nodded, glad that he was next to her. They were only a few seconds away from exiting. She quickly turned to Frankie.

"Up and to the right, Frankie."

Frankie nodded, and everyone braced as the ship groaned and strained through the exit of the transgate.

The shields were up on the Acadia, as they usually were through a transgate. As they exited, the ship bucked and shuddered as weapons fire hit them. Kiara attempted to shield the Acadia but was struggling to focus. Every time she attempted an energy field, the stone would pop into her head, breaking her concentration.

So far, the shields were holding as Frankie maneuvered them around, and Jax fired at the Mercenary ships. Jax motioned Kyle to take over for him, and quickly unbuckling from his seat, he jumped in front of Kiara, sensing her struggles.

"Kiara, focus!"

Kiara looked at Jax in distress. She tried again, but once again the stone popped into her head, breaking down her energy field. Frankie yelled that the shields wouldn't hold much longer, and she could hear Blackburne trying to get help from the space station.

Jax grabbed her hands, forcing Elvis onto her shoulder and Kiara to look at him.

"Come on, Kiara, we need you! Focus!"

Kiara closed her eyes and shut everything out. Jax was still yelling at her to open her eyes and focus when she realized that she was going about this all wrong. Instead of trying to shield the Acadia, she should destroy the Mercenary ships. The stone tried to insert itself into her mind's eye, but instead, she forced an image of Elvis into her mind. She felt her bond with the little drayek grow stronger, and using it, she pictured the battle against the Mercenary ships. Gathering her strength, she sent pulses of energy at the Mercenary ships. It took multiple tries, but the first one, then another ship, exploded. Her next pulse of energy weakened the last ship, and Kyle was able to destroy it.

Kiara tried to stand up, but her knees felt weak, and her vision was starting to grey out around the edges. Jax grabbed her arm and sat her back down, and Kiara could hear Elvis chirping in her ear.

"Are we okay?" she finally managed to ask. Jax was trying to force her head between her knees to keep her from passing out, but she was fighting it.

She heard Frankie give a status update to Blackburne, and it sounded like the shields were holding.

"Scan the area; make sure we don't have another ambush coming!" Blackburne bellowed out.

"I'm okay, now," Kiara told Jax. She wanted him to quit pushing at her.

Jax squatted down in front of her, and he could see her eyes were finally clear and focused on his. He gently cupped her jaw and nodded at her before getting up to discuss their situation with Blackburne. Kyle moved over to stay with Kiara.

Kiara could hear them discussing the status of the shields, their engines, and their route. She needed to be in on the discussion about their route, but wasn't sure her legs would hold her yet. Trying so hard to focus past the stone and use her abilities to destroy the Mercenary ships had sapped all her strength. She looked around the room and saw Cory, still strapped to his seat, looking as if he might throw up. What a way to start the young man's trip. He was probably wishing he were back home.

She looked up at her dad. "Dad, I have some ideas about the route we can take." She jerked her head toward Cory. "I think Cory needs a little help."

Kyle motioned Blackburne and Frankie over to her chair and went to help Cory. A few reassurances, a few deep breaths, and Cory had his equilibrium back.

"Now that we aren't at the space station at Earth Delta Nine, we can take any route we want," Kiara began.

"We don't want to delay too much, Kiara; the stone's hold on you is getting stronger," Jax said from behind her. He put his hand on her shoulder in a comforting gesture.

"I know," Kiara said, ducking her head. She felt guilty for nearly getting them killed, again. "We have another route, with a different transgate. It will only delay us half a day." She looked at the faces around her. "They won't be expecting it."

"Show me," Blackburne demanded.

Kiara moved her chair to her navunit, keyed in a few commands, and brought up the new route. Blackburne and Jax studied it, looking for potential traps or other dangers. The new route would take them through an area with dead planets, so if anything happened to them, they wouldn't be able to get help. It was a risk, but everyone agreed that the opposition wouldn't be expecting it.

Blackburne and Frankie checked the fuel and other supplies, and, feeling they had a cushion on both, decided to take Kiara's new route. Kiara set up the route and sent the navigation information to Frankie.

Feeling stronger, Kiara got up from her chair once Frankie got them underway and walked over to Cory. He was starting to look calm again.

"Are you okay?" Kiara asked him quietly. She didn't want to embarrass him.

His cheeks pinked up a little bit, but he didn't look too uncomfortable as he nodded.

"Feel up to helping me get the shields back up to full strength? That battle probably burned out some circuits that we can try to repair."

Cory looked relieved to be able to do something to help, so he unstrapped from his chair and followed her to the panel with the shield generator. Curly was in the hallway, obviously thinking the same thing. Curly was too big to get into the panel, but she was there to help in any way that she could.

Kiara opened the panel and scooted in on her back, Elvis taking up his position on her stomach. "Let me get a look in here, and we can figure out what we need for a repair." Kiara's voice floated out from the panel.

Kiara, seeing some burned-out components and other areas that needed repair, rattled off the parts and tools she needed. Curly headed down the hallway to get the parts as Kiara scooted out from the panel. She motioned Cory to take a look. He got down on his back and wiggled his way in. Kiara could tell that he immediately felt at home. She handed him a diagnostic scanner, and he checked circuits and connections, mumbling as he did it. Kiara smiled. That's how he had been at his home when he was working on her armor.

He scooted out from the panel, a slight frown on his face.

"What did you find?" Kiara quickly asked him.

'Oh, nothing bad," Cory quickly assured her. As Curly came back with a container of parts, he looked from Curly to Kiara. "I think I can make some improvements to protect some of those circuits. It might give us a little extra time in a fight."

Kiara remembered the last time she made modifications to the Acadia and didn't run it by Blackburne first. She didn't want his wrath again, so she told Cory to send his suggestions to Blackburne first. If he approved, she'd help Cory implement the changes. In the meantime, they'd do what they could to get the shields back up to full strength.

Working together to repair the damage, Cory showed Kiara where he could make improvements. Kiara agreed and helped him send his suggestions to Blackburne. She also sent something separately to Blackburne to let him know she approved of the changes.

Kiara was getting the panel secured when Blackburne came down the narrow hallway. "Let me see what you guys are proposing. If we have the parts, I think you should do it now, before we run into more trouble."

Kiara opened the panel, and Blackburne squeezed his large frame in as far as he could go. With Cory explaining his modifications, Blackburne grunted his approval at what he was seeing. Finally, he scooted out, his look slightly less severe than usual.

"Do it."

As Blackburne walked away, Cory looked at Kiara in bafflement.

"You'll get used to it," Kiara said with a laugh.

As their journey continued, Kiara and Cory worked together every chance they got to fine-tune the body armor. They increased its deployment speed, refined how it looked, and worked to keep it from interfering with Kiara's abilities. Each time Kiara felt the stone start to creep in, she would focus on Elvis and use their bond to beat it back. Each time was more difficult than the time before, and Kiara knew the stone was getting closer and closer to taking control of her altogether.

Kiara was immensely relieved that her new route was successfully keeping them out of harm's way. She worried about trying to protect those around her, since she felt the stone was close to taking her over completely. Looking down at Elvis, she resolved to stay strong for as long as it took. The thought of breaking her bond with Elvis, which would lead to his death, was more than her heart could bear.

They arrived at the Trandorian colony without further attacks. Once they were in orbit around the planet, Kiara and the others prepared to head down to the surface. Jax had contacted the colony, and they were sending a shuttle up to the Acadia to transport the crew to the surface. For this trip, only Kiara, Jax, and Kyle would head to the surface. Cory and Blackburne would stay on board to help with repairs, upgrades, and the defense of the ship.

Kiara was nervous. She needed this to work for her sake and those around her, but she was also nervous about meeting other Trandorians. She'd never had the opportunity to meet someone else from Trandor, since there were so few of them left. Unfortunately, her current situation was overshadowing the momentous occasion. She grabbed a small bag of her belongings, moved Elvis to her shoulder, and headed out. As she approached the bridge, she could hear Frankie talking to the shuttle pilot and felt the small knock on the hull as the shuttle docked with the Acadia. Her dad and Jax were waiting for her, and after a brief conversation with Blackburne, the three of them boarded the shuttle. Kiara tried to peek around Jax as they boarded; she wanted to see if the pilot was a Trandorian. She tried to hide her disappointment when he wasn't. Jax, of course, wasn't fooled.

"Don't worry, there will be plenty of Trandorians to meet on the surface," he whispered to her.

Kiara smiled and strapped in for the bumpy ride to the surface. Jax always knew what she was feeling.

The shuttle was a small one, with no windows, so Kiara wasn't able to catch a glimpse of the planet as they descended. She suddenly realized that she didn't even know the name of the planet. When Jax had been giving them information on how to get there, he'd called it the colony. Turning to him, she asked him the name of the planet.

Jax smiled. "We call it Trandor Prime."

"Oh." Kiara thought about that for a second. "What do the original inhabitants call it?" Before Jax could answer, she shot another question at him. "Who are the original inhabitants?"

"I believe the planet's name was something unpronounceable in the native language and sounded like gibberish whenever anyone attempted to translate it. When others from Trandor were looking for a place to land, they found this planet, with an atmosphere and climate suitable for them." Jax looked sad for a moment. "Most of the native population had been decimated by a plague before they were able to eradicate it. When they found the planet, the population was starting to recover, but there were vast areas that were deserted. Apparently, the original population had moved most of their survivors to consolidated areas to help them and keep their society going." The shuttle bumped through some upper atmosphere turbulence before smoothing out again. "The original inhabitants were actually excited to have someone occupy several of the deserted cities, and help keep their planet and economy going."

Kiara's forehead wrinkled. "What about the plague? I know you said they eradicated it, but if I remember my biology right, some viruses and other diseases can remain dormant for long periods of time in the soil, or other areas."

"Quite right." Jax nodded, his look serious. "I know they did extensive testing, and they found that it was still there in some areas, but it wasn't compatible with the Trandorian physiology, or any other known species, for that matter. The original inhabitants have a vaccine for it and inoculate their population, much as Earth's inhabitants did with polio and other early diseases. I know that it is something we constantly monitor for them."

"What about drayeks?" Kiara looked down at Elvis, curled up in her lap. "Should I be worried?"

Jax looked thoughtful for a moment. "Let me check the archives." He brought up his com unit and quickly searched for the information. "I'm sure he'll be fine, but I didn't think to check for drayeks."

Kiara watched him for a few tense seconds before Jax nodded at her. "As I suspected, his species is listed here under the ones known to be incompatible with their plague."

Kiara let out the breath she had been holding. She knew that she would need Elvis for the ceremony, but she would have left him behind rather than put him in danger. "They were fortunate to find this planet."

"True, but most travelers through this system avoid the planet, knowing that the plague was there. No one had attempted to contact them for many years due to the fear it caused. It actually worked in our favor, since most travelers through this area still avoid it."

"How big is the colony?"

"The colony itself is about five thousand, but not all are Trandorian. I would estimate that there are several thousand Trandorians here. It has taken us many years to find that many."

Kiara nodded and turned to look at her dad. He was intently looking at his com unit, and Kiara knew that he was worried about his Ranger friends and the fight they were in.

They landed with a soft thump, and Kiara unhooked her safety harness and stood up quickly, her nerves making her a little jumpy. She heard the pilot clear them with control and tried to be patient as she waited for the door to open. She hadn't asked Jax, but wondered if there would be anyone here to greet them. Did they know she was coming? Did they understand why she was here? She felt a slight wave of embarrassment. She knew she had been foolish, and now, more than just the crew of the Acadia was going to be inconvenienced.

The pilot finally opened the door, and bright light flooded in. Kiara shielded her eyes until they adjusted, and as she walked down the shuttle ramp, she could see they had landed on a tarmac, surrounded by low buildings. All the buildings looked modern, made of stone and glass, and Kiara briefly wondered whether they were new or built by the original inhabitants. She could feel the heat and humidity hit her as she descended. Her gaze swung back around to the base of the ramp, to the hooded figure standing there. Stryker! Her heart bumped a little wildly in her chest, and Elvis let out a small huff. Stryker still had the ability to scare her, even though she knew he was on her side.

Jax reached the base of the ramp ahead of her and greeted Stryker. Jax moved to the side, and Stryker stepped forward toward Kiara.

"Kiara." He said her name quietly, his eyes probing her face.

She didn't know why, but the way he said her name made her want to cry. Stryker stepped forward and enveloped her in a hug, his musky scent wrapping around her. She felt comforted and recognized that his scent was similar to Jax's. She could hear Elvis chirping at him, her emotions flooding through the little drayek.

When he let her go, his gaze bored into her. "We will fix this."

He turned to Kiara's dad. "Kyle." His voice held warmth and respect.

The two men greeted each other before Stryker waved them toward a nearby building. As they walked, Jax and Stryker walked together, their voices low, and Kiara assumed they were updating each other. She took the opportunity to look around. She couldn't see much vegetation, hills, or mountains, and felt slightly disappointed. She'd been hoping to see something that looked like her home world, from her dreams with Mirona. She knew it was silly, but there it was.

They entered the cooling comfort of the building, with the windows providing shielding from the light. The building appeared deserted, which confused Kiara. Jax walked over to her.

"The colony is some distance from here, but to keep it safe and hidden, we never take the shuttle straight to it from the orbiting ship. We have an underground tram that will take us to our final shuttle point."

They followed Stryker to an innocuous-looking panel-like door. It didn't even have a handle or anything that Kiara could see to open it. Stryker waved his hand in front of the wall next to the panel, and a screen appeared. Something scanned his face, and the panel slid silently open. It reminded Kiara of some of the spy videos she used to watch with her dad. She searched her mind for one of the famous spy names that they made so many videos of. Her dad came up behind her.

"Just like James Bond, huh?"

Kiara smiled back at him. That's the name she was trying to remember. Leave it to her dad to know what she was thinking.

They followed Stryker down a dimly lit corridor, and at the end, he did the same panel trick, opening a door into a small room. They entered, and Kiara discovered it wasn't a room at all, but a lift. They entered the small room, and Elvis let everyone know that he didn't appreciate being in the cramped space with his disgruntled huffs. They descended for a few seconds before the doors opened into an area that held a platform and a small tram on rails.

Once Stryker had the tram moving, Kiara moved to a bench on the side wall and sat down. She was beginning to feel fatigued, and she knew that was dangerous. She was on guard, all the time, beating back the influence of the stone, and it was taking a toll on her, both emotionally and physically. Her dad immediately sensed the danger and sat next to her, engaging her in conversation and keeping her focused on the present.

When the tram finally slowed, Kiara perked up. From what Jax had said earlier, this should be the colony, and she was excited and nervous to meet others from Trandor. She stood up nervously. Would they accept her? Would they welcome her?

They exited the tram, and Stryker took them through several hidden panels and into the lift that Kiara guessed would take them to the surface. As they drew closer to the surface, Kiara began to sense something. She struggled to identify it. She wasn't sensing thoughts from anyone in the lift, and she didn't think it was the stone.   Suddenly, she knew.   She was sensing Trandorians! Hundreds and hundreds of them! Their presence, as she drew closer, seemed to warm her and strengthen her. The feeling flowed through her and into Elvis. She felt as if it was strengthening her and her bond with the little drayek. She turned to Jax, the joy and wonder of it on her face.

"Why didn't you tell me?"

Jax smiled at her. "Not all who come here get to experience it; I didn't want to prep you for something that may not happen."

"Are they expecting us?"

"Yes," Jax said as he moved closer to her. "We sent a message ahead; we wanted one of the Trandorian officials from this colony to meet us. They will be able to gather the group together that we need for the ceremony."

"It's like an exorcism." Kiara thought about old videos and books she had read from Earth. There was a period of time when people were obsessed with demons and possessions.

Kyle looked at his daughter, worried. He supposed it would be like an exorcism, but instead of being possessed by a demon, she was being taken over by a stone.

Jax frowned. He had heard of exorcisms, and he didn't like the term for what they were doing. "I do not think we should call it that; let's call it a ceremony." At her doubtful look, he continued, "Perhaps think of it like a joyous occasion to meet others from Trandor."

Kiara smirked at him. She knew he was trying to alleviate her fears.

The lift finally stopped, and Kiara couldn't keep her hands from fidgeting. The door opened, and Stryker stepped out first. Kiara peeked around him and saw a large, bright atrium with colors of blue and green, much like she remembered from her dreams with Mirona. Her eyes dropped from the ceiling area, and she let out a gasp. A sea of blue faces, most of them smiling, were facing the lift. Stryker moved to the side, letting the crowd see Kiara, and Kiara see them. Tears filled her eyes as her heart swelled with emotion. She had never met a Trandorian before, and to be presented to so many at once was overwhelming.

A dignified, tall, older Trandorian stepped forward, extending his arm. His skin was a dark blue, his short hair framing his serious face, and he wore a dark shirt and trousers instead of a skinsuit. Gold accents on his clothing indicated his status in the colony.

Instinctively, Kiara knew to grab his arm in the traditional Trandor greeting that she had seen Mirona do. He seemed pleased by her actions. He greeted her in a deep, dignified voice.

"Welcome, Kiara. I am Linto, First Regent of Trandor Prime. We are honored to have you visit us."

Kiara smiled broadly. "Thank you, First Regent, Linto. I am honored to be here."

The rest of Kiara's party was introduced before the First Regent turned to introduce Kiara to some of the others standing behind him.

"Kiara, this is my wife, Sonal. She will be leading the ceremony that Stryker has asked us to perform." The First Regent gently brought his wife forward to meet Kiara. The First Regent's wife was nearly as tall as Kiara, with a short bob of dark hair framing her face. She wore flowing clothes in gold and green.

Kiara could sense some power in Sonal. She greeted her warmly.

"Kiara, we are honored to have you here. We will do our best to help rid you of the influence of the stone." Sonal looked at Kiara, kindness and sympathy in her eyes. "Stryker was not able to give us many details for the ceremony; I hope you can give us more."

Sonal looked at Elvis, still clutching Kiara's shoulder.

Kiara nodded. "My ancestor, Mirona, gave me instructions." Reaching up, she gently touched Elvis' feet. "This is Elvis."

Sonal looked fondly at the little drayek. "Will he need any special accommodations or food? Stryker said you are bonded, and that he will be needed for the ceremony."

Kiara smiled, grateful that her little drayek was accepted so readily. "He stays with me, and eats fruit if you have it, but I also have food for him."

Nodding, Sonal took Kiara's arm, leading her into the group, introducing her to others as they went. Kiara smiled and nodded, but she knew she would never remember everyone's names. She hoped they would be patient with her.

Amid the group and introductions, Kiara felt a malevolent force hit her. She stumbled back from the force of it, Elvis tightening his grip on her shoulder to steady himself. Sonal tried to steady her, asking if she was okay, but Kiara was looking around, frantically trying to see or sense where the energy had come from. Turning in a circle, she couldn't see anyone who looked angry with her, and she couldn't sense anything. Jax came up and took her other arm, leaning in close.

"What is it?"

"Someone here is not happy with my presence," Kiara whispered.

"Is that why you stumbled?"

Kiara nodded, still searching the crowd.

"I haven't seen anyone looking particularly angry with you," Jax responded to her, still leaning in, but he, too, was scanning the crowd. "Have you tried to sense them?"

Kiara nodded again. "I can't sense anything, so they must be hiding their feelings." Kiara looked up at Jax. "Whoever it is, they must have abilities similar to mine."

"I will have Stryker make some discreet inquiries."

They finally made it through the crowd, and Sonal directed them to a small shuttle. "We have rooms prepared for you in the guest quarters of our residence. I hope that will be sufficient for your needs."

Kiara beamed a smile at Sonal, "Thank you, Sonal. I hope we aren't causing you too much trouble. We are grateful for any help and any accommodations you have for us."

Sonal returned Kiara's smile, relaxing at Kiara's assurance. Sonal had noticed that something had happened in the crowded area, and she wasn't sure what to make of it. Stryker had emphasized Kiara's importance, and since she and everyone in the colony were indebted to Stryker and his team, they would all do whatever they could to help.

The shuttle touched down on a landing pad behind the First Regent's residence. It was a grand building, made of stone in blues and greens, and reminded Kiara of the buildings in her dreams with Mirona. Gardens surrounded the multi-story building, with a small pond near the back entrance.

Once they were settled in their rooms, they met in the large common area of the First Regent's home. Sonal had refreshments laid out for them, for which Kiara was grateful. She was used to traveling, but this trip was taking its toll on her.

The First Regent and his wife shared the refreshments with their guests, asking mundane questions about their travel. Sonal wanted to make sure they were comfortable before asking the tough questions about the ceremony.

"Do you have details about the ceremony?" Sonal asked.

Kiara opened her com unit, bringing up a display so that everyone in the room could see it.

"Mirona called it a modified 'Protection' ceremony." Kiara turned to Sonal. "I am hoping you know about the Protection

Ceremony?" At Sonal's nod, Kiara continued. "We will need twelve in a circle, around me. Mirona has said that Jax can be one of the twelve."

Sonal studied the display, noting the differences in the ceremony. "What about Elvis? Will he be with you, or in the circle?"

"Mirona said he needs to stay with me. Because we are bonded, we will be treated as one in the center of the circle."

Sonal nodded again.

Kiara looked down, feeling like she should be honest with those in the room. "I must confess, all of this is new to me. My exposure to Trandorian culture and history has been very limited." Kiara looked around the room, expecting to see frowns or disapproval from the First Regent and his wife. She was surprised to see a look of understanding.

"We see this quite a bit," Sonal told her. "We've had to work hard to recover the history and traditions that we have. So much was lost during the war. Those that come here help us to recreate what was lost, and preserve what we can."

The First Regent nodded and added to his wife's comments. "We learn something from everyone that comes here, even if it is just friendship or community."

Kiara felt relief, and looking at the display she had brought up, she turned back to Sonal. "Do you have enough people to make up the circle?"

Sonal looked thoughtful for a moment before nodding. "I believe we do. We had a few community meetings before you came, and asked for volunteers. At that time, we had more than enough, but sometimes people change their minds."

"My ancestor, Mirona, said that tomorrow evening would be the best time for the ceremony. Do you think we can be ready by then?"

Sonal looked at the display and asked a few more questions. She turned to her husband. "I believe so. We received a list of supplies from Stryker," she nodded at Stryker as she said it. "And we have most of them. We have a ceremonial area to the west that should suffice. Linto? What do you think?"

The First Regent was also nodding. "We should take some time in the morning to get the right people, inventory items, and make sure we all know what our roles in the ceremony are."

Sonal addressed Kiara. "In a Protection Ceremony, the ancestors of those needing protection are called upon for their power and support. Will we be calling upon your ancestors?"

"Yes," Kiara nodded enthusiastically. "Mirona has alerted those in our family line; they will be ready."

Chapter 9

Kiara slept fitfully but couldn't pinpoint a reason for her restlessness. Mirona had been there to keep the stone's influence at bay, and Jax and Kyle had also taken turns watching her. Even so, she'd had dreams where she could feel something evil just out of reach. She really hoped that this ceremony would work.

Kiara met with Sonal, and they spent the morning reviewing the ceremony, the props needed, and everyone's roles. Sonal introduced her to the others who would be in the circle. Kiara tried to sense if any were feeling animosity toward her, but all she could feel was support and empathy. Luckily, the ceremony was primarily in her and Sonal's hands. The others were there for power and support.

Shortly after lunch, Sonal took Kiara and Elvis around the colony. Sonal explained how Stryker had found this deserted village, but all the buildings were in serious disrepair. They had to spend the first few years living in temporary houses while they worked to fix up the buildings.

"You would not believe the arguments we had those first few years," Sonal said as they walked in an area filled with shops, restaurants, and patrons. "Some wanted to create a village that looked just like ones on Trandor. Some wanted everything to look completely different because of the trauma they felt when they thought of our home world."

Sonal stopped in front of a small shop, and Kiara could see that the shelves were filled with the supplements that Trandorians needed. Elvis peered at his reflection in the glass and made small chirping noises.

"It seems like you did something that was a compromise. I see some areas that look like dreams with my ancestor, Mirona. Some look very foreign to me." Kiara looked around her, seeing glass and metal in the familiar blues and greens, as well as areas that looked like sandstone buildings. She was also intrigued to see rustic-looking wood buildings sprinkled throughout the village.

Sonal smiled. "Of course, we had to compromise. It was the only way for us to move forward. Trandor is gone. We cannot live in the past, but we also cannot abandon who we were and who we are." Sonal opened the door to the small shop they were standing in front of. "We also recognized that all Trandorians that come here would need these supplements." She gestured around the small shop. "We make them available for all, at no cost."

The shop owner smiled at Sonal with respect, a common theme throughout the village. Kiara could tell that those in this village respected the First Regent and his wife.

They stepped back out of the shop, and as Sonal turned to walk back, a wave of animosity hit Kiara. It struck her with such physical force that she was shoved back into the door she had just come out of. Sonal let out a slight noise of concern, reaching for Kiara to steady her. Elvis was clutching Kiara's shoulder and let out a screech of alarm.

"Are you okay?" Sonal asked Kiara. Sonal was already reaching for her com unit, thinking perhaps that the stone had somehow gotten to Kiara while they were out walking. Jax had assured her that they would be fine, but what if he was wrong?

"I'm okay," Kiara quickly rushed to assure Sonal, and with her thoughts, reassured Elvis. Kiara looked around, trying to find the person with intense animosity toward her. Surely, she could find them – they weren't in a large crowd this time.

"Someone doesn't want me here," she finally whispered to Sonal.

Sonal looked around them with concern. "I thought perhaps I had imagined that yesterday."

"You could feel it too?"

Sonal nodded. "Not with the force that you did, but, yes, I felt it as well."

Kiara fully straightened up. "I can't keep getting ambushed this way. Let's see if I can find her." She was sure it was another female Trandorian with powers similar to her own. She reached up and touched Elvis' feet, silently communicating with him. Expanding her power, she searched for the one who had such hatred toward her. Within a few seconds, she'd found her.

Kiara turned to Sonal. "She's this way."

"You found her?" Sonal struggled to keep up with Kiara's purposeful striding. "How did you find her?"

"I used my power to search for her."

"You can do that?" Sonal shook her head, her breathing becoming slightly labored. She had some power, but nothing like Kiara's.

Kiara turned into a small café-type shop, looked around, and headed straight to a small table next to the window. A very sullen-looking, young, Trandorian female sat by herself at the table. At Kiara's approach, she jumped to her feet, her alarm at seeing Kiara approach turning to a look of anger and hatred. Kiara stopped a few feet from the table. Now that she was here, her adrenaline was fading, and she wasn't sure what to say. The girl seemed so young. Medium-length dark hair framed a face full of hatred and teenage emotions. She wore a light skinsuit, and Kiara was surprised at the amount of enhancers the young girl had painted on her face.

Sonal finally caught up to Kiara, her eyebrows shooting up at the sight of the girl standing in front of them.

"Talia?"

Kiara turned slightly to look at Sonal. "You know her?"

"Yes, of course. Talia came to us about a year ago. She's been living with a foster family on the other side of the village."

Kiara could feel the power in the young girl building again and feared she might do something that could hurt others in the café. Taking a deep breath, she calmed herself and attempted to send calming thoughts to Talia.

"Your powers won't work on me!" Talia gritted out between clenched teeth.

Kiara could feel that what Talia was saying was true. Talia threw her hand up at Kiara, and Kiara did the only thing she could think of. She enveloped Talia in an energy bubble.

Unfortunately, Talia's burst of hateful energy bounced around in the bubble; the result was Talia knocking herself out. The tables around Talia shattered into pieces, and the floor beneath her cracked. Sonal gasped in shock.

Kiara sent a quick message to Jax, hoping he could come and help her figure out the situation.

Sensing that Talia's energy had dissipated, Kiara dropped the bubble and cautiously approached the girl. Sonal dropped down next to her.

"What happened? Why was she trying to hurt you?"

Kiara shook her head and quickly checked Talia for a pulse. It was there, strong and steady.

Talia's eyelids fluttered. As she opened her eyes, her gaze darted between Sonal and Kiara. Her pupils dilated slightly at the sight of Elvis on Kiara's shoulder.

"Are you okay?" Kiara gently asked.

Talia looked away and refused to answer.

Sonal reached under Talia's shoulders and gently helped her to sit up. "Talia, what is going on? Were you trying to hurt Kiara?"

Talia, sensing sympathy from Sonal, decided to play on that.

"I'm so sorry," she whimpered. "I didn't mean to."

Sonal immediately hugged the young girl. Sonal couldn't begin to comprehend that anything malicious could be happening, not in their village.

Over Sonal's shoulder, Talia met Kiara's gaze. Hatred, pure and simple, directed at Kiara.

Kiara stood up, frowning. Why would this young girl hate her so much? Elvis's claws pinched Kiara's shoulder, and Kiara could hear a low, growl-like noise come from him, as he, too, felt the young girl's hatred.

She opened her mouth to ask again, but Jax touched her shoulder. Kiara turned to him, hurriedly whispering what had just transpired. Jax looked past Kiara and tried to reconcile the pitiful young girl being held by Sonal with Kiara's description. He had to admit, it was difficult, but the situation didn't feel quite right. He could feel deception.

Turning back to Kiara, he quietly told her to switch places with him so that Kiara was facing Talia, and his back would be toward the young girl. Chances were good that the young girl didn't know that he had some empathetic ability, and he could use it now. Once in position, he closed his eyes and gave Kiara a nod to look past him at Talia.

His breath shot out in a whoosh. Opening his eyes, he realized he probably didn't need much empathetic ability to sense that much hatred. He quickly apologized to Kiara for doubting her and turned back to the young girl. He quietly asked Sonal to step away and gently helped the young girl to an unbroken chair.

"Talia, why so much hatred for Kiara?" Jax asked her, keeping his tone sympathetic.

Sonal opened her mouth to protest, but Kiara silently stopped her with a touch.

Talia looked at Sonal, and sensing that her ally was no longer going to help her, turned back to Jax, her face twisting with the hatred she had inside.

"What makes her so special?" She spat the question at Jax. Before Jax could answer, Talia continued. "She's just another orphaned Trandorian. She shouldn't be getting special treatment! Special shuttles! Special ceremonies!" She sent hateful looks at everyone around her as she said it.

"She is here for our help, Talia," Jax said quietly, hoping his tone would convey some calmness to her.

"I hope she dies!" Talia jumped up, shouting and pointing at Kiara. "I hate you!"

Jax reached out to Talia, hoping to keep the situation from spiraling out of control. Talia pushed his hand back with a pulse of power before turning and running out of the back of the shop.

Sonal looked at the back of the shop where Talia had disappeared, her mouth hanging open in shock. She knew people got angry, but she had never witnessed such hatred before, not in their community. Sonal turned toward Jax and Kiara, ready to apologize.

Kiara held up her hand, silently asking Sonal not to apologize. Shaking her head, she turned to Jax. "She must be the one I felt animosity from when I first arrived." When Jax nodded, Kiara whispered, "She's very powerful, and very angry."

Jax looked thoughtful. "We will need to talk to her again, but we don't have time before the ceremony." He turned to look at Sonal. "We will need to make sure she doesn't interrupt the ceremony."

Sonal nodded. "I will speak to Linto; we will take care of it."

Jax guided Kiara out of the shop, keeping his hand on her back to reassure and calm her. He could sense the turmoil coming from her and knew that she needed to have a clear head for the upcoming ceremony.

"Why do you think she hates me so much?"

"I believe it has more to do with envy and jealousy than anything else." Jax kept her headed back to the First Regent's house.

"Do you think I should try to talk to her?" Kiara felt sick to her stomach. She'd battled other ships and others that had hated her for her race, but she had never expected to have another Trandorian hate her so much.

Jax touched her arm, bringing her to a halt. "Kiara, I need you here, in this moment. There is nothing you can do with her, or for her, at this point. We need to complete the ceremony and remove the influence of the stone."

"I know, I know." Kiara forced her feet to move and attempted to clear her head of the last image she had of Talia, wishing her dead. Jax was right; she needed to be focused on the ceremony.

When they arrived at the First Regent's house, the security staff immediately met them and pulled Jax and Stryker into another room. Kiara assumed it had to do with Talia. Sonal had most likely called the First Regent to involve security. Kiara had seen Sonal on her com unit when they left the shop, while trying to console the shop owner and help clean up the mess Talia had left. Kiara headed up to find her dad, but he met her halfway.

"Are you okay?" Kyle asked her.

Kiara nodded and quickly hugged her dad. "What did you hear?"

"Sonal called the First Regent and told him that you had found a young Trandorian girl who was responsible for the angry feelings that had been directed at you." At Kiara's nod, he continued.

"There was some damage to a shop? And Jax wanted protection for the ceremony?"

"Sounds like you have most of it."

"Stryker was here when Sonal called. He is helping organize additional security for the ceremony. I don't think they've found the young girl."

"She didn't go home?" Kiara asked with some distress. She hated that the young girl was so angry, but she didn't like the thought of her wandering around alone.

Kyle shook his head. "The foster parents told the First Regent that they had been having trouble with her for a while."

Kiara looked sad, knowing how fortunate she was that Kyle had found her.

"Kiara, how dangerous is she? The First Regent said she was young, but I didn't get many other details."

"Dad, I'm not sure how dangerous she is, but she's pretty powerful, even at her young age. She's perfectly capable of disrupting the ceremony."

Jax joined them, his expression unreadable.

"Did they find her?" Kyle quickly asked him.

Jax shook his head. "We will be okay," he assured them. "Stryker has moved the ceremony to a different location, and it is unlikely that Talia will find it. We will be able to complete the ceremony as planned."

At that moment, Talia was hiding out in the basement of one of the unfinished buildings in the town center. She was pacing back and forth, muttering, trying to control her power as her anger seemed to fuel itself. She shot a pulse of energy at an empty bottle on the floor, obliterating it with her rage. Why was Kiara so special? Talia shot another pulse of energy at the wall, punching a hole in it. Everyone in town was talking non-stop about the 'Guardian' coming to visit, and how special she was. Talia stomped her foot, cracking the floor she was standing on. She didn't even notice it in her angry state. She shot a few more pulses of energy out before finally starting to calm down. She wished she knew where the ceremony would be held. She figured that after her little display of power today, they had probably moved the location. Too bad, she thought. Her face twisted into an angry grin. She would have loved to disrupt that stupid ceremony. She focused on a small rodent running across the floor, and, pretending it was Kiara, annihilated it with a pulse of energy.

On Earth Delta Nine, one of the Director's aides sent him a high-priority report. The Director entered his credentials and read the report. He had directed his staff to monitor all communications and flag anything that mentioned Trandor or Trandorians. The report was an intercepted communication between what appeared to be a young Trandorian female and someone she was venting to. Two things caught his attention. The first was that the young girl seemed to be complaining about another Trandorian female, and from the description, he guessed it was the same one who had been interrupting their operations. The second thing that caught his attention was the young girl's constant reference to her own power.

There wasn't enough information to determine where the female was, which frustrated him. However, maybe it wasn't a total loss. He sent off a message to one of his aids. If they could somehow open a dialogue with the young girl, maybe they could use her and her anger. The Trandorians were a tight-knit community. They protected each other at all costs. With all his resources, he still hadn't been able to find their secret community. He'd never heard one of them complain about another in power, especially not with the fervor that he detected in the communication he was reading. He didn't care about the secret

Trandorian community, just the female Trandorian that kept interrupting his operations.

A plan began to form, one that could use the angry young girl and possibly find an end to the thorn in his side.

The time to hold the ceremony had finally arrived, and not a moment too soon, as far as Kiara was concerned. She was fatigued, and fighting the pull of the stone was becoming too much of a strain. Jax was constantly at her side, shoring up her defenses, but she could also tell that he was starting to tire as well. She felt as if she was walking through a narrowing tunnel. The sides of the tunnel were the stone's influence, constantly closing in. She didn't want to close her eyes because then she felt lost, even with Jax supporting her.

She exited the shuttle Jax had used to get them to the ceremony site. Elvis clutched her shoulder, almost painfully, and Kiara could tell that the little drayek was also trying to help her. Kiara reached up and touched the toes clutching her shoulder, thanking the little drayek for doing all that he could.

They approached a dark hillside, and Kiara realized that they were no longer near the city. She'd been concentrating so hard on keeping the stone at bay that she hadn't been paying attention on the way over. She looked around her and realized that she couldn't see any lights at all. The hill loomed up sharply in front of her, silhouetted by the darkening sky. As her eyes adjusted to the approaching darkness, she could make out large boulders dotting the hillside, with small shrubs here and there. She looked at Jax, confused. There were no buildings, and they were walking directly toward the hill. Where was the ceremony supposed to be? She stumbled over some loose rocks, and Jax shot out a hand to steady her. She stopped for a moment and took a deep breath, letting it out slowly.

"We are almost there," Jax said quietly, keeping his hand on her arm. "I should have brought the shuttle closer."

"It's okay," Kiara told Jax, just as her dad came up from behind to support her on her other side.

Jax steered her around a large boulder that was larger than their shuttle, revealing a hidden entrance into the hillside. As they entered the tunnel behind the boulder, Kiara could see flickering light bouncing off the walls and hear echoing voices from the opening.

The further into the tunnel they went, the heavier Kiara's legs felt. She could feel panic welling up inside her and an almost uncontrollable urge to run back to the shuttle.

"I can't, I can't," she gasped out, her knees starting to buckle.

Kyle looked over her head at Jax and gave an almost imperceptible nod. Jax had warned him that this might happen. They hadn't told Kiara; Jax hadn't wanted to worry her more than was necessary. Jax had sensed that the stone was embedded in Kiara's subconscious, and it wouldn't leave willingly. Both men kept a firm grip on Kiara, guiding her farther into the tunnel. Elvis gripped her shoulder, flapped his little wings, and did everything he could to help.

They emerged from the tunnel into a dimly lit cavern. The cavern was small, with a ceiling height barely above Kiara's height, and a dirt floor. Kiara, her legs still heavy, could see several Trandorians in the cavern. Distracted by the feelings in her legs and head, she wanted to count to see if the required number of people were there, but finally gave up and left it to Jax or her dad to figure out. They found a chair against the wall, and Kiara gratefully collapsed into it.

Jax surveyed the room, finding Stryker, Sonal, and the First Regent, and a quick count showed approximately twenty Trandorians in the cavern. The ceremonial symbols and crystals were on the floor, used to focus the energy of the ancestors and those in the room. The circle was small, and Jax was grateful to see that they had also placed a chair in the middle for Kiara. Leaving Kyle to watch over Kiara, Jax crossed over to speak with Sonal.

"Sonal," Jax spoke her name quietly.

"Jax," Sonal breathed out his name in a sigh of relief. She looked around him to see Kiara slumped in the chair against the cavern wall. "Is Kiara alright?"

"For now, but I think we are going to need to hurry and get the ceremony started."

Sonal nodded and led Jax to a small group of people. Introductions were made, and Sonal began moving people to their places in the circle. Jax headed back to Kiara.

"We're ready," Jax told her quietly.

"I'm not ready," Kiara told him in a slightly whiny voice he'd never heard from her before. Elvis was on her shoulder, making small clicking noises.

"It's okay," Kyle told his daughter. With help from Jax, they walked her over to the chair in the middle of the cavern. Elvis, with a firm grip on Kiara's shoulder, kept up the clicking noise.

Jax squatted down in front of Kiara and willed her to look at him. "Kiara, we need your help with the ceremony. You're the key to contacting your ancestors."

Kiara struggled to concentrate. Her brain felt like it was wrapped in cotton, and her eyes wouldn't focus on any one thing in the room. She finally found Jax's concerned face and drew strength from his eyes and his grip on her hands. She nodded at Jax and, freeing one hand, reached up to touch Elvis. His strength flowed into her, and she concentrated on the clicking noise he was making. She timed her breathing with his clicks, realizing that it was the little drayek's way of helping.

With one final squeeze of her hands, Jax pulled away from Kiara and headed to his spot in the circle. He could see Kyle worriedly pacing just outside the circle. Jax looked at Sonal, then Kiara, and gave a quick nod.

Everyone in the circle joined hands, and Jax could feel the energy in the room grow. He looked again at Kiara, willing her to contact her ancestors.

Kiara, one hand holding Elvis' paw, closed her eyes and silently called for Mirona. At first, nothing happened. She didn't hear Mirona's voice, and she struggled to keep the panic at bay.

"Mirona!" Kiara screamed it into the room.

Kiara's scream startled the group, but Sonal and Jax tightened their grip on the hands they held, willing the group to stay connected.

Sonal was holding Jax's left hand, and Jax could feel her twitch slightly, just as the energy in the room seemed to change.

Kyle, outside the circle, stopped pacing and looked around, confusion on his face. Stryker joined him and placed a comforting hand on his shoulder.

Jax looked at Kiara, and he could see her sitting straight up in the chair, her skin flushed a dark blue, her eyes closed. Elvis, too, had turned a matching dark blue. Jax felt pressure in his ears, and the room seemed to warm.

"Mirona," Kiara breathed her ancestor's name out in a sigh of relief.

My child, I am here. I can sense the others in the room with you. Are we ready?

Yes, Mirona, we're ready.

I will make the connection to our other ancestors, and we will attempt to break the stone's hold. Please let them know to keep their focus. We will need all their energy to make this work.

"Please stay focused, don't break the circle," Kiara whispered.

Kiara could feel her connection to Mirona strengthen, and then she felt her other ancestors join. The energy she felt was nothing like before. Stronger, deeper, it flashed dark blue across the back of her eyelids. Kiara could feel Mirona probing her mind as she searched for the stone's influence.

Mirona focused her power, searching, searching. There was no doubt when she found it. Dark, oily, insidious; it had taken over a large part of Kiara's mind. Mirona was the scalpel; she used the power of those in the room, and her ancestors, to cut away at that oiliness. It was hard, exhausting work, and she could feel that darkness beat back at her.

Kiara, my child, help me with this. Help me beat this back!

Kiara pushed her energy to Mirona and felt Elvis join her. The darkness in her mind began to recede. Kiara pushed harder.

Jax could see Kiara grimacing, but he felt they were making progress. His abilities were pushed to their limit, sweat breaking out on his brow. Sonal's hand clenched his almost painfully, and he knew that everyone in the circle was supporting Mirona and Kiara's effort to the best of their ability.

After what seemed like hours, Kiara collapsed off the chair onto the floor, Elvis screeching as he flapped his little wings to gain his balance. Several Trandorians in the circle also collapsed to their knees. Jax rushed to Kiara, Kyle reaching her at the same time.

"Kiara!" Jax gently rolled her to a sitting position, with Elvis hopping up and down behind her, intermittently chirping and screeching.

"I'm okay, I'm okay," Kiara mumbled. She reached behind her and pulled a very distressed Elvis into her lap. With her free hand, she alternately patted Jax on his shoulder and then her dad.

Kyle rolled his eyes. Leave it to Kiara to be worried about them, while they were worried about her.

Kiara took a few deep breaths and asked Jax if everyone was okay.

"Yes, we are all okay, just exhausted." Jax looked hard at her, trying to discern if they were successful in ridding Kiara of the stone's influence.

Kiara finally looked back at Jax, knowing precisely what he wanted to know. She slowly shook her head.

"I don't know if we were successful." Kiara took another deep breath. "It was taking everything we had, and I blacked out before we finished."

Jax looked worriedly at Kyle.

"What do we do now?" Kyle demanded. He didn't know how he would handle it if the ceremony didn't work.

Kiara leaned against her dad. "It's okay, Dad, we'll figure it out. As soon as I rest up a bit, I'll contact Mirona again and see what she has to say." Reaching up with her free hand, Kiara scrubbed at her face, trying to clear the fog. "Right now, I can't feel the stone."

Kyle took some comfort in that and told himself to be patient while he waited for a better answer.

Jax got up to see to the others in the circle, and with Stryker's help, assisted them into chairs and handed out water. They all looked exhausted, but hopeful. Sonal joined him, looking a little shaky, but determined.

"Were we successful?" Sonal quietly asked Jax.

"Kiara is not sure, but she does not feel the stone's influence at this time. She will contact Mirona again when she has her strength back."

On Earth Delta Nine, the Director was in the park outside of his office building. His Galdorian contact was seated behind him, watching some of the locals stroll through the garden. The Galdorian had sent an urgent message to meet.

The Director, facing the opposite direction, cleared his throat. He was a busy man, and his impatience came through in that one noise.

The Galdorian let out a quiet sigh. "She tried to rid herself of the stone's influence in a secret ceremony."

The Director raised his eyebrows. "How do you know? More importantly, was she successful?" He kept his voice low, but it took quite a bit of effort.

"We know, because the stone belongs to us." He waited an additional few seconds before answering the next question. He loved to torture the Director. "Time will tell if she was successful."

The next morning, Kiara woke from the first restful sleep she'd had since coming into contact with the stone. Her dreams had been peaceful, and as she looked over at Elvis, he, too, looked relaxed. His color was normal, and he was making little chirping noises in his sleep. Kiara closed her eyes, reaching her mind to him, just to be sure. She caught images of fruit and flowers. She giggled. Of course, he was hungry. Her stomach made a gurgling noise, and Elvis woke with a jerk. He reached out with his two front paws and touched Kiara's face. They both let out a long breath and touched their heads together. Kiara smiled. She felt normal.

Later that morning, she sat on the bed, Elvis in her lap. Taking a few deep breaths, she reached out for Mirona.

Mirona.

I'm here, child.

Were we successful? I can't feel the stone. I've searched my mind, but I don't feel it.

Kiara, I cannot sense the stone either, so I believe it is gone, but I cannot be sure it won't come back.

Mirona, what do you mean?

I called upon my other ancestors. They were doubtful that the ceremony would be completely successful. They asked me to pass on a warning to you, my child. Be alert! If the stone's influence comes back, your only choice will be to destroy it before it destroys you!

Kiara broke the connection to Mirona and searched her mind again. She didn't feel the stone, but Mirona's words left her feeling uneasy.

Kiara hurriedly dressed and searched for Jax to tell him what Mirona had said. She found Jax sitting outside, enjoying the warm weather in the area behind the First Regent's house. Kiara joined him on the low bench he was sitting on and slowly told him what she'd learned from Mirona.

Sitting in silence, Jax digested the information. He reached his arm around Kiara and pulled her close to his side.

"But you do not feel the stone?"

"No." Kiara leaned her head onto Jax's shoulder.

Jax nodded, looking thoughtful. "Your father has been asked to go and help some of the Rangers."

"I thought so."

"Yes, but this morning, the plea for help was more urgent." Jax pulled back slightly and looked at Kiara. "This may not be what you want to do, but I think we do not let him know about the possibility of the stone coming back. Your father is needed, and he will not leave if he thinks you are still in danger."

Kiara smiled guiltily. "I was thinking the same thing. I don't feel the stone, but I also don't need my father hovering over me, waiting for a disaster that may never happen."

Jax nodded in agreement. He didn't want to lie to Kyle, but justified it by telling himself it wasn't really lying; they were just withholding a little information.

"What about us, Jax? Can we get back to completing missions again?" Before he could answer, she rushed on. "Will you be able to trust me?"

Jax looked thoughtful. "Will you be completely honest with me if you start to feel anything?"

Kiara nodded forcefully.

"Then let us get back to it. We have had several requests for help since we have been here."

Kiara let out the breath she had been holding and leaned back into Jax. Elvis chirped happily on her shoulder.

"What's going on here?" Kyle's voice came from behind them. He'd been watching them for a few minutes, noticing their closeness. He knew they'd developed feelings for each other when they had first met, and it appeared to him that those feelings were deepening.

Kiara had sensed her dad's presence, so his voice hadn't startled her. She slowly pulled back from Jax, enjoying his warmth and comfort. She smiled at her dad as she got to her feet.

"I contacted Mirona, and we think the ceremony worked! Neither of us can feel the stone!"

Relief flooded through Kyle as he embraced Kiara. He'd been fearful that the ceremony hadn't worked. "You're sure?"

Kiara nodded against his shirt.

Kyle sighed with relief and gave Kiara an extra squeeze before releasing her. He looked at Jax, saw the same confirmation on his face, and turned back to look at Kiara.

"Kiara—," he started to speak, but stopped, unsure of how to tell her that he had to leave.

"It's okay, Dad." Kiara squeezed his arm. "I know the Rangers need you. I'm okay, so, you can go now."

Kyle looked resigned. Of course, she would know.

"The messages are more urgent. The attacks are growing bolder and more frequent, and they need some leadership in some of the remote areas that have been hard hit."

Kiara looked from her dad to Jax and opened her mouth to offer her help as well.

Kyle cut her off. "You can't come. I don't want you anywhere near this, because you'll be a magnet for every attack. Even with the armor, you're not invincible."

Kiara snapped her mouth shut, irritated momentarily, but realizing he was right. Besides, the missions for Jax and Stryker were what she had wanted to do anyway, but she would worry about her dad, just as he would worry about her.

Talia watched Kiara and the others leave through the secret passage that led to the shuttle pad. Her anger was still there, but she had been working hard to control it so that she wouldn't be detected. She'd been hiding since her blowup with Kiara, and as far as she was concerned, she was done with this place. She'd been working on a plan to stow away on one of the transport ships, and now she just had to put that plan into action. She headed back to her hiding place to continue to practice her power. She wanted to be ready if she ever ran into Kiara again.

Chapter 10

Back on the Acadia, Kiara had just finished a challenging workout with Elvis and was heading to the small kitchen area to get some snacks. Stryker had a mission for them, and they were on their way to a space station orbiting one of the moons of Satoria. They'd been traveling for a few days, and so far, Kiara couldn't feel the stone's influence. Even her dreams were peaceful.

She entered the kitchen to find Cory there, one hand shoveling food into his mouth, the other hand swiping at his tablet screen. He barely glanced up when she walked in, and Kiara smiled. So different from when they first met. He was comfortable with her now, as well as the rest of the crew. Kiara grabbed her snacks and headed for her bunk to change clothes before proceeding to the bridge.

On the bridge, she waved at Frankie and nodded at Blackburne. Frankie's shirt today was an eye-popping neon green with purple streaks, which made Kiara blink. Sitting at her navunit, she did a quick check of their status. They were on course and due to arrive at the space station in a few hours. The trip had been uneventful, both from a stone perspective and from an attack perspective. Whoever was controlling the CyRAINs and gunning for her seemed to have backed off for the time being. Blackburne was also being cautious, covering their tracks and taking routes they wouldn't be expected to take.

Her com unit signaled, and Kiara saw that Jax was ready for them in the flex-space to go over more details of the mission.

Stryker had traveled ahead of them to prepare for their arrival, and Kiara assumed that Jax had probably heard from him.

Kiara entered the flex-space, followed by Cory and Blackburne. A few seconds later, Curly entered, and Kiara smiled. The flex-space was a fairly good-sized room, but when the Bendanite entered, the area felt cramped. Curly had volunteered for this mission. The peace-loving Bendanite, once she found out what the mission was, immediately volunteered. Kiara was pretty sure that once the bad guys caught sight of Curly, they were going to wet their pants.

Jax cleared his throat and enlarged the screen so everyone could see.

"As we first told everyone a few days ago, we received information through our network about illegal animal trafficking in this sector. The proper authorities were notified, but due to the remoteness of this sector and the ongoing conflicts with the CyRAINs, no action has been taken." Jax moved the screen to show the harsh climate on Satoria. "There are rare, horse-like creatures that call this harsh planet home." Jax switched the screen to show the animals he was discussing.

Curly emitted a low noise that Kiara had never heard before. Kiara reached over and touched Curly's arm. Curly kept her eyes glued to the picture on the screen but covered Kiara's hand with her large, furry one. Kiara could feel Curly's sadness.

"These animals are in demand from wealthy collectors – they are cute, rare, and very docile, making them the perfect collector's item." Jax continued. "Standing about one meter tall, and as you can see, perfectly suited to the harsh, cold climate on Satoria. Their fur is a dense, pearlized white color, so if the collector doesn't want to keep them alive, the animal's fur is also in very high demand." Jax showed another view of the planet. "The sun in this sector is weak, and Satoria doesn't rotate on an axis as some other planets do. The side facing away from the sun is at a constant -40° C. The core of the planet is superheated, which is why it is not just one big ice block. It is also why the animals can survive."

Jax switched the view to show a large number of caverns at the base of an icy cliff. "This is one of the breeding areas for the animals. The name for them in this sector roughly translates to Pearls."

"How can we stop this kind of animal trafficking if the demand for the animals is still strong?" Kiara asked into the silence.

Jax nodded. "That is a concern, so we are taking a couple of approaches to this. The first is to get the group that has been gathering up the most Pearls. We're sure that this isn't the only animal they are trafficking, so stopping this group will help in other areas. The second approach is to genetically change the Pearls to make them less desirable."

Kiara raised her eyebrows. Genetically altering the species didn't sound like a good plan. Jax saw the look on her face and gave a quick shake of his head. Kiara took that to mean he needed her to be patient.

"We planted a couple of scouts on the space station to help us gather information. We know who the main traffickers are," Jax said, as he brought up pictures of ten people on the screen. All humanoids, most of whom looked mixed-race or mixed species, were primarily men, though a few women as well.

Curly looked at the screen and let out a growl, which Elvis echoed. Kiara could feel the anger coming from both of them, and it burned in her heart as well.

Jax nodded, as he was also angry. What he hadn't shown them was the pictures of the mangled carcasses left behind by these traffickers and the heartless collectors.

"These animals have been hunted to near extinction, so we need to do everything we can to help. Our scouts have determined that the traffickers are due back within a week to make another gathering of the Pearls." Jax looked around the room. "We're here to stop them this time."

Kiara felt like she had been patient enough. "What about the genetic alteration? That doesn't sound good. What about long-term ramifications? Will it make them more susceptible to predators?"

Jax smiled. "We had some of the best genetic scientists working on this for the last couple of months. We were able to recapture several of the Pearls a while back, which was a big help for the scientist. What we were trying to accomplish was a way to make the Pearls less desirable. With the genetic alteration, once the Pearls leave their home planet, their fur changes to a dirty brown color and emits an odor that is toxic to most species."

"Were you able to test it out? Does it hurt the Pearls?" Kiara asked, her worry evident in her voice.

"It doesn't affect them at all," Jax assured her.

"It seems like collectors would still want the fur. What if they just kill them and take the fur?" That question came from a very serious-looking Blackburne.

Jax nodded. "We thought of that as well. Their fur, in addition to turning brown and stinky, will become brittle and fall off the hide of the animal, rendering it useless."

"So, as long as the animals stay on their planet, nothing changes for them?" Kiara wanted to make sure she understood.

Jax looked at Kiara, his gaze full of patience and sympathy. "We made sure that their lives wouldn't be changed on the planet."

"When and how does that happen for the Pearls?" Cory quietly asked. He could tell how much this mission meant to those in the room, but his logical brain wanted to know the logistics as well.

"Outstanding question, Cory," Jax smiled at the young man. He had hoped that Cory would not just stand on the sidelines with his computers but become part of the group. "One of the main sources of food for the Pearls is a fungus that grows in the caverns they spend much of their time in. We had the scientist release the serum into the atmosphere a few weeks ago. It will make its way into the planet's ecological system and into the Pearl's systems after that. We expect full protection within a few months."

"That's fast!" Cory said with surprise.

"Indeed," Jax acknowledged. "We installed some scientists in the space station in this sector to help deploy the serum, monitor the effects, and make any adjustments that are necessary."

"Are we expecting the traffickers to show up on the planet or the space station?" Blackburne wanted to know.

"Our scouts tell us that the traffickers usually spend a few days on the space station, drinking and partying, but we want to be prepared for both scenarios, just in case they get suspicious and change their routine." Jax brought up a picture of the planet. "We have a sensor net around the planet, so if they go there without stopping at the space station, we will know."

Jax turned his attention to Cory. "Cory has been working on some advancements for our communications when we are on missions. Cory?"

Cory stood up in front of the group, his attention on the tablet in his hand, his feet shuffling. Kiara smiled. So much for being comfortable!

Cory cleared his throat and tried not to fidget with his clothes. "I've been working on this for about a year, with no practical application until I met all of you," Cory said into the silence. "It's a way for us to communicate, without speaking." At the puzzled looks, Cory grabbed a small box from the bench he had been sitting on, and handed everyone a small disk, about the size of a pea.

"Place this on your temple," Cory demonstrated with his own disk, "and I'll sync it up to your com unit." Comfortable again, since he was talking about technology, Cory went to each person to make sure their disk was secured in the right place. He made a few swipes on his tablet and, with a nod, tested it out.

"Can everyone hear me?"

Kiara's eyebrows shot up. She could hear a synthesized version of Cory's voice in her head, but Cory's mouth didn't move!

Cory smiled. "Go ahead, Kiara, say something in your head to the rest of us."

"That was amazing!" Kiara's synthesized voice reached out to everyone in the room. Kiara looked at Curly to see if the Bendanite had heard her. Curly's eyes had enlarged, so Kiara assumed it had worked for her as well.

Cory, seeing Kiara and Curly exchange glances, broadcast to their minds. "Curly was the one I had the most difficulty with, due to her physiology. It's good to see it working. Curly, can you say something, so we know it works for us to hear you?"

The Bendanite looked around the room, and one word came through loud and clear. "Pearls."

With the briefing finished, Kiara headed to her bunk to prepare for docking with the space station. The space station around the Satoria moon was one of the larger ones in this sector, with hangers for visiting ships, but Jax wanted to dock the ship instead. Kiara knew it was because he wanted a quick way to chase the traffickers or protect the Pearls. Elvis could sense Kiara's emotions and kept chirping in her ear and touching her hair. Kiara appreciated his attempt to comfort her and told herself to relax. She was nervous, though. This was their first mission since the stone's influence, and she wanted to make sure she was an asset to the team.

She joined the crew on the bridge, helping Frankie communicate with the space station and get the ship docked. Once docked, they went through security at the space station and joined

Stryker in a private room behind the space station's administrative offices. The officials on the space station were reluctant participants. They didn't have the staff to help, but they made their surveillance equipment available to the team and agreed not to broadcast that Jax's team was here. As far as everyone was concerned, they were just a cargo ship, here to drop off supplies.

After a quick lunch, Stryker let them know that the traffickers hadn't arrived yet and that the sensor net was active and working. He quickly brought up a live feed of a couple of the known areas that the Pearls inhabited. Kiara could see a bit of movement, but the Pearls were so well camouflaged that it almost looked as if the icy layers on the planet were shifting a bit. The group conducted a quick communication check, and Cory checked Kiara's body armor. All systems checked out, so they split up. The sensor net alarms were tied to Stryker and Jax, and the space station officials were connected to Blackburne's com unit.

Kiara headed into the space station, Elvis on her shoulder, and Jax's parting words echoing in her ear. "Stay away from the gift shops." She grinned as she headed out, barely keeping herself from rolling her eyes. However, she did think she needed some more chocolate. She'd have to make time to find some before they left.

From the space station directory, Kiara knew this place had a small garden where fresh produce was grown for the station's restaurants and shops. She wished more space stations would do that, but she also knew it was a significant investment that not all space stations could afford. She briefly wondered how this small station could afford it, but left that mystery for another day.

As they were approaching the gardens, Elvis suddenly let out a noise Kiara had never heard before. It sounded like a cross between a growl and a chirp. Kiara stopped and touched his toes to connect to him. At first, she could only get alarm and panic from him. She sent calming thoughts and waited for him to calm down. Once he was calm, she got a picture of a small drayek from him. Kiara frowned. It wasn't Elvis; she could tell from its shape and color. Before she could try to determine what he was telling her, Elvis jumped from her shoulder and headed away from the gardens, toward the shopping area.

Kiara ran to catch up to him. He looked back at her a couple of times as he was running, sending chirps to her, asking her to keep up.

"Where are you going?" Kiara muttered. She sincerely hoped he wasn't heading to another shady shop with stones in it.

Knowing she was following him, Elvis slowed down as they entered the shopping area. The area had very few customers, and Kiara was grateful. The few patrons in the area gave both her and Elvis curious looks. When Kiara caught up to him, he turned and climbed up to her shoulder, chirping as he went. Kiara could still feel the urgency and alarm coming from him. Elvis sent her directions in her head, between the images of the small drayek he kept sending her. He stopped her in front of a large shop that boasted unique gifts for every traveler.

Elvis made the growling/chirping noise again and sent Kiara a more urgent picture of the small drayek.

"Okay, okay," Kiara whispered and entered the shop. At least this shop looked legitimate and was well-lit.

Several clerks and one patron immediately noticed her and Elvis. They were staring, and one of the clerks, a small, mixed-race male with a pointy nose, hustled over to her.

"No, no, we don't need another one," he declared in a loud whisper.

"Another one?" Kiara asked in alarm. "You have a drayek you're trying to sell?"

"Of course," the clerk answered in a snooty voice. "We pride ourselves on offering unique items."

Elvis growled at the clerk and tugged on Kiara's braid. His anxiety about the other drayek was coming across, loud and clear.

Kiara wasn't sure if selling a drayek was even legal, but she knew, from Elvis' panic, that she'd better see it for herself.

"Can I see it?" She asked the clerk, trying her best to appear like an interested consumer.

"Ohhh," the clerk exclaimed with a smile. "You want a companion for yours! Excellent! Right this way!"

Kiara followed him toward the back of the stores and stopped in front of a glassed-in cage. She estimated the enclosure to be a few feet wide and tall. A small drayek, grayish-brown in color, was curled in a ball in one of the corners. It was the drayek that Elvis had been sending her pictures of. Its breathing was shallow, and Elvis' concern for the drayek was now flooding Kiara's brain.

"Is it sick?" Kiara quickly asked.

"No, no," the clerk hurriedly assured her.

The little drayek became aware of their presence and jumped up, looking around wildly. When it spotted Kiara and Elvis, it let out a shriek and jumped to the front of the enclosure, its tiny front paws swiping at the glass separating it from the outside world. Kiara's heart broke at the sight of the animal in such distress.

Elvis sent Kiara a picture of him with the little drayek, but Kiara was concerned. What if the drayek was sick, and made Elvis sick? Elvis sent a negative thought, which Kiara assumed meant the drayek wasn't ill.

"Was it bonded to someone before?" Kiara asked the clerk. Maybe it was dying from being separated?

The clerk looked confused, so Kiara assumed he didn't know about bonding and probably didn't know much about drayeks.

Elvis again sent her negative thoughts. Kiara thought maybe he knew that it hadn't bonded with someone.

Kiara looked at the price proudly displayed on the cage and knew she couldn't afford to buy the little drayek, but she also knew she couldn't leave it here. The little drayek was still pawing at the glass, and Kiara could barely make out little chirps coming from it. Kiara moved a small table over to the glass and placed Elvis on it so he could offer some comfort to the little one.

Stepping back from the glass, she pulled her com unit out. She quickly checked whether selling a drayek was legal. To her relief, it wasn't, and that meant she had some leverage. She promptly sent a message to Curly and Blackburne asking them to join her in the shop. She made sure they knew it wasn't an emergency, and it didn't involve a stone. But, she did ask them to hurry. She didn't want the clerk to get suspicious. She immediately received replies – they were both on their way. She sighed in relief. Now, to stall the clerk.

"Aren't they cute together?" She asked the clerk. "It's important that they get along."

Relieved that he might be making a sale, the clerk smiled and nodded.

Kiara watched Elvis and the other drayek touch their paws through the glass while Elvis made clucking and chirping noises. She had no idea what she would do with another drayek, but she also knew she couldn't leave it here.

Within minutes, she heard murmuring behind her and felt the floor shake slightly. Curly had arrived.

She turned to greet Curly and noticed that not only had Curly and Blackburne made their way to the shop, but Jax was also with them. That might work in her favor, since the shop was illegally selling drayeks.

Kiara moved to the side so Curly could see Elvis and the other drayek. Curly let out a small, high-pitched moan.

"Who are these people?" the clerk demanded, but he also took a step back at the sight of Curly.

Blackburne was silent, but Jax stepped forward in his most menacing posture. He turned to look at the clerk.

"It is illegal to sell drayeks," Jax said in a deceptively quiet tone.

The clerk looked confused for a second and clearly wasn't sure how to proceed. He took another step back before grabbing his com unit and sending a message.

"I'm not authorized to handle this," the clerk said in a timid voice and hurriedly left.

Another clerk, or perhaps the manager, approached them from behind. Nearly as tall as Kiara, the man had dark skin, black eyes, and a bald head. His scowl could match Blackburne's scowl on any given day.

"Is there a problem here?" he asked in an authoritative, booming voice.

"It is illegal to sell drayeks," Jax repeated for the new clerk.

The man looked around Jax at the drayek in the cage, then at the group standing before him. He shrugged. "It is not for sale."

Jax pointed to the sign listing the price.

Again, the clerk merely shrugged. "It must be a mistake."

"Then we will take it," Kiara said.

"I am sorry, he is not for sale, and you cannot just take him," the clerk said emphatically. "I must ask you to leave."

Up to this point, Curly had been silent, except for the noise she made when she first saw the drayek. At the clerk's statement, Curly turned toward the clerk, stood to her full height, and puffed out her chest and fur. The action made her appear nearly twice as big. She took a step toward the clerk, and Kiara could hear a low growl coming from her.

The clerk backed up a step but attempted to hold his position. "I am sorry, but you cannot take the animal." His voice cracked on the last word.

Kiara smiled. The veneer was cracking.

"I suggest you give us the drayek," Kiara said quietly, and stepped toward the clerk. She silently called Elvis to her. When he landed on her shoulder, she connected with him and, using her power, lifted the clerk off the floor.

The clerk let out a shriek that was inconsistent with his earlier bravado, and Kiara took another step toward him.

"I suggest you give us the drayek, since it is not for sale," Kiara said again. She looked at Curly and motioned the Bendanite forward with a slight tilt of her head.

Curly stepped toward the clerk and opened her mouth, showing her teeth and letting the growl grow louder.

The clerk looked panicked but had not yet agreed. Kiara was going to escalate her pressure, but Jax stepped forward.

"Curly, here, is concerned about your care of the drayek. Sometimes, her concern leads to bodily harm. She may decide to relieve you of one of your limbs, in her concern for the drayek. I would hate to see it come to that," Jax quietly informed the clerk.

Kiara sensed a threat from behind their group and immediately threw up a protection field. She turned to see the danger and found three security guards behind them, weapons pointed at Curly.

Curly, her gaze never leaving the clerk, took another step forward. One of the security guards shouted at them, and Kiara knew she needed to take action to get this wrapped up quickly.

"Your security guards are ineffective against my power, so do not look to them to help you," Kiara said as she quickly crushed each of the weapons they were pointing at the group. "Give us the drayek, you will not be harmed, and we will not turn you into the GTA for illegally selling drayeks."

The now panicked clerk nodded at Kiara and motioned for the security guards to leave. Kiara watched out of the corner of her eye as the security guards, relieved, ran back to the front of the shop.

"Key?" Blackburne asked with a fierce scowl and a resigned sigh. Apparently, they were getting another crew member.

The clerk brought up his com unit, his hands shaking, and punched in the code to open the cage.

The little drayek, knowing it was free, shot out of the cage straight to Curly. Curly caught the little animal and cradled it into her massive arms. With one last look at the clerk, Curly turned and lumbered out of the shop, making clicking and cooing noises at the little drayek.

Jax stepped toward the clerk. "I will be personally checking this shop in the future to make sure that no other drayeks are for sale."

The clerk nodded again as Kiara finally released him. He landed with a soft thump on the floor and struggled to get his legs to support him.

The clerk, now quiet and subdued, scurried over to the other clerks huddling behind a counter. They watched in silence as Kiara and the others left the shop.

Kiara caught up to Curly just as she was exiting the shopping area. Elvis immediately hopped and flapped to Curly's shoulder, chirping at the drayek in Curly's arms. Kiara could hear the answering chirps from the little drayek.

"Is it okay, Curly?" Kiara asked. She was still worried that it was sick.

Curly turned warm, brown, emotion-filled eyes to Kiara.

"She is okay."

Kiara looked at the little drayek in Curly's arms. It was now the same color as Curly's light chocolate brown coloring and looked about as content as she had ever seen Elvis look.

"Oh," Kiara murmured. It seemed the little drayek had chosen Curly to bond with. "It's a little girl?"

Curly nodded. "She is too young. She should have mother."

Kiara's heart broke, again. People could be so cruel to animals.

The little drayek poked its head out of Curly's arms and chirped at Kiara, then at Elvis. To Kiara's surprise, she could feel the little drayek's thoughts of safety and contentment. Maybe her connection to Elvis made it easier to connect to the other drayek?

Elvis jumped back over to Kiara, and she could feel gratitude coming from him.

"Elvis, my little man, you saved her, you know that?" Kiara crooned at him.

Elvis chirped at her and touched her hair.

Once they were back onboard the Acadia, the crew followed Curly back to the cargo bay. Cory's eyebrows raised when he saw the little drayek, but he didn't say anything.

Blackburne approached Curly. "Are you keeping it?" he asked in a resigned voice.

Curly looked down at the tiny creature in her arms. It looked even smaller against Curly's massive bulk. She had lost one in a war many years ago, and her heart wouldn't let her let this one go. It was as if the universe had sent her another.

"I keep," Curly said quietly. She looked sad for a moment as her gaze went from Blackburne to Kiara. "I can go," she said even more quietly. It was apparent she thought adding another drayek might be too much for Blackburne and was willing to abandon her position on the Acadia, and her friendship with Kiara, to keep the little one.

"Absolutely not!" Blackburne bellowed.

The little drayek screeched at the shout, before burrowing further into Curly's fur. Kiara and Elvis both jumped.

Kiara smiled. "You're a fluffy," Kiara said.

Blackburne frowned at her. "Softy," he corrected gruffly. "I am not a softy!"

Kiara went to the kitchen to get some food for the new arrival, and Elvis had wanted to stay with Curly to keep an eye on the little drayek. Kiara could sense big-brother-type feelings from Elvis. Now that they had rescued the little drayek, her heartbreak was beginning to heal.

Once she had provided the food for the newest arrival to Curly, Kiara headed to her bunk, Elvis on her shoulder. Stryker had secured lodging on the space station for those who wanted it, but Kiara had always felt most comfortable in her bunk. It was cramped, but it was hers. With Curly in her own space in the cargo bay, Kiara's bunk was a comfortable haven for her and Elvis.

Once she got settled in her bunk, with Elvis softly snoring on the bed, she contacted her dad via the ship's encrypted line. The signal was weak, so Kiara just sent a quick message that she was okay. She waited a few minutes, hoping Kyle would send something back so she would know he was okay, too. She was just about to disconnect when the message came through. Her dad was on a mission with other Rangers, but was okay. Kiara let out the breath she had been holding.

Kiara fell asleep quickly and dreamed about gardens with apple trees and drayeks, and at one point, Mirona joined her in the garden. They walked in her dream, sharing stories and each other's company.

When Kiara woke, feeling refreshed and ready for whatever the day was going to bring. She felt a sense of anticipation, or, at least, she thought it was anticipation. She didn't want to dig too deep, but she assumed it was eagerness for the mission. The Pearls had stolen her heart, and she wanted to do whatever she could to keep them protected. She checked her com unit for updates, and so far, all was quiet. Grabbing a quick breakfast, she headed to the flex-space to get a quick workout in. When she entered, Cory was sitting in the room, swiping at multiple screens. He jumped when she entered, and Kiara hastily apologized.

"It's okay," Cory quickly assured her. "I get so involved in the programming; I don't pay attention to what's happening around me." At Kiara's questioning look, Cory sighed. "I wanted to give Curly and her new companion some bonding time. I heard about the cage it was in, and I wanted it to feel good about being here."

Elvis chirped and hopped his way over to Cory. Kiara reflected on Cory's reaction and fear when he first met Elvis, and now the two truly adored each other. Kiara suggested that since Cory was in the room with her, she might as well do the workout with her body armor. She'd been wearing it daily now, getting used to having it on, and she supposed she should take advantage of having Cory here to monitor it.

The workout was time well spent, with the body armor performing well. Cory was continually making adjustments, and every time she deployed the armor, she felt more comfortable than the time before. Even Cory seemed pleased this time.

Kiara's com unit signaled. Stryker had sent out an alert that the traffickers had arrived at the space station. Looking up, she saw Cory had gotten the same message. Kiara nodded at him and left to join Stryker and Jax on the station. Cory would stay on the Acadia and monitor the group.

Kiara met up with Jax outside a bar on the station. Stryker and Blackburne also joined them. Curly, with her new companion, was stationed outside the hangar that housed the trafficker's ship, in case they made it that far.

"Are they in there?" Blackburne casually asked the question, doing his best to appear nonchalant.

Kiara wanted to laugh at the absurdity of it, but instead focused on Jax and the intensity he was giving off. Elvis was on her shoulder, holding her braid, and looking around at the group. He was unusually quiet, and Kiara thought he must be picking up on the group's emotions.

Stryker sent pictures of the traffickers spotted in the bar to everyone's com unit.

"Wait, there's only four of them," Jax quickly commented.

Stryker nodded. "Our scouts on the station said that this is their ship, so we are not sure why there are only four. The scouts were watching as the traffickers left the ship, and a quick scan of their ship did not show any other humanoids on board."

"Should we wait to see if more of them show up? Kiara looked around the group. "If we only get a few of them, the others will still be able to keep trafficking – if not here, then elsewhere."

"My thoughts, exactly," Stryker said. "However, we need to keep an eye on them."

Blackburne volunteered to take the first shift and contacted Frankie to help with the next shift.

Kiara joined Jax and Stryker as they walked down the hall. She was just about to ask them what they thought about where the rest of the traffickers were when Stryker's com unit signaled. Looking at it, he frowned.

"The sensor net on the planet just went off."

They turned as one and ran back to the Acadia. Stryker sent a message to Blackburne to keep the four traffickers in the bar on the space station, and a message to Frankie to get the Acadia ready. As soon as they boarded the Acadia, Frankie had them undocked and headed to the planet. Stryker directed him to where the sensor net had been triggered. Frankie had the engines straining as he pushed the ship to get there faster.

Stryker's com unit signaled a message from Blackburne. The traffickers in the bar had taken note of the Acadia's departure, laughing and nodding. Blackburne warned of a trap. Stryker relayed the information and looked hard at Kiara.

Kiara closed her eyes and sent her thoughts ahead, looking for enemies, looking for explosive devices, or anything out of the ordinary. In her mind, she saw the ship at the same time that Frankie yelled out a warning. Knowing that Frankie had the ship in his sights, she continued to look for anything else, Blackburne's warning about a trap in the back of her mind.

Frankie engaged the ships' shielding as they got closer to the other ship, and Jax attempted to contact it. His hails weren't answered, and Frankie maneuvered the ship to make it less of a target as they approached the other ship.

Kiara's eyes popped open. "It's a decoy," she looked at Stryker as she said it. "There's another ship on the surface already."

"Avoid that ship!" Stryker yelled, but it was too late.

Kiara watched, in what seemed like slow motion, as the ship between them and the planet's surface exploded. Kiara immediately enveloped the Acadia in a protection field, not sure if the ship's shields would be enough to protect them.

The shockwave from the explosion hit them, throwing the Acadia off course, and everyone on the Acadia that wasn't strapped in was thrown to the floor, including Kiara and Elvis. Frankie struggled to keep the Acadia under control, as the ship's structure groaned and creaked under the strain.

After a few tense seconds, Frankie got the ship under control and quickly checked the Acadia for damage. The shockwave and subsequent spin had knocked out some circuits, and the shield generator was fluctuating. Structurally, the ship was sound.

Frankie set the ship to hold its position and went around the bridge to make sure everyone was okay. He'd been the only one strapped in when the other ship exploded, so Jax, Stryker, Kiara, and Elvis were on the floor. As Frankie approached Kiara, he noted Elvis jumping up and down, chirping and shrieking. Elvis was agitated but otherwise appeared okay. Kiara was motionless on the floor, and Frankie quickly looked over at Jax and Stryker. Both were picking themselves up off the floor, so Frankie continued to Kiara. Just as he reached her, she began to move her arms, and Elvis quickly jumped to her side, touching her face, making small clicking noises. Frankie surmised that Elvis had been so agitated because Kiara was unconscious.

"Kiara, are you okay?" Frankie asked as he helped her to a sitting position.

Kiara rubbed the back of her head and grimaced in pain. "I'm okay. Is the ship okay?"

Frankie rolled his eyes at Jax and headed back to his chair. Stryker joined Jax in helping Kiara to her feet. She appeared steady on her feet, so Frankie did another check of the ship. The shield generator was steady now, and the circuits that were knocked out weren't affecting anything significant.

"Everybody okay?" Frankie yelled while still looking at his diagnostic screen. He heard three affirmatives and one chirp. He smiled fiercely and turned the ship toward the planet. "Then let's go get the bastards!"

Kiara sat at her navunit, scanning the surface for the other ship. She scanned one of the caves the Pearls used, figuring the traffickers would know where it was as well. Her scan pinged a big metal object outside the cave, so she sent the location to Frankie and nodded at Jax and Stryker. Her head hurt a little, but more at the point of impact than an actual headache. She took that as a good sign.

Kiara sent a quick message to Cory and was relieved that he responded that he was good. He'd been strapped in a seat in the cargo bay and was only a little bruised. She let Stryker know and relayed to Cory that they were heading to the planet to intercept the actual traffickers. Cory acknowledged and let Kiara know that he was ready to monitor her body armor and that she could deploy it at any time.

Kiara took a deep breath and deployed the armor. It flowed around her without a hitch, and she realized that she felt better, knowing it was on.

The Acadia bumped and jolted its way through the atmosphere, and Kiara briefly wished that Curly had accompanied them. The Bendanite's fur would have helped to protect her, and Kiara was sure that the Bendanite's size would have worked to their advantage. However, since Curly had her own little drayek, it was probably best she stayed on the space station.

The Acadia finally cleared the rough part of the atmosphere, and the cave complex came into view. On the view screen, they could see the trafficker's ship outside the largest cave. Frankie shot the Acadia straight at the other ship, firing reverse thrusters in a maneuver that jolted everyone on board. Kiara was ready for it; she knew they had to move fast. If the traffickers thought they were going to be caught, they might try to make a run for it.

Jax, Stryker, and Kiara were waiting at the door of the ship when it bumped onto the ground. All three had special insulated suits and dark goggles. Kiara's armor was underneath her insulated suit, and Elvis was on her shoulder, encased in an energy bubble to keep him from freezing. They hadn't had time to create an insulated suit small enough for him, but they had found a small pair of goggles to protect his eyes. The door released, and Kiara jumped out, not waiting for the ramp to deploy. She cushioned her fall with an energy bubble and shot across the icy landscape toward the trafficker's ship, Elvis on her back, holding her braid of hair. She knew that Jax and Stryker would be right behind her; they could move faster than she could.

Just as they reached the trafficker's ship, Kiara could see the ramp retracting, and the thrusters on the ship fired. She could hear Stryker yell at Frankie to intercept the ship, but Kiara worried that the trafficker's ship would outrun them if it got off the ground. Focusing on one of the thrusters, she shot several small bursts of energy at it. The thruster sputtered and stopped, and the ship, a couple of feet off the ground, tilted precariously as one side of the ship hit the icy landscape. Kiara shot energy pulses at a second thruster, bringing the ship down hard.

Kiara scanned the ship for weapons and saw a couple of outer guns turning toward her, Jax, and Stryker. At the same time, the ramp was extending again. Stryker saw the guns as well and gestured at Kiara to take them out, while he and Jax ran toward the ramp. Kiara fired a couple of energy pulses, taking out the guns with ease. As soon as the door to the ship opened, weapons fire shot out. Jax and Stryker dodged and weaved, easily outmaneuvering the slow weapons fire. Kiara encased Elvis and herself in an energy bubble and rushed up the ramp. She counted five bodies coming down the ramp, firing wildly. A couple of the shots hit her energy bubble, slowing her progress. Out of the corner of her eye, she could see that Jax and Stryker were still safely dodging the weapon's fire. Stryker reached the ramp, extended his baton, and took out the trafficker closest to him.

Jax took out another, causing the other three to run back up the ramp, turning periodically to fire wildly behind them. Jax and Stryker were under the ramp for protection; it was too dangerous to try to go up the ramp. The traffickers were hiding behind the doorway of the ship, sticking their weapons out and firing. Kiara joined Jax and Stryker, looking to Stryker for the next move.

Breathing hard, Stryker looked at Kiara. "Can you encase them in an energy bubble?"

Kiara shook her head. "They're dodging around so much, I can't get a read on them."

"I am worried they will become desperate, now that we have disabled their ship," Jax said grimly.

The weapon's fire above them stopped. Kiara was just about to step out and see if she could see anything when a voice above them spoke out.

"I will kill all the Pearls on this ship if you don't let us leave!"

Kiara looked desperately at Stryker. Before Stryker could answer, a low growl came from behind Kiara's head. Kiara could feel the anger coming from Elvis. Looking at Stryker, Kiara smiled fiercely. Stryker immediately understood and nodded. Kiara sent a silent message to Elvis, increasing the protection level on his bubble. She handed him over to Stryker. Jax moved to the other side of the ramp, and Kiara shot a couple of small energy bursts on that side. Weapon's fire hit that side, and Stryker stepped out from behind the ramp and tossed Elvis onto the ramp.

Kiara closed her eyes and connected with Elvis so she could see what he was seeing. Elvis shot up the ramp, emitting a growling noise that raised the hair on the back of Kiara's neck. She could see surprise through the mask on the first person's face, before Elvis hit him, teeth and talons striking swiftly. Elvis didn't wait but jumped toward the second person. Kiara could hear an exclamation of surprise, right before Elvis hit him. She heard screaming as Elvis ran down the corridor and took that as their cue to get into the ship.

Jax stayed at the doorway, while Stryker and Kiara ran inside. Kiara followed the path of destruction left by Elvis. Blood, torn clothing, bits of plastic, and metal littered the hallway. Kiara could still feel Elvis's anger and sense that he wasn't hurt. She asked him to come back to her, but he refused. Surprised, Kiara connected to him and saw that he had cornered one of the traffickers in the small cargo area, and the trafficker had a weapon pointed at a Pearl and what appeared to be a baby Pearl. The trafficker was yelling at Elvis and moving his weapon from adult Pearl to baby Pearl, and then to Elvis.

Alarmed, Kiara told Elvis to hold and hoped that her energy bubble for him would withstand weapons fire from that close. She ran down the corridor until she reached him. The trafficker, his hand shaking, pointed his weapon at Elvis, clearly thinking the small animal with the bared teeth was the bigger threat than the tall blue woman who had just entered the room. Kiara could see he was desperate. He had the Pearls between him and Elvis, trying to use them as a shield. Kiara glanced at the Pearls, surprised that they didn't seem alarmed, and in fact, were contentedly chewing on some fungus that had been brought on board for them. Well, at least she didn't have to worry about a panicked animal while trying to keep them safe.

Kiara started to raise her hands, in what she hoped was a placating gesture. Instead, it panicked the trafficker. He fired at Elvis and pulled a dagger from his clothing, and threw it at Kiara. The energy bubble around Elvis held, but the dagger went right through Kiara's protection bubble. The last time that happened flashed through Kiara's mind, and she had a moment of panic. The dagger hit her body armor and bounced harmlessly to the floor. In her ear, she could hear Cory yell something positive, but she was still trying to process that she wasn't hurt. She looked down at the dagger on the floor, and then into the shocked face of the trafficker. Kiara tamped down her surprise and used her anger to fuel the energy pulse she threw at the trafficker's face. He crumpled into a ball at the feet of the Pearl.

She contacted Stryker, and he let her know that he had the pilot contained as well as two of the injured traffickers. Jax chimed in that he had the two traffickers from outside, and the trafficker in the doorway who threatened to kill all the Pearls was unconscious, but alive.

Jax and Stryker moved the traffickers to the Acadia, binding their hands and feet with energy strips. Kiara searched the trafficker's ship and found a total of six Pearls. She attempted to communicate with them, as she had with the Amdrolans from Havernon 3. However, when she touched them, all she got was contentment. Their hair was thick and dense, her hand disappearing into the lush fiber. The hair shimmered under hand, and Kiara could see why their fur was in such demand. However, the Pearls just stood there, oblivious to the danger they were in. No wonder they were such easy targets.

Kiara gently pushed and herded the Pearls toward the door of the ship, with Elvis helping as well. Kiara smiled at Elvis. He was following her silent commands, which reminded Kiara of a video she had seen from Earth of herding dogs. The Pearls didn't seem to be afraid of Elvis either. Once they were off the ship, they wandered toward their caves, their fur helping them blend into the landscape.

Kiara joined Stryker and Jax on the Acadia and nodded at Frankie as she entered the bridge. Cory was sitting off to the side, looking somber. She could sense an extra layer of tension as she entered.

"What's wrong?" Kiara shot the question at Stryker.

"Frankie was wondering how the traffickers knew to divert us," Jax responded.

Stryker looked angry. "It appears that the space station leaders betrayed us."

Kiara looked alarmed. "Did you check on Curly and Blackburne?"

Jax nodded. "They are fine. The traffickers are still in the bar."

Kiara let out the breath she'd been holding, and Elvis, on her shoulder, tugged on her hair to let her know that he, too, was relieved.

"If the space station is in on it, what do we do with these guys?" Kiara looked at the others. "I mean, it is weird. If the space station knew about the measures put into place to protect the Pearls, why didn't they warn the traffickers that it wouldn't be worth it to take them anymore?"

"Too many unanswered questions," Stryker answered her. "We will get those answers on the space station. Frankie, destroy their ship."

Stryker strode out, anger in every step. Jax made sure that the traffickers were secured, and Frankie lifted off. They headed to the space station, the trafficker's ship a smoldering pile of rubble behind them.

Kiara heard Frankie alert the space station that they were docking, so she helped scan for threats as they approached. If the space station was helping the traffickers, they could be flying into a trap.

They docked without incident, and Stryker sent a message to Blackburne to pick up the other traffickers and bring them to a meeting room off the space station's main administrative section. Kiara and Elvis went to meet Blackburne and Curly at the bar to help if needed.

Kiara stopped at the bar entrance and watched Curly lumber down the hall toward her. She almost laughed when a tiny drayek head popped up over Curly's shoulder. The little drayek looked entirely at ease, like they had been together for years. Kiara sensed Blackburne approaching from behind her. She peeked into the bar, verifying that the four traffickers were still in the bar. If they had been drinking the whole time, getting them to the meeting might be a challenge.

Blackburne volunteered to go in first, and Kiara talked him into taking Curly with him. The two entered the bar, heading for the traffickers. Kiara reached up, touched Elvis' toes, and sent an energy bubble around Blackburne and Curly, and Curly's drayek. This whole operation seemed rife with traps, so Kiara wanted to be prepared.

As Blackburne approached the table with the traffickers, everything in the bar went quiet. To Kiara, it reminded her of an old Earth movie, a 'Western'. She smiled. Except, in this instance, the two heroes who had just entered the bar were protected by her. The three men and one woman at the table were looking at Blackburne and Curly, and Kiara could tell the moment they realized that Curly was heading for their table. Eyes went wide, and the woman at the table tried to scoot her chair backwards.

Kiara couldn't hear anything, but she could see Blackburne trying to keep the situation calm with his gestures. He was trying to convince them to come with him, but so far, he wasn't having any luck. She could see heads shaking, which turned into angry looks from the traffickers. The situation escalated quickly. All four of the traffickers stood up, pulling their weapons as they did. Blackburne dove toward a table, yelling at Curly to move. All four traffickers fired, their shots bouncing off the shield Kiara had put up for Blackburne and Curly. Curly, realizing instantly that she was protected, bared her teeth and let out a roar that shook the floor. She grabbed the two closest traffickers and smashed their heads together. They crumpled at her feet. The other two threw their weapons down and held up their hands in surrender. Unfortunately for them, Curly wasn't feeling very merciful. She grabbed them and threw them toward the door of the bar. They landed in a heap, dazed and confused. Blackburne got up, following Curly toward the exit. She had a trafficker under each arm, her little drayek riding high on her shoulder. Before they reached the door, the man and woman at the doorway attempted to get up and run. As they gained their feet, they came face to face with Kiara, Elvis on her shoulder, with his teeth bared. The man clumsily tried to throw a punch at Kiara, which just bounced off her energy bubble. He yelled in pain and grabbed his hand. The woman looked at Kiara, then Elvis, then back at Curly approaching them.

She threw up her hands again. "I'm sorry, I'm sorry!"

Kiara was sorely tempted to hit her with an energy pulse, just because.

Shepherding the two conscious traffickers while Curly carried the other two, they entered a small room in the station administration area. Jax and Stryker were there with the ones from the surface, and Curly unceremoniously dumped her two on the floor near the back of the room.

Kiara approached Jax. "Did anyone talk? Do we know who tipped them off?

Jax nodded. "One of our scouts was also working with someone on the space station staff. The traffickers made a deal with them to stay in business."

Kiara looked confused. "But your scouts knew about the genetic modification, didn't they?"

Jax smirked. "Yes, they thought to get one more big payout before the traffickers discovered that the cargo was useless. We caught the scout and the space station employee, just as they were trying to board a freighter."

Kiara looked at the traffickers in the room. Their looks ranged from rage to fear to disappointment.

"Are you sure that we have everyone who was in on it?" Kiara wasn't convinced that there were only two others involved.

"My thought, as well," Stryker said as he walked up. He looked over at Curly. "We will let Curly ask a few questions."

Hearing her name, Curly lumbered over, her expression radiating anger. Kiara smiled at her, and tilting her head toward the trafficker with fear all over his face, she asked Curly to move over to him. Stryker followed.

Kiara looked at the trafficker, then at Stryker, then at Curly. Her gaze going back to the trafficker, she took the lead.

"Stryker wants to know everyone involved in the trafficking of the Pearls. Who on the space station, and anyone else here that might have been involved." The trafficker started to open his mouth, but Kiara raised her hand to stop him. "Stryker wants an answer, but Curly, here, she just wants to rip you apart." She saw the trafficker visibly swallow. Curly bared her teeth, her little drayek doing the same. "I would think very carefully before answering."

"Y-y-you won't let her hurt me, there are rules, you know," the trafficker stammered out.

Kiara nodded. "Yes, there are rules, but you already broke those rules. And Curly, here, she wants justice for the Pearls. We probably won't be able to control her if she thinks you are lying." The trafficker looked at Curly, and Kiara could tell he was trying to judge how she would know if he was lying. "Oh, and to be clear, I'll know, with my telepathic ability, if you are lying, and I'll be sure to let her know."

One of the other traffickers yelled at him not to talk, but Kiara could tell that her last statement had gotten through to the fearful one. He turned to Stryker, giving him the names of the two they already had in custody, plus another that worked in the hangar on the space station. Kiara, thinking they had the info they wanted, was just about to turn away when the trafficker took another deep breath and started naming names on other planets for their distribution, and even some of the buyers that he knew. Kiara raised her eyebrows and noticed Jax recording everything on his com unit.

Suddenly, one of the other traffickers jumped toward the one who was talking, murder in his eyes. Kiara was going to throw an energy pulse at him, but watched in fascination as Curly shot forward, and with a short growl, grabbed the trafficker by the throat before he got close. Kiara was always amazed at how fast Bendanites could move when they wanted to.

Curly brought the trafficker's face close to hers and let out a roar that had the trafficker screaming in terror. Curly's little drayek was alternately growling and hissing at everyone in the room. Curly squeezed the trafficker's throat, cutting off the scream, and then dropped him before she hurt him permanently. The first trafficker was still spilling everything he knew, almost blubbering in his terror. While that trafficker kept talking, Stryker grabbed Blackburne and headed out to grab the employee who worked in the docking hangar.

When the trafficker finally stopped talking, Jax went around and secured all the traffickers, checking to make sure that the three that Curly had handled were okay. Kiara kept an eye on them, and Elvis hopped around making hissing noises at all of them.

As Kiara walked by one of the traffickers, he locked eyes with her. Kiara stopped, curious as to why this trafficker felt so bold. As she looked at him, his expression changed. His eyes glazed over, and he didn't seem to be seeing her any longer. Goosebumps popped out on her arms, and the hair on the back of her neck stood up. His lips turned into a snarl, and Kiara stumbled back half a step, but she couldn't seem to break the connection with his eyes. She could see that he was whispering something. She felt compelled to move forward to hear what he was saying, all the while locked with his gaze. As her face got closer, she could hear him repeating the same word over and over. Death.

Elvis screeched at her, breaking the connection. Kiara stumbled back, Jax leaping forward to catch her. Jax helped her stand, turning to confront the trafficker, his baton out and ready. The trafficker held up his bound hands in a futile attempt to protect himself, submissiveness in his body language.

Jax put his baton away and turned back to Kiara, a questioning look on his face. Elvis was on her shoulder, stroking her hair and making small noises at her. Elvis' behavior looked a lot like it did when Kiara had been under the influence of the stone. Jax grabbed both of Kiara's arms and forced her to meet his eyes. She looked absolutely traumatized.

"Kiara, what is it? What happened?"

Kiara closed her eyes and finally took a deep breath. When she opened her eyes back up, there were tears there.

"Kiara?"

"He kept repeating one word. Death."

Jax looked at her and then back at the now complacent trafficker. Jax turned back to Kiara, his eyebrows raised.

Kiara's chin dropped to her chest, and her breath whooshed out. On a sob, she said, "his eyes were the stone."

Chapter 11

Stryker walked back into the room and immediately knew something was wrong.

"What is it, what has happened?" Stryker asked as he surveyed the room, checking to ensure that all traffickers were secure and that no one was hurt. Blackburne hurried in behind, the docking hangar employee in his custody.

Curly shoved their newest guest into a corner of the room and took over the watch so Stryker and Jax could talk to Kiara. Elvis was alternately clutching Kiara's hair or combing it with his paws.

"It can't be happening again, it can't!" Kiara wailed.

Jax and Stryker each reached out with one hand, gently grasping one of Kiara's arms. They used their limited empathic abilities to help calm her down.

"Breathe, Kiara, breathe," Jax gently soothed her. He helped her regulate her breathing, coaxing her with his eyes to look at him.

After a few deep breaths, Kiara could feel herself regaining some control. She had felt overwhelming panic when she saw the trafficker's eyes turn into the stone. And the creepiness of him muttering 'death', over and over. Even now, just remembering it made goosebumps pop out on her arms.

"We will take care of it, Kiara, we will," Stryker soothed from her other side.

Kiara nodded, feeling a bit steadier.

"Tell me exactly what happened," Jax softly commanded.

Kiara nodded again, telling them both about the trafficker's eyes and his chant. Stryker stepped away, quietly questioning the trafficker. Jax led Kiara to a chair away from the traffickers, gently sitting her down, and continuing to help her regulate her breathing. Elvis looked a little less worried as well. Stryker joined them a few moments later.

"He did not know what I was speaking about," Stryker said, with some confusion.

"It is possible that the stone spoke through him," Jax said.

Stryker nodded, and Kiara felt a sense of relief. They both believed her, which had been a concern in the back of her mind. Her story seemed so weird, even to her.

"Your ancestor warned us that the ceremony may not be entirely successful," Jax reminded them. He looked at Kiara's face, trying to decipher the look he was seeing.

"What are you thinking?"

"I was wondering how this will progress. Will it be like last time?" Tears filled her eyes, and she reached up to touch Elvis' toes. "Will it be worse? Will I hurt Elvis?"

"We will not let you hurt Elvis," Jax assured her. "We will monitor you as before, until we rid you of the stone's influence, this time for good."

Kiara took some comfort in the confidence that Jax spoke with.

"If I remember correctly, Mirona said we will have to destroy the stone this time," Jax said, but what he didn't say was what they were all thinking. How could they destroy the stone? How would they even find it?

"I'll contact Mirona and see if she has any insight into how to destroy the stone," Kiara said calmly, even though she was feeling anything but calm.

Jax nodded and looked at Stryker. Stryker nodded back. He would find out what he could about the stone's location and any additional information on destroying it.

Stryker delivered the traffickers into custody, while the Acadia crew boarded their ship and headed to Earth Delta Nine.

On the Acadia, Kiara went to her cabin and, with Elvis sitting in her lap, closed her eyes and contacted Mirona.

Mirona!

I'm here, child.

Mirona, we think the stone still has an influence over me. Kiara described the incident after they had rescued the Pearls. *Mirona, I'm scared.*

Kiara, I am here. You are not alone. However, I cannot sense the stone's influence.

What does that mean? Was I hallucinating because I am worried about it?

No, my child. I am sure that it happened. I believe that the stone is trying to gain another hold over you, but that it hasn't yet. You and the stone are still connected, but it is not strong enough for me to sense it.

Will it get stronger? Will I be back to where I was before?

Yes, my child. It will get stronger, but you still have time. Because the stone is not with you, its influence is diluted. It will take time to rebuild. When you had the stone the first time, its influence was easily transferred. Not so, this time.

Kiara let out a breath that she didn't realize she had been holding. *How much time do you think I have?*

Weeks or months, it is hard to determine. This will give you the time you need to find the stone again. You must destroy it!

Mirona, how do you know this? You didn't seem to understand this much the last time we spoke about it.

I was worried about you and the ceremony being successful. We pulled together all our resources to find as much information as we could. In the end, it was one of my ancestors who gave us the information. She remembered more because she once had a friend who was from Galdor. Our two planets used to be as one. The war and strife destroyed all that.

Mirona's sadness came through to Kiara. So much had been lost!

Mirona, how will I destroy it?

Kiara, my child, this will be the biggest test you will face. Only you can destroy it. However, the closer you are to it, the more it will try to influence you and take you over. You will need to be stronger than you could ever imagine.

Can't I just blow it up with explosives or a laser or something? To Kiara, it seemed so simple. Find the stone and blow it up. She could even send Jax in to do it.

Kiara, I wish it were that simple for you. Through the years, others have tried to destroy the stone in a similar fashion. At one point, it was thrown into a live volcano. And yet, here it is again. Only you can destroy it. You must do this, not only for yourself, but for future Trandorians.

Kiara broke the connection and looked down at Elvis in her lap. She hugged him tight, tight enough to make him huff at her in protest.

"Sorry, little man. I'm just so relieved!"

Elvis looked into her eyes, communicating his worry.

Kiara closed her eyes. "Yes, I know. I still must figure out how to destroy it, but I'm relieved that we have time, and I won't be hurting you." Elvis chirped in agreement. "Let's go find Jax and let him know."

As the Acadia headed toward Earth Delta Nine, Talia was arriving at a remote space station, several sectors away. Worried that she would be recognized, she wore a covering over her face and hair, gloves, and a long cloak, completely concealing her skin. She'd stolen money from several residents on the Trandorian colony to get here. Her friend, whom she had been communicating with, had directed Talia to this space station. Talia was supposed to meet her friend here, but she was cautious. She knew she couldn't trust anyone. Because she was traveling on her own, there had been several times when someone had tried to take her money or grab her. She had discreetly snapped them back with her power, disguising it as a shove. She was confident in her power but also didn't need to draw attention to herself.

Finding a corner away from the crowds, she pulled out her com unit and attempted to contact her friend. At first, she didn't get an answer. She tried again, this time sending a quick message. She received a response, but it confused her. The message said to stay where she was. The next message said to follow the man in the red hat who was approaching her. She saw the man in the red hat but was apprehensive. The man stopped in front of her.

"Talia?" His voice was deep, and he towered over her.

"Yes?" Talia tried to put some confidence behind her voice, but it still came out a little squeaky. She began to build up some power, ready to strike out if needed.

He seemed to sense it and put up his hands in a placating gesture. "Please do not be alarmed. You are safe, I will not hurt you."

"Where's Kam?" Talia demanded. She was feeling a little more confident, now that she knew her power had alarmed him.

"She is not here, but I am here to take you to a safe place. If you come with me, I can explain further." At her hesitation, he gestured toward an open eating area. "We can sit over there where you will be in full view of other patrons, but it will give us some privacy so that I can clarify what is happening."

Talia nodded and relaxed slightly. She followed him to a sitting area away from others. She noticed several men around the table, keeping others away. She began to worry a bit more.

"Please, sit." He gestured toward the chair.

Talia sat, keeping her eyes on him and the other men.

"My name is Rend. I work for the GTA Director. You have caught the attention of the Director."

Talia raised her eyebrows. "Is that good or bad?"

"It is very good," Rend told her with a small smile. "He is very interested in you and your power."

"Why?" Talia asked suspiciously.

"Let me just say that you and the Director have an enemy in common."

"Kiara," Talia breathed out her name.

Rend smiled.

Talia smiled back, a vicious smile.

Even though Mirona had told her that she had time, Kiara still worried. It was like that old Earth saying, 'waiting for the other shoe to drop'. Jax was a constant, steadying presence, for which Kiara was grateful. He was always ready for a quick hug or a touch on her cheek when he could sense her faltering, and she didn't know what she would do without him.

The Acadia was currently waiting its turn to go through a transgate on its way to Earth Delta Nine. Jax was staying in touch with Stryker and his journey. Stryker had taken a more direct route to drop off the traffickers and get to Earth Delta Nine; the Acadia had taken a more indirect route to keep them safe and avoid detection. The Acadia was flying under a different ship name and identifier, and so far, it was working. Their journey had been quiet, so far—no attacks on the ship, and no issues with Kiara. Jax and Blackburne had been shadowing Kiara constantly, looking for any signs of the stone's influence.

Kiara appreciated their concern, but it was getting a little tiresome to have them shadowing her everywhere she went. In one instance, she had to push Jax out of the bathroom when he accidentally followed her in.

Kiara had also been reluctant to tell her dad. She'd been in touch with him many times since they had rescued the Pearls, but so far, had declined to tell him about the stone. Even though he was working with the Rangers again, he was safe. Kiara knew he was needed, and she knew that if she told him about the stone, he would fly back to her in an instant.

While they were waiting at the transgate, Kiara was constantly sensing ahead for danger, and Frankie was monitoring communications. Being on constant alert was wearing on Kiara. She was tired and irritable. Elvis was snoring lightly on her lap. Waiting for a turn through the transgate could be boring, and add to that the strain of constant sweeps.

This particular transgate was located in a very busy sector, with a large, populated planet nearby. The planet's population had also expanded out to its two moons, with the larger moon doubling as Transgate Control for the sector. It all added up to a long wait. Not only were there large numbers of ships from the planet and moons, but this transgate was also a bustling hub for those ships passing through.

Kiara could hear Frankie, in his bright yellow shirt with red flowers, tapping his toes in his chair. When she glanced over, she could see that he was doing another sweep of the area. Taking a cue from him, she sat up straighter and searched for any signs of trouble near them.

At first, she sensed nothing, but suddenly, she detected faint feelings of alarm. She turned to Frankie. "Are you getting anything?"

Frankie shook his head as he ran another scan. Kiara gently shook Elvis so she could tap into his strength to see if she could tell where the alarmed feelings were coming from. Elvis was immediately alert and brought his face up to Kiara's face. Kiara closed her eyes and searched. Jax crossed over to Kiara, waiting to see what she would find. When Kiara opened her eyes, she looked a little confused.

"What is it, Kiara? Is there an attack on the transgate?" Jax searched her face, trying to discern what was going on.

"It's not the transgate," Kiara said, her look still confused.

Jax waited.

Kiara took a deep breath and met Jax's eyes. "It's one of the colonies on the smaller moon." At the questioning look from Jax, Kiara shrugged her shoulders. "From what I can tell, there's a colony of Lamoranites on the smaller moon. They are under attack, but I can't tell who is attacking them."

Jax turned to look at Frankie. Frankie was searching, but he shook his head. "I'm not getting any distress signals. Communication with the Transgate Control and other ships in the area is normal."

Blackburne joined Jax at Kiara's station. "Is your telepathy expanding so much that you are getting smaller crimes or people in need?"

Kiara frowned. Was it the stone? Was it something else?

Jax reached out and touched her shoulder, trying to see if he could discern what was happening with her. He could sense confusion, but little else.

Kiara took a deep breath, closed her eyes, and held Elvis' toes. She closed her mind to everything except what would be a threat to them. The cries from the colony came through even louder.

"It has to have something to do with us," Kiara told the others on the bridge. "I'm sure of it."

Blackburne nodded at her. "Send the location to Frankie, then pull our ship from the transgate queue." He sent Jax a serious look, expecting an objection. Instead, Jax was also nodding.

"I could sense that she had focused her power to only receive threats to us. We must investigate. I will send Stryker a quick message."

After Kiara sent the location to Frankie, he pulled the Acadia from the transgate queue. Kiara concentrated on gathering as much information as she could, so they would be prepared. Her telepathy was only picking up panic, so she did a quick search on the computer for information about the colony.

"How long, Frankie?" Blackburne asked as the Acadia executed some sharp turns and navigated through the other ships waiting at the transgate.

"About ten minutes."

"I've got something," Kiara said quickly. "The Lamoranites have a mining colony on the moon. What they mine isn't listed, which tells me it is something very valuable."

"Agreed," Blackburne responded. "Let's see how that ties into us."

Frankie maneuvered the Acadia into the moon's thin atmosphere, heading toward the colony. The smaller moon was sparsely populated, and as the Acadia flew over the landscape, Kiara could pick out small pockets of civilization, followed by large areas of desolation. The moon's atmosphere was thin, but Kiara was able to determine that it had enough oxygen for them to exit the ship without supplemental oxygen. Plants were few and far between, and from what she could quickly find out, most of the water resources were underground. Several humanoid species populated the moon. The Lamoranites were known for their mining expertise and were most comfortable living and working underground.

As the colony came into sight, Kiara could distinguish several ships clustered around the colony buildings. Most of the colony was built underground, so there were fewer than five above-ground buildings.

"Can you make out any markings or other identifiers for those ships?" Blackburne barked it out while he surveyed the scene. "Make sure the shield generator is working!"

Jax checked the shields, while Kiara tried to determine who the ships belonged to. They were all similar in design but lacked markings. Very suspicious.

Jax tried to contact the colony but got no response.

"Let's do a fly-by, see if we can make anything out," Blackburne directed Frankie. "Kiara, are you getting anything?"

"This is definitely where the attack was, but it's quiet now. I'm getting a lot of fear, but that's about it."

Frankie was bringing them back around when weapons fire hit the Acadia. Frankie took evasive action as the Acadia bucked and shuddered from the impact.

"Where's that coming from?" Blackburne yelled.

Jax responded, "From the main building. It looks like the colony defense system."

"Frankie, get us closer, I'll take out the guns," Kiara yelled.

Frankie zigzagged them toward the building, then spun around to face the bunker the shots were coming from. Kiara quickly shot a couple of energy pulses at it, and the firing stopped.

"We got someone's attention," Blackburne muttered.

"It's not the Lamoranites," Kiara said. "Most are being held below the surface in one of the mining caverns. They are the ones I'm getting all the fear from."

Frankie landed the Acadia as close to the buildings as he could. Kiara touched base with Cory, then quickly deployed her armor. Blackburne directed Frankie and Cory to stay on board, so Frankie could protect the ship if needed.

Jax, Blackburne, and Kiara, with Elvis on her shoulder, shot down the ramp of the ship and sprinted toward the main building. They were still a few hundred yards from the door when Kiara sensed danger. She threw up an energy bubble around them, making sure everyone was close. Elvis was on her back, holding her braid, his back feet steadying himself as he alternately hissed and chirped.

Shots hit the ground in front of them, and Jax looked back at Kiara, who was slightly behind him. Kiara gave him a quick nod, and Jax took that to mean that she was shielding them. Jax touched Blackburne's arm, and they increased their speed, counting on Kiara to protect them. As they got closer, shots bounced off the energy bubble, and Kiara concentrated on keeping it up.

They finally reached the building, which afforded them some protection. Jax pulled his baton, and Blackburne brought out his weapon.

"Kiara, can you sense anything?" Jax asked her as he struggled to catch his breath. There was oxygen, but it was thin. Jax looked at Blackburne, who was in distress as well.

Kiara had her eyes closed as she struggled to breathe, maintain their protection, and sense what lay behind the door. Elvis quietly huffed in her ear, and she nodded. Opening her eyes, her look intense and focused, she glanced at Jax and then at the door.

"There are two hostiles inside to the right, two more up the stairs to the left. There are several more with hostages in the next room, in case we get past the first four. There are two more down in the caverns with hostages."

"Blackburne, you take the two on the stairs, I'll get the two to the right. Kiara, you and Elvis, disable the ones holding the hostages." Jax gave out his instructions in a now steady voice. "Yell out if you need help or find more hostiles."

They all nodded and prepared to enter. Kiara took a deep breath, strengthening her protection around the group. Jax popped the door with his baton and shot in low and to the right. His cloak billowing behind him, he had the two hostiles to the right unconscious before Blackburne had even cleared the doorway. With Kiara's direction on the location of the other two, Blackburne had his weapon pointed up and to the left as he jumped through the doorway. The two on the stairs hit the ground shortly after the two on the right.

Kiara was heading through the doorway directly across from the entrance, and the sound of falling bodies behind her followed her into the room. She took in the room dynamics in an instant. The Lamoranites, short, stocky, robust-looking men with abundant facial hair, were being used as shields for the hostiles behind them. Two of the hostiles, seeing a woman enter the woman, started laughing. The third, however, seemed to realize who she was. A look of horror crossed his face, and he tried to hide behind the Lamoranites a bit more. He nervously looked at the other two, but they were too busy laughing in their overconfidence.

"Who the hell are you?" One of the hostiles yelled at Kiara, spit flying out of his mouth.

Kiara didn't want to put anyone else in danger, so she didn't think his question was worth answering. Her right hand flew up, and like an old-time western movie, she shot three quick energy pulses out. She shot them with such precision; her energy pulses hit each of the hostiles in the head, knocking them back about six feet—even the one who was trying harder to hide.

The Lamoranites jumped forward to put distance between them and their captors. One cautiously approached Kiara.

"Thank you," he said, hesitantly. Kiara could tell that he was trying to speak her language.

She nodded at him as Jax and Blackburne walked into the room, Jax dragging the two that he had taken out with his baton.

The Lamoranites, who had been approaching Kiara, now backed up at the site of Blackburne and Jax.

"They are with me," Kiara hurriedly assured them. "We are here to help."

The Lamoranites still looked at Jax and Blackburne cautiously, and the one who had approached Kiara first approached her again.

"How? We could not send a distress."

Kiara wasn't sure how to answer that. She looked at Jax, then back at the Lamoranite. "It is hard to explain," she said slowly.

"You are," he struggled to find the right word.

"Guardian!" One of the other Lamoranites exclaimed excitedly. "You are Trandor!"

Kiara's eyebrows shot up in surprise. "How do you know that?" As far as she could remember, she hadn't been on this planet or its moons, and she didn't remember meeting a Lamoranite before.

"We know you help others," the Lamoranite told her. "Then, when these," he gestured to some of the men on the floor, "show up, they say they do not want the Guardian here."

Before Kiara could answer, he excitedly turned to the others, telling them something in a language that sounded like tapping. The other Lamoranites looked between the one talking and Kiara, excitement growing on their faces.

The one who had been talking turned back to Kiara. "I am Kurn." He bowed low at the waist. "We are honored."

Kiara, unsure exactly how to proceed, decided to bow and murmured a thank you, Elvis holding her braid and chirping quietly. She could tell how hard it was for Kurn to get the words right, but she knew it was important to him. When she straightened, the Lamoranites looked happy, so she supposed she did the right thing.

"Kurn, I sensed two more holding your people in the caverns," Kiara said.

Kurn nodded. "Can you help?"

"Of course," Jax said with a nod. "You will watch these?" Jax pointed to the men on the floor.

Kurn directed a couple of the other Lamoranites to handle the men on the floor, then asked Jax and Kiara to follow him. Blackburne nodded at Jax to let him know he would stay behind.

Kurn took them through the building and down a narrow flight of stone steps. As they approached the bottom step, Kiara could hear shouting echoing off the cavern walls. Kiara touched Kurn's shoulder, asking him to hold.

"I will go first," she whispered to Jax.

Jax nodded, but Kurn looked concerned, even though he had just seen her take care of the hostiles up above. Kiara tried not to roll her eyes. She remembered reading that the Lamoranites were a patriarchal society.

Kiara put up a protection field and stepped into the cavern. The light from the stairs didn't reach into the cavern, and she didn't have a light. She could hear the shouting ahead of her, but couldn't see anyone.

Before she could ask, Elvis touched her cheek. He was still on her back, holding her braid, his back feet planted against her shoulder blades. She knew this was his favored battle position.

Closing her eyes, Kiara reached out her mind and brought in the layout of the caverns and tunnels. The group she was looking for was ahead, through two smaller tunnels, and off to the right. They were being held in a larger cavern. She could also see several other Lamoranites in a cavern behind her. They appeared to be readying for an attack to rescue their comrades.

She turned back to the stairs. "Kurn, several of your comrades are down that way," Kiara pointed behind her, "and appear to be ready to mount an attack. Please hold them off for now."

Kurn opened his mouth to say something, but the yelling coming from the hostage area had him instead, hustling down to stop his comrades.

Jax nodded at Kiara, so she turned, closed her eyes, and headed to the hostages.

"Ready, little man?" Kiara whispered. Elvis clenched his feet in response.

Kiara picked up speed through the second tunnel and shot into the cavern where the Lamoranites were being held. She completed a front flip over two Lamoranites, extending her leg and connecting with one of the hostages, sending him flying. The other hostage taker, fumbling with his weapon after being startled by the attack, didn't stand a chance. Kiara hit him with a roundhouse kick that sent him flying one way, his weapon the other way.

The Lamoranites, recognizing the opportunity to subdue the hostiles, jumped into action, with several sitting on the men, and others picking up the weapons. They clicked at her, in their language, and several bowed to her.

"Is everyone okay?" Kiara asked, not sure if they would understand her. From the blank looks she received, she supposed they didn't.

Kiara sensed Jax coming in behind her and quickly threw a protection field around him. She was glad she did when, as he entered, one of the Lamoranites panicked and shot at him. Jax looked startled for a second before nodding at Kiara.

Kiara put her hands out in a placating gesture, but the Lamoranites were still looking angrily at Jax. Kiara walked back to Jax and put her arms around him. It was the right move, as all the weapons were lowered.

Kurn soon joined them with the other Lamoranites from the back cavern. He tapped and spoke to the ones in front of Kiara, then turned to her.

"We are grateful for your help," Kurn told her. "And Tonga would like to apologize for shooting your friend."

Kiara turned to look at Jax to make sure he knew they had apologized.

Jax bowed to the Lamoranites.

Kurn escorted Kiara and Jax back to the surface building, where Blackburne was anxiously waiting.

"We are good," Jax told him.

Blackburne nodded.

"Kurn, do you know why they were here?" Kiara asked, pointing to the men on the floor.

Kurn nodded. "They want," he paused as he struggled for the right word. "They want important rock."

The image of the stone shot into Kiara's head, and Elvis screeched on her shoulder. All the Lamoranites jumped at the screech, and a couple of them made angry tapping noises back at Elvis.

Kiara looked at Jax, her face filled with distress. Jax moved slowly forward, his com unit in his hand. He showed Kurn the pictures of the stone Kiara had found, both the rough and the smooth images.

Kurn studied the images for a moment. "Yes." He looked at Kiara. "You are afraid?"

"It has power that can hurt me," Kiara said quietly.

Kurn nodded again. He turned to the other Lamoranites, and a lengthy discussion proceeded—lots of tapping noises, a few grunts, and even a few stomping feet.

Kurn finally turned back to Jax and Kiara. "We take these," he said as he gestured to the men on the floor.

"Do you have someplace we can put them?" Kiara looked around the room, not sure where they could put them. "Also, what happens to them after that?" Her worry, as Jax would understand, was that if GTA sent them, then calling the authorities wouldn't exactly help.

Kurn nodded again as a couple of the Lamoranites left the room and came back in with a small hoverlift. They made quick work of the men, the stocky bodies of the Lamoranites easily moving them.

"Is that all of them? Are there more in the mines?"

"This is all," Kurn said. He gave a signal, and the Lamoranites moved the hoverlift out of the room. "We have security," Kurn said as he watched the others leave the room. "They will take them." Blackburne followed the others out of the room to make sure that the Lamoranites stayed safe.

Kurn turned back to Kiara and Jax. "We are thankful."

Jax bowed to Kurn. "Kiara had sensed you were in trouble, and at first, we could not understand why she would sense your trouble. Now we know it has to do with the stone." Jax looked worriedly at Kurn. "Did they find it?"

Kurn shook his head. "They do not have stone."

Kiara and Jax let out the collective breath they had been holding.

"They hear stories about the stone is here, so they came." Kurn shook his head again. "We say, no stone, but they are angry, and yell. They hold my brothers, and tell us find it, or they hurt us." The anguish in Kurn's voice came through, even though he wasn't speaking in his native language.

Kurn looked straight at Kiara. "This stone can hurt you?"

Kiara nodded. "I encountered one that was similar, and it nearly destroyed us." Kiara reached up and touched Elvis. He had been very quiet since he had screeched.

Kurn eyeballed Elvis. "What is this?" He gestured at the little drayek.

"He's a drayek," Kiara told him. She attempted to explain how they were bonded, but because of the language barrier, Kurn didn't understand what she meant. Finally, after trying to explain it in different ways, Kurn seemed to understand. Kiara explained what happened when the stone took over. The concern on Kurn's face showed that he understood that part.

"We do not have 'bonding', we have –," again, at a loss for words, Kurn firmly grasped both of his hands together, showing it to Kiara and Jax.

Kiara nodded, assuming he meant they had something like a brotherhood.

"We do not let stone hurt you," Kurn said emphatically. "Where is stone?"

"We believe the GTA has it," Kiara said quietly.

Kurn looked confused. "This is good?"

Kiara shook her head. "It still has the power to hurt me. My ancestor has told me that I must destroy it."

Kurn looked concerned. "How you do this?"

Kiara let out a little laugh. "We haven't figured that part out yet. We have to find it, then destroy it."

Kurn nodded, his expression thoughtful.

A few of the Lamoranites came back in, followed by Blackburne.

"Their security has them, so the mine is safe again," Blackburne said.

Kurn joined his fellow miners, and Kiara could hear their tapping and grunting as they held a discussion on the other side of the room.

"They were very grateful for our help," Blackburne said. "Most of them can't speak anything but the tapping noises, but the ones that could kept saying 'Thank you', over and over. They thought they were going to be killed."

Kurn returned to the group. "We want to help you, to repay."

Kiara started to tell him that that wasn't necessary, but Kurn shook his head.

"We have stone they want."

"What?!" Jax yelled into the quiet.

Kurn nodded. "We have, but we knew, do not give to them. We hide. It will help you."

"Help me?" Kiara squeaked out. Elvis, on her shoulder, let out a loud hiss.

Kurn looked distressed. He could clearly sense the fear and anger in the room. It suddenly dawned on him that they didn't understand what he was trying to tell them.

"Wait, please," he implored Kiara.

Kiara, her breathing fast and shallow, struggled to control her panic. Images of the stone were suddenly front and center in her mind, and she fought to beat it back. Elvis touched her face, and Jax touched her shoulder. Kiara swallowed hard and forced the image from her mind. Her breathing still a little fast, she focused her gaze back on Kurn.

"I am sorry," Kurn quickly apologized. "I do not mean distress." He looked from Kiara to Jax. "We want you," Kurn paused as he thought of the correct words. "Use stone to practice destroy."

Kiara hitched a breath in. Could they do that? Could she practice on the stone that was here?

Kurn's expression turned hopeful. "Yes? You try?"

Jax stepped forward, as Kiara let out the breath she had been holding. "I do not think we can take the risk of her failing," Jax said worriedly. "This new stone may take her over as well."

Kurn shook his head. "We can destroy stone, we know this. We do not help your GTA stone, but Guardian try, here."

Jax looked at Kiara. "It is your choice."

Kiara closed her eyes. Ever since Mirona had told her that she had to destroy the stone, she had worried about how she would do it. She worried that once she saw it again, it would just take her over, and she wouldn't even get a chance. She also worried that even if that didn't happen, she wouldn't be powerful enough to destroy it. Perhaps this was the answer to all of that.

Opening her eyes, she directed her gaze to Kurn. "We should try to destroy the stone. But first, can you tell me how you were going to destroy it?"

Kurn was relieved. "Yes, yes!" He was nearly jumping in his excitement and relief. Kurn brought up his com unit, showing Kiara and Jax the frequency and amplitude to use against the stone. "We put web on stone and destroy." Kurn showed them the webbing. It was wirelessly connected to a controller.

"Can you attach the webbing before Kiara comes near the stone?" Jax was trying to make this experiment as safe as possible.

Before Kurn could answer, Kiara jumped in. "How do you know how to do this?" She looked over at Jax. "We had a difficult time finding any information about the stones, so how do you know about them and how to destroy them?" She was trying not to sound accusatory, but it seemed suspicious to her.

Kurn was not the least bit offended. Nodding, he responded to her. "We found one many times ago," he said in his attempt to speak in their language. "We thought, good money."

"What changed?" Kiara prompted when Kurn didn't immediately continue.

"One of elders say danger. We looked." Kurn gestured to his com unit. "We see," Kurn said as he pointed at Jax. "We do not want danger. We do not want death." Kurn looked at Kiara. "We try many times to destroy. We hit, we –," he made a gesture like an explosion. "Nothing destroy. Until this," he pointed at the webbing.

"How many have you destroyed?" Jax wanted to know.

"We destroy two. The second one, fast, we knew how."

Kiara let out a sigh of relief.

"Perhaps we can use the webbing on the one at the GTA?" Jax asked.

Kiara shook her head. "Mirona was emphatic that I must destroy it, with my powers, or the stone's influence will stay with me."

Jax looked disappointed but resigned.

Kurn gestured to the doorway. "We can try now, or wait."

Kiara looked thoughtful for a moment. Jax thought she might want to wait, but instead, she surprised him.

"Let me talk to Cory first." At the quizzical look from Jax, she shrugged. "I think he can help me think through a strategy, based on Kurn's information."

Kiara moved to the side and contacted Cory. She explained the situation and sent him the frequency and amplitude information from Kurn. As she hoped, Cory had ideas for focusing her power to destroy the stone. They discussed back and forth for a few minutes until Kiara felt comfortable enough with the information to disconnect from Cory and join Kurn and Jax.

"Ready?" Jax asked.

Kiara nodded but turned to Kurn. "We need to try without the webbing."

"No!" Jax was emphatic. Elvis screeched at his shout.

Kurn looked startled.

"Hear me out," Kiara said soothingly. "Kurn can be close by with the webbing, if needed, but Cory thought that having the webbing would give me an advantage here, and we won't have it when we find the other stone."

Jax sighed. Of course, she was right. "We need to protect Kurn, in case the stone starts to influence you."

Kurn looked startled by Jax's statement. Blackburne stepped forward. "You protect Kiara, I will protect Kurn."

Jax nodded and got a nod from Kurn. They followed Kurn to another room, where the stone was sitting on a small table. Clear panels were set around the table; Jax assumed they were there to contain the blast when the stone was destroyed. Blackburne shadowed Kurn as they entered. Jax stayed slightly behind Kiara, his baton at the ready. Jax, using his limited empathic abilities, did his best to monitor Kiara as they entered.

At first, he felt nothing from her. He felt Elvis's worry, understandably so. He realized, as he shifted forward, that Kiara's eyes were closed. He waited to see if she would open them, then realized she didn't need to open her eyes to accomplish the task, which probably reduced her risk. Jax nodded at Kurn and Blackburne to let them know that she was good.

Kurn shifted his weight, bringing the webbing up in front of him. He had handed the controller to Blackburne so that once he threw the webbing, Blackburne could immediately start the destruction process.

Taking a deep breath, Kiara focused on the energy she felt in front of her. The stone. She could feel the energy, but no influence. Focusing on the energy in front of her, pushing all thoughts of the first stone from her mind, she did some deep breathing and began to focus her energy. She could feel Elvis's energy as she focused and did as Cory had suggested. She pictured the frequency and amplitude as Kurn had shown them and pictured wrapping it around the stone like the webbing.

Jax watched her hair start to float, her breathing deep and even. The skin on her face turned a deeper blue, and he knew that if he could see her eyes, they would be a deep purple. He felt no stone influence, but he could *feel* the power in the room. It was almost a deep hum. He looked at Kurn, awe and respect in the Lamoranite's gaze.

Kiara pictured the stone and, wrapping her power around it, she increased her energy. Her hands rose toward the stone, palms outward. Elvis clenched her shoulder, his small front feet touching her face, his nose pressed against her cheek. Kiara channeled the extra power from Elvis and pushed it to the stone.

At first, she thought she wouldn't be able to do it, then she heard Kurn.

"Yes! Yes!"

Kiara took that affirmation and pushed every last bit of her power.

The humming in the room grew louder, and Jax could see the edges of the stone blur as the vibrations affected it. The hum rose sharply, and Jax found himself squinting and bracing for the final destruction. It happened with a loud crack and a massive pulse of energy that pushed him back a couple of steps. He steadied himself and made sure that Kiara was okay.

Kiara was swaying slightly, and Jax knew it was from the energy she had just used. He found a chair, quickly brought it over, and let her collapse into it. Kiara opened her eyes, assuring Jax that she was okay. Elvis was stroking her hair and making soft chirping sounds. Jax patted the little guy's head and turned to see if Kurn and Blackburne were okay as well. Blackburne was standing behind a broadly smiling Kurn, so Jax assumed they were doing fine. He looked at the table where the stone had been and stopped. There was nothing there—no rock fragments, no dirt, no sand, nothing. The table was shattered into pieces on the floor.

"What happened to it?"

Kurn came forward. "It is gone."

"But how can that be?" Jax was looking around suspiciously.

"It has energy," Kurn explained. "Too much energy. The webbing, or Guardian," Kurn gestured to Kiara, "no place for energy to go."

Jax nodded. "The energy turns on itself?"

"Yes!" Kurn exclaimed.

Jax turned back to Kiara. She was looking a little steadier. He squatted down in front of her, ready to ask her if she could tell if the stone was really gone.

Kiara anticipated him. "I can't sense it at all. I've tried, multiple times."

Kurn came forward, bowing low before Kiara and Jax. "The stone is gone. We use—," Kurn motioned to some equipment in the room, "but no stone, no energy. We try with second stone. We could see energy—" he was once again at a loss for words and instead demonstrated with his hands the squeezing of space.

"It imploded?" Jax filled in.

Kurn thought for a moment and then nodded enthusiastically.

Jax helped Kiara up, and they headed back out to the front of the building.

"I need to get Kiara to the Acadia, get her some supplements," Jax said quietly.

Kiara was trying to be strong, but she felt like her knees were going to buckle at any moment.

"You go, you go," Kurn hurriedly assured them. "You help us, and we are forever in your debt." He smiled as he said it, and Kiara smiled back. Kurn bowed low and handed Kiara a small silver-and-blue amulet.

"You heard that somewhere, didn't you?" Kiara said quietly. He said it too perfectly.

Kurn smiled sheepishly. "Yes."

Kiara graciously accepted the small token. "I am forever in your debt," she whispered back to Kurn.

Jax and Blackburne helped Kiara to the ship, and Jax got her settled with food and supplements. Elvis curled up close to her. Jax was cradling her in the bunk, making sure she was taken care of.

Kiara knew she was going to fall asleep quickly. Her eyelids were already trying to close. "Jax, wake me if there is trouble at the transgate."

When he hesitated, she snapped her eyes open and grabbed his hand. "Promise!"

Jax nodded and let her fall back as the Acadia's engines rumbled to life. He would only wake her in a dire emergency.

Chapter 12

Kiara wanted to stay asleep, comfortable in her bunk, but finally forced herself to get moving. Elvis was sprawled out on her chest, snoring quietly. She struggled to a sitting position, waking up Elvis as she did. Elvis rumbled at her and moved to the bed. Kiara swung her legs to the side and shook her head. Images of stones, old and new, were still swimming in her head. She hoped it was just a leftover from their adventures, and not a foreshadowing.

Slowly standing up, Kiara felt a wave of dizziness wash over her, and she plopped back down on the bed. Elvis immediately jumped into her lap and peered into her face, trying to judge what was wrong. Kiara blinked a couple of times, trying to clear her mind and stop the room from spinning. Elvis placed his paws on both sides of her face and touched his forehead to hers. She could feel a steadying energy coming from him, and taking a couple of deep breaths, felt her head clear.

"Thanks, little man," Kiara whispered.

Slowly standing again, she was relieved to feel steady on her feet. Looking at the side of her bunk, she could see that Jax had left her some supplements and gel, and a short note.

You're beautiful when you sleep. Take your supplements. -J

Kiara smiled and grabbed the supplements. Looking at her com unit, she checked the ship's location. From their position, she could tell that they had already passed through the transgate and were on their route to Earth Delta Nine. She didn't know if she should be relieved or angry that Jax hadn't woken her up. In the end, knowing how tired she had been, she was relieved.

On Earth Delta Nine, the Director's com unit signaled a high-priority, encrypted message. The first part of the message contained the news about Talia. Rend was bringing her to Earth Delta Nine. Rend described Talia's power as 'raw' and 'uncontrolled'. The Director quickly sent a message to Rend, asking him to find someone to train her. She would be of no use to him in her current state.

The second part of the message had him frowning. His people watching the stone reported that it periodically changed from a rough exterior to a smooth one. When it was first delivered to Earth Delta Nine, it had a rough exterior and remained that way until now. Even when his Galdorian contact had informed him that the Trandorian had tried to rid herself of the stone's influence, the stone hadn't changed.

The Director arranged a meeting with his Galdorian contact. He needed to know what was going on with the stone. He was relieved when the Galdorian agreed to meet right away.

They met in their usual place in the park. The Director quickly relayed what he knew about the stone's behavior. To his surprise, the Galdorian just chuckled.

"She thought she had rid herself of the stone's influence, but she failed. It will mean her death."

"What do you mean?" The Director quietly asked.

"The stone's influence is coming back stronger; it is why the stone is changing. The stone's power is building slowly, but in such a way that she will not be able to defend against it. When this happens, she will go insane before taking her own life, and those who are with her. This is the stone's purpose." The Galdorian slowly stood, his laugh taking on an evil tone.

As the Galdorian walked away, the Director could hear him swearing and cursing Kiara and all Trandorians. The Director had picked the right man. He needed someone with that much hatred to see this through.

On the Acadia, Kiara headed slowly to the kitchen area. She was still feeling sluggish and hoped some food and supplements would help. Even Elvis appeared to be tired. Kiara fleetingly thought she should be alarmed, but was just too tired to follow through.

Grabbing some fruit for Elvis, she looked listlessly at the rations for the crew. Finally, after deciding on a small protein bar, she sat at the small table and ate it without really tasting it. When Elvis was finished, she headed back to her bunk, almost without thinking. Her mind seemed to be devoid of all thought. Once she was back in her room, she found herself standing in front of the small mirror on the wall. She blinked as if she were coming out of a trance. She had no memory of walking back into her room.

Elvis climbed down her arm and hopped over to the bed. He dug around in the bedding for a moment, then flopped down with a sigh.

Kiara was staring at her reflection but not really seeing it. When her eyes met her reflection's eyes, the room behind her seemed to fade away, and it was just her and her reflection.

"You are a failure." Kiara's reflection quietly sneered at her.

Kiara blinked, but her reflection's eyes stayed open and steady.

"I'm not a failure," Kiara whispered back. A small part of her brain acknowledged that her reflection's mouth didn't move either.

"You are a failure, but you already knew that," her reflection said again. The eyes in her reflection turned black, the face contorted in rage. "You are worthless, you are not helping anyone!"

"No," Kiara whispered back, but she was beginning to doubt herself. Because of the stone, she hadn't been able to help as she should have. It was her fault that the stone had influenced her. It was her fault that everyone around her had to stop what they were doing and take her to the Trandorian colony for the ceremony.

Kiara's reflection laughed at her. "Because of your failures, everyone is in danger. They are better off without you."

Kiara held back a sob. Because she wasn't strong enough, she had put everyone in danger. Maybe they were better off without her.

"Kiara?" Jax had been walking by her room when he'd heard whispering. Kiara's door was open, and looking into the room, he saw her standing in front of her mirror, her face looking impossibly sad.

When she didn't answer him right away, he stepped into the room and immediately noticed that her eyes looked glassy. Alarmed, he reached out to touch her, and as he did, he saw her reflection in the mirror. He stopped in horror. That wasn't her in the mirror. A distorted figure, with black eyes and a twisted face, stared back at Kiara. What sort of magic was this? Was Kiara doing this? Should he shock Kiara with his baton, or shake her? He turned to look at Elvis on the bed, but the little drayek appeared to be peacefully sleeping. He didn't understand this at all.

He sent a quick code red alert to Blackburne and decided that shocking her with the baton would be the best option. He heard racing footsteps in the hall as Blackburne hurried toward them. As soon as Blackburne entered the room, Jax popped out his baton, took a quick look back at the ship's captain, and touched Kiara's shoulder. Blackburne's expression probably mirrored his own.

As soon as the baton touched Kiara's shoulder, she collapsed. The reflection, however, howled and screamed. Jax caught Kiara, and Blackburne intercepted Elvis as he shot off the bed and made a beeline for Kiara. Elvis, in Blackburne's arms, reached for Kiara. As he did so, he must have caught sight of the reflection, which was still screaming in anger and what sounded like pain.

Elvis hissed and let out his own screech.

The reflection finally faded, along with the sound. Elvis was still hissing and baring his teeth at the mirror. He would stop for a moment, touch Kiara's arm, then turn back to the mirror to hiss.

Blackburne and Jax, now on the floor with Kiara, exchanged a look over her head.

"What was that?" Blackburne whispered.

"If I had to guess, I would assume it is something that Kiara created with her powers," Jax whispered back. He looked at Kiara. "I would also assume that it means the stone's influence has returned."

Before Blackburne could respond to that alarming statement, Kiara's eyelids fluttered, and she moaned out a long, drawn-out 'nooooo'.

Elvis wiggled out of Blackburne's grasp and gently jumped onto Kiara's chest. He held her face, peering into her eyes. He was making little chirping noises and turned his concerned face toward Jax.

Jax nodded. "I know, little man, I know."

Kiara raised her arms to hold Elvis and immediately felt pain where Jax had touched his baton.

"Did you shock me again?!"

Jax sighed. Her indignant shout relieved him. She was back to normal, at least for now. "What do you remember?" He asked her. He would not apologize for using his baton.

With help from Jax, Kiara moved to the side of her bed and sat down heavily. She scrubbed at her face, trying to clear the cobwebs.

"My reflection was talking back to me," she finally whispered, her head still down. "It's the stone, isn't it?"

"I believe it is," Jax confirmed her fear.

"This is so different than last time." Kiara shook her head. "I didn't even feel its influence."

Blackburne hovered in the doorway, his frown severe enough to scorch the floor. "What did the reflection say to you?"

Kiara looked down, ashamed to say anything. The reflection had been right about one thing. She was putting everyone in danger, again.

"Kiara," Jax gently prodded her. "Tell us what the reflection said." When she still didn't answer, he bent his head closer to hers. "I can feel what you are feeling."

When Kiara closed her eyes, a single tear squeezed out. She could feel support coming from Jax and Elvis, and it helped to push back the shame.

Jax grasped her hand, giving it a quick squeeze. He could feel the tide turning in those negative emotions. He reached up and wiped the tear tracking down her cheek.

"That reflection kept telling me how worthless I was, and how I was putting everyone in danger." She let out a tiny sob. "It said I wasn't good enough to protect those around me."

Kiara turned a tearful face to Jax and then Blackburne. "I never wanted anyone to get hurt."

Jax immediately pulled her into his arms and tried to send her feelings of strength and comfort.

"We are a team," Jax whispered. "You are saving and helping people, not putting others in danger."

"We are a team," Blackburne said emphatically.

Kiara took a deep, cleansing breath, the negative feelings slowly flowing out of her. She could finally tell that those feelings weren't hers.

She pulled back a little from Jax. "It's frightening how easily that reflection had me doubting myself."

"This must be the next tactic that it takes. Destroy from within," Blackburne said with a scowl. "It won't work! You are a valued member of this team, and we will do whatever it takes to keep you safe!" He pounded his fist into his other hand for emphasis.

Kiara sent him a watery smile and pulled Elvis close. "The problem is, if it attacks me this way again, I don't seem to have a defense for it. I was completely sucked into the story it was weaving."

"I know you don't want to hear this, but we won't be able to leave you alone until the stone is destroyed."

Kiara sighed. "I won't lie, having someone shadow me constantly is not my favorite way to spend my time, but after what just happened to me, I would welcome it."

Frankie cleared his throat noisily from the doorway. When everyone turned to look at him, he quickly informed them that they were nearing the next transgate. He also quietly said he would gladly take a turn keeping an eye on Kiara.

Blackburne nodded at Frankie. "Are we still broadcasting the fake transponder signal?"

Frankie nodded.

"Have we received any questions about it?" Blackburne asked.

Frankie shook his head and proceeded back to the bridge.

"I should help scan the transgate," Kiara said while she slowly stood up.

"I think we can handle the transgate this time," Jax said, trying to push her back down to the bed.

"I need to feel useful, and not like a burden," Kiara said, and pushed Jax back with a quick pulse of energy.

Jax nodded, following her closely to the bridge. Kiara tried hard not to be annoyed, but it wasn't easy. She turned to say something to Frankie, and instead, bumped into Jax.

Kiara sighed, Elvis chirped, and Jax looked unapologetic.

"I know you want to keep an eye on me, but I should at least have enough room to breathe," Kiara muttered at Jax.

Jax backed up a half step.

Kiara sighed again and turned toward Frankie. "The transgate looks clear."

"Agreed," Frankie said, his bright blue shirt in contrast to his somber reply. He looked to Blackburne for the signal to move through the transgate. Blackburne nodded.

Kiara turned back to her console, scanning for threats and monitoring communications. As she sat there, it dawned on her that she was, once again, heading to Earth Delta Nine for a big battle. What did her dad call that? She frowned slightly as she tried to figure out the right word.

"What's wrong?" Jax asked, scanning her face and using his limited abilities to check her mental state.

"What?" Kiara looked up at Jax. "Nothing is wrong."

Jax didn't look convinced and continued to study her face.

Kiara turned back to her console and suddenly blurted out, "Déjà vu!"

Jax jumped back, and Elvis jumped from her lap to her shoulder, as if he was looking for someone named déjà vu.

"Who the hell is déjà vu?" Jax yelled and looked around the bridge, as if he too was looking for someone by that name."

Frankie and Blackburne looked confused.

Kiara looked around the bridge and started laughing. Talk about a language barrier!

"Déjà vu, Jax. It means that you feel like you've already done this before." Jax and Elvis relaxed slightly. "I was trying to remember what my dad called it."

Frankie let out a snort, which sent Kiara into another laughing fit. The mood, as they entered the transgate, was a little more relaxed.

Kiara studied her console and realized that this transgate was one of the unusual ones. Because they were avoiding the usual, busy routes, they ended up taking the less-traveled, sometimes more dangerous transgates.

"Frankie, transfer some of the shield energy to the starboard side of the ship. The forces in this transgate aren't symmetrical."

Frankie nodded his acknowledgement, and Kiara watched the stats for the ship shift slightly.

Kiara's eyes shifted slightly to the left, and she could see her reflection in the shiny console. Before she could shift her eyes away, her reflection began to twist and distort.

"Jaaaaxxxx!" Kiara wasn't sure that she said his name, because the reflection was still just sneering at her.

Jax grabbed her face and turned her to look at him. Kiara felt herself snap to the present, and the reflection's hold on her was broken. She let out a breath, her eyes locking onto Jax's eyes instead.

Jax watched the focus come back into her eyes and let out the breath he had been holding. Elvis was on Kiara's shoulder, trying to cradle both of their heads at the same time, and making little chirping noises. Jax steeled himself and looked over at the console, expecting to see that scary, sneering version of Kiara in the reflection. He saw nothing but the console.

"Is it gone?" Kiara whispered.

Jax nodded.

"Everything okay?" Blackburne's voice interrupted them.

Kiara snuck a quick look at her console, relieved to see it was blank for her, too. She turned to look at Blackburne and gave a quick nod.

"Kiara, I need some help here." Frankie's calm, pilot-like voice interrupted all of them.

Kiara shot down into her chair, just as the ship began to vibrate and shake.

"What's going on?" Blackburne demanded.

"The stresses in this transgate are changing too fast for me to compensate," Frankie responded, his voice still calm.

Kiara checked her scans and frowned. She couldn't see anything that could be causing their current problems. She'd had Frankie compensate for the asymmetrical stresses of the transgate, and she could see that those settings were still in place.

The shaking grew into actual bucking, and Kiara could tell from her console that every move that Frankie made to compensate only lasted a few seconds before the ship began to jerk and shake again. Blackburne and Jax buckled themselves in, and Elvis latched onto Kiara's shoulder with a painful grip.

Kiara's fingers flew over the console, trying to narrow down the problem, but it eluded her.

"The shields aren't going to hold us together much longer," Frankie quietly informed them. "I see failures in the cargo bay and near the engine compartment." Frankie's voice was quiet, but Kiara could hear a hint of panic.

Kiara was getting nowhere with her console. She closed her eyes, touched her fingers to Elvis' toes, and searched for the reason they were coming apart. At the same time, she expanded a shield around the entire ship. She heard a quick 'whew' from Frankie when the ship's integrity stabilized.

Kiara searched the wormhole and found instability along the entire path. The wormhole was falling apart, and she could tell it was only a matter of time before the instability destroyed everything in the path, including them and both transgate entrances. She'd never had to bail out of a wormhole before, and the stories she'd heard had always ended in total destruction and death for those inside.

"The wormhole is coming apart!" Kiara yelled over the increasing groaning and banging from the ship. "We're going to have to bail out!"

"No!" Blackburne yelled. He knew the stories as well.

"We have to!" Kiara yelled back. "I can't protect us if the wormhole falls apart with us in it!" With her eyes still closed, she turned to yell at Frankie. "I'm sending you the bailout point, Frankie! Don't miss it!'

"Got it!" Frankie yelled.

Alarms started going off, and several consoles around the bridge shorted out, plunging the bridge into near total darkness.

"I've lost power!" Frankie yelled. "I can't steer us into the bailout point! Engines are failing!"

The ship tilted, and the artificial gravity began to fail. Thankfully, Kiara had strapped herself in, but Elvis was struggling to hold onto her shoulder. She had to get them safely out of the wormhole, or they were all going to die. In her mind, she pinpointed the bailout point, which was coming up fast. The ship was making so much noise that even if the others on the bridge were trying to communicate with her, she didn't think she'd hear them. Pushing everything out of her mind except the bailout point and keeping a shield around the ship, she used her energy to push the ship out of the wormhole. Cracking, explosions, and thunderous noises she couldn't identify assaulted her. She grabbed Elvis with both hands and wrapped them in a secondary bubble.

271

It all happened so fast; there was no time to think about whether they would survive. She just did everything she could to keep them safe. She used all her energy, blacking out before the ship cleared the wormhole.

Kiara woke to the sound of fire suppression systems going off. Her secondary energy bubble was still intact, but Elvis was unconscious. The forces exerted on them and the ship were too much for everyone. She couldn't hear anyone else and quickly touched Elvis' face to check him. He was breathing and didn't appear to be hurt. She pulled her hand away and realized that they were floating in what remained of the bridge. Emergency lights had come on, but there was smoke and debris everywhere. The artificial gravity was still offline. Closing her eyes, she searched out Jax, found him alive, but the oxygen level in the bridge was dangerously low.

She found the rest of the crew in a similar state and quickly enveloped the ship in a weak forcefield. Her energy was low, and she didn't know how long she could keep the ship safe. She moved her and Elvis to her console and quickly worked on trying to restore power and shields. The engine appeared intact, and with her energy, she was able to restore connections. She gave the engine a quick shot of power to jumpstart it. To her relief, the engine rumbled to life, restoring power to the bridge. She quickly activated the ship's force fields, stabilizing the oxygen levels.

Kiara dropped her bubble, landing with a soft thump on the floor of the bridge. The artificial gravity had kicked in as well. She gently placed Elvis in her seat and went to check on the others. Jax was starting to sit up when she reached him.

"Are you hurt?" Kiara asked as she helped move debris off him.

"I am only bruised," Jax said with relief. "Are you hurt?" he quickly asked her, trying to judge for himself as he looked her over. "Where is Elvis? Is he hurt?"

"Elvis is unconscious, but unhurt, as far as I can tell." Kiara helped Jax into an unbroken seat. "I need to check the others."

Jax stood, only a little wobbly, and headed for the seat Blackburne had been occupying. Kiara headed for Frankie. Both had only minor injuries; Blackburne seemed to have the worst, with a possible dislocated shoulder.

"Have you checked on Curly and Cory?" Blackburne gritted out. His shoulder was starting to throb.

"Heading that way now," Kiara said. As she reached the doorway of the bridge, she sensed Elvis waking up. She turned to look at him and watched him stand up and shake his body, as if to shake off the effects of the accident. He saw Kiara across the bridge and made a beeline for her, jumping across the floor and up her arm to sit on her shoulder. He cupped her face with his front paws, chirping and warbling at her.

"I'm okay," she whispered to him. "Let's go check on Curly and her little drayek." Elvis chirped his agreement. As she headed out, she could hear Blackburne barking orders to check the ship's status and make sure they weren't in any danger where they were sitting.

Kiara found Curly in the front of the cargo area. Curly had strapped herself against the wall but appeared to be unconscious. Her little drayek was holding onto Curly's shoulder and chirping at her. Kiara was relieved to see that the little drayek appeared unhurt. Kiara didn't see any obvious signs of injury to Curly, so she approached her friend slowly to see if she could rouse her.

"Curly?" Kiara softly spoke her friend's name and gently touched Curly's arm. Bendanites were notorious for being very grumpy when they were abruptly woken up, so Kiara was staying alert.

Curly came awake with a start and a roar. When she saw Kiara, she snapped her mouth shut and blinked a couple of times. She looked from Kiara to Elvis and back to Kiara. Her head swung to the side to find her little drayek, and Kiara could see her relief that the little one was okay.

"You are okay?" Curly asked Kiara, her expression full of concern. When Kiara nodded, Curly quickly asked about the others.

"They are okay, just some minor injuries." Kiara worked on getting Curly out of the straps. "Are you hurt?"

Curly closed her eyes and pointed at her midsection. Kiara gently patted her arm.

"The straps probably broke your ribs. Let's get you to the med-bay and get you fixed up."

"I go," Curly said. "Go help Cory."

Kiara nodded and headed to Cory's bunk. She had sensed that he was alive, but he'd been unconscious, so Kiara had no idea how badly he might be hurt.

She reached his bunk, and at first, she didn't see him. There was so much debris from all of his equipment and pieces of the cabin on the floor. He wasn't in his bunk.

"Elvis, do you see him?" Kiara asked the little drayek.

Elvis chirped, jumped from her shoulder, and shot down to the pile on her right. Burrowing his snout into the debris, he made another chirping noise.

"Found him, did you?" Closing her eyes, she determined she had enough energy left to move the debris with her powers. Poor Cory was buried under several feet of debris. Once she had him freed, she checked for a pulse. He had one, but his breathing was shallow and labored, and Kiara could see blood. She pulled out her com unit, signaling Jax that she needed help moving Cory to the med-bay right away.

Jax arrived quickly, and together, with her powers and Jax steadying him on a portable cot, they moved him to the med-bay.

Blackburne was just coming out, moving his shoulder, and looking more comfortable.

"It's going to be tight – Curly is still in there. She's got a couple of broken ribs, a concussion, and some major bruising. But she's going to be okay."

Curly heard them and lumbered out, her drayek perched on her shoulder. She took one look at Cory's bloodied body on the cot and gestured to take him in first.

"I am good, I wait," she said.

They transferred Cory to the bed and let the computer check him: multiple broken bones, some internal bleeding, and a concussion. The internal bleeding was a concern, but thankfully, it was something the computer could handle.

Once they had Cory fixed up and strapped into the med-bay bunk, Kiara helped Curly get the attention she needed. Curly kept touching her little drayek to check on her.

"Curly, did you name her?" Kiara asked.

Curly nodded. "Daisy." At her name, the little drayek climbed up to the top of Curly's head and chirped.

Kiara stopped what she was doing. "Daisy? That's so cute! Where did you come up with that?" Kiara didn't expect Curly to use an Earth name.

"I saw, in your bunk."

Kiara thought for a moment, and then she remembered that she had a print picture above her bunk. It was a field of daisies with some dogs running through it. She smiled. Her dad had given her that picture a few years after adopting her.

Curly pointed to her com unit. "I looked for the name."

"It's perfect," Kiara murmured.

Curly said she would stay with Cory so Jax and Kiara could help with repairs.

Kiara and Jax headed to the bridge. Jax handed Kiara some supplements and food, and a piece of fruit for Elvis.

"Are you sure you're okay?" Kiara asked Jax in between mouthfuls of food. Elvis, on her shoulder, dribbled fruit juice onto her shirt. She was thankful she was alive to get dribbled on.

"Yes, I am good," Jax assured her. "I checked myself in the med-bay to make sure nothing was broken, or that I did not have bleeding." He smiled at her. "I promise, it is just bruising." Jax reached out and cupped Kiara's chin. "You two should be checked out."

"We need to get the ship into a safe state first," Kiara said emphatically. "I need to figure out what happened and make sure we weren't being attacked."

Jax was ready to argue, but decided against it. She seemed to be fine for now, and he would make sure she and Elvis were checked out as soon as possible.

"Does anybody know where we are?" Jax asked as they entered the bridge.

Frankie had cleared off his chair, but the rest of the bridge was still filled with debris and fire suppressant.

Frankie nodded. He'd had to hook up a portable console to his station. His console was currently shattered beyond use.

"We only made it about halfway through the wormhole. We jumped out into a very unpopulated area of space. Only a few planets in this sector."

Kiara sat at her console, which was still in relatively good shape, with only a crack down its center. She began to confirm Frankie's findings and checked her scans for other ships or reasons the wormhole had collapsed in the first place.

"We need to get to a space station, stat!" Blackburne barked out the order while he tried to clear a path through the debris. "Anything at that nearby planet?"

"Checking." Kiara's fingers flew over her console. She was having trouble pinpointing exactly where they were.

"Finally." Kiara turned to look at Blackburne. "If we can get to that planet, we'll be able to work on repairs, but the planet itself doesn't have a space station or docking port. It does have an atmosphere that can sustain us."

"Early civilization?" Blackburne asked.

"Yes, it's one of the planets listed as off-limits by the GTA."

Blackburne frowned at that news from Kiara.

"However, the planet is very sparsely populated, so we'll be able to get in and get out without being noticed."

"That'll have to do for now," Blackburne said quietly. "We need to get stabilized and finish assessing damage." He turned to Frankie. "Can we get there? Can we get through the atmosphere?"

Frankie was nodding. "If we don't do any fancy flying or run into enemy ships, we shouldn't have any problems getting there." Frankie assessed the shields and looked over at Kiara. "We may need a little help from Kiara holding the shields together."

Blackburne gave his approval, and the Acadia limped its way to the nearby planet. Frankie hovered over the southern atmosphere as he prepared to make the descent.

"Shut down everything you can and keep as much power to the shields as possible," Blackburne instructed Frankie.

Frankie looked at Kiara, got a nod of assurance, and began the descent to the surface. Jax had gone back to make sure that Curly and Cory were strapped in, and she was glad that he did. Even with her powers, the ride was bumpy, and the hull overheated in several places.

Kiara let out a sigh of relief when the Acadia softly thumped to the ground.

Frankie brought up the screen to show the outside around the ship. Low green-purple vegetation covered the ground as far as they could see in every direction.

Kiara double-checked the oxygen level and found it was within their tolerance, but she felt reluctant to leave the ship.

Blackburne must have felt it too; he made a ship-wide announcement that everyone should stay aboard and help with repairs.

"The engines are our priority," Blackburne informed them as he headed off the bridge. "Set a continuous scan for any native life outside. Also, set a scan for anything coming at us from space."

Kiara and Frankie nodded as they followed him. Kiara had already set the scan, and other than a few insect-like creatures, they were alone. They ran into Jax coming out of the med-bay.

"They're okay," he whispered.

Hours later, dirty, grimy, and very tired, Kiara, joined by the others, squeezed into the kitchen to see if any of the food was still edible. They'd made considerable progress with the engines. Frankie guessed they had a few more hours left, and they'd have them at just about optimum. The rest of the ship was going to take considerably longer.

They had all been quiet while they worked on the engines, other than occasionally asking for a tool or a grunt as they moved something heavy.

Kiara sat down heavily at the table in the kitchen. Elvis, in his usual place on her shoulder, leaned against her head and made quiet chirping noises. She looked up as Jax placed some food in front of her and handed some slightly squished fruit to Elvis.

"Thank you," she whispered. She heard Elvis slurping at the fruit, but she felt too tired to eat, even though she knew she should. She finally shoved a bite into her mouth and made herself chew.

"Kiara, were you able to determine why the wormhole collapsed?" Blackburne quietly asked. He could see how tired she was, but he was also concerned about being attacked. They were still very vulnerable.

"I narrowed it down to something that happened at both transgates, at the same time." She brought up her com unit, tapped into the ship's computer, and went back through the logs of their journey. She was able to pinpoint the exact moment that the wormhole began to collapse. With that information, she was able to see that both transgates were destroyed, simultaneously. Without the transgates keeping the wormhole stable, it began to oscillate and tear itself apart. She showed Blackburne the data.

"Any idea if we were the target?" Jax looked worried.

"I honestly don't know," Kiara said. "It seems like a reasonable assumption that we were the target, but no one knew we were here. We've been using a fake transponder signal, and it hasn't raised any flags yet." Kiara shook her head. "I'll be able to tell more when we get the computers fully operational."

On Earth Delta Nine, the Director received a new, high-priority, encrypted message. He quickly scanned it. Rend had used Talia to check on Kiara. Talia had sensed that Kiara was on her way to Earth Delta Nine. For a moment, the Director felt a sliver of panic. Until he read the rest of the message. With Talia's help, they'd been able to determine which sector Kiara was in and, from there, make an educated guess about the specific transgate. They hadn't been able to see a manifest for the Acadia, but presumed the Acadia was running under a different name anyway. Rend's team had destroyed both transgates that controlled the wormhole, and any ship within it. Rend, anticipating the fallout from such a high-profile destruction, had his men make it look like an accidental circuit overload.

The Director nodded to himself. There would still be questions, but he would be able to deflect those questions with the information he had.

Kiara finally took a break from the repairs and went to her bunk to rest. Frankie was taking the first shift to monitor scans while the others slept. She was so tired, she figured she would immediately fall into a dreamless, deep sleep. Her head hit the pillow with Elvis curled against her back. She turned her thoughts to why the wormhole collapsed, but fell asleep within seconds.

Kiara had been asleep for about 30 minutes when she suddenly shot up in bed, breathing hard and startling Elvis. She looked wildly around the room for a second before jumping out of bed and grabbing her com unit. She signaled Jax, and while she waited for him to join her, she worked to calm her breathing. She could hear Jax's running footsteps in the hallway and immediately felt relief.

"What happened?" Jax demanded as he entered. "Did you see that reflection again?"

"No, no, that's not it," Kiara choked out, still working to control her breathing. "I think I know what happened to the wormhole."

Jax sat next to her on the bed and waited for her to explain.

"It's Talia, the Trandorian we met at the colony."

"Talia?" Jax looked confused. "What would Talia have to do with the wormhole collapsing?"

"They have her looking for me," Kiara said as Elvis climbed into her lap and made small clicking noises. "While I was sleeping, I felt her reaching out."

Jax thought through what Kiara just told him and reached the same conclusion that she had.

"She's trying to confirm your death."

Kiara nodded.

"You said you felt her reaching out? Did she confirm that you were still alive?" Jax worriedly asked.

"I don't think so," Kiara responded. "There's no way to know for sure, but I attempted to disguise my thoughts as one of the Trandorians from the colony."

Jax let out a sigh of relief. "Maybe that will buy us some time." He stood up from the bed. "You'll have to be on guard for that, as well as the stone. We will need to brief Blackburne."

On the bridge, after briefing Blackburne, Kiara sat on the floor with Elvis in her lap and waited to hear the questions from her captain. Before Blackburne could ask anything, Jax piped up.

"Wait, wait. You said 'they' have her looking for you. Who's 'they'?"

Blackburne and Jax both faced Kiara; their matching frowns would have made her laugh under any other circumstances.

Kiara thought back to her statement and her thoughts while she had been sleeping.

"I was dreaming and talking with Mirona, my ancestor," Kiara said quietly, as she looked inward. "Mirona alerted me that another Trandorian was searching for me." Kiara shook her head. "I think she could sense it first, due to the nature of our connection."

Kiara furrowed her brow as she thought back and brought up the details. "Mirona said that 'searching' for another Trandorian is a highly skilled task, and she didn't understand who would be doing that, and why. This will be hard to explain, but Mirona pulled my consciousness out of Talia's path, and we attempted to observe her. We could tell someone was instructing her, but we couldn't tell who. Mirona helped me disguise my thoughts as someone from the colony, and then we let her 'find' me. I woke up right after that, so I'm not certain we were successful."

"I've been monitoring communications, and so far, nothing would suggest that anyone knows we're here, or that anyone is looking for us." Frankie updated the group. "Of course, we aren't able to intercept as much in this sector as we usually do, so there's a chance we're missing something."

Blackburne looked slightly relieved. "The engines are almost ready, and luckily, the shields were relatively easy to stabilize. They'll be at optimum with the engines."

Frankie and Jax nodded their agreement with the captain's assessment.

"We still need to get the outer hull repaired before I'll feel safe heading through the atmosphere." Blackburne looked at Kiara. "How are we doing with food and water?"

"We've got a couple more days of each. We'll need to ration some, to make sure we have enough to finish repairs and make it to the next space station or refueling station." Kiara looked at some data on her com unit. "I scanned the surface here to see if we could find any supplies, and the water on the planet would take several weeks to purify, and the food sources are scarce." Kiara could see Blackburne's frown deepen at her report. She was just about to make it worse. "Also, there are no fuel sources that we could use to enhance our fuel, and no precious metals to use on the hull."

"Nothing?" Blackburne asked with some disbelief.

"There are some possibilities, but none that could be done quickly. We'd run out of food and water before we'd get anything usable."

Blackburne nodded, his mind already working through scenarios and possibilities.

"Frankie, determine what we need to fix the outer hull to get us to the nearest station. Kiara, find us the nearest, safest place to finish our repairs."

"I did find what I think is the best place to go, but it is in the opposite direction from Earth Delta Nine," Kiara quickly informed the group. "There is a space station slightly closer, but I think it would be more dangerous, and more conspicuous."

Blackburne looked at the data that Kiara moved over to one of the side screens in the bridge. Jax and Frankie joined them.

"This might work in our favor," Jax said into the silence. "If they are still looking for us, they won't expect us to be going in that direction."

"Agreed," Blackburne said.

"I think we can strip some of the inner cargo area plating and use it to patch the hull, temporarily," Frankie told Blackburne.

"Do it."

Later, as Kiara flopped into her bunk, she let out a huge sigh. Frankie and Curly were finishing up the hull repairs, and they would be able to head out tomorrow. She hadn't had any other incidents with the distorted reflection, and for that she was thankful. She attributed it to her being too tired to do anything but work on the ship, eat, and sleep. When she slept, Mirona helped to protect her.

Elvis was already letting out small snoring sounds, and Kiara fell asleep quickly with a slight smile on her face.

"Elvis? Where are you?" Kiara stumbled around her cabin, looking under furniture, tossing blankets and clothes aside as she looked for him. Panic was in her voice as she called him, again and again.

Maybe he left the cabin? Kiara turned toward the door, but it wasn't there. She spun around, looking for the door, looking for Elvis. She couldn't find either. As she turned in a circle, the room began to change. The furniture disappeared, her belongings disappeared, and the room turned into a giant mirrored space. Kiara's heart rate accelerated as she anticipated her distorted reflection to appear. Where was her com unit? She needed to call Jax for help. And where was Elvis? She hadn't hurt him, had she?

She opened her mouth to yell for Jax, but no sound came out. As she spun around the room looking for Elvis, the door, her com unit, she saw her reflection, and the distortion it had become. Her heartbeat accelerated, and sweat broke out on her brow. The reflection began to scream at her, a howling scream that pierced Kiara's brain. She doubled over, the pain in her head moving down to her stomach. The nausea was overwhelming. She tried to fight it, to find her way out, but the howling just went on and on in her head.

On the bridge, Frankie and Blackburne were doing some last-minute checks of the ships' systems when Jax joined them. Jax looked around the room, wondering where Kiara was. He sent a message to her com unit but got no reply.

His brow furrowed, and he tried to sense her.

"What's wrong?" Blackburne asked.

Jax turned to answer him, but before he could say anything, Elvis shot into the room without Kiara. Elvis was making a high-pitched squealing noise that raised the hair on the back of Jax's neck. The little drayek was pale blue and appeared severely distressed. Jax immediately knew that something was wrong.

Elvis saw Jax and, with a burst of energy, jumped straight into Jax's chest. Elvis grabbed both sides of Jax's face while Jax tried to steady him. Jax's head filled with images of Kiara lying on her bunk, unresponsive and barely breathing.

"Let's go, Elvis," Jax said and ran out of the room with Elvis, Frankie, and Blackburne right behind him.

When they entered Kiara's room, she appeared just as Elvis had portrayed to Jax. She was on her back; her breathing was shallow. Elvis jumped onto the bed, getting as close to Kiara as he could, making little chirping noises. Elvis stroked her hair and face, and

Jax noticed that the little drayek's color hadn't improved with him being close to Kiara. That told him that the bond between Elvis and Kiara was breaking.

Jax bent over and picked Kiara up from the bunk and headed for the med-bay. He thought that whatever was happening had something to do with the stone and the distorted reflections, but he wasn't sure. He hoped they hadn't missed an injury from earlier, and they could do something to reverse this in the med-bay.

Blackburne, having sized up the situation, was ahead of Jax. Blackburne entered the med-bay and prepared the emergency diagnostic bunk for Kiara. Cory, on the opposite side of the room, was sleeping comfortably. Blackburne sectioned off the area where Cory was so they wouldn't disturb him and waited for Jax to bring Kiara in. Jax placed her gingerly in the bunk, Elvis on her stomach, still trying to connect with her. While the computer ran its diagnostics, Jax attempted to sense Kiara with his limited abilities. He closed his eyes, held his breath, and pushed harder to find her when his first attempt came up empty.

Jax opened his eyes when he heard the quiet beep that signaled the computer had finished its diagnostics. He looked at Blackburne, but Blackburne looked puzzled.

"The computer didn't come up with anything wrong with her." Blackburne scrolled through the computer screens before stopping on one. He made a low humming noise.

"What is it?" Jax couldn't see what Blackburne was looking at from his position next to the bunk.

"These levels here suggest that her brain is in a constant state of fear or terror. I should be seeing elevated adrenaline levels, but I see exactly the opposite." Blackburne frowned at the screen. "None of this makes any sense."

Jax turned back to Kiara, picking up her hand. Closing his eyes, he tried again to sense her. At first, there was nothing. He was about to give up when Elvis jumped on his shoulder and put his little paw on Jax's cheek. Jax felt a slight rush of power and knew that Elvis was trying to push Jax's limited abilities.

Jax concentrated, and finally, he could sense her. He couldn't reach her; instead, he felt a wave of overwhelming fear, and just before he let go, he heard that unmistakable howling scream that he'd heard from the distorted reflection.

"The stone has her," Jax said into the quiet of the room. "I can sense her fear, and I could hear that horrific howling from the distorted reflection, but I can't reach her." His mind scrambled to come up with a solution. He couldn't just leave her in that state.

"We can't contact her ancestor without her, can we?" Frankie asked.

"I don't see how," Jax said as he shook his head. "We've got to do something; we can't just leave her in that place of fear."

"Perhaps we should put her deeper into a coma, and get her past the point where the stone can reach her?" Blackburne threw out the idea. It was the only thing he could think of.

Jax nodded. "Let's give it a try; we can always reverse it if needed." He looked at her vitals being monitored by the computer. Her heart rate and breathing were continuing to fall.

Jax held her hand while Blackburne initiated the procedure. The computer strapped Kiara in and administered the required drugs. All three watched the monitors. At first, nothing changed, but slowly, ever so slowly, her heart rate returned to normal, and her breathing deepened and leveled out.

Blackburne let out the breath he didn't realize he'd been holding. The scans of her brain showed less activity that represented fear, and normal levels for a coma.

"I think we've got her stabilized for now," Blackburne said. He looked at Elvis. The little drayek was curled next to Kiara's head, quietly breathing. His color, while still pale, seemed to have stabilized.

Kiara, still doubled over with the pain and nausea brought on by the screaming, slowly fell to her knees. Where was Jax? Where was Elvis? She crumpled to the floor, not sure how long she would be able to tolerate the pain and fear. She tried to scream again, but felt as if she couldn't draw in enough air to fill her lungs. She couldn't even raise her head. She tried to summon enough energy to stand, to scream, to do anything. Even as she did, the howling increased, beating her back down. A terrible thought fleetingly entered her mind – she was dying. However, she couldn't seem to do anything about it. For an instant, as she felt like she was slowly dying, she thought she felt Jax and Elvis. She tried to raise her hand to signal them, but the howling increased again, and her hand and head flopped back down on the floor. She was dying.

Suddenly, the howling scream began to fade, and Kiara felt as if she could breathe again. It was such a blessed relief. As the howling faded, the world around her faded away into a black void, and she fell into a quiet nothingness.

Chapter 13

On the bridge, Jax, Blackburne, Curly, and Frankie were huddled together around Frankie's seat. Both Jax and Blackburne had Kiara's monitors tied to their com units. Before leaving the med-bay, Blackburne awakened Cory and had him keep an eye on Kiara as well. Cory was doing better every day and was grateful for a way to help.

"She's stable for now, but we don't know how long that will last," Blackburne informed the group. "We know the stone is responsible, but we can't destroy the stone without her."

"I could attempt to contact her ancestor, with Elvis' help, but I don't have much hope it will work," Jax said quietly.

"Other ideas or suggestions?" Blackburne asked the group.

"I think we should call her dad," Frankie said, looking at Jax. "And, maybe we should ask Stryker for help?"

Jax nodded. "I sent an encrypted message to Stryker, but it will take some time for him to get it and respond. We still need to keep our position a secret."

"I'll contact her father," Blackburne volunteered for that duty. He wasn't looking forward to it. "However, we need to decide whether or not we continue to Earth Delta Nine, or if we should plot a course to somewhere else to find help for Kiara."

"It is my thought that we should continue to Earth Delta Nine and try to determine a way to revive Kiara and beat back the stone's influence on the way," Jax said. "Even if we head back to the Trandorian colony and find a way to help her there, she will still be in danger until the stone is destroyed."

Blackburne and Frankie nodded.

"Frankie, will our repairs hold us for now?" Blackburne asked. Time was not on their side, and a long delay for repairs would not help Kiara.

"Yes, they'll hold for now. We'll monitor for any deterioration."

"It's decided. Frankie, let's go."

On Earth Delta Nine, the Director received the news he had been waiting for. They could no longer detect the Trandorian that had been plaguing them, so she was either dead from the wormhole collapse or the stone had destroyed her.

With her out of the way, he could push on with more of his plans.

Kiara's dad, Kyle, was making his way back to his ship that was currently docked in a space station several sectors from Earth Delta Nine. He was tired, and his ship was looking a little worse for wear. He'd been involved in several battles with the CyRAINs, the last one at the space station he was currently docked at. He and the other Rangers had successfully defended the station, this time. He frowned as he thought about how the attacks were becoming more vicious and more frequent.

He boarded his ship and was immediately notified through the ship's com system that someone was trying to reach him. His heart went into overdrive as he worried that something had happened to Kiara. He checked the system and saw that Blackburne had sent him an encrypted message. He opened the message with dread. He sat down heavily in his chair after reading it. Why hadn't she let him know? He could have helped; he was her father! For a moment, his anger and grief nearly overwhelmed him.

When he could think clearly again, he sent an encrypted message back to the Acadia. He set a meeting point near Earth Delta Nine and let them know when he would be there.

On the Acadia, Elvis was still curled into a tight ball next to Kiara's head. Both were pale, their breathing shallow, but steady. As soon as Blackburne had induced the coma in Kiara, she had steadied, and Elvis hadn't left her side. It was as if Elvis was in a coma as well.

Cory checked her vitals on the computer, noting that they were steady and unchanged. Moving over to the bunk they had Kiara strapped in, he slowly reached out to pet Elvis. He was incredibly sad to see both in this state. Elvis didn't stir, even with Cory touching him.

Cory looked up when Jax entered the med bay.

"Any changes?"

Cory shook his head. "They're both the same."

Jax replaced Cory next to the bed and placed his hand on Elvis, searching for the little drayek's consciousness. He was just about to pull his hand away when he found him. He was barely there, but the little drayek sent him a quick feeling that he was okay. Jax sent a reassuring feeling back, hoping the little drayek received it. Bending down, he kissed Kiara's forehead and reminded himself to stay focused. His anger and despair at her current state wouldn't help her, and he needed to make sure he was there for her. He acknowledged that his feelings for her were strong, and he pushed any thoughts of losing her out of his mind. She would get better, she had to!

Jax joined Blackburne and Frankie on the bridge. Before he'd gone to check on Kiara, they'd been discussing how to proceed.

He nodded at Blackburne as he sat heavily at Kiara's station.

"We've heard back from Kiara's dad," Blackburne informed him. "He gave us a meet point on the way to Earth Delta Nine."

"I knew he would find a way to join us." Jax smiled. "We can use all the help we can get."

"Did you hear back from Stryker?" Blackburne asked him.

Jax nodded. "I received a quick reply that he received my message, and that he is trying to find the actual location of the stone. He trusts us to do the right thing with Kiara and get to Earth Delta Nine."

"We'll be at the meet point in about twelve hours," Frankie put in.

Blackburne nodded. "We can get her father's take on our plan, but I think it's our only shot at reviving her and beating back the stone long enough for her to destroy it."

Kyle paced in the small storage area of his ship. It was really only big enough for two small steps in any direction, but he had too much energy to sit in the pilot's seat. He was currently docked at a small refueling station, waiting for the Acadia. He'd pushed his ship to the limit and had arrived early.

He checked his com unit, for probably the hundredth time in the last two minutes, as he took another step and bumped into the wall in the storage area. He let out a sigh and turned, just as his com unit signaled. He quickly grabbed it, noting the short message. The Acadia was here, refueling in dock three. Letting out another sigh, Kyle jumped into the pilot's seat, fired up the engines, and quickly undocked from the fueling station.

Taking a roundabout track, he headed for one of the nearby, desolate moons. Nearing an abandoned colony on the moon, he set his ship down gently to wait for the Acadia.

Frankie brought the Acadia down next to Kyle's ship and unlocked the remote hatch near the cargo area. Kyle climbed aboard and quickly took off his space suit as soon as the hatch area was pressurized.

Kyle was halfway to the med-bay when Blackburne and Jax caught up to him.

"How is she? Any change?" Kyle asked as he kept moving toward the med-bay.

Jax shook his head. "She's still comatose. Elvis is with her, and Cory has been keeping an eye on them."

Kyle nodded and entered the med-bay. She looked so pale! He wanted to scream or punch something. How could this happen? Taking a deep breath, he struggled to force those emotions into something positive to help her. He approached the bed and put a hand on Kiara's head and one on Elvis. Both were breathing steadily, and he took some comfort from that.

"We have a plan," Jax spoke quietly from the doorway.

Kyle nodded again. Leaning over, he whispered to Kiara to stay strong, then quickly kissed her forehead.

Kyle followed Jax to the bridge.

Frankie was already lifting off from the moon, scanning the area to make sure they weren't seen. Frankie, in a dark blue shirt, briefly acknowledged Kyle as he entered the bridge, then went back to scanning the area.

Once the Acadia was on its way, Kyle joined the crew next to Frankie's chair so they could discuss the plan. Kyle acknowledged it was the first time he hadn't seen Frankie in a brightly colored shirt. He supposed it showed the pilot's worry for Kiara.

"It's risky, but we think it's our only shot at reviving her," Blackburne said.

Kyle nodded. Adrenaline. They were going to pump her full of adrenaline and hope that it would be enough to not only revive her but also give her enough fuel to beat back the stone's influence.

"We have to time it out right," Blackburne continued. "If we do it too soon, the effect may wear off before she can get to the stone. If we do it too late, we may be discovered before she is ready."

Frankie looked doubtful. "Do we know how much to give her?"

Blackburne shrugged slightly. "We used the computer to calculate the dose, and Cory helped as well." Blackburne sighed, a sure sign that he wasn't convinced they had it right. "There just isn't enough information out there on her race."

"We'll need the exact location, or else this is all for naught, anyway." Kyle voiced what they were all thinking.

"Stryker has been working on it," Jax put in. "He thinks he is close to figuring it out."

"Do we have a place to land, without being noticed?" Kyle asked, trying to catch up to the plan.

Blackburne nodded. "I contacted a buddy on Earth Delta Nine; he's meeting us on the outskirts of the city. We're still flying under a different transponder, so landing shouldn't be an issue. He'll shuttle us to the city."

"Do you trust him?" Kyle asked worriedly.

"With my life." Blackburne turned to Frankie. "Give us notice when we're a couple of hours out, so we can prepare to treat Kiara."

Kyle sat in the med-bay, watching Kiara, looking for a change, double-checking the calculations of the drug dosages they were going to give her. Cory, sitting on the bunk near him, looked over Kyle's shoulder and nodded. Cory was healing quickly, and not a moment too soon, since he would be needed on this mission.

"You came up with the same dosages that we all did," he said quietly. "I think we can take some comfort in that."

Just as Kyle nodded, his com-unit signaled a message from Jax. Stryker had found the stone's location. And just in time, Kyle thought.

Frankie signaled they would be landing in a few hours.

Jax appeared in the doorway. "Blackburne and I think it is best to wait until we land before we attempt to revive her." At Kyle's questioning look, he explained a little more. "Kiara thought the young Trandorian from the colony was tracking her. With her being in a coma, she can't be tracked. Most likely, they think she is dead or otherwise incapacitated. If that is the case, and our fake transponder is working, they won't know we are coming."

"And are you sure she can destroy the stone?"

"She was able to destroy one, so, in theory, she can destroy the one with the hold on her." Jax paused, as he voiced the worry that all of them had. "We just don't know what her state of mind will be when we revive her."

"Can we help her focus when the time comes? Shore up her defenses and give her strength?"

"We will try."

Frankie set them down in a small depot outside the city where Stryker said the stone was being stored. With Kyle's connections, they'd been able to get permission to land the Acadia on the planet, instead of docking out in space. So far, the fake transponder had kept their identity hidden, and the security in this small depot was lax, making it the perfect spot. Automation moved their ship into a hangar, where they prepared to revive Kiara.

"Is our ride into the city here yet?" Kyle asked Blackburne.

"Two minutes out."

Kyle took a deep breath. Now or never. He administered the meds with the help of the med-bay computer, then stood back.

Kiara jackknifed to a sitting position in the bed, screaming as she did so. Everyone in the room braced for a pulse of energy that never came.

Kiara looked wildly around the room; Elvis clutched tightly to her chest. Her heart was racing, her breathing shallow and fast.

"Dad?"

"Easy, baby girl, I'm here," Kyle approached her slowly, keeping his voice low and soothing. "Are you okay? Are you with us?"

Kiara nodded. "Dad? What happened?" She could barely get the words out. Her heart was still racing, and it was difficult to catch her breath.

"The stone had taken you over, and we had you in a coma," Jax said from the doorway.

Kiara squinted her eyes as she struggled to remember. The memories came flooding back quickly. She looked at Jax in a panic. "Don't let it take over again!"

"Can you feel it?" Jax asked worriedly.

Kiara shook her head. "My heart is racing, why?"

"We dosed you with adrenaline," Kyle said. "We hoped it would bring you out of the coma, but also beat back the stone, at least for a time."

Elvis whimpered into her chest, and Kiara realized she was squeezing him. She looked at his face and quickly checked their bond. Good and strong.

Kiara closed her eyes and tried to self-assess. Her heart was racing, but she didn't feel out of control, and she didn't feel the stone's influence. She didn't feel Talia, either. Opening her eyes, she brought her hands up, enveloping her and Elvis in an energy bubble. The bubble came up, strong and steady. She increased it slightly until it bumped her dad, pushing him back a step. Kiara smiled. She could do this.

"You might want to bring some of that adrenaline with us," she told her dad when she dropped the energy bubble.

Jax and Kyle breathed a sigh of relief to see her seemingly in control.

Blackburne's voice floated down the hall. "Our ride is here!"

With everyone loaded into his friend's shuttle, Blackburne turned to look at the group and tried to judge their mental state. Kiara looked steady, but slightly darker blue, he presumed from the adrenaline. Elvis, on her lap, was staring at Kiara's face, and Blackburne noticed that the little drayek had a death grip on her hair as well. Kyle was studying his daughter, looking for any problems, as was Jax. Blackburne hoped that Kiara would hold up under all that scrutiny. Cory was working on his com unit, preparing to help Kiara in any way that he could. Cory was still a little pale, but he looked steady. Curly, cramped in the back of the shuttle, had insisted that she go along. Her little drayek, Daisy, was firmly planted in Curly's arms. Curly didn't want Kiara to be left unprotected. Frankie had stayed behind to guard the Acadia.

Blackburne turned back around to look out the front of the shuttle. His friend, Darin, was competently piloting the shuttle to the warehouse district where Stryker said the stone was being stored. Stryker also sent as much information as he could gather about security at the warehouse. It appeared security was mostly automated, with technology being the weapon of choice. The warehouse had minimal human security. Blackburne ensured Cory had the information and hoped he could help them navigate through security to reach the stone. Stryker couldn't get all the information, so Blackburne knew there would be variables they couldn't account for. Cory had insisted that he was up for it.

Darin looked over at Blackburne. "There will be security around the warehouse, so we won't be able to land near it."

Blackburne nodded. "How close can you get us?"

Darin brought up a map of the warehouse district. He pointed to a shuttle lot, about a mile away from the warehouse they wanted.

"If I land here, we'll stand a better chance of not being noticed."

"That's quite the distance." Blackburne looked at Kiara. "I'm not sure that's going to work. What are our other choices?"

"If we're quick, and the stars align, you can jump out in the lot behind the back of the warehouse." Darin looked grim. "It's not a shuttle lot, so we'll have to hope there's enough room to get close to the ground." Darin shook his head. "And we have to hope that security doesn't stop us."

Blackburne studied the building's layout and the lot—quite a few unknowns. "We'll use that shuttle lot for our exit. You can wait for us there."

Cory cleared his throat behind Blackburne. "I'm pretty sure I can tap into the security at the warehouse and get a view of the back lot."

"Can you do it without getting detected?" Blackburne quickly asked.

Cory nodded.

"Do it, we're only a few minutes out!" Blackburne turned back to the rest. "Get ready! We're jumping out in the back lot of the warehouse, in about two minutes!" He looked hard at Kiara. "Ready?"

Kiara had been focusing on Elvis, trying to breathe steadily, even through the adrenaline. Her heart was still racing, but she could feel darkness creeping in. She looked up at Blackburne, her look slightly panicked, her color changing to a lighter blue.

The shuttle dove to the right, jolting the passengers.

Darin muttered something about security poles, and Blackburne knew that his friend was doing some fancy flying to get them to the right spot.

"Adrenaline!" Blackburne shouted at Jax.

Jax had already sensed that Kiara was starting to falter, and he had been reaching into the med bag to grab the shot when he heard Blackburne's shout.

Jax turned to Kiara, ready to administer the drug, but froze. Kiara's face was distorted, and a guttural growl was coming from low in her throat. Jax realized that they had waited too long, and now that they were close to the stone, it had easily taken her over.

Kyle, on the other side of her, saw what was happening and knew that Jax would not be able to administer the drug while Kiara was focused on him. Kyle quickly reached out and grabbed her other arm, pulling her toward him.

Kiara's head swung around toward her dad, screaming and growling. Elvis was hissing and pulling on her hair. Jax quickly took advantage of her diverted attention, slamming the drug into her arm.

Kiara turned and knocked Jax off his seat and onto the floor, but the adrenaline was already working. Kiara's face returned to normal, and the screaming and growling stopped.

Breathing hard, she slowly became aware of her surroundings. Jax was shaking off the hit she'd just given him, Blackburne and Darin were yelling up front about security and landing, and Cory was madly working on his com unit to get them information on the landing area. Her dad softly touched her face.

"Hon, are you with us again?"

Kiara nodded and answered, gritting her teeth. "I'm here, Dad." With a quick nod at Cory, Kiara deployed her armor.

Cory turned back to give directions to Darin, and the shuttle dipped and dived as they approached the warehouse.

"We're going to have company shortly," Cory yelled into the back. "There's no way to disable the air security in time before we land, so the shuttle will set off the alarms."

"What kind of automated security will they have?" Blackburne asked.

"I'm working on it," Cory muttered, his fingers working his com unit as quickly as he could. With a few extra swipes, Cory synchronized everyone's com units to enable silent communication.

"Ready to disembark, in three, two, one!" Darin shoved the shuttle down to the ground with a hard thud, opening the side door at the same time.

Kiara briefly thought the picture of them jumping from the shuttle was worthy of an Earth twentieth-century superhero film. Elvis was anchored to her back, holding onto her braid as she jumped down. She turned back to look at the shuttle, just as Curly, with Daisy on her back, jumped down. The shuttle rocked back and forth as Curly's weight left the small ship.

Cory was still working his com unit, so Blackburne grabbed his shirt at the shoulder and, with Cory giving directions, headed out, making sure Cory was going in the right direction.

The shuttle lifted off behind them, leaving the yard eerily quiet as they followed Blackburne and Cory.

Suddenly, Cory halted, and Blackburne shot up his hand in the universal signal to stop.

Kiara, still struggling to get her heart rate under control, bumped into the back of Jax. Jax quickly steadied her with his free hand, his other hand already holding his baton. Jax looked at Kiara, silently willing her to get in the game. It worked. He saw her eyes focus on his face, her brow settling into a fierceness he could appreciate.

Cory's voice entered everyone's head. "The shuttle set off some alarms. I can't disable them. The back door of the warehouse is ahead. I'm disabling motion sensors as we go, but keep an eye out for security from the alarms."

Cory's head dipped slightly to let Blackburne know that they could move.

As they headed to the warehouse back door, Kiara focused, scanning for threats. She sensed the security shuttles before she heard them. Shouting in her head, she yelled, "Run!"

As a group, they ran for the door, Cory trying to turn off sensors ahead of them.

"I can't get the door!" Cory's voice shouted through the com units.

Jax jumped ahead, ready to hit the door with his baton, but Kiara beat him to it. Enclosing the security panel in a bubble, she punched the door open with a pulse of energy. As soon as everyone entered, she slammed the door and released the security panel.

Collectively, they held their breath to see if alarms would go off. Outside, they could see the yard light up as the security shuttles swept the area.

After a few minutes, when they didn't hear any alarms and the yard went dark again, Kiara started to breathe normally again. Well, as normal as could be with the adrenaline still pumping through her system.

Cory's voice entered her head. "That was the easy part."

Kiara looked around them as her eyes adjusted to the darkness. They couldn't risk a light.

Suddenly, Curly's voice entered her head. "I lead."

Cory shook his head, but Kiara understood.

"She can see better in the dark than any of us," Kiara broadcasted.

Cory nodded his understanding, and with Curly on one side of him and Blackburne on the other side, he quickly pointed the direction they needed to go.

Jax and Kyle flanked Kiara as they followed Cory. Kiara, scanning for threats, yelled, "Stop!" into the communications channel. Lasers? She pushed the question.

Cory shook his head.

Yes! Kiara pushed the thought back. She realized that Cory couldn't see the threat.

Kiara threw up a bubble around the group, just as the lasers started firing. She was thankful it wasn't knives, as her force field was holding up well against the lasers.

Cory looked panicked, but Blackburne pulled on his shirt, silently telling him to keep moving. Blackburne could sympathize. Being in Kiara's protective bubble was unnerving.

"We need to move quickly," Kiara pushed the thought. "They know we are here."

Cory changed his tactic. Instead of looking for security to disable, he now focused on opening doors and disabling locks.

They were moving fast now, and security lights lit up the area. Alarms went off, and an automated voice told them to hold their position. Stryker estimated it would take at least five minutes for additional security to reach them. Cory guided them to the left, up a set of metal stairs, through two sets of doors that he unlocked as he reached them. At every turn, a new set of lasers fired at them, and an automated voice continued to yell at them.

Jax looked at Kiara, judging her mental state and energy level. Her color was dark blue, Elvis touching her cheek with one hand, and Jax knew the little drayek was doing his best to assist her. Kiara returned his look and, with a slight nod, let him know that she was good.

Cory stopped in front of an innocuous-looking door, and before he could say anything, Kiara spoke.

"It's in there." Kiara looked at Jax, then at her dad. "I can feel it."

"Are you ready?" Jax asked her. He didn't want to push, but they didn't have much time.

Kiara nodded. Cory unlocked the door, then stepped aside so Kiara could enter.

The room wasn't large. Maybe ten feet by ten feet, with dark gray walls and a dark gray floor. In the center of the room, in a glass case on a pedestal, was the stone. It was currently fluctuating between the smooth stone and gray rock. Kiara assumed her proximity was the reason it was changing. Elvis hissed at it, his feet clenching against her shoulder.

There were no lasers or other security measures in this room. Kiara thought that whoever was after her would assume that if she made it this far, the stone would finish her. Her heart rate accelerated, and Kiara could feel it pushing against her consciousness.

Dropping the protective field around herself, she encased the others in protection and brought up the memory of how she had destroyed the previous stone. She pictured the frequency and amplitude, as she had before, and pictured it wrapped around the stone with her power. She pushed her power at it, but could feel the stone resisting.

She knew overcoming this stone would be more difficult than destroying the other stone. This stone was connected to her and was actively resisting her efforts. As she pushed her power around the stone, it began to scream and growl at her. She didn't know it, but the sound was not only in her head, but in the room as well. She pushed harder, picturing her power wrapped around it like the webbing that the Lamoranites had used. She closed her eyes and felt Elvis touching her cheek, giving her all the power he could. She began to falter. The stone, taking advantage, pushed back, sending images of Kiara, a face twisted with hate and rage, into her mind. The screaming and growling intensified, and the image grew bigger.

Jax, sensing her trouble, grabbed Kyle's hand and placed it on Kiara's shoulder. Yelling over the horrific sounds in the room, he told Kyle to send supporting thoughts of strength and love. Jax put a hand on her other shoulder and used his limited abilities to strengthen her.

The others in the room covered their ears and silently willed Kiara to destroy the stone.

Suddenly, Cory started chanting through the com unit. "Kiara!"

Blackburne and Curly joined in, hoping their voices in Kiara's head would reach her and strengthen her.

Kiara, on the verge of failing, felt her father first, then Jax. Soon, she could hear Curly, Blackburne, and Cory chanting her name. She felt wrapped in love and caring, and as she pictured the stone, she used those feelings to strengthen herself. This stone would not defeat her! She straightened her almost buckling legs, threw her shoulders back, and her arms out in front of her, palms out toward the stone.

Her power wrapped around the stone, and as she pushed her power, a low hum in the room joined the deafening sounds of screaming and growling.

Outside the room, Cory, still chanting Kiara's name, checked the security feeds to see how much time they had. He could see groups of heavily armed security personnel outside the two main doors. He knew they would breach at any moment.

Blackburne could see the information on Cory's com unit, but he wasn't sure security personnel would be their primary concern. The automated lasers were still firing, and he wasn't sure if Kiara's protection was going to last much longer. She was using everything she had to destroy the stone.

Curly, also sensing that Kiara's protection was weakening, reached into the room and grabbed the door. With a roar worthy of her race, she ripped the door off its hinges and used it to shield herself, Blackburne, and Cory, just as the protection bubble fell.

Inside the room, the low hum increased in intensity. Kiara pulled every last bit of energy she had, every last bit she could draw from Elvis, and pictured her power squeezing the stone into dust. The hum, the screaming, the growling, rose to a deafening crescendo. Kiara screamed, and the stone imploded with a loud crack.

The pulse of energy from the stone blasted out, knocking Kiara and the others in the room into the wall. Kiara had no energy to catch herself or the others. She lay in an unconscious heap against the wall, her dad holding her, Elvis on top of her. The blast was so powerful that it opened holes in the walls and ceiling. The case and table the stone was on were obliterated.

Kyle slowly gained consciousness, still cradling Kiara, as he had tried to protect her as the blast had knocked them back. He quickly checked for Kiara's pulse and found it, weak, but steady. Elvis was on her stomach, looking dazed but unhurt. He looked around for Jax but didn't see him. As he pushed up to a sitting position, he could hear Jax and Blackburne over by the door. Kyle could see that the door was missing, and he could hear the lasers still firing in the hall. Blackburne and Jax were in a heated discussion about how to stave off the attack from the security troops headed their way.

"How much time?" Kyle managed to croak out.

Jax limped over to him. "A minute or two. We can hold them off for a little while, but we are cornered up here."

"Is Cory able to disable the lasers?"

Jax shook his head. "He's working on it, but he can't get to the system that controls them. Curly is using the door as a shield, but it won't hold out much longer."

Kyle pulled Kiara into his chest. He had his weapon, as did Blackburne, but it wouldn't be enough to get them out of the building. They needed Kiara, but he didn't know whether they could revive her or, if they did, what kind of energy reserves she would have left.

Kyle looked up at Jax. "Can you sense her at all?"

Jax shook his head.

"Can we risk another adrenaline shot?" Kyle asked as he stroked her hair.

"No," Kiara whispered into her dad's chest.

"Kiara? Are you okay?" Kyle asked as he moved her head so he could see her.

Jax could sense her, but he could tell she was weak, and a little disoriented.

"No more adrenaline," Kiara whispered.

"Okay, baby, we won't give you any, but we're in a bit of a jam. We don't have a way out." Kyle told her.

Kiara nodded. She pushed away from her dad and pulled Elvis close. His energy helped to clear her head. For the first time in a long time, she was completely free of the stone, and it felt great, minus the aches and pains from getting slammed into the wall.

"How much time do we have?" Kiara asked. Elvis was holding her face, quietly chirping at her. She took a couple of deep breaths and reached out her consciousness. She was pleasantly surprised that she could see the security troops entering the warehouse.

"Maybe a minute?" Jax told her.

Jax turned and looked at Blackburne. Blackburne was leaning over Cory, trying to will him to turn off the lasers somehow. Curly was holding the door in the opening, helping to shield them.

"Jax, do you have any of that energy gel?" Kiara asked him.

Her voice was stronger this time, and Kyle breathed a sigh of relief.

305

Jax quickly handed her some, and Kiara swallowed it, feeling stronger with every breath.

"I have an idea," she told her dad. "We're on the top floor of the warehouse, right?" At his nod, she continued. "I can blast through the ceiling, and then protect us in a bubble, but I'm not strong enough to do that and run." She smiled. "Not yet, anyway."

Jax looked at Curly and smiled as well. He was glad that Curly had insisted she come along.

"Once we're on the roof, I'll shield us, and we can make our way to the shuttle lot." Kiara looked at Cory. "Maybe Cory can do something to create a diversion, so we have some time?"

"Let's do it!" Kyle said as he levered up to his feet. Everything hurt, but seeing Kiara improve gave him a boost of energy.

"Curly, jam that door into the doorway, and help buy us some time," Jax ordered. He quickly explained to Blackburne and Cory what they were planning. "Cory, what can you do for a diversion?"

Cory smiled now, as well. "I can set off alarms going the other way, and that should lead them away from us."

Curly, Daisy on her shoulder, slammed the door into the doorway with a loud bang, and immediately went to Kiara and picked her up off the floor.

Kiara laughed. Curly picked her up like she was a feather.

"Everyone ready?" Kiara asked.

At everyone's nod, she held Elvis close, closed her eyes, gathered what little power she had, and sent a pulse through the ceiling. The ceiling exploded outward, helped along by the holes created when the stone had imploded. Once the dust cleared, Kiara could see the night sky.

Curly grunted something like 'hold on', and with minimal effort, she threw Kiara up through the hole. Kiara laughed as she landed with a thud on her backside. She laughed some more when, one by one, Curly threw the rest of the team onto the roof. She imagined they all had the same look of surprise that she did.

"Curly, can you get up here?" Kiara worriedly asked back down through the hole. She knew that Curly had massive strength, but she couldn't remember ever seeing her jump.

"Yes, I jump now," Curly grunted at her.

Kiara moved back, not knowing what to expect. She heard a loud grunt, then Curly's head and arms came into view. Daisy jumped from Curly's shoulder to the roof. Curly grabbed the ragged edges of the roof to pull herself up. Blackburne and Jax immediately jumped to help her. Kiara smiled again as she watched both Elvis and Daisy help to pull Curly up. After a few seconds, they were once again, altogether on the roof.

"Cory, you're up," Blackburne told him.

Cory nodded and set off alarms for open doors, heading away from them.

Curly picked up Kiara, made sure Daisy was settled on her shoulder, and headed off in the direction of the shuttle lot. Kiara closed her eyes, held tight to Elvis, and enveloped the group in a protective bubble. She didn't think there were lasers up here, but she wasn't taking any chances. Blackburne once again steered Cory while helping Kyle keep up behind Curly's long stride. Jax limped along in the back, watching their backs.

They could hear shouting from somewhere deep in the building, and Kiara doubled down to keep the protection around them.

Cory let out a slight laugh as he worked his com unit. "I've got them chasing door alarms, and all the doors that lead back to us are locked with a new code." Cory nodded again as Blackburne steered him in the right direction. "I've bought us a little extra time."

When they reached the shuttle lot without incident, Kiara began to relax. When Darin had them in the air, and they weren't being pursued, she realized they'd made it. She looked around at the group, wounded, hurting, dirty, and dusty, and felt a wave of gratitude that they had stuck it out with her. The stone was destroyed, and she had her life back.

Chapter 14

Darin dropped off the Acadia crew and, with a few last-minute directions from Blackburne, made a quick exit. Blackburne had been in constant contact with Frankie to let them know when they would reach the ship and to monitor communications to see if they were being pursued.

Frankie met them on the ramp to board the ship. "They've sounded the alarm. Ships are in the air looking for you."

Blackburne nodded grimly. He turned to look at the rest of the crew. Curly was still carrying Kiara, Kyle and Jax were holding each other up, and Cory looked shell-shocked.

"Any idea if they know who we are, or tracked Darin's shuttle?" Blackburne wanted to know.

"Not so far. Security has put out a general alert for thieves who broke into the storage facility." Frankie shook his head. "I don't think you're all going to fit in the med-bay."

Blackburne grunted as he walked past Frankie and headed for the bridge.

"Frankie, get us in the air before they ground all ships!" Blackburne bellowed.

Frankie hurriedly closed up the ship and ran to the bridge.

Curly took Kiara straight to the med-bay, with Kyle and Jax right behind her.

"Curly, are you hurt?" Kiara croaked out. Whatever energy she had received from the gel Jax gave her was now gone, and she was unbearably hungry and thirsty! She could hear and feel the engines rumble to life, hoping that Frankie could get them off the planet before they were discovered.

"Curly is not hurt," Curly assured her as she placed Kiara and Elvis on the bed and moved her bulky frame into the hallway to make room for Kyle and Jax. Daisy, still on Curly's shoulder, chirped at Elvis.

Kiara pushed off the bed to make room for her dad or Jax. She was still weak, and every muscle in her body hurt, but she thought she looked better than those two. Closing her eyes, she connected with Elvis to check on him again. He was being very quiet, and she was worried. Elvis' thoughts blasted into her head. Hungry! Kiara smiled and sent a thought back – let's wait for my dad. Elvis chirped his agreement, and Kiara finished checking the little drayek over. He appeared unhurt, and she was thankful.

Jax quickly assessed Kiara and, with a quick nod, pushed Kyle onto the bed. Kyle protested, but weakly. Now that his adrenaline was wearing off, he didn't have the energy to argue.

The med-bay computer assessed Kyle with broken ribs and a concussion. Jax administered the protocols to Kyle and switched places with him. Jax was pretty sure that beyond the concussion, he probably had a few broken bones as well. He was right. He also had some torn ligaments and damage to one of his ears. All in all, considering what they just accomplished, it wasn't too bad.

Kiara, seeing that her dad and Jax were taken care of, headed to the kitchen. She needed to refuel quickly, or both she and Elvis were going to crash, right there in the hallway.

She found Curly and Daisy in the kitchen, setting out food for the crew. Curly had already set out a bowl of fruit and some protein cubes for Daisy and Elvis. Elvis saw the bowl and Curly, and even though he wanted to jump and flap his way to both, he waited for Kiara to get him to the table.

"Thank you, Curly!" Kiara exclaimed as she sat Elvis next to Daisy and the bowl of food. Elvis immediately started slurping his way through his food. Daisy, sitting next to Elvis, ate a few bites, then chirped at Elvis, then ate some more. Curly pushed some food at Kiara.

"Did you eat?" Kiara asked Curly.

Curly nodded while she set more food out. She looked at Kiara. "You are good now?"

Kiara understood the question. Curly wasn't talking about the food, or even if she was okay, now that they were back on the ship. Curly wanted to know if Kiara was totally free from the stone's influence. Kiara slowly stood up, muscles still screaming at her, and put her arms around Curly.

"Thank you, my friend. I am good now." Tears choked her voice with emotion. Without Curly and the others, she knew she wouldn't be here.

Curly, careful not to squeeze too hard, hugged Kiara back.

As Kiara hugged Curly, she heard a noise coming from her Bendanite friend that she'd never heard before. The sound, a mix between a growl and a purr, was coming from deep within Curly's chest. Kiara nearly broke down. It was a noise reserved for a Bendanite's family. She hugged Curly tighter and felt Elvis and Daisy join in.

Kiara finally sat down at the table and shoveled food into her mouth. Out of the corner of her eye, she could see Elvis and Daisy still eating. She was nearly finished when Jax and her dad looked in the doorway. Curly gestured to the food on the table and lumbered out of the kitchen, Daisy on her shoulder.

Jax and her dad sat at the table, both letting out a huge sigh. Jax moved his chair closer to Kiara; he just needed to be close to her. Before Kiara could ask how they were, Jax shoved another packet of gel at Kiara. At her questioning look, he cautioned her. "We may need your help."

Kiara nodded and took the gel. She was already feeling better, but Jax was right. She might be needed.

In the Director's office, he was slowly reading the report in front of him, his face growing redder as he went through the document. She wasn't dead! He couldn't believe that she was able to get past all their security and destroy the stone. He briefly wondered if destroying the stone would eliminate the effects on her, but decided he would have to ask the Galdorian.

The Director slammed a couple of drawers in his frustration. He couldn't push for security forces to hunt her down without bringing unwanted attention to himself and his cause.

According to the update in front of him, the security at the storage facility was treating the break-in and destruction as simple vandalism, since nothing was stolen. With a few choice words, he stormed out of his office. He still had some contacts that weren't 'official'. He'd get them involved. Since she was on this planet, now was a perfect time to eliminate her. Using his personal com unit, he contacted Rend and told him to get Talia ready.

Kiara, feeling better, joined the others on the bridge, Elvis riding her shoulder. Frankie still had the Acadia engines idling, but they hadn't moved yet. Kiara sent a questioning look to Blackburne.

"Some patrols came through this area a few minutes ago. We're waiting for them to clear out."

"I have an idea," Kiara said quickly. She sent a message to Cory, hoping he was up for the challenge. She hadn't seen him since they boarded. Cory responded that he was on his way.

When Cory joined them on the bridge, Kiara thought he still looked a little unsteady, but the color was coming back into his face. Jax was behind him, a comforting hand on the young man's shoulder.

"Cory, we could use your help, if you're up for it."

"Sure, Kiara. I'm okay, it was just a lot..." Cory trailed off, looking embarrassed.

"It was a lot!" Kiara exclaimed. "But we couldn't have done any of it without you!"

Her words of praise had the desired effect; Cory visibly perked up. Kiara thought maybe he'd been embarrassed that he'd looked so shell-shocked after the adventure. She'd meant every word, though, and imagined that they had all looked a little shell-shocked.

With a nod at Cory, Kiara brought up a map of the area around the storage facility they'd just passed. In a densely populated area opposite the depot where they were currently idling, Kiara circled an area.

"Can you create some fake sightings of us in these areas, using the descriptions sent out by security?

Cory immediately brightened and pulled out his tablet, his fingers flying over the screen.

Blackburne nodded at the plan, while Kiara monitored communications.

"Frankie, get us ready," Blackburne instructed the pilot. "Everyone, strap in!" He yelled on the coms for the rest of the crew.

"It's working!" Kiara said excitedly. "Keep it up, Cory. Make it look like we're heading to the depot on the other side of the city."

Cory nodded.

With the path clear of security forces, Frankie lifted off and headed to the area reserved for ships leaving the planet.

A few minutes into the flight, Kiara detected two small ships heading to intercept them. She scanned them, noting that they were not broadcasting any transponder data.

"Frankie? Do you see what I'm seeing?" Kiara asked the pilot.

"Yep. Very strange – they aren't broadcasting transponder data."

"Bring our shields online," Blackburne instructed.

"Oh no!" Kiara shouted. "Talia told them I'm on this ship!"

"Is she with them?" Jax wanted to know.

Kiara shook her head as she tried to detect where the other Trandorian was.

"How long until they intercept us?" Blackburne asked.

Kiara closed her eyes, touched Elvis' toes, and used her senses to track the other ships. Talia's thoughts had blasted into her head, telling her that those two ships were coming for them. Kiara blocked out Talia the best that she could and focused on the two ships approaching them.

Not Mercenary ships, and not security ships. They belonged to whoever was behind the attacks on the transgates. Kiara wasn't getting a name, though. Either the pilots knew how to hide their thoughts, or they didn't know who was directing them.

The first blasts from the attacking ships hit the Acadia with minimal impact. Kiara frowned. The firepower from both ships wasn't enough to damage the Acadia.

"It's got to be a trap," Kiara mused out loud.

Jax heard her. "Agreed! Anything else in the area?"

Kiara couldn't sense any other ships, but she did sense they were trying to herd them in a specific direction.

"Frankie, they're trying to push us in a certain way," Kiara muttered. She was trying to sense what was ahead of them.

Frankie veered them to the left, and the ships instantly fired on that side.

"They aren't doing much damage, but they will eventually, if they just keep firing at us," Frankie said.

Kiara shot an energy pulse at one of the ships. No effect. She frowned. Could Talia be protecting them from a distance?

Jax approached her seat. "Can you take them out?"

"My energy pulse had no effect, so I'm thinking Talia is protecting them. I don't know how, though."

"We're coming up on a warehouse area. If this is an ambush, that would be where they would do it," Frankie said. He slowed the ship slightly to give Blackburne time to work on a plan.

"Frankie, we need to get to an area with little to no population," Blackburne instructed. "Let's show them what the new engines on the Acadia can do for maneuvering, and Kiara, you do what you can. Let's get on the offensive. Jax, take a weapons station."

Kiara sent Frankie a course to take them over a deserted area, moving Elvis to her lap. "Let's do this!"

Frankie shot the ship nearly vertical and banked to the right, heading to the coordinates Kiara had sent him.

Kiara let out an evil laugh. "They had some anti-aircraft cannons hiding in one of the warehouses."

Blackburne nodded. They may have survived an initial blast from the cannons, but not with the other ships firing at them.

The smaller ships were catching up quickly, firing wildly at the Acadia to get it to turn back.

"Kiara, ready?" Frankie asked.

"Yes!"

Frankie shot the Acadia straight up and then arced over the two pursuing ships in a move so quick that neither ship could react right away. As they arced over the top, Jax began firing at them. Kiara focused on one of the ships, looking for a weakness in the shielding. She found it and, with precision worthy of an old west gunfighter, fired a small but powerful energy pulse. The pulse shut down all power on the ship, and it dropped out of the air like a rock, completely disintegrating in a fireball on the ground. The other ship began flying wildly, trying to avoid the same destruction, and Kiara could hear his panicked shouting. He was trying to tell someone what was happening, but Kiara still couldn't sense who he was talking to.

With Jax still firing, Kiara looked for weakness in this ship. She couldn't find one, so she took a different tactic.

"Frankie, get me a little closer," Kiara said as she gathered her energy. Once she felt she was close enough, she enveloped the smaller ship in an energy field and then forced the energy field toward the ground.

Frankie, understanding what she was doing, followed closely. The pilot of the other ship, in a complete panic now, pushed the engines on his ship past maximum in his attempt to get free of the energy field. The ship exploded within the energy field.

Frankie immediately broke off pursuit and shot them away from the planet. Blackburne nodded his approval. The hell with sanctioned egress points, they needed to get off the planet, now!

Days later, Kiara and Elvis were standing in a secluded area on a small space station, observing the stars and the nearby planet. They'd made it here with no other attacks or drama, and Kiara was grateful. Stryker had secured a safe place for them to lie low for a while. They could rest, fix the ship, and decompress.

They'd grabbed her dad's ship as soon as they were off Earth Delta Nine, bringing him with them. The crew was healing, and Kiara knew her dad would head out soon. The Rangers still needed him.

Kiara's thoughts turned to Jax. He was still with them, healing and resting as well. Her feelings for him were growing, and she sensed that his feelings were similar. She didn't know what their future would be, but she couldn't imagine being without him again.

She sighed, and Elvis quietly chirped at her. No more stone. When she looked back, it seemed like a dream. She hoped she never ran into another Galdorian stone! With her ancestor's help, she'd been able to shore up her defenses to keep Talia out of her head as well, but she was still worried about the other Trandorian. She had brought her worry to Jax. Talia was advancing in her powers quite a bit faster than Kiara was, and it appeared that whoever was orchestrating the attacks was planning on using Talia against Kiara.

Kiara sighed again. That was a worry for another day.